NOT MARRIED,

KT-230-673

Carol Clewlow's first novel *Keeping the Faith* was short-listed for the Whitbread Prize, while her second, the best-selling *A Woman's Guide to Adultery* was translated into 15 languages and turned into a TV mini series. A further novel, *Love in the Modern Sense*, plus a number of her short stories have been broadcast on Radio 4 and a fourth, *One For The Money*, performed at the Edinburgh Fringe Festival. She is a founder member of Operating Theatre, a ground-breaking organisation which brings health professionals and members of the performing arts together. She lives and works in the North East of England.

Visit www.AuthorTracker.co.uk for exclusive information on Carol Clewlow.

NOT BOTHERED

Also by Carol Clewlow

A Woman's Guide to Adultery
Keeping the Faith
Love in the Modern Sense
One for the Money

CAROL CLEWLOW

Not Married, Not Bothered

An ABC for Spinsters

HarperCollinsPublishers

This novel is entirely a work of fiction.
The names, characters and incidents portrayed in it are
the work of the author's imagination. Any resemblance to
actual persons, living or dead, events or localities is
entirely coincidental.

HarperCollins*Publishers*
77–85 Fulham Palace Road,
Hammersmith, London W6 8JB

www.harpercollins.co.uk

This paperback edition 2005
1 3 5 7 9 8 6 4 2

First published in Great Britain by
HarperCollins*Publishers* 2005

Copyright © Carol Clewlow 2005

Carol Clewlow asserts the moral right to
be identified as the author of this work

ISBN 0 00 720401 9

Typeset in Sabon by Palimpsest Book Production Limited,
Polmont, Stirlingshire

Printed and bound in Great Britain by
Clays Ltd, St Ives plc

All rights reserved. No part of this publication may be
reproduced, stored in a retrieval system, or transmitted,
in any form or by any means, electronic, mechanical,
photocopying, recording or otherwise, without the prior
permission of the publishers.

This book is sold subject to the condition that it shall not,
by way of trade or otherwise, be lent, re-sold, hired out or
otherwise circulated without the publisher's prior consent
in any form of binding or cover other than that in which it
is published and without a similar condition including this
condition being imposed on the subsequent purchaser.

Spin-ster (spinsta) *n.* 1. an unmarried woman regarded as being beyond the age of marriage. 2. *Law* (in legal documents) a woman who has never married. Compare **feme sole**. 3. (formerly) a woman who spins thread for her living. [C14 (in the sense: a person, esp. a woman, whose occupation is spinning; C17: a woman still unmarried): from SPIN-STER] –

spinster-,hood *n*, – spinsterish *adj*.

A is for . . . Attitude

If you ask me how all this got started, I'd say it was with Magda deciding to marry herself.

You may wish to read that line again.

She was packing up one of her *Spells for Beginners* for a customer when she caught me.

'RILEY! IMAGINE! JUST THE PERSON!'

Magda used to be in television, which is why she speaks in one of those loud overenthusiastic TV researcher's voices. Then one day she found her hair was too high and her fingernails too long. Now she runs Hocus Pocus at the bottom of the High Street.

Deciding to get married was a big thing for Magda.

'After all, I've been single all my lives.' (She was previously a vestal virgin and after that a witch. Obviously this was before she went into television.)

Magda got the idea of marrying herself from some Weirdo of the Day paragraph in her morning paper. Except, of course, being Magda, she didn't think it was weird at all.

'I THINK IT'S WONDERFUL. TOTALLY *EMPOW-ERING*.'

Apparently the woman who married herself said she'd lived with herself for forty years. She felt she *knew* herself. She felt *ready* for the commitment.

'Um . . . where did this happen exactly?'

'California.'

Only in California.

Only in the loony tune town of my birth.

Over cappuccinos in her coffee shop, I said, 'So how will it work, Magda? Will you promise to obey? Will you have a joint account? You're a woman of substance. I hope you'll insist on a prenup.'

She said, 'I'm sorry you feel the need to mock, Riley. I'm surprised you don't see it. I'm making a statement. For all of us.'

'Us?'

'Single women.'

And then she said it: '*Spinsters*, Riley.'

And that was where it started. Because it was like I was hearing it for the first time. That much-maligned, charming, noble, splendid old word.

Courtesy of Magda MacBride. *Spinster* of this parish.

Magda said, 'It's time for a new attitude, Riley.'

'Damn it, she's right,' I said later to Danny.

This after I found the spinster sites on the Net: *Be at peace with your singleness. Do not apologise for your chosen life-style* . . .

'For God's sake. It's all so goddamn craven.'

It was after that I started noticing things. What things? Well, this for instance, from one of those 'Things I Wish I'd Known' columns by some doyenne of the women's movement.

I wish I'd known that breaking off my engagement didn't mean resigning myself to eternal spinsterhood . . .

'*Resigning* herself?' I said. '*Excuse* me.'

And this too, from a celebrity journalist (female, to her shame) interviewing a hot-shot female film producer.

Despite, perhaps because of, what they are, a certain air of loss, of sadness will always cling to such women . . .

'A *certain* air of loss and sadness . . .' My Ss spat out on to the table. 'Ssssimply because she can't *produce* a husband and children.'

So that all of a sudden I'm beginning to get that old Jonathan Aitken feeling, that whole *If it falls to me* thing. I want to swish that old Sword of Truth in the air. And why? Because the more I think about it, the madder I am, and this because as far as I can see, it's spinsters that have kept this damn country going. Teachers, civil servants, nurses, secretaries, plus a hundred other occupations, years of faithful service from the single woman and not just after World War One either. And for what? To go on being patronised and condescended to, to have her life considered so much of less worth than that of her married sister. Worse – and this in the new millennium – to continue being the subject of grubby jokes and prurient conjecture, to be caricatured as fey, grey and miserable on stage and screen and in all those fey, grey miserable novels.

'We're the last minority group,' I said to Danny. 'We suffer from prejudice. We need a campaign. T-shirts. Car stickers.'

Look. Once upon a time, spinsters were just that – women who spun for a living.

'See . . .' I said, jabbing a finger down on the dictionary, open like a Bible. 'Once spinsters were just ordinary working girls.'

'Still are,' Danny said, diving a hand into his pocket. 'Here's your gas bill, Spinning Jenny. They stuck it through my door by mistake.'

From all this you will deduce that Danny is my neighbour. He's also my workmate, both of us being employed – me as reporter, he as a photographer – on our weekly newspaper. More importantly, however, he's my Obligatory Gay Male Friend and I am his . . .

'What am I to you, Danny?'

'My help in ages past, my hope for years to come . . .'

Danny comes from good Methodist stock and sometimes the past comes back to haunt him.

Over the years of our friendship (ten), and over many bottles of wine and/or the odd joint, Danny and I have debated all the major questions – whether there's a God, if Keanu Reeves can act, if Google really is the only search engine.[*]

Gay men and spinsters will always be natural allies, according to Danny.

'Gay men look at spinsters and know that's pretty much where they're going to be.' He lays a hand on his heart. 'Take me, for instance. Without you, I would never have known how truly rich and fulfilling life could be for the single person in their twilight years.'

Yes. Thank you, Danny.

Still, you can pretty much bet that any single woman of uncertain years these days will have a friend like Danny. Not that my years are remotely uncertain.

I was born at the turn of the decade, the year of Korea, the year they gave the Nobel Prize to Bertrand Russell, principally for his book on marriage (with three of his own

---

[*] Answers in reverse order: Yes, No and How could we know?

he'd been able to research it closely), the year George Bernard Shaw died, who wrote, among other things, 'All great truths begin as blasphemies' (something to bear in mind, dear Reader). Also the year in which Peggy Ashcroft played Beatrice and to much acclaim at Stratford. Beatrice, that great spinster heroine, a woman with *serious* attitude, not curst like Kate, who also I love, but not half as much as Beatrice, who was just so much more damn *merry* about the whole thing.

Born in a merry hour, surely?

No, sure, my lord, my mother cried . . .

'Damn right. What a time I had of it with you . . . You were bloody hours coming.'

Oh, why not? She's like Banquo's ghost, after all. Don't invite her to the feast and she'll show up anyway.

Might as well start where all spinsters start.

Folks . . .

My mother.

Once in the back garden my brother-in-law, Fergie, put his arm comfortingly around his wife's shoulder. He cast his eyes up into the soft sweet Somerset night.

'Ah yes . . .' he said. 'Somewhere up there the mother ship is circling and it's looking for Babs Gordon.'

Because our mother is barmy Our mother is bonkers. Our mother is barking, dippy, daft as a brush. Our mother is Madame Defarge at the foot of the guillotine, but in the words of the late great Freddie Mercury, only knitting on that one solitary needle.

Not that the comparison with the revolutionary Ms Defarge would at all suit our mother, she being one of those old-fashioned, unreconstructed Thatcherites doing such a stirling job holding back the party. (Oh thank you, thank you, *thank you* mother.)

And yet, and yet . . . if only this was the end of it.

If only the gods in their wisdom, in their compassion, had given Cassie and me a straightforwardly mad hang-em-and-flog-em Fascist for a mother. For instead Babs Gordon *oscillates*. Babs Gordon is a human fan, swinging eternally left to right, and for no discernible reason, blowing out the first vacuous, entirely illogical and idiosyncratic opinion that drops into her lovable Carmen-curled head. And while you, in your folly, might think it adds a certain piquancy, a certain *frisson* to life to walk up your mother's front path of a morning never knowing, when the door opens, whether you'll be confronted by Mother Theresa or the winner of the Genghis Khan Most Promising Newcomer Award, trust me, it doesn't.

Shall we, for instance, be sympathetic to single mothers this fine morning?

'Well, of course, I am. I've been one myself haven't I?'*

Or shall we, by contrast, be taking a stronger line?

'It's all taxpayers' money. You and me, we're paying for them. You know that, don't you?'

Or – I know – asylum seekers. An oldie but goldie. Shall we be extending the hand of friendship today?

'I mean, I feel *so* sorry for them. Imagine having to shop with *vouchers*.'

Or shall we be in favour of putting them up against the wall and shooting them?

'Don't be ridiculous, Adeline, I really resent the way you do that.'

---

* Author's note: Cass was 29 and I was 26 by the time our father passed peacefully and gratefully away from our mother.

'Do what?'

'You know.'

'What?'

'Make me out to be some sort of . . . oh, I don't know . . .'

'Burbling, featherbrained, six-short-of-a-box reactionary old swinger?'

I lied.

Regrettably this is not something I've ever managed to say to my mother.

Meanwhile please note the reference to shopping in her sympathetic response to asylum seekers. To say that shopping plays a big part in Babs Gordon's life is to indulge in the deplorable British habit of understatement. Shopping is Babs Gordon's faith, her hope, the nearest, viz. the voucher argument, she'll ever come to charity. Brought up as a wishy-washy Baptist, Babs Gordon thereafter converted to shopping. A card-carrying member of the Royal Society of Shoppers (Visa, Mastercard, Debenhams, John Lewis, but in particular M & S), at least once a month she drives the thirty miles to our nearest out-of-town Marks, a massive thing the size of the British Museum, there to walk the aisles in the same spirit, a dutiful tourist looking at all the exhibits and making her way through women's wear, footwear, underwear, handbags and shoes, home furnishings and, of course, menswear, the last for which she heads expressly just so she can flutter her eyelashes like some sixteen-year-old virgin, and say with that deceptively careless, entirely self-satisfied and proprietorial air: 'I'll just slip in. See if I can get anything for Tommy.'

A word now about Tommy.

What is Tommy to my mother?

In other circumstances you might call Tommy my

mother's lover. But I don't believe it. Not for one minute. And if you think this is the response of an anally retentive spinster daughter, well, frankly I don't give a toss. Suffice it to say on the matter of sex, I wish my mother was having it, I wish I was having it, I wish you were having it, I wish we were all having it, I'm that generous. Still I'd lay a pound to a penny that my mother is not and never has been *en flagrante* with Tommy. Or with anyone else. Including our father. For while I recognise that the existence of Cass and myself would indicate some form of interchange between our mother and our father (I think we can safely rule out any of that early test tube stuff with the sperm of actors and vicars), I have every confidence that, at least on my mother's part, we represent entirely token copulations.

Not that Babs does not like men. No, no. Our Babs *adores* men, a fact she is given to asserting frequently in her cups at parties.

'I've always got on so much better with men.' That's one of her particular favourites, accompanied by those eternally fluttering lashes and that familiar hand laid deprecatingly upon bosom.

In short, there's a word for what my mother is but I don't intend to use it. Let's just settle for flirt, a quaint old-fashioned term that would thrill my mother to her skinny marrow should she overhear it being used to describe her. For were you to venture, machete in hand, through the impenetrable jungle that is my mother's mind, you would find there a scary image, the one she bears of herself, a Mata Hari figure, a *femme fatale*, condemned (hand fluttering upon bosom again) to wreak havoc and confusion in the hearts of men. As for Tommy, well, I guess the best thing to call him is her consort, the man she goes bowling with, on chaste single-room coach-tour holidays to the Swiss Alps, the Scottish Highlands and the Dutch Bulb Fields, as well as to all and every event at the Conservative Club, where Tommy is bar steward and chairman of the entertainments committee. And the fact that this entirely sexless relationship unquestionably suits Tommy down to his last buffed-up blazer button is not something my mother feels a need to take on board. And strange as it may seem, neither do I. It is one of only a handful of things for which I feel a need to defend my mother, and this because I am, at heart, a sixties person and therefore a fully paid-up member of the Whatever Is Your Bag/Whatever Turns You On Party. Furthermore, if it is the case that in an age and a world different from the one into which he was born, Tommy might otherwise be more merrily engaged flicking a towel at the firm buttocks of a handsome young pool boy . . . well . . . that's his business. And long may the pair of them, my mother and he, ignore it.

This is a small town and with a small-town mentality. Despite, or possibly because of, this, as far as their friends and neighbours are concerned, Babs and Tommy are respectably *à deux*, occupying their own remarkably similar, chintzy, cushiony, squeaky-clean homes, each with matching pine block freshner down the toilet, pink seat cover and frilly Kleenex holder.

It's been this way since our father died the best part of thirty years ago when the funeral baked meats, metaphorically at least, began to coldly furnish forth the marriage table.

'Don't go there,' has been Cass's advice from the first, counsel I followed reluctantly at first but, as time passed, increasingly easily.

To all intents and purposes, Tommy is now part of the

family, not least thanks to thirty years of Christmas Days spent together. In essence, he still looks the way he looked at our father's funeral, like some old-fashioned stiff-upper-lipped colonel with a stick beneath his armpit. His back is still ramrod straight, or at least it would be was it not for the shaking that has begun to afflict him and that may or may not be the onset of Parkinson's. This shaking gives him the air of a man trying to control his anger but nothing could be further from the truth. In fact he's an astonishingly peaceable man, miraculously so bearing in mind he spends so much time with my flighty, wildly irritating mother.

All of this would be fine was it not for the fact that, in clear contradiction of her own eminently comfortable lifestyle, she still feels the need occasionally to harass her spinsterdaughter

'Hey, I've not noticed you're in that much of a hurry to get hitched again, Mother.'

'I'm not talking about getting married, Addy. No one has to get married these days.' (Babs likes to think of herself as *excessively* modern.) 'There just never seems to be anyone in your life, that's all.'

'Well, thank you for mentioning it. I don't believe I'd noticed that, Mother.'

A strict diet of booze and fags plus the odd lettuce leaf pushed in a desultory way around her plate at what passes for meal times ensures that my mother's size 8 figure never gets any bigger. Despite this unhealthy life-style she gets a clean bill of health every time she goes to the doctor (and while we're on the subject, why do you go to the doctor, Mother; is it because he's young and good-looking, you shameless hussy?). Given half a chance, she'd still do that Cleopatra thing of hopping forty paces through a public

10

street. Robbed of the opportunity, she contents herself putting in a full day's shopping at Marks & Spencer on a pair of heels that would provide training for a stilt walker.

Like Cleopatra, my mother believes with passion and spirit that age cannot wither her, an opinion most often expressed when she stands before her hall mirror patting her washboard stomach and uttering the now familiar words: 'Haven't put on a pound since I was sixteen,' this always followed by a critical stare in the direction of whichever daughter has the misfortune to be caught in the mirror next to her, and the rider, 'Darling . . . do I dream it . . . or are you a size 14?' (Or 16 in Cassie's case.)

I have learnt over the years that all my mother's snips and snides are prefaced by the word 'darling'. As in:

'Darling . . . do you *have* to buy such clumpy shoes?'

'Darling . . . is that a *motorbike* jacket you're wearing?'

And now, of course: 'Darling, all I'm saying is, do you *really* think your hair suits you that short?' (The italics in all cases, I promise you, are my mother's.)

As regards my hair, I've always worn it long. I've had every style known to man or beast (perms, pleats, plaits, highlights, low-lights, etc., etc.) but still it's never risen much above my shoulders. Thus the day I came in with it ice white and shorn, my mother fell back against the sink like she was having a heart attack.

'Oh, what have you done . . . what have you done?' she moaned, clutching her chest.

'I've had an arm amputated. I've shot the Prime Minister. Oh no. I've just remembered. I've only had my hair cut, Mother.'

She continued keening for a while. 'Oh, your hair . . . your beautiful hair.' But in the way of these things, grief soon turned to anger.

11

'It was your saving grace, Adeline, you know that, don't you?'

'Oh, and I thought it was my crowning glory.'

Please note here my mother's use of the name Adeline to address me, she being the only person on the planet to do so, and this on account of it being the one she gave me – a fancy French name, according to my dictionary of first names, although not in this instance, since I was named after an Adeline from Bromsgrove whose bridesmaid I later became and who had the bed next to my mother's in the barracks in Cairo.[*]

The name was and is entirely unsuitable, one I would have had to wear like a bolt through my neck was it not for my father, God bless him. In a move that my mother would forever regret, she deputed him to register my birth, something that allowed him to pull one of only two known flankers over her in the history of their time together (the other was when he died to get away from her).

Afterwards he would claim that the middle name he gave me was that of a close friend killed in the war. He'd even take the trouble to look suitably mournful when he said it. Once, though, bending beneath a bonnet in his ramshackle old tin-roofed garage on one of our long evenings together, me standing beside him handing him his spanners, he told me he'd named me after his favourite car, a Riley Sprite he'd owned in the halcyon days of his youth, which translated means those days before he met my mother.

'Lovely thing, she was. Four cylinder push-rod-operated overhead-valve engine.'

I assume he was talking about the Riley.

Thus I am Adeline Riley Gordon, but to all and sundry

---

[*] Among many others. See B for Bridesmaids.

ever since (except, natch, my mother), *Riley*, not least because my father, keen to compound his crime and irritate my mother whenever possible – the revenge, *raison d'être* and principal calling of his married life – referred to me as that from Day One, firmly instructing my sister Cassie, three at the time, to follow his example.

In all this I count myself lucky. Not just because Riley suits me infinitely better than Adeline ever could (or, the horror . . . the horror . . . the appalling 'Addy'), but because if I'd had the misfortune to be born a generation later, God knows, I might have had to put Golf or Mondeo or Fiesta at the top of my O level paper.

Anyway, I like Riley. It suits me. It has a jaunty, freedom-loving air that I like to think entirely encapsulates what I am. I think, I hope that, like Beatrice, a star danced when I was born.

'Not from where I was looking it didn't.'

Yes, thank you, Mother.

Anyway, I'm more than happy, just like Beatrice, to pay for my state by leading apes in hell when I die, this being the mythological punishment for spinsters, but one that holds no fears for me, coming of age as I did at a time and in a place where men were still getting used to the upright position. Confronted by the word 'clitoris', there's still a few would guess at one of the lesser known Greek islands.

All in all I'd say the only downside, if downside there be to my name, is the jokes it provokes. Or rather, The Joke. Because there is only one. I've heard it a thousand times but, trust me, that's not something that ever spoils the enjoyment of the joker.

'Ri-l-ey . . .' he'll say, and I'll watch as that geeky smile dawns and behind the skin of his face those old wheels and cogs start turning. 'I suppose you live the life of Riley, then?'

And if you want know what all this Spinster's Alphabet stuff is about I'd say it's just that.

Because as a matter of fact, I think I do.*

---

* As will be clear by now, the aim of this book is ever to inform. Thus you may be interested to know whence comes the term Life of Riley. It first appeared in a popular song performed by one Pat Rooney in 1880s America, 'Are You the O'Reilly', which describes all the things said O'Reilly would do if he was rich. Another song, 'The Best in the House is None Too Good For Reilly', shortened the name to the one we know and introduced the notion of R(e)iley as a carefree soul. The actual words the 'Life of Riley' appear in a third and later song, 'My Name is Kelly'.

> Faith and my name is Kelly Michael Kelly,
> But I'm living the life of Reilly just the same.

With 'My Name is Kelly' the metamorphosis was complete. Reilly had become the idle, ne'er do well of popular fiction, and in particular of my mother's morning newspaper for whom the phrase is indispensable, especially when applied to that vast amorphous body of people whose sole unifying feature is that they're all somehow not just getting something for nothing but something due, by rights, to readers of said paper. This body includes but is by no means confined to:

- single mothers
- students
- gays
- lesbians
- blacks
- any teacher, vicar, lawyer, film or theatre director deemed by her morning newspaper to be 'trendy'
- anyone with a good word to say for the sixties
- criminals (unless they're actually members of the Tory Party)
- and last, but definitely not least, anyone receiving Unemployment Benefit.

'Scroungers,' is my mother's rallying cry as she waves her paper in the air. 'On the dole. Lying in bed all day. Leading the Life of Riley.'

14

B is for . . . Bridesmaid
(as in 3 times a . . .)

According to *The Guinness Book of Records*, the world's most prolific bridesmaid is believed to be one Euphrenia LaFayette of Big Flat, Arkansas. A combination of a large family and lack of good bridesmaid material in her mountain home is said to have led to Ms LaFayette being called on no less than sixty-three times. Interviewed by the *Arkansas Sentinel* upon her retirement at the age of forty-four, Miss LaFayette said, 'Ah been up that damn aisle in every kinda dress, n' carried every damn kinda posy. I've had every damn kinda contraption on ma head too, and dang me, if a gal caaaint get tired o' that sorta thang.'

Ms LaFayette has never married.

I lied.

There is no Most Prolific Bridesmaid category in *The Guinness Book of Records*. Which is a pity.

I could have been a contender.

When I told Cass about Mad Magda deciding to marry herself and asking me to be one of her bridesmaids, she

15

said, 'Well, it's not like you don't have the experience.'

It's a weird thing when you think about it that once upon a time the best way to bless the bridal pair, to wish them good luck in their marriage, was to have them met upon the church steps by a raggedy, smutty-faced boy chimney sweep complete with pneumoconiosis and brushes. You can still find the scene depicted on wedding cards, although it's harder to lay your hands on the real thing these days, boy chimney sweeps having gone the way of so many of our great traditions – children down the mines, nimble-fingered seamstresses working by candlelight, blind and starving match-girls on every street corner. However, whereas we now balk at sticking young boys up chimneys, we show no such compunction at grabbing some innocent young female, thrusting her into a bad dress and bonnet, and pushing her, posy in hand, up the aisle behind the bridal party.

I know. I was that bridesmaid.

Look, the way I see it is this. Some people are born bridesmaids (particularly if they're cursed with blonde ringlets); some people achieve bridesmaidhood; others, thanks to what can only be termed sheer dereliction of duty on the part of their sisters, have the bridesmaid thing thrust upon them. (Cassie, are you listening?)

Because if that whole 'Three times a bridesmaid, never a bride' thing* really is the ancient curse that Archie alleged all those years ago at Cass and Fergie's wedding, then all

---

* Discovering the derivation of this old saying, '*Three times a bridesmaid, never a bride*' has proved surprisingly difficult, in particular why or how the figure of three came to be established as the one at which all hope should be abandoned. Listerine, the US mouthwash company, used 'Often a bridesmaid but never a bride' for its adverts in the 1920s, this itself an adaptation of the old British music-hall song 'Why Am I Always the Bridesmaid?' made famous by Lily Morris a few years earlier.

I can say is my fate as a spinster was sealed early on. Six times – and this before the age of ten – I was forced into taffeta and tulle, to my mind a human rights abuse of the first order. In part this was due to Cassie cleverly throwing up on her frock within sight of the altar on her first booking (you're pretty much finished on the bridesmaid circuit after that). But mainly it was due to all those Buffies and Madges and Snowies.

There's a picture on the mantelpiece in my mother's front room. More than a picture, an icon. Because the fact is that she looks wonderful in that photograph. They should have used it for a recruitment poster.

'They did. How many times must I tell you?'

There's not a ruck or a tuck or wrinkle in that uniform. The cap sits squarely on her head as she gazes straight-backed and grave into the camera. She sheds a tear over that picture sometimes and, trust me, my mother sheds a tear over very little.

'All this will go when I go,' she says, dabbing at her eyes pitifully with one of her customised floral Kleenex. 'You two'll just throw it away.'

'Never, Mother, never.'

'We'll hang it on the wall.'

'Light a candle beneath it.'

'We'll have one of those dippy little finger bowl things underneath so we can flick holy water on our foreheads as we pass.'

Why am I always the bridesmaid
And never the blushing bride?

The very question this volume seeks to answer.

17

'Oh, you.' But there's real pain in her voice.

It's one of the few occasions when I feel genuinely sorry for my mother. For herein lies the source of my mother's madness, the reason for all that lunacy. My mother, you see, never got over the war.

One night, helping her to the car from some wartime reunion night at the Conservative Club, Tommy on one side, me on the other, she clutched at his arm as he lowered her into the front seat.

'They don't understand, do they?' she said. Her eyes were full of tears but, more than that, a terrible yearning sorrow. 'I was twenty years old, Tommy. I was in *Cairo* . . .'

'It's alright, Babs, it's alright,' he said very gently, and in that moment I did understand, not just all that madness, but also her relationship with Tommy, and what this too might be about, this secret that belonged only to themselves and others of their ilk: what it had been like to be plucked from a small country town, not even full grown, and dropped down into a foreign, utterly exotic place – in my mother's case Egypt; for Tommy, India. All this with that added ingredient of war. That what? *Frisson?* No, no, so much more that that. Something we've never known, please God will never know. Something that, for all the books and the films, we still can't really imagine.

Ask my mother about the war, and you won't hear anything about those bit part players like Hitler and Churchill. Instead you'll get, 'Did I ever tell you about the night Madge and I got caught by the curfew and had to climb in through the window after we'd been out all night at the Deck Club?' Or, 'Did I tell you how Buffy and I hired a truck and went out dressed as sheikhs to the Pyramids?' Or, 'Did I tell you about the night Snowy got drunk on arak and almost threw up over Larry Adler?'

Oh, yes. Many times. So many times, Mother.

As a child, I measured out my life with those visits from the Madges and Buffies and Snowies.

Upstairs in her bedroom, revelling in her round National Health glasses and her straight coarse blunt-cut hair from which slides and flowers and Alice bands would slip as if deliberately, Cassie would sit bent over her book, point-blank refusing to come down and join the party. Thus it would always be just me standing outside the lounge door waiting to be paraded on the rug in preparation for yet another outing as bridesmaid. Through the crack I'd hear the plop of the sherry cork, the sound of all that merci-less, melancholy Chalet School laughter.

'There we are, look ... in that funny little place we found that day near the Continental Hotel. There's you, Buffy, and you, Madge. And is that Snowy?' A blood-red fingernail would stab the page of the photograph album in something I recognised even then as resentment.

They look so damned happy in those pictures, those young women, that's the thing. All that leaning in, all that loving and laughter. They make war look such *fun*. Which is not their fault. The best of times in the worst of times among those elegant potted plants and wicker chairs in the pictures. Blame the table tops full of glasses if you must blame some-thing, or the rakish nature of uniform. Blame *Carpe Diem* written in the wreathes of cigarette smoke over every table.

Our father is in those photographs. George Gordon, leaning forward, laughing. Battledress most rakishly unbut-toned of all. The man who betrayed our mother, double-crossed her with the oil-stained overalls that became his uniform after the war, that would replace the dashing airforce blue in which he had wooed her.

'How many times must I tell you not to wear those

19

bloody things around the house?' she would rage at him. 'You only do it to annoy me,' which probably was the truth of it.

I asked my father once, in a blaze of teenage bravery, 'Why did you marry her?'

He didn't raise his head from beneath the bonnet. He said, 'I was mad about her.'

As always he tried to make a joke of it. 'Must have had a touch of the sun,' he said, 'desert fever,' only then he turned serious. He raised his eyes, gave me a hard look across the engine. 'It doesn't do to be too romantic, Riley,' he said.

According to my mother – this told with relish when he was alive – my father pursued her against her will, even after the war was over and they returned home from Cairo.

'What could I do?' she liked to simper. 'Eventually I relented.'*

To say that our father disappointed our mother is to indulge again in that appalling habit of understatement. All their married life she made it clear that she despised him. Even the way she looked at him said she'd been fooled, deluded, cheated.

'Oh . . . George,' she'd say, this so often that as a child I thought this was his name. *Oh . . . George.* Always accompanied by a disgusted click of the tongue and a contemptuously raised eyebrow. Or sometimes a derisive snort and the stab of a bitter red fingernail on the photo album for those Buffies and Madges and Snowies.

They used to say in our home town that George Gordon could mend an engine with a piece of string and a six-

---

* In fairness it should be pointed that at the time (see D for Divorce) she was in dire need of a husband.

inch nail. Old-timers I bump into in the street still some-times repeat it, a fine thing, I always thought, to have chiselled on your tombstone. Not so my mother. She hated our father's business. Each month on bill day the air would be full of her fury. It swirled around, mingling with the blue of her cigarette smoke as she sat there poring over the invoice books on the kitchen table. Over at the sink my father would be Swarfegaing his hands calmly, running them under the tap like some grease monkey Pilate.

'How much?' my mother would ask, her pen poised on the bill head.

'Oh, I don't know . . . charge her a tenner,' whereupon a howl of wrath would rise up to the ceiling.

'No . . . no . . . no. How much . . . ? How much . . . ? How much did it cost you to do the bloody job for her?' And it was so often a *her* because there's no question that my father could be a soft touch when it came to elderly single women, convincing my mother that it was the spin-sters of our town who were ruining my father's business.

'Bloody old maids, they pull the wool over your eyes,' she'd yell at him. 'Well, they're not doing the same to me, I can tell you.'

As far as she was concerned, the entire Spinster World was engaged in some sort of conspiracy.[*]

'See . . . see . . . ?' she would scream, thrusting the local paper at him, folded at the wills page where the horrible truth was revealed – that yet another of my father's 'impov-erished' customers whose car he had mended for next to nothing had bequeathed her small fortune to a cat's home

---

[*] A nice touch, this, from a woman who not that long hence would prove to be so much happier being single.

or some charity rescuing pit ponies. Worse still, though, was when Olive Jepson died and left the lot to the Communist Party.

It's a tribute to Olive Jepson that the mere mention of the word 'spinster' will bring her instantly to mind. She remains for me the Ur, my über-spinster, which I guess is what she also was for my father.

He liked to take me to see Olive Jepson. I figure now there were a number of reasons for this, not all of which I want to go into. Once, in the summer, as I sat on her lawn drinking lemonade, I saw my father clash closed the bonnet of the Austin-Healey, and walk up beside her where she sat sipping gin and tonic in her deck chair. As he got to her, he reached his hand down and she reached up hers, and for a moment their two hands were clasped in the air in the sort of strong, firm comradely grasp that I knew, even then, was unimaginable between him and my mother.

Olive was the town's librarian. She drove a large green growling Austin-Healey, and in the summer did her gardening in a checked bikini no bigger than a brace of pocket handkerchiefs.

'Honest to God . . . sixty if she's a day . . .' my mother would say with a sniff, and 'mutton dressed as lamb,' this last said too loudly once as Olive pulled weeds up in her front garden. Unabashed, Olive raised herself and gave a long mocking baaaaaaa over the hedge, something for which my mother never forgave her.

Olive was secretary of the local Communist Party, a small outfit, probably with scarcely more than a dozen members. She'd been in Spain with the International Brigade, where, rumour had it, her fiancé had been killed.

'Actually he ran off with another comrade.'

I was fifteen when she told me this. It was the last time

I saw her. She died from cancer very suddenly a few months later. It was winter, with a hoar frost on her lawn and I was sitting in her lounge. Outside the window, my father was blowing on his fingers beneath the Healey bonnet. She picked the picture up from the top of her grand piano: her and her fiancé sitting on some hard-baked earth, in fatigues and with packs on their backs, smiling. She smiled back as she looked at it.

She said, 'Sometimes it's really useful to have a dead fiancé, Riley.' She put the picture back on the piano top, turned to look at me. She said, 'This is a small town, Riley. I don't know why but some people just seem happier if you can give them a good reason why you're single.'

That day I heard my mother call Olive a 'skinny sex-starved old woman'. I saw my father's hands clench and unclench at his side. There was a set look on his face and, spying from the top of the stairs, I thought he was going to hit her. But then he went to the sink, turned on the tap, began lathering his hands under it. When he spoke his words were very clear and very cold and deliberate.

He said, 'Well, you'd know all about that, wouldn't you, *Barbara*?'

That was how it was at home when we were kids. A terrible ongoing argument that raged along like a swollen stream, all the time underground but sometimes bursting out above the surface.

Meal times were the worst. Our father could be cruel and very cutting.

'Maybe you could tell your mother to pass that grey slop she likes to call mash,' he said once. Another time, tasting one of her stews (and they were pretty bad), he strode to the sink and spat it out. 'For God's sake, woman,' he said, 'are you trying to poison us?'

The serving spoon was still in her hand. She held it up as if wanting to strike him with it and her eyes were white with fury.

'I wish I could. I tell you, I wish I could poison you. It would be worth going to gaol for.'

Once, when they were arguing, Cass put her hands on the side of her head. She must have been about eight; I was three years younger. She began screaming, 'Stop it, stop it, stop it . . .' over and over.

In the end our father jumped up and put his arms around her. Tears ran down his face. He nursed her, crying, 'I'm sorry. I'm sorry, Cassie.'

Mostly I solved the problem by eating very fast, throwing it all down, getting down from the table as soon as possible.

It's a habit that continues to this day. I still eat far too fast. I remember it was one of the things Nathan noticed about me. That first time he took me out for a meal he stared curiously across the table.

'You eat like a caveman, Riley,' he said. 'You throw your food down. You must hardly taste it.'

When he said it, I felt the tears prick behind my eyes. I picked up my napkin, slapped it petulantly down on the table.

I said, 'Don't criticise me,' and he stretched a hand immediately across.

He said, 'I'm sorry. I'm just interested, that's all. I wondered why you ate so fast.'

But it's too early for Nathan.

More, much more about Nathan later.

Cassie and Fergie's wedding was my last outing as a bridesmaid. It was a wedding much of its time. Proof of this is the photograph that stands on the mantelpiece of their front room, a courageous act, bearing in mind the presence of their two children.

'God, you look bad, Dad.'

'Thank you, son.'

He does too, clad in the sort of cheap-looking white suit with a width of flare and lapel that could only have been expressly designed to engender scorn and derision from any fruit of the loins that would follow him.

Not so Cassie and I. In fact we look pretty good, both of us in Biba, with big floppy hats, Cass in cream and me in that unsurpassable Biba mulberry.

Fergie likes to say that his father would have paid Cass to marry him. A bewhiskered old major-general in the old tradition, he sent Fergie to boarding school in the same way he'd been sent. In the same way, Fergie was as thoroughly miserable.

According to Fergie, it left him with the same inability to communicate with women that had afflicted his father, which is why he still regards himself as being rescued the day that new art teacher Cass Gordon turned up in the staff room of the local comprehensive where he was already teaching science.

'No sooner looked than they loved . . . no sooner loved than they were screwing like bunnies.'

'Yes, thank you, Archie.' This from my sister, Cass.

'Such a charming sentiment and written in such large letters, as I recall, on the wedding card Fergie's mother opened.'

True too. Fergie and Cass moved in together a bare few months after they met, a radical thing in our Land That Time Forgot back in the early seventies. A year later the major-general died so that Fergie was able to put down a deposit on a rambling cottage in Haviatt, a small village several miles to the west of our loony tune town, all of this occurring while I was out of the country on my travels.

They were married a year later in their local parish church, St Michael's where, thirty years on (God, can it be that long?) Fergie is now Tower Captain. On practice nights during the summer I sometimes bike out, and sit on the wall beneath the shadow of the church to listen to the bells and watch the evening fall on the mellow mustard-coloured stonework. Afterwards Fergie and I walk across the fields to the pub where the talk will be of the mystery of sallies and bobs and touches, bell-ringing being a foreign language to those who don't speak it.

From this you may deduce that I delight in the company of my brother-in-law, that I love him close on as much as I love my sister. I could call him a big cheese in his home village of Haviatt, only this would be a terrible pun on account of the fact that the place is famous for its prize-winning Cheddar. A parish councillor, Fergie also runs the pub skittle team and its folk club. This last I refuse to attend on account of a congenital dislike of beards and sandals, but, more importantly, miserable one-hundred-and-eight-verse ballads where women no better than they should be get rolled in the hay, and pregnant and/or dead afterwards. (Fergie says it's not like this any longer but I'm not willing to take a chance on it.)

It was a lovely wedding at St Michael's, I'll say this – although weddings are definitely my least favourite cere-monies – a balmy late September day with a first fine twinge of autumn about it.

I liked Fergie from the first; not so Archie.

We met at the rehearsal the night before. His first words, having been told of my travels, were; 'So, Bangkok,' this with a distinctly lecherous look in his eye. 'Was it like *Emmanuelle*, then?'

Scarcely have a best man and a bridesmaid had so little to say to each other at a reception. Forced eventually on to the dance floor with him, I said – rather cleverly, I thought – 'Fergie's such a nice guy. How come you ended up friends?'

He just grinned, refusing to be insulted. 'Cut and thrust of the rugger field, darling,' he said. 'All that male bonding in the showers.'

Archie was delighted to learn this was my seventh outing as a bridesmaid. Flapping his hands and faintly bending his knees in what passed for dancing in the period, he said, 'It's a curse.'

'Really?'

'Absolutely. Only one way to get rid of it.'

'Surprise me.'

'Violent sexual congress with the best man at the immediate conclusion of the reception.'

As Fergie revved up his battered old Ford Capri in the fond but as it turned out faint hope that it would actually carry them as far as Scotland, Cass hurled her posy in the traditional devil-may-care manner back over her shoulder. Archie, towering above the rest of the crowd of well-wishers, caught it, neatly deflecting it into my accidentally upraised hands. In a moment my mother was upon me cooing.

'Oh, darling . . . oh, darling . . .'

'Oh, darling . . . *what*?' I tossed the posy over to her like it was radioactive.

It was the early hours of the morning and I was collecting my coat from the hotel cloakroom when Archie finally caught me.

'So?'

'So . . . what . . . ?'

'Are you going to bed with me or not?'

'That depends.'

'On what?'

'On whether the alternative is having my toenails pulled out one by one without the benefit of anaesthetic.'

My mother took the wedding posy home, put it on the kitchen windowsill in a vase where it withered and wilted and fell apart in the manner of Miss Havisham's on that bridal table. The mortal remains she pressed and put in her favourite photograph album.

Some people take the sight of a primrose as the first sign of spring, others the cool clear sound of the cuckoo. For me it will always be the moment each year when, regular as clockwork, my mother reaches up to the sideboard for that album. Opening it up, she pulls out those crumbling remnants, holds them up to the light.

'Oh, you,' she will say in tones of irritation, which have grown more intense with each passing year, and which, faced with the horrible truth of Archie's financial elevation, now threaten to overwhelm her.

'Oh, you . . .'

'Oh, me . . . what?'

'You . . . you . . . you could have *married* Archie.'

C is for ... Cliché

It was Danny who gave me the idea to reclaim the word 'spinster'.

'Why not? I mean, you reclaimed queer, after all.'

Which is true.

Queer.

Dyke.

Nigger.

Personally I've always thought the last a little premature, bearing in mind not everyone in the world has a burning desire to use it with affection. And I was about to say *But that's another story* ... And then I thought maybe not. Because all insults come from fear, after all. Witness my cousin Fleur in her Frau Goebbels days, her shoulders doing those delicate little convulsions beneath her cashmere cardigan.

'I'm sorry, Riley, but I'd just be *terrified* at the thought. I mean, to be on my own. When I got older.'

I decided to do a little research on the subject of the spinster. One evening I drove the twenty-five miles to Bristol to use the library of the university where I did my degree as a mature student what seems like yesterday, but is actually twenty years ago. I always go in the evening. It's almost empty then. You could have full sex in Philosophy and no one would notice. I tapped in 'spinster', expecting a list to show up. You know the sort of thing, textbooks pretending to be something more interesting with racy covers and titles: *Niggers with Attitude: Black Pride in the Nineties; Queering the Pitch: The Law and the Homosexual; Finger in the Dyke: A History of Anti-Woman Humour* . . .

Instead it came up 'WORD NOT RECOGNISED'.

'I felt like I'd committed some crime against the state. I thought a grille was going to come down, some card-carrying cadre was going to escort me from the building.'

Danny grinned. He said, 'I guess someone PC-ed the PCs, girlfriend.'

'Listen, they got so scared of spinsters back in the 1850s they hatched a plan to ship them off to the colonies.'

'Wooooh. Imagine it. All those brawny farmers.'

'Hey, hey. It wouldn't be like *The Piano*, you know. There'd be all that ringworm and tapeworm. And it wouldn't be like Harvey Keitel or Sam Neill would be waiting for you.'

Most people think of post World War One as the high spot of spinsterdom (or the low spot, according to which way you look at it) but the rot had set in long before then. In the 1850s, thanks to a demographic imbalance, there were 400,000 more women than men. One in four women was single and one in three would never marry, a situation referred to in the letters columns of the daily papers as a 'disturbance' and a 'mischief', and debated in Parliament under the title The Problem of Surplus and Excess Women. The spinster became the scapegoat and all-round repository for society's perceived ills, among her most vocal critics being her married sisters. Consider, for instance, this little number, from the allegedly liberationist *Freewoman*, in which the spinster is described as 'a withered tree . . . an acidulous vessel under whose pale shadow we chill and whiten . . . silent, shamefaced, bloodless and boneless, thinned to the spirit . . . our social nemis . . .'

It's amazing just how much the spinster has been left out of history, feminist history in particular, more's the shame of it. Plenty of married women in there, gay women galore, but precious little of the defiantly straight and single. All I managed to turn up in Women's Studies that day was one measly chapter on spinstas. Still it contained details of that old spinster Export Plan. It foundered in the end, that plan, but only on the rock of sheer impracticality, the problem, according to one regretful letter in *The Times* being 'the mechanical conveyance of these women to where they are wanted, given the average passenger limit of fifty persons per ship,' a shame, this, since it almost certainly deprived some waggish old salt of the chance of urging every last woman on board with a cackle of laughter and some corny crack about not wanting them to miss the boat second time round.

'Missing the boat' is a cliché when applied to spinsters. So is 'left on the shelf' and 'old maid' and that very word 'spinsterish'. But then, spinsters attract clichés.

'So what? So do married women.' This from my sister, Cass.

'No they don't. At least not in the same way.'

Which I believe to be true. Because while it may be the case that somewhere in an alternative reality, accessible only to ad men through some wormhole of time, there are indeed mothers whose major concern in life is the softness of the wash and the germ-free nature of their kitchen floor (as opposed, for instance, to how they can slide into work late without anyone seeing them because they had to take little Johnny to the doctor, or how they can get away from some garrulous over-shot meeting to pick him from the child-minder), still clichés no longer cling to the married woman the way they do to the spinsta, sticking to her like burrs, and turning her into some metaphorical horse chestnut.

'Hummph . . .'

It's the nearest I can get to the sound Cass makes but from it you can deduce that she is unimpressed with my campaign to reclaim 'spinster'.

'It's a horrible word. No matter how you spell it. Nobody uses it any more.'

'John Major does.'

'I rest my case.'

You may not remember this but some years ago our former Prime Minister had a dream of Old Albion which had all to do with warm beer, the sound of leather on willow from the village green, but most important and heart-warming of all, the sight of a spinster, all tweed and lisle stockings, pedalling through the early morning mist to Holy Communion on her sit-up-and-beg bicycle.

Tweeds and lisle? Sit-up-and-beg bicycle? Excuse me?*

Yeah, C is for cliché alright, also for Caricature, that picture of her as 'bloodless and boneless, thinned to the

---

* For the record, I've never set foot in a Holy Communion service, this mainly thanks to my mother who neglected to send me to confirmation classes. I do, however, have a bicycle. It's a Rock Hopper. Twenty-four gears, chrome alloy frame. A thousand quid's worth of off-road riding.

'Look . . . you want it, you don't want it. What?' – Lennie, like Autolycus. A snapper-up of unconsidered trifles . . . Again, more (oh so much more) of Lennie later.

spirit,' this being anti-spinster speak for 'celibate' under which she's listed in *Roget's Thesaurus*, also for Cardboard Cut-out, the picture of her in tweeds and lisle stockings peddling through the early morning mist, also for Calumny – another cliché, this, a favourite of film and play and novel, the lonely spinster with nowhere to go on Sunday afternoons but the homes of relatives, married with children.

Ha!

Behind every successful single woman there are other successful single women. Show me a spinster and I'll show you the proud and grateful possessor of a fine circle of female friends – in my case Mad Magda, for instance, who you've already met, Sophie and Connie who have yet to appear, others too who you won't meet but only because they have no particular part to play in this drama. I think of them as a sort of Greek chorus, standing at the back of the stage and carrying the narrative of life forward with visits to the cinema, the theatre, Ikea, dinners out, dinners in. Because the fact is that far from being lonely and with a duff social life, the spinster can generally be counted on to have a wider circle of friends than those who spend their lives as part of a couple, this for the obvious reason that she has more time and energy to expend on her friendships than those with partners and/or children. More likely than not, her friendships will be long and deep, this because she knows the truth of the thing – that friendships, the ones that count, are relationships too, and go through the same traumas and tensions, and require the same amount of time and energy, faith, hope and charity to keep them going.[*]

---

[*] An interesting point is that single men generally do not possess this supportive 'Greek chorus', something reflected in the grim reality of the mortality figures. According to Department of Health statistics, single men living alone after the age of forty-five, particularly those

In all this, these canards, these cock-and-bull stories, C stands for contempt, for a curl of the lip. On the other hand, C also stands for Cat, biggest of all spinster clichés.

Which is why I won't have one, despite all Cassie's urging.

'Cats are not just for Christmas, Cass,' I say when she starts in on me as fat old Hughie, her favourite, leaps up and starts purring contentedly on my lap. 'It's all that responsibility. Bringing them up. Finding the right schools. Putting their paws on the right path in life. I just don't feel I'm up to it.' And there's more than a scrap of truth in all this.

'But you like cats,' she says reproachfully, and I do, I do.

But cats are like husbands to me.

I just prefer them in other people's houses.†

A word about my sister, Cass, now.

Cass, full name Cassandra, was named after Lady Cassandra Something or Other who clacked away at her

---

single second time round, post divorce or separation, are twice as likely to die prematurely as single women in the same situation. They're also more likely to succumb to a whole range of 'quality of life' illnesses – rheumatism and diabetes that sort of thing – allegedly because their evenings are more likely to be spent playing the couch potato, washing down a takeaway curry with beer, this as opposed to the spinsta, who's probably out with friends at the gym or an exercise class, returning home to share low-fat lasagne and a pot of yoghurt.

'How awful . . .' This from Magda with a shudder. Magda won't do any sort of exercise that requires special equipment or clothing. She does yoga (of course), some special variety known only to herself and some swami halfway up the Himalayas.

† Some late news *re* cats and spinsters. According to some new research, a cat can make a woman more sexy and attractive, this thanks to a parasite that can leap from little Tigger on to humans, causing a

typewriter next to my mother in Cairo. My mother still likes to refer to her in the manner of a bosom buddy.

'Poor old Cassie. Getting divorced again . . .' This like she'd just heard it from a mutual friend as opposed to reading it in the gossip column of her morning paper.

In fact Lady Cassandra dropped all that social levelling crap the minute the war was over. Wedding Number One was in Westminster Abbey, to which my mother and the rest of the girls from the Nissan Hut Nine were not invited, and where Lady C wore a mile-long train carried by a dozen bridesmaids, although not including me despite my long and distinguished service. Number Two, to some zillionaire Nazi gaucho was in some Chilean registry office, and Number Three (to her personal trainer, it lasted a week) in a Las Vegas wedding chapel.

None of this matters, however, since it's our Cassie who concerns us here, not Lady Cassandra; Cass to me on most occasions, Cassie who I have come to the conclusion I love more than life itself, something I discovered thanks to a dark period in our lives when she got cancer.

The day Cass told me she had cancer, I shook my fist at heaven, cursing the fact that there no *system*, no Great Cosmological Swap Shop where we were allowed to trade

---

condition called *Toxoplasma gondii*. This condition, which may be infecting up to half the population, is good news or bad, depending on whether you're male or female, i.e., whereas females who catch it may well begin to suffer from the sex kitten effect, men become more scruffy and grumpy. Apparently, in the most serious cases *Toxoplasma gondii* has been known to lead to entire personality changes – depression, antisocial behaviour, but most interesting of all schizophrenia, the last of which, it seems to me, could have serious implications for Magda. She has, after all, four cats, so there's every chance she has, in fact, contracted *Toxoplasma gondii* and is now suffering from schizophrenia. This would explain her decision to marry herself.

our lives to save another's. I knew then that I'd give my life cheerfully for Cass, which was no big deal. It's just the same thing that's been discovered, and in similar circumstances, by countless other people.

I still feel humbled, inadequate at the memory of the stern courage with which Cass faced her cancer, the extraordinary determination not to be brought down by anything, chemo, hair-loss, contemplation that she might not be here in the future. Still, I think it was Fergie who was the big surprise.

People talk about others in time of trouble as a 'rock' but that's exactly what Fergie was, a slab of absolute determination, refusing to accept under any circumstances that Cass could do anything but live. The day they told her she was clear – I mean really clear, no more check-ups, go away, don't come back – we drank champagne beneath that sweet soft Somerset night in the back garden and I clinked my glass against his while Cass was in the house.

'You were fantastic too,' I said, but he shook his head.

'Nah. Purely selfish.'

'Selfish? No. I don't think so.'

'Yes. Absolutely self-interested.' He turned to face me. 'I knew that I wouldn't survive without your sister.'

I didn't give up the spinster thing with Cass. I said, 'Now here's a thing I bet you didn't know. The actual definition of spinster is a single woman *beyond* the age of marriage.'

'That's me.'

'What?'

'Beyond the age of marriage.'

'But you *are* married.'

Now I know Cass is married, and not just because I was

the bridesmaid at the wedding. The real clincher on this occasion was that only moments earlier I had been in the kitchen with the man I know to be her husband discussing plans for his retirement party.

'Of course. But what I'm saying is, I've done the marriage thing now. And I don't know what it's supposed to be but, by and large, I reckon with the kids and Fergie and everything, I've had just about as good as it gets.'

'So?'

'So if anything happened to him, God forbid, I wouldn't bother doing the thing again, that's all. I'd make a new life for myself. Do something different.'

And then she said it.

'I'd be perfectly happy on my own.'

Because it turns out that C is also for compromise, this according to Cass who says, 'It's wrong to separate out the married and the single. You do it all the time.'

'What exactly?'

'Make the mistake of thinking that people who marry and people who stay single want different things from life.'

'Don't they?'

'No. Everyone wants the same thing at the beginning.'

'Which is?'

'A mixture. Companionship with solitude. Intimacy, but with distance.'

The way Cass describes it, there's this long line, and we're all standing on it, and through that line goes another one bisecting it like a cross. And one side of that central line is labelled Companionship and the other side Solitude.

'And everyone – at least every sane person – wants a bit of both.'

'Only you can't have it.'

'Well, you can but never in equal measure.'

And that's the bastard of the thing, isn't it? In the end that's what shocks you. That life has such a damned limited amount of options. That in the end you have to fall one side of that bisecting line or the other.

Of course, you can pretend, if you like. You can tell the world you've found some grand, adventurous new way of living, get yourself interviewed for one of those life-style features and boast about how you and your Significant Other have cracked the whole companionship and solitude/intimacy and distance thing, how you have this perfect relationship, which allows you both space and comfort, sanctuary and safety. And you can even imagine, if you like, that anyone out there is believing you when all they're really asking is how significant is that Significant Other anyway, when what you really want is to go off and fuck other people.

I said, 'I guess what everyone wants is the best of both worlds. To have their cake and eat it.'

'And why the hell shouldn't we?' Her words were combative, deserving of an answer. She said, 'Life's a compromise however you look at it. Single or married, it's all the same. Doesn't mean we didn't start off wanting the same thing. Doesn't mean we still don't, one way or another.'

Meanwhile, truth to tell, I wasn't that thrilled at the prospect of celebrating Fergie's retirement. Not that I had anything against him retiring. Quite the reverse. I was delighted for him. I figured he deserved it, teaching science for close on thirty years.

'Selfless years, dedicated years.' I clinked my glass against his in the Apple Tree.

'Cherishing young minds . . . nourishing them.'

'Ripping off all their duty-free allowances so you could bring back all that wine and Stella.'

Some people, politicians mainly, like to retire to spend more time with the family. Fergie was retiring to spend more time in his shed at the bottom of the garden. It's there he makes lovely mellow imitation Shaker chairs and tables, which he sells for such wonderfully inflated prices to owners of weekend cottages, the reason he'd been pushing for early retirement.

He's a craftsman, is Fergie. Watch him lathing and planing. Watch the way he runs a hand along with something approaching joy, something so much more than satisfaction. It's the same look I'd see on our father's face, bending inside a bonnet, which was why, I guess, the pair of them got on so well from the moment Cass and Fergie first got together. They'd spend hours together in the garage, Fergie alongside my father, learning, working on whatever was his current old banger. Taking tea out to them, you could feel the mutual appreciation, the companionable nature of the silence.

Anyway, like I say, I wished Fergie well in his new life. I just wasn't that crazy on the idea of a party to celebrate it.

'Oh God, it'll be full of teachers moaning about their pensions.'

Look, the way I feel about teachers is this: whereas it's just possible that putting the proverbial monkeys in a room for a trillion years with a bunch of typewriters might result in the plays of Shakespeare, teachers would still be talking about their pensions.

I'm only jealous, of course. I don't have a pension. Something of which my mother constantly likes to remind me.

'I don't know what you think you're going to do. There won't be anything from me, you know. I'll need the money from this house for a nursing home.'

'No you won't.'

'What do you mean?'

'Oh, I'm sorry. I thought I'd mentioned it. I fully intend to murder you.'

For the record I have made no provision for my retirement, my only plan being a note in my diary to steal a supermarket trolley and put it by, this because I expect there to be a run on them from the several million or so old sixties swingers who, when we all come finally of age, will start moving, pensionless, around the country, probably in marauding gangs, our progress charted each night just before the news using those little triangular symbols rather like the ones for rain, and sleet and snow, which will be slapped onto the weather chart then as now by one of those eternally smiling, highly irritating young women clearly enjoying flaunting her fingernails.

From all this you will deduce that my economic position can best be described as precarious, a major reason why the news that Archie had been invited to the party fell like a dead hand on my heart.

'Oh God. Not Archie.'

Cassie raised an eyebrow in that elder sister way she has, denoting disapproval. 'Of course. Why not?' There was an edge of irritation in her voice. 'Really. I don't know. What is it with you and Archie?'

Precisely how Archie got his squillions is a mystery to me, but then high finance has never been my chosen subject. All I know is (I have chosen not to know more) he was involved in some dot com company selling pet food, or perfume, or toys or something on-line. When it went public

40

he became a zillionaire along with everyone else including the tea lady. Not, you understand, that I am remotely jealous. Something I constantly have to make clear to my mother.

'See . . . see . . .' she said the day the news broke on the financial pages. ('*See* . . .', such a small and insignificant word and yet so pregnant with meaning.) Just in case I should fail to appreciate every last nuance of her wrath, she thundered a pan down on the stove top.

My mother is unable to mention Archie's name these days without adding the rider, 'He's worth a fortune now. You know that, don't you?' And of course I do know it. I know it very well and it doesn't improve my temper, so that to save face I have to come back with a lofty little rejoinder.

'Really, it's of no conceivable interest to me, Mother.' Which is totally untrue because in my heart of hearts I'm as mad as hell, in fact possibly even more pissed off than my mother. Something Danny understands perfectly.

'I mean, the least you can expect from an ex-lover is that he'll have the decency to remain an abject failure.'

'It's not like you're asking for skid row or anything.'

'He doesn't have to be in the gutter.'

'Just respectably hard up.'

'Decently overdrawn.'

'But not, definitely not, a fucking dot com millionaire, darling.'

Despite all the above, Fergie remained firmly unashamed of his decision to invite Archie to the party.

'Never thought he'd accept, if you want to know the truth of it.' He smiled amiably, clutching a pint of his beloved Butcombe to his chest. 'I mean, these days it's practically impossible to get him off that island of his.'

'Of his. *His?*' My mood was getting decidedly nasty. 'You'll be telling me next he owns the bloody thing.'

'No, of course not. He's just got a villa there, that's all.'

'Oh, a villa. Excuse *me*.'

'Well, probably it's not really a villa.' He was backtracking now and I knew it. 'Probably it's just a house. A very small house. Really no more than an apartment.'

'Bollocks. It's a villa. You know it's a villa. And I bet it's got its own pool.'

'I wouldn't know.'

'Yes you would. You'll have seen pictures of it.'

'OK. Yes. It's got a swimming pool.'

'And I suppose the whole thing is surrounded by olive groves.'

'I believe I saw olive groves, yes.'

'And I'll warrant it's set on the side of a hill overlooking the bay.'

'It's true. You can see the sea.'

'And, no doubt, just for good measure, it has one of the terraces where you can sit out in the evening with a glass of wine in your hand and smell the bougainvillaea.' I positively spat the 'b' out at him.

'Well . . .'

'And it'll be furnished with antiques – wooden chests and expensive rugs and brass incense lamps, the sort of stuff you see in *House and Garden*.' And since I was spitting blood by now I thought I might as well end with a flourish. 'And for sure there'll be a fucking maid who comes in every day so you don't have to lift a finger.'

'Ah, now there you're wrong.'

Fergie had found something to take issue with. A relieved

smile flooded across his face. 'There's definitely not a fucking maid.'

His head bent to mine as his voice became distinctly gossipy and conspiratorial. 'Matter of fact he was quite open about that last time we spoke. Said things were a bit thin in that department.'

D is for ... Death, Divorce and Moving House

It may seem trite, it may seem like something straight off the self-help shelves, it may even, in its own way, appear radically revisionist in these dangerous Me-generation times. But still I believe it's worth taking a Count Your Blessings approach to Life, focusing on the plus points rather than the minuses. In this vein, think, oh, think, oh lucky spinster, more to the point, thank your lucky stars.

Divorce will always be something that happens to other people.

You'll never have to:

divide up: the dishwasher
            the washing machine
            the fridge freezer

separate out: the duvet covers
             the cutlery and crockery
             the garden implements

sort through: the holiday snaps
         the DVDs
         the CDs
         the videos

You'll never have to fight for that complete set of Jeffrey Archer.

It's amazing how many Ds you can find to go with divorce.

'Discord . . . dissent . . . dismemberment . . .'

'Dissection . . . disruption . . . um . . . dissolution . . .' Nathan, with his lips drawn back in the eternal faintly mocking smile as we played the game together.

That was the night he told me he was divorced; Nathan, like an old iceberg, only a small jagged part of him poking up out of the water.

'I didn't know.'

'There was no reason why you should. I hadn't told you.' The way he leant back calmly in the plastic-strung chair, a hand curved around his chin, his face all white and bright from the street stall's fizzing gaslamp dangling above us.

'So who was she? How did you meet?'

But his lips were clamped closed now and the shutter had dropped down over his face. Nathan. The Man in the Iron Mask.

'It doesn't matter, Riley. It was a long time ago.' Buttoned-up Nathan. Tight-lipped Nathan. Nathan, with what seemed to be a loathing of sharing this *tittle-tattle* about himself, as if he believed it was frivolous, idle, unnecessary gossip. 'It's of no consequence.'

Nathan, with this formal, old-fashioned way of talking. Drawing his tentacles in with it, covering himself like one of

45

those sea anemones. And all this the reason why it's so hard to reconstruct him now, making me realise how very little in the end in those four months together in Bangkok I really got to know him. Nathan with his *It doesn't matter . . .* and *It's of no consequence.* And *It's nothing to do with us, Riley.*

I said to him that night, 'My parents should have divorced,' perhaps playing for his sympathy. There was concern anyway, a warmth in his eye when he looked up.

'I'm sorry.'

'Are you? Why?'

'Because it's not good. To have unhappy parents.'

It was the first time I'd heard that, I remember. Almost thirty years ago when such things were not said so easily. When people were more *stoical*.

'Isn't it. Don't lots of people have unhappy parents?'

'Some do, yes.'

'And you?'

'Maybe. Yes. But they were already middle-aged when I was born.' Again that look, his fork suspended in the air as if he was considering it. 'I guess by the time I got old enough to really look at them, they were old too. Too old and too traditional to show it.'

I don't know why our parents didn't divorce when I come to think about it now. God knows, my mother threatened it often enough.

'I'm off. You see. I don't need to be stuck here with you.'

'Good. I couldn't be happier.'

'The girls'll come with me. You know that, don't you?'

'Not a chance.'

'Did he really believe that?' I said to Cass. 'That he could take us?'

'I don't know,' she said. 'But I guess, in the end, that's what kept them together.'

All this was in a different age, like I say. A time, I guess, when people did stay together. Unlike now, when forty per cent of couples in this country divorce, fifty per cent in America. Of those people in this country who do weather the storm, eighty per cent say that they've given splitting-up serious consideration. Maybe it's the thought of all that long division that stops them.

In the trauma stakes, divorce ranks second only to death and even this is up for debate. A recent survey carried out by Norwich Union found that forty-six per cent of people who'd divorced said it was more stressful than bereavement. A full forty per cent said they were determined not to marry again because of it.

Death, divorce and moving house. The great triumvirate of trauma:

'Although as far as I'm concerned, one and two are definitely overstated.'*

You could have knocked me over with the proverbial feather when Fleur said that, wiping an exasperated hand

---

* Actually there's some truth in what Fleur says. The question of whether Death should be at the top of the Death, Divorce and Moving House triumvirate is definitely up for debate. In essence, it depends upon precisely who the rating applies to. The definition of trauma, after all, is 'a powerful shock with long-lasting effects'. Thus, while death can certainly be judged to be traumatic for those loved ones left behind, the question has to be asked whether death, i.e., the act of slipping into oblivion, into that bourn from which no traveller returns, can in any logical sense be judged to be traumatic for the person who's died. To me, the answer would seem to be absolutely not.

  'Really?' Magda's voice was decidedly chilly when I made the mistake of discussing it with her. 'Well,' she said (distinctly offended). 'All I can say is, *you* get buried alive as a vestal virgin and then get woken up fifteen hundred years later only to be burnt as a witch, see how *you* like it. See if *you* don't think death is bloody traumatic.'

47

over her forehead. This was mainly because it was the first time in our lives I'd heard her say anything remotely witty. A precursor of things to come, I couldn't help thinking, and almost certainly, I realised afterwards, a direct result of the change in her circumstances.

It was a couple of days after Fergie had heard about his early retirement, and I was returning from the Town Council when I came upon Fleur haranguing the two removal men outside the new block of flats beside the abbey. They were carrying a white sofa up the path, which if I'd looked carefully I would have recognised. I didn't, though, because I thought she must just be helping some friend move house. But then she caught sight of me and waved me over furiously.

'I told them *clearly*. Kitchen stuff *last*.' She flung a hand distractedly up to her Liberty bandanna. 'Now the blasted tea bags are in some tea chest at the back of the wagon.'

'There's a corner shop over there,' I said, pointing towards it. She put a hand up to her forehead, shading her eyes like some newcomer to the colonies gazing over a clearing in the jungle.

'A corner shop?' she said as if I'd used a foreign phrase she'd need translating.

'Best let me go,' I said. 'I speak the language.'

Later, sitting at the kitchen table drinking mugs of tea (she'd made the smaller of two removal men wriggle through to the offending chests to find the mugs plus the kettle), she fixed me with a severe eye.

'I thought you'd have heard.'

'No.' Because I hadn't.

'Really?' A satirical, and I must say entirely warranted expression shot her eyebrows up into her hairline.

'Auntie Barbara *is* slipping.'

Time now I think for you to meet The Other Side Of The Family.

Imagine.

Two households, both alike in dignity . . .

Not.

It's a simply tale, corny too, but none the less poignant for that.

Once upon a time there were two sisters.

One married a humble motor mechanic, the other the son of our town's only major employer.

If you'd opened up the glossy magazines in the fifties you'd have seen full-page ads for Frasers Fine Leathers, the gloves looking more like silk than skin, laid out elegantly like the spokes of a wheel. When the sixties arrived, and no one but the Queen wore gloves any more, Frasers was forced to diversify, which it did and highly successfully. The proof of the pudding is still there in the foyer, a glimpse of the past: John Lennon wearing that famous leather cap, and Patti Boyd, all gap-toothed smile in a Fraser leather skirt the width of a pelmet.

Those were the long-gone glory days of Frasers. Six hundred people worked there then, now it's down to no more than a hundred, the skirts and bags and gloves that still bear the Fraser name turned out in the sweatshops of Eastern Europe and Asia, a boon for its sales manager, a.k.a. my Cousin Royston, younger brother to Fleur, who before Carlotta took him in hand liked to take full advantage in recreational terms of visiting suppliers.

I was still at school and Royston had yet to be even a gleam in his parents' eyes when I had a Saturday job at

Frasers. I worked in the shop, which was run by Miss Eames, a serious spinster who wore a net over her hair, which she'd blue-rinsed so many times it had turned a glorious funky purple.

The shop was just off the foyer then, busy enough to cover two floors and connected by a narrow curving staircase where Cousin Freddy, elder brother to Fleur, caught me one Saturday and tried to stick his tongue down my throat in an effort to widen his sexual experience. I like to remember this thirty years on, watching him tapping his pinky finger against his wine glass, and sticking out his Toad of Toad Hall chest and making one of his pompous head-of-the-firm little speeches at family parties.

Frasers has been part of our town for close on two hundred years. It became part of our family one day in 1946 when my Aunt Fran met my Uncle Hugh in Millington's Café at the bottom of the High Street (now the Avalon Alternative Health and Therapy Centre). She was introduced by her sister, Babs, a lesson to us all. i.e., when pursuing the man of your dreams take care not to be accompanied by your younger, better-looking sister.

Required to explain what happened that day in Millington's, I suspect the words 'We wuz robbed' would best suit my mother. At family gatherings, after her fifth gin and tonic, she likes to murmur in a noble and meaningful voice, 'Of course, I got to know Hugh first.' This closely followed by, 'We met when we were *serving*.'

To this day my mother regards herself as having been cheated over Hugh Fraser. She'd like to bring Life to account for it, accuse it of having lost the plot, and I have some sympathy with her over this. Because not only did she meet Hugh before Fran, but they met in circumstances that it was fair to expect would have led to the most

50

romantic of conclusions, i.e., a junior officer and a typist from the same small country town cast up in the middle of a war a couple of thousand miles from home in North Africa.

And all this while Sister Fran was back in Blighty and doing no more for King and Country than rolling bandages.

At Fraser family gatherings my mother gets very drunk, drags at Hugh's arm, dredging up memories of Cairo.

'Remember, Hugh, oh, remember . . .' this clapping her hands girlishly. 'Those mad nights at Groppi's, Hugh. Martinis at Shepheards. Oh, and those *wonderful* Sunday night concerts . . .'

In all this she likes to imply to anyone willing to listen, and to those who aren't, that something more passed between Hugh Fraser and Babs Gordon née Garland in Cairo than the mere exchange of pleasantries when the junior officer caught the West Country burr of his typist.

'Of course, I'd met George by then,' she'll say with a brave smile and a demure droop of her eyes, this designed to imply a love story tragically foreshortened.

And indeed she had met our father – met him and almost certainly ruled him out of the picture. But when fate took a hand via Hugh and Aunt Fran she needed to save face and quickly. So it was that when George came to visit next time she snared him like a spider, this so that when her sister walked up the aisle she was able to watch from her pew with the satisfied feeling of her fingers tucked into husband's elbow.

Hugh, meanwhile, always acts the perfect gentleman when she puts on her pantomime at family parties. For Hugh is a nice man. A good man. A decent man. He lets our mother reminisce for a while, before patting her hand and then gently disengaging it. But while Hugh is kind to old Babs Gordon, his only daughter, my Cousin Fleur, has never felt any similar compunction.

At the firm's parties, where my mother likes to play the family card, act like Lady Bountiful with the workers, Fleur's chilly little favourite is: 'I see your mother's enjoying herself,' the phrase normally accompanied by a thin smile and a nod in the direction of Babs growing steadily more raucous in the corner.

(Oh God, if only our mother would get *tired* and emotional.)

'I'm only surprised your mother hasn't heard,' Fleur said, that day she dragged me in for tea, a bitchy remark but one entirely well-founded, my mother being the human equivalent of a sniffer dog when it comes to searching out family scandal and misdemeanour.

'HA!' my mother said with a smile the size of a water-melon when I passed on the startling news about Fleur leaving Martin.

'Old-Poker-Up-The-Arse' this being the *nom de guerre* Babs Gordon coined for her niece close on thirty years ago when Fleur, still only fifteen, strayed fatally beyond her years to ask at one of those family parties, 'Don't you think you've had enough, Auntie Barbara?' Suffice it to say that my mother did not approach the question in any sense as rhetorical, and that everyone standing within a radius of fifty feet took the answer to be in the negative.

To put all this into context, i.e., to appreciate the significance of Fleur leaving Martin, you need to be aware of the way in which Fleur has played the little wifey during the twenty-three years of their marriage. On the night they got engaged, for instance, she informed me in all serious-ness that she considered the occupation of wife and mother 'a woman's highest calling' (she used those words precisely).

'Gosh,' I said. 'You and Joseph Goebbels.'

Fleur was nineteen when she got engaged to Martin. They were married two years later.

'I've been the perfect wife,' she said that day at her kitchen table, looking over the top of her mug at me, and I couldn't argue. Apart from anything else, she's even looked the perfect wife – her long straight fair hair sitting impeccably behind a velvet Alice band, her lobes graced with no more than small pearl earrings. She brought up her children too with this same degree of perfection, three of them – Mark and Hannah and James – all of whom have that same perfect straight fair hair and perfect teeth, and who have so far failed absolutely to do the slightest thing to disgrace their parents (Hannah at some fancy cooking school, Mark and James both at good universities).

I suppose it was always inevitable that Fleur would play the part of older wiser women with me, and this despite being seven years younger.

'Relationships are something you have to work at, Riley,' she told me severely on another occasion, hearing that another one of mine had bitten the dust.

'I've got a job,' I said. 'Who needs another one?'

Over the years, Fleur's conversation has been entirely dominated by *Martin and I*, and *our* house . . . *our* car . . . *our* holiday . . . *our* children. Her tongue would slick along those pale pink lips in self-satisfaction as she said the words. To all outward appearances she and Martin were joined at the hip. A few years ago, for instance, she offered me a free weekend in Paris she'd won in some upmarket shopping competition.

'I can't go,' she said. 'Martin's working.'

'Go with a friend,' I said. 'All else fails, I'll go with you.'

She looked at me like I was suggesting group sex or

experimenting with hallucinogenics. 'I *couldn't*,' she said. 'I simply couldn't. Martin and I do *everything* together.'

Only not any more, apparently.

'He's become so *boring*.'

Now this was a shameful lie. A total untruth. Martin had not become boring at all. Martin was always boring. Martin is a country estate agent. He drives a Volvo. He's a member of Rotary. He's *supposed* to be boring.

In her new kitchen that day, as the small army of women washed up and put stuff away around her (apparently *all* in the *wrong* places), Fleur clattered our mugs together and got up from the table with the air of someone setting out on a journey.

'I told Martin now the children are away I want time for ME . . . time to find myself, time to get my head together.' (Time to find a new scriptwriter. R. Gordon.)

She said, 'I need space . . .' a particularly nice touch, this, I thought, since she was leaving behind an executive home with half a dozen bedrooms, a games room in the basement, an ensuite with sauna, a swimming pool and a lounge the size of Wembley Stadium.

Listening to Fleur that day I felt as though I'd slipped into some alternative reality, like someone had wound the clock back. I was hearing phrases that day I thought never to hear again, that I'd thought safely dead and buried by the end of the seventies. And if I was hoping that somewhere along the line Fleur would see the irony of all this, bearing in mind all that *kinder, kirche, küche,* stuff she'd put the rest of us through over the years, I was about to be disappointed. Clearly Fleur didn't do Nazi allusions.

'I've worked my fingers to the bone for him over the years.' Her grey eyes were innocent, open wide. Challenging disagreement. 'I've been nothing but a wife and mother.'

That was when it occurred to me that something seriously sinister might be happening, that maybe Fleur had been the subject of some spooky personality transplant, a kind of Stepford Wife reversal, or maybe – this would work – maybe *it wasn't Fleur at all*. Maybe she'd been substituted overnight by a lookalike, possibly as part of a plot involving an alien species.

'I'm going to do all the things I've never done, all the things I've never had time to do.' There was something severe, dedicated, *nun-like* in her face. She was staring into the distance. I swear to God she was *pledging*.

'Like what?'

'I'm not sure yet. There's so many things. I thought I might take art classes, perhaps even do a foundation course. Or there again,' and here she paused and there was a small gleam of something that might have been spite,' I thought I might do what you do – write some kids' stories.' Her arms were crossed against her chest in a self-satisfied fashion as we stood on the landing and below us the lift began clunking upwards.

'The children have been on at me for years to do it.'

'Really?'

'Oh, yes. I always told them stories, you know. When they were young. They loved it.'

I was musing on the horror of this when suddenly her face was right there beside me.

'I'm going to tell you something now.'

Her voice had changed. It was girly, confidential, which is when I thought: oh God, no. Please, God, no. Not one of those horrible marital secrets.

She said, 'In the whole of my married life . . .' and I thought, no, no. Please, no. Nothing personal. Nothing horribly intimate like she never had an orgasm with Martin, or he wanted to wear her shoes or he would only have sex with her in the back of the Volvo. Please, God, nothing that's going to flash up over Martin's head next time I bump into him in the High Street.

But all she said was, 'Do you know, in the whole of my married life I've never even *seen* a gas bill.'

She pronounced the words with wonder, laying her crossed hands upon the upper part of her chest. There was about her a palpable mixture of excitement and self-satisfaction.

And while in my work I attempt at all times to follow Elmore Leonard's Fourth Rule of Good Writing, the one which states an adverb should never be used to modify a verb, still on this occasion I find myself forced to transgress it.

'Life's going to be one big adventure,' I said. And I have to admit that I said the words drily.

E is for . . . Eleutherophobia

It's a strange thing to come from where the sea should be. I have this theory that it leaves you with an odd sense of impermanence, nothing between you and the ocean but a dozen or so miles of moorland and the few hunks of Ham stone that make up the sea defences. I have this recurring dream. I think it might be racial memory. I'm standing on a shingle beach with the sea piling up in a high grey wall and dropping down dead in front of me.

I'm bred to the bone in this town. My mother's family goes back six generations. I've lived most of my life here. Still I'm convinced most of the time the place doesn't suit me, in particular the moors, which are just too damn low, too damn *brooding*. As a kid I'd be scared, waking up to a lake where the fields used to be with just the tops of the gates poking up and the spiky willow branches like clutches of drowning fingers. I dislike the rhines too (pronounce them reens); distrust them. They may look harmless enough, just innocent ditches with their covering of irises and marsh orchids, but they can swallow a car whole. One did, when I was a kid, taking with it a mother and her two children.

They unsettle me, the moors that surround my home town, that's the truth of it. I always think that, walking to the office window, looking out at them. I feel the weight of history from those old trackways, the featherlight dust of the bones of a thousand dead Monmouth rebels, the more so driving across them. I don't care for the low roads. I feel like I'm always looking over my shoulder, expecting the sea to come back, just to take a notion one day to crash through those paltry sea defences, or the river to suddenly breach, bursting through the banks that rise higher than the car roof, pouring down on top of me.

'This place. It's just so damn *ancient*, that's the trouble,' I said to Sophie one day, staring out through her cottage window. 'I mean, when you think about it, prehistoric creatures once roamed those moors.'

'Well, you should know,' she said. 'You went out with most of them.'

A word about Sophie now.

Sometimes people I haven't seen for a long time or who don't really know me will say, 'Are you still friends with Sophie?' and I won't know what to say. It's like the words don't make sense to me. Like they've got their syntax wrong or they're speaking a foreign language.

I mumble something usually. 'Sure . . . yes . . . of course. Naturally . . .'

What I really want to say is: Am I still standing here? Am I still breathing?

Sophie Aitchison and I met over the old green baize desks in the newsroom of the *Free Press*, our local weekly newspaper. Until I left at twenty-two to travel – hence her knowledge of my prehistoric sex life – we also shared a flat together.

As with so many things in my life – jobs, affairs – I fell into journalism. I'm an aspiration-less bastard, if you want to know the truth of it. In addition I'm lazy, bone idle. I see myself as a sort of Friday afternoon person, juddering along that old Assembly Line of Life. Suddenly someone calls out and the Angel Assistant turns. And, hey presto, there I go, juddering on past and out into the world minus that vital component of ambition.

Unlike Cass, whose name, even to this day, is emblazoned in gold in the hall of the distinguished old girls' grammar school we both attended, I failed miserably at everything, exiting with barely an O level. In the local careers office they went through a thick book of career options from nuclear physicist at the front (not enough O levels) to Stand and Tan assistant at the back. (I lie. Stand and Tan had yet to be invented.) They said, 'Is there *nothing* you want to do?' and I didn't feel it was appropriate to say that was exactly it, that the only thing I really wanted to do was nothing. Luckily butterflies were even at that moment beating their wings. Not on the other side of the world either but slap-bang outside my father's garage.

It's a truth universally acknowledged that a man stuck with a daughter around the house who shows no sign of getting a job will grab the first opportunity to do something about it. George Gordon was no exception. He moved swiftly the day that old khaki Ford Pop puttered to a halt. He knew that car and more importantly he knew its owner. Head bent beneath that upraised bonnet that day, he gave the sort of horror-struck intake of breath that would have won him Best Actor from the Academy of Motor Engineers if only the judges had been there to hear it. Its owner, with four children to support and a too substantial mortgage, blanched at the sound and at the mournful shake of the head that accompanied it.

Thus it was that Harry Oates, editor of the *Free Press*, got his car mended for free and I got a job on this paper.

My current incarnation here is my second. It's a nice irony, although not by any means an accident, that that same Sophie Aitchison is now my editor.

Sophie and I have now spent a considerable part of our lives working together. Not long after I left to travel, she also departed, to a down-table sub's job on the Bristol evening paper. She was still there, although rising up the table, when I returned from my travels. No sooner had I set foot in my home town, than certain circumstances necessitated a flight from it (all will be explained), so that for a while – for the second time in our lives – we lived together. Her position with the paper meant she was able to put in a good word for me when a job came up and I subsequently spent the best part of seven years there in the end, first on news and then as a features writer. I left for what would prove to be an unhappy spell in freelance public relations, something which at least had the advantage of propelling me into that English degree at the university. It was here that I started to write, producing the first of the 'Aunts' books for which I am now (mildly) famous.

After some success I was able to give up the day job (I had moved the twenty-five miles back to my home town by then; bought this cottage). Over the years the media group that owned Sophie's paper had acquired various weeklies, one of them being the *Free Press*. When the job of editor came up she applied for and got the position, which proved to be a godsend for me, since by this time my life, for various reasons, no one reason, had fallen into financial disrepair and I was in dire need of some extra income. Treating accusations of nepotism with the contempt they deserved, she offered me a job so that today my life has come full circle. I'm back where I started, something which no longer worries me.

Thus now I work three days a week at the *Free Press* (Mondays, Tuesdays and Wednesdays should you wish to contact me). This helps cover the bills and at the same time leaves me plenty of time for my writing. Lest you should think I am the subject of any favouritism from my editor, given our previous association, I can assure you this is not the case. I get the same treatment, the same bum jobs as everyone else in the newsroom, something confirmed one Wednesday a couple of weeks after the Fleur episode when I found myself marked down to cover the latest example of New Age lunacy in my home town – the opening of Bad Ponytail Peter's new phobia clinic.

OK: some facts about my home town. First off, I won't be naming it because there's a pair of genuine olde worlde sixteenth-century stocks at the bottom of our High Street and I don't want find myself sitting in them.* And while I don't believe in all this witchcraft crap, still, with a coven on every street corner (each with accompanying website) you can't be too careful.

You see it's Flake City, my home town, the Wacko Capital of the Kingdom. Other places have the Town Band, the Soroptomists, the Gardeners' Club. We have the Tantric Drummers, the Wicca Society and Friday Night Channelling.

---

* Still, if you've done the West Country tour, which I'll warrant more than a few of you have, you won't have too much trouble identifying it.

Some people believe the ley lines conjoin in my home town. Some think we've been visited by aliens (something I give more credence to than most but only because of my mother). Some think that Joseph of Arimathea visited, that King Arthur is buried here.[*] What's certain is that the myths are pressed down hard, layered like the peat in the moors, and that now we dig them up and shovel them out the same way in every New Age shop and emporium. It's been this way since the mid-sixties when the first tepee went up, the first long-haired aristo clip-clopped in on his horse-drawn caravan.

Today, you can buy fifty-six different varieties of Tibetan Bell in the High Street of my home town along with every conceivable shape of crystal and candle.

The problem is you're screwed if you want half a pound of tomatoes.

Bad Ponytail Peter's already on the pavement outside the Avalon Alternative Health and Therapy Centre[†] when I arrive with Danny snapping away in front of him. Once approaching him from the back like this would have been the best way to observe the long straggle of greasy grey from which he got his name. But then one day, possibly because of that grey, he shaved it off.

'Shocking,' Danny said the first time we saw him without it. 'The loss of a national treasure.'

It was more as a tribute than anything else that we

---

[*] Even though those who know say all this is just early spin-doctoring on the part of the abbey.

[†] Previously, you may recall, Millington's Café where Aunt Fran shamelessly stole Uncle Hugh from my mother.

decided to keep the name. Thus, shaven-headed as he is, he remains Bad Ponytail Peter, a.k.a. Peter Tarantine, Reiki Grand Master, author,[*] Thought Field Therapist, re-birther, channeller, chakra cleanser, aura diviner, director of the Wicca Academy . . .

'He's also a Grand Vizor . . .'

'I'd never have known.'

Which is why Bad Ponytail Peter will be conducting the ceremony at Magda's wedding.

This being the Flake Date of the Month it's no surprise that Magda's here drinking her dandelion wine, biting into her lentil vol-au-vent, or that there are more aromatherapists, reflexologists, Indian head massagers, I Chingers, crystals healers and white witches that you could shake a stick at (shaking a stick somehow seeming an appropriate piece of imagery for this bunch with their assorted weird *modus operandi*).

'So, you think there's a demand?' I asked Peter (my standard business start-up question). He gave me a pitying look through the new rimless glasses he's adopted, probably to make him look more like a therapist.

'My dear,' this is in his smooth, creepy Aleister Crowley voice, 'the world is *awash* with phobias.'

Now, before we go any further, I should like to point out that whereas I don't have the first idea where my chakras are, I do know I'd have to be held down by a team of ten before I let Bad Ponytail Peter cleanse them, plus I wouldn't let him near my aura.

---

[*] *Nettles for Health*, *Your Aura and You*, *Chakra Cleansing for Beginners*, *Mysteries of the Tarot*, etc., etc., all Demeter Press, available from the Avalon Alternative Health and Therapy Centre, Hocus Pocus and by mail order.

'Many people's lives are ruined by phobias, not least because they don't even realise they have them,' he said, and I pretty much knew what was coming. 'For instance, they may have problems with *relationships*.'

He pronounced the word in the manner of an accusation, so that I figured if I could open up his forehead, pull it down like a hatch I'd see the vision he has of himself, in *Joy of Sex* mode, leading some luckless female through an ecstatically gymnastically challenging position. He's pitiless when it comes to sex, according to Magda, who had an deeper than usual channelling session with him one Friday night.

'He's just so *serious*,' she said after one glass of wine too many. 'He won't give in. You just feel this terrible *responsibility* to have an orgasm.'

Meanwhile, it seems there's no end of the weird things people can be scared of. The list on the leaflet I picked up from Peter was full of them – clowns, chickens, feathers, chins . . .

Chins?

'I mean, how can you be scared of chins?'

But Danny's looking sideways in the office mirror. 'Easily.' He slaps a hand at his throat. 'Particularly when you think you might be getting another one.'

It's tough life being a gay man, the way I hear it from Danny. He's ten years younger than me but still he says, 'On the scene, let me tell you, I'm past it.' Not that he's really interested in the scene. He only goes occasionally to clubs although he does do the odd personal ad and on-line dating.

I nag him sometimes. 'You're burying yourself down here in the country. You should get out more. Go up to town. Meet more people.'

He says, 'Look who's talking.'

He's been pretty much single since he moved down here nine years ago, and this in part to start a new life without Doctor Jack, the big love of his life, who spent most of their time together turning him over emotionally before finally dumping him.

'You're getting too *comfortable*, too contented, that's your trouble,' I say to him sometimes. 'Trust me. I know about these things. I'm a spinsta.'

Sometimes I'll wave exotic job ads in front of him, and he'll take them with a show of interest but somehow he never applies for them. More often than not he'll use his parents as an excuse. 'I like to be near them.'

Danny loves his parents, not least because of the way his father handled Danny's coming out, which occurred with supremely bad timing at his sister's wedding.

Danny got rather drunk at Ruth's wedding, having not long been dumped by Jack. Thus when he was asked by an ancient aunt when he too would be getting married, he answered glumly that he couldn't say, first because Jack had just dumped him, but more importantly because as yet it wasn't legal. His mother, standing close by and over-hearing this, thus had her worse suspicions confirmed. She promptly burst into tears, refusing to stop until Danny's father shouted in exasperation, 'For God's sake, woman, stop your snivelling. The boy's queer, not dead.' Thus instead of pointing a quivering finger at the door and quoting Leviticus (a particularly useful Old Testament book, apparently, especially if you're in two minds about how to sacrifice your bullock) he merely gave Danny a severe dressing-down for the way he'd broken the news to his mother.

'Totally thoughtless.'

Which as a matter of fact, growing more penitent, not to say sober, by the minute, Danny agreed with.

Ten years later, Danny's brother-in-law now being a high-flying academic and his sister all over the place (they're currently *en famille* in America), Danny, the gay son (as is so often the case) is the mainstay of the family. Truth to tell, he plays the spinster daughter, visiting his parents once a week (they live in Bath) and accompanying them on their annual cultural trips to Europe (Italian painters, Echoes of Byzantium, etc., etc.). More often than not it'll be some single attractive woman he makes friends with, and I can't help imagining the disappointment they must feel with this handsome forty-two-year old, with his serious air and his cropped head and his rimless glasses. Because apart from the odd eye-rolling moment, he hates the whole campy thing and is undemonstrative in the main. A gay man would spot him, of course. Eye contact would do that. But for a straight woman . . . how sad.

'Don't worry,' Danny says, patting my hand. 'They soon get the picture when they realise we're after the same waiter.'

Meanwhile there are fears from Arachnophobia to Zemmiphobia on Peter's list. Zemmiphobia? Fear of the Great Rat?

'Fear of the Great Rat?' Danny shook his head, reading out from the list. 'What the hell's that about?'

'I don't know,' I said. 'But I guess if I'd had it, I'd have been ready for Lennie.'

'Deipnophobia? A fear of after-dinner conversations. Wooh, that's weird too.'

'Not at all. It's the reason I don't do personal ads and on-line dating.'

That was when I felt a tap on my arm and found Fleur standing beside me.

The phobia clinic opening was the last place I was expecting to see her. Turned out she'd given up the art course idea, and writing a children's book (for this, much thanks). Instead she was thinking of signing up for a course in aromatherapy.

'I have to think of ways of making a living,' she said. 'I'm on my own now.'

'Well, not exactly,' as I said later to Cass, 'bearing in mind Martin's renting the flat for her, and that Fraser family money.'

But Fleur was enjoying herself, I could see that. There was a definite air of nobility about her.

'I married so young,' she said, a hand on her chest now and faintly tragically.

'What?' as I said to Cass. 'Like she'd been given in marriage at thirteen to some European crown head.'

'Of course, I realise it's going to be hard at first,' Fleur said, 'paying my own way and everything, strange too after all our years together.' She gave me one of those flat-faced challenging looks, the sort you get from government ministers in unsound regimes when they're shamelessly rewriting history for the cameras. 'I'm just *so* looking forward to having time to myself,' she said, 'to being on my own.'

'Un-bloody-believable,' I said, reporting it. 'This from the woman who used to shiver at the mere thought of it.'

'I can't tell you,' Fleur said, 'how much I'm looking forward to being *single*.'

'How dare she?' I said. 'Calling herself *single*.'

'Well, I suppose she is.'

'Not at all. She's just *claiming* the title.'

But the final outrage, as far as I was concerned, was still to come. I was crossing the road from the Avalon Centre, glad to be getting away from her, when suddenly there she was again, beside me.

'I feel wonderful,' she said, thrusting her arm chummily through mine, making me feel like I'd been caught by a stalker. She flung her head back, face to the sun in a grand flamboyant gesture. 'Ah . . . freedom,' she said, and there it was, the final insult, the ultimate profanity.

Freedom.

My lodestar. My guiding light. *Appropriated* by Fleur as part of her new-found persona.

There's a name for fear of freedom. I found it on Peter's list. It's eleutherophobia. A fancy word for the fear of it, but no mention – mark you – of a term for the terror of losing it.

'I just want to feel free,' I said to Nathan one night, not long before the end.

He said, 'It's just a word, Riley.'

I said, 'I just want to do what I want to do, that's all . . . go where I want to go . . . live the life I want to live.'

In the silence the air conditioner clattered while somewhere in the distance, a mah-jong piece was slapped down heavily on a table.

He said, 'I'm not trying to tie you down. That's not what love's about, Riley.'

I don't know why I went travelling. All in all, I could have just stayed at home. Waited for all that bead-and-bangle hippy shit to come walking up the High Street.

Still the facts of the case are that in 1972 I did what it seemed at the time like half the country was doing, at least those of my age and inclinations. I bought a large orangey-red rucksack with a steel frame that bit into my back and rose up over my head like the beak of some giant bird, packed it full of toilet rolls and soap and shampoo and salt tablets, although not all the other weird stuff – mosquito netting and the malaria pills – which Tommy, with his war service in India, insisted I'd be needing.

Some said we did this thing because of a war, others because of a lack of one. Whatever. I did the same as everyone else anyway, went on the Hippy Trail, joined that crazy, grand, absurd, pretend peace and love diaspora.

It was the day before I left Nepal for Bangkok when it came to me, that thing about freedom. I'd hired a bike, cycled out of Kathmandu. I was lying down on the grass verge with the scent of the pines in my nostrils, the wheels of the bike still whirring and clicking beside me.

As I stared up into the crystal-blue canopy above me, I thought about everyone back home and, in particular, I thought about them working and I felt a deep, satisfied sense of pleasure that I was here doing nothing.

I thought, this is what freedom feels like. And the revelation seemed so real and so true I could have reached out and touched it.

It seemed to come right out of the heart of all that blueness.

F is for . . . Finances

I guess I should go back to Bangkok now. Because that's what writers do, isn't it? When they want the past and the present to collide in their head. They go back to the scene of the affair. Which is what I should do – hole up in some backstreet hotel, beat out the story on an old upright Smith Corona with the sounds of the city outside the window, and the sun slanting through the dirty dusty Venetian blinds and making patterns on the wall, all of which would remind me conveniently of Nathan's hotel room and our afternoon lovemaking sessions. Except that I don't remember us making love in the afternoon, and anyway I can't go back because I never go anywhere now. For one thing I can't fly.

'Can't?' Archie's look was curious over the top of his glass as the hubbub of Fergie's party rose and fell around us.

'No.' I could feel myself growing defensive. 'Look, it's no big deal. I just don't like flying, that's all.'

He said, 'No one *likes* flying, Riley.'

Being an aviophobe (thanks, Peter) or if you prefer it a pteromerhanophobe, isn't the only thing that keeps my feet on the ground. The other reason I don't travel is that I can't afford it. Not a problem that afflicts the former, now reformed Frau Goebbels.

A week on from the phobia clinic opening I met her in the High Street. She was all Nike-ed up on her way to the gym. In training. For her holiday. Seems she'd done another rethink, this on the aromatherapy course. Now she'd signed up for one of those heavy-duty hi-adventure holidays, white-water rafting, hang-gliding round Everest or something. In Hocus Pocus, where she dragged me for a coffee, she thrust a brochure in my face. It was full of bronzed surfer types with very white teeth doing exciting things in lifejackets and baggy shorts and very black sunglasses.

'Ah, bless,' as I said to Cass. 'And Martin, the poor mutt, still thinks she's coming back to him.'

I know this is what Martin thinks on account of the fact that he told me. I bumped into him by chance a few days later although 'bumped into' is scarcely the right term. Alerted by the merry strains of the accordion and seeing the knot of visitors in the Market Place, and thus the lie of the land, I leapt into a shop doorway. But too late. Mid-leap he caught my eye above the crowd and gave his hand-kerchief an extra loud snap in the air to show that he'd seen me.

Against all the odds, Martin is a morris dancer, although perhaps not, bearing in mind that for him morris dancing represents the raffish and unpredictable side to his nature. Like so many of his kind (i.e., the bank manager, two solic-itors, surveyor and accountant who constitute the rest of the troop) he thinks it's evidence of the fact that he's not boring, an allegation apparently that Fleur not only made to me, but more cruelly flung at him at the time of their parting.

71

'Boring. Can you believe it? That's what she called me.'

There's a sorrowful confusion on his face that would have touched my heart if I hadn't remembered just in time that he was an estate agent.

Even Martin's ankle bells had a mournful tinkle to them that day. His mood could be detected in the half-hearted way he flapped his handkerchief.

'It's just a phase she's going through,' he said, using it to mop his brow as we sat on the town hall steps. 'She just needs a break, that's all – a bit of space. That's why I agreed to get her the flat.' The misery was beginning to subside by now and his eyes were becoming matter-of-fact and hopeful. 'What do you think, Riley?'

I couldn't answer, not for the lump in my throat – there wasn't one (like I say, in the last analysis Martin *is* still an estate agent) – merely for the memory of all those beautiful baggy-shorted young men and Fleur's lustfully glowing enthusiasm.

'I should have thought this would be the sort of thing you'd fancy, Riley,' she said that day, pushing the page towards me from which a particularly appealing tousle-haired young Icarus stared out at me, dark glasses exploding into stars of sunlight.

'Not me,' I said, flipping the brochure closed and pushing it back across the table. 'Me, I get all the adrenalin rush I need just opening the post in the morning.'

Listen, do you ever get the feeling that Life's a card game, and that you're the only one at the table busking it because you don't know the rules? Well, that's pretty much the way I've always felt watching other people get married. I'd poke in and around my own heart, trying to find something, a yearning, an inclination, finding only a gap, an absence where both were supposed to be. At the same time I'd know it had to be me, that there had to be a good reason why people got married, since most of them did it. And now I've discovered it. The explanation. The reason it's so popular. The hitherto unspoken, undisclosed Official Secret that everybody else knew but forgot to mention to me. The biggest cliché in the book. So bloody obvious it was staring me in the face.

Two can live as cheaply as one, right? And while it's not Isaac Newton and the apple, or Archimedes and the bath, still it explains why any sensible human being should want to get married.

You wouldn't think it would take so long to dawn on me, would you? This simple truth. Or that it would appear in the manner of that Great White Light on the Road to Damascus. But that's exactly what happened as I complained to Cass about Fleur's cavalier use of the word 'single'.

'Look, I've earnt the title. I've paid all my own bills all my life.'

Which is the precise moment when it exploded over my head like some sort of revelation, the simple fact that all those marrieds and cohabitees, being *à deux*, only have to find the cash for half of the bills that drop down on their doormat every month while I, being one alone and single, have to fork out for the whole damn lot of them.

Question: if two people can live as cheaply as one, then how much is one alone paying as compared with one living as part of a twosome? Write on both sides of the page, preferably using graphs and pie charts.

'When you think about it, it really *costs* to stay single,' I moaned one day to Sophie.

'So what?' she said. 'Everything in life costs one way or another.' And I see that. But still . . .

According to a recent survey[*] the average married fifty-year-old with a mortgage, pension and all the other joint accumulated financial paraphernalia assembled after the best part of thirty years spent together, is worth about fifty grand. By contrast the average never-married single of the same age is likely to be worth only half of that (in my case, if only, but that's another story), good grounds for getting married, I can see that (although personally I'd want at least a couple of mill, plus a peerage and the thanks of a grateful nation).

The main reason why married couple's finances are supposed to be better in general than those of single people – and this according to the same survey – is that coupledom forces those involved to do more financial planning, this because most will be wanting children, and therefore know that up ahead somewhere, sometime they'll be faced by major financial considerations like university fees and, in the case of daughter or daughters (unless they can be persuaded to elope), large and expensive white weddings.

Being part of a couple, it's alleged, acts as a brake on spending, because individuals in the relationship have to account for their purchases to a partner and are thus unlikely to indulge in splurges in the manner of single people. 'Absolute rubbish,' according to Cass, citing somewhat tersely as evidence her discovery only minutes earlier of Fergie reading the paper, in his dirty overalls on the new white sofa she'd bought in her lunch time and had delivered. His excuse, shouted in an injured tone

---

[*] Carried out for BestInvestment.com and reported in my mother's paper.

74

from halfway up the stairs where he'd been sent to change, 'Well, no one mentioned a new sofa to me,' appears to further bear out her argument.

Tie the knot at thirty, according to the survey, and merely by doing so you'll increase your personal financial potential by some fourteen per cent. Come seventy-five, and the Marks and Spencer's slippered pantaloon, oh, married sister, you'll be worth a full thirty per cent more than the spinster.

There's a catch to all this, though, and I'll warrant some of you have already spotted it and quite possibly from bitter experience. To stay in the money, you have to stay married.

For spinsters, as it turns out, are not at the bottom of the pile financially. That honour goes to the newly single, those people currently in the middle of a separation.

Clearly there are exceptions to this rule. I'm sure we can all name one from within these pages. In general, however, the income of a woman, especially one with a young child or children, nose-dives on the break-up of a marriage.

Widows may also suffer the same fate. On the other hand, they may just emerge from their husband's death doing the Merry Widow waltz. Which you might say is what happened to our mother.

George Gordon died one wet Wednesday afternoon returning from a car auction in his well-loved, much-mended old Humber Snipe, a tank of a car, which when it left the road on the bend, managed to crash through a hedge and fence before hitting a tree, and all this with only a small dent to its bumper.

George's death was his finest hour, as far as Babs was

concerned, thanks to the discovery of the insurance policies in the bottom drawer of his desk. This, plus the sale of the much-depised garage, left her what she always wanted to be, comfortably off and still respectably married in the eyes of the world, but without the day-to-day irritation of a husband.

Words cannot describe the speed and dexterity with which our mother metamorphosed from carping, miserably mis-married wife to tragic heartbroken widow. *Oh . . . George . . .* achieved with his death what he could never have achieved in his lifetime. He became 'Poor George', and 'Dear George', and finally, 'My George', this a last self-satisfied little sideswipe at all those damned spinsters.

Cass and Fergie had been married only six weeks when our father died. Still, it was lucky in its way, this because at least it meant that Fergie was now a member of the family and was thus able to officially identify the body. It was his first experience of mortality being still a young man. He came back shaken and with Archie who'd come down to help.

'Why are you here?' I said to Archie, unreasonably angrily.

'Why do you think?' he said, which I thought didn't answer the question.

In fact he did prove to be helpful, not least to me. He provided me with a butt for my anger. I was hurting inside and out over my father's death. I wanted to vent all that hurt on someone and Archie seemed eminently suitable.

'What *is* the matter with you?' Cass said, angry herself after I'd shouted at him to leave me alone when he'd tried to comfort me.

'He shouldn't be here,' I said. 'It's family.'

'Don't be so bloody unreasonable,' she said. 'Can't you see how useful he is, particularly for Fergie?'

At our father's funeral, our mother carried her wreath before her like the Queen at the Cenotaph on Remembrance Sunday. Afterwards she stood at the lich-gate in her new little black suit and her six-inch heels and her Jackie O pillbox, dabbing at her eyes through the veiling.

The line of mourners stretched down the church path. Most were customers, people whose cars he'd repaired for next to nothing with that string and those six-inch nails, among them a small flotilla of spinsters.

'Paying their respects,' our mother snarled in an aside, dropping the tragic widow act for one blissful moment. 'Why not? They paid for bugger all else in his lifetime.'

I wanted to shout at her then, I remember. I wanted to shout, 'So what? What does it matter?' I wanted to tell her right there, under the lich-gate, what an awful human being I thought she was. How much better I believed he was than she. How angry I was that by sheer bad luck the only decent part of my parentage was now dead with the stupid, rotten vain part left behind. I stormed away, up the path, beside the line of mourners to get away from her, to be alone. I found a quiet spot hidden from view in the furthest corner of the graveyard where I sat on an ancient gravestone that had fallen flat, and was resting under a tree, which is where Archie found me.

'I'm sorry . . .' he said, the words hesitant. 'Cass sent me. They've left for the house. I've to give you a lift.'

'I don't want a lift with you,' I said, astonished because I hadn't been crying before but now I was. Suddenly tears that had not been there a moment before were running down my face. 'I don't want to go with you. You of all people. I never wanted to see you again, you know that.'

He took a step towards me. He said, 'Look, Riley . . . please . . . I just want to say something.' But my shouted words stopped him in his tracks.

'I don't want you to say something. Don't you understand? I just want you to go away.' I laid a hand on my heart, feeling suddenly faint. Violently sick. 'Go away . . .' I said. 'Go away. How many times do I have to ask you? Just leave me alone, will you?' and I dropped down on the stone.

I heard his steps receding behind my back as I threw up in the long grass beside it.

I didn't join my mother in that large overwrought wreath. Instead I bought a dozen red roses. When I'd finished being sick, I went back to the grave where the gravediggers were just picking up their shovels.

I threw one of the roses in and it landed on the coffin with a soft empty swish and an air of finality.

I stood there beside the open grave that day listening to the unforgiving sound of the spades and the whump of the earth as it landed on the coffin. I felt as if something had been cut away from me.

To be frank, it's a feeling that's never left me.

G is for . . . Gamophobia

I am not the only one to suffer from fear of flying. The list of famous aviophobes is long and distinguished: Twiggy, who takes Dr Bach's Rescue Remedy for it (it's never worked for me); Stanley Kubrick, who had to recreate the Vietnam War in Pinewood because of it; Dennis Bergkamp, the Arsenal and Dutch player who leaves several days ahead of the rest of his team to get to European matches, plus some American female rock star who can't tour because of it but whose name, unfortunately, I can't remember. On behalf of all of them, I'd like to ask – and particularly of Bad Ponytail Peter who insists it must be cured – what is so damn phobic about being scared of being locked up in some aluminium tube half a mile in the air, and this in the full knowledge that any moment some crazy might take over the cockpit or Jonathan Livingstone Seagull do a nose dive into one of the engines. From this you will deduce I don't regard fear of flying as remotely phobic. To me aviophobia is like ballistophobia (fear of bullets and missiles) or lilapsophobia (fear of hurricanes and tornados) or nucleomituphobia (fear of nuclear weapons), all of which are on Bad Ponytail Peter's list, and all – as far as I can see – utterly inapplicable as phobias since they concern things which by their very nature only a complete idiot would not be scared of.

I feel much the same way about gamophobia.

Fear of marriage.

I used to think I was some sort of oddity, some beast with a brand on my forehead with regard to my gamophobia but now I don't think so. Tell you the truth, I think that, as a condition, it's getting as common as measles. For a start, people are putting it off. The average age for marriage now is thirty for men, twenty-eight for women, a rise of five years over the last quarter of a century.[*] The way things are going, in fifty years' time, people will be hitting the big four-oh before they clamber into their wedding clobber.

As much as anything, of course, this has to do with the increased social acceptance of cohabiting instead of, or prior to, marriage. A quarter of the nation is now shacked up without benefit of clergy – or Living In Sin as my mother prefers to call it – a figure expected to double over the next ten years. As a result of this more than forty per cent of the nation's babies are now born to cohabiting couples, a ten per cent rise over the last decade. Cue a bout of enthusiastic tutting from my mother when she read it in her morning paper.

'All those children born out of wedlock.'

'*Out of wedlock*. For God's sake, you'll be saying "wrong side of the blanket" next. We're not living in a Catherine Cookson novel, Mother.'

Meanwhile there're no prizes for guessing just why society

---

[*] Figures from the Office of National Statistics.

got a taste for cohabitation as opposed marriage. It's because it's *not* marriage, that's why. Because it's not quite that final. Because it represents a resting place, a place to draw breath, to hold back, think twice. A place where there's still a let-out clause, a light still shining at the end of the tunnel. All the marriage-shy spinster does, as usual, is raise her head that bit higher above the parapet.

'We're living too long, that's the problem.'

This is Sophie's theory about society's increasing inability to contemplate a future without that light, however faint, glimmering at the end of the tunnel. 'Let's face it, if you know there's a racing chance you're going to get carried off by cholera, or stabbed in the back in a street brawl, you're not going to waste your time agonising about whether you're *really* settling down with the right person.'

I reckon there's truth in this. After all, back when old age was kicking in anywhere from the late thirties onwards, we didn't have to worry about our futures and whether they were open-ended or otherwise. All we had to do was to listen for the sound of those winged chariot wheels at our back and get the hell on with it.[*]

'I blame medical science. It's gone ahead extending our lives physically without giving us the mental and emotional resources to cope with it. Human kind cannot bear too much reality.'

'Well, not when you realise you might have to bear it under the same roof with someone till you're ninety . . .'

What I believe is that we're a scientific age and what we'd really like is some sort of True Love test. Why they

---

[*] Not, I hasten to add, that that greaseball Andrew Marvell would ever have got his hand on my knee with that old winged chariots at our back argument.

bother taking us to the moon when this is what we really want I simply can't answer.

'We need a sort of Love Thermometer to take its temperature,' I said to Sophie, 'or piece of litmus paper that would turn pink.'

'Or a beaker of something,' she said. 'Stick the thing in and see if after thirty years that it would still be fizzing.'

But that's the trouble with love, isn't it? Somewhere along the line it has to become a relationship. When it comes to luuurve, it's praxis that's the problem. It's not theoretical. It can't be investigated, experimented with in the laboratory. The only way you get to see if it works, if it's the Real Thing, is to try it out in the field. Test it to destruction. Commit. Shack up. Move in together. Get married.

I said to Sophie once, 'Do you love Denis?' and she turned in surprise.

'Good God, no.' She looked genuinely shocked.

'How do you know?'

'Because if I loved him, I'd do something about it.'

'Like what?'

'What do you think? Live with him. Make a life together.' And I can tell you, that was an answer that shocked me.

Denis Dalassis is policeman, one of those disconcerting ones who look too much like the part they're playing. Only last week one of our more distinguished local drug dealers up before the Bench claimed he'd only resisted arrest on account of the fact he thought he'd seen Denis on *The Bill* a week earlier.[*]

---

[*] Far from being embarrassed about this, or seeking in any way to exert undue influence on Sophie not to use the story, he was delighted when she put it on Page One. Something that should tell all you need to know about Denis.

Sophie met Denis at one of those death-by-buffet official functions she was attending as editor. By the end of the evening they were in bed together.

'You disapprove. Why don't you admit it?'

'Not me. You know me. I'm too lazy to disapprove of anything.'

About Denis, I say, 'I don't know what you see in him,' but it's not strictly true. I've never really done chunky, bald and sexy but if I did, well, probably I'd go for Denis.

Sometimes I think Sophie was designed to be a mistress. She's large and handsome and lush. She's a bit like Denis in this respect. She looks like the part she's playing. She was always this way. We had an elegant ground-floor flat in those early junior reporter days, high ceilings, swagged curtains, and in the case of Sophie's bedroom, French windows leading into the back garden, something particularly useful even then, given that her lovers were both numerous and married.

'Married men suit me,' she told me the first time one came in through the window. 'You'll just have to accept it.'

Whether I have or not is a matter of dispute between us. She says I haven't and maybe she's right. Whether adultery is right or wrong in any moral stroke religious sense I can't say. I've had no religious training, and this thanks to my mother.* I think I can safely say I'm not up for anyone being stoned for it. I've tried to figure out how I feel about it in my heart, and in the end I'm forced to confess that Sophie's probably right. I do disapprove, and this because, advanced gamophobe that I am, I don't understand how any two

---

* 'Oh, right it would have to be my fault, wouldn't it?'
  'Of course it would. Dammit, you are my mother.'

people, same sex or otherwise, are crazy enough to contemplate attempting to live under one roof together. I wouldn't try it in the same way I wouldn't try bungee jumping, or hang-gliding or any of that other white-knuckle stuff that Fleur has signed up for, and all for the same reason. That the potential for something going wrong, for serious damage to one's person, is clearly enormous. That some people do contemplate this folly, this Impossible Dream, I consider nothing short of a miracle, so that the least I can do is give them a round of applause and cut them some slack, this rather than circle round them like some blood-sniffing piranha.

As in: 'Well, anyone can see the marriage is not really working . . .'

And: 'They've never really been happy . . .'

And, my personal favourite: 'Of course, he only stays for the children.'

None of which I'm happy to say my friend Sophie ever uses.

In fact she's Miss Moral Majority when it comes to men leaving their children.

'I *totally* disapprove. *Completely* unnecessary. The last thing I'd want is for him to walk out on his family.'

'That's because you're not interested in anything but your twice-a-week liaisons.'

'Absolutely. And that suits him too. The last thing he'd want is to move in with me.'

Still I can't leave it.

'Affairs are so *yesterday*, don't you think? Just so damn corny. If he died you'd have to do that thing the mistresses do.'

'What's that?'

'You know. Like in the movies. Turn up to the funeral

in some bad Marlene Dietrich mac and stand under a dripping umbrella on the edge of the mourners.'

'Pooh . . . I wouldn't go.'

'Good. 'Cause you needn't think I'm coming with you.'

Theoretically, spinsters should be good adultery material, I can see that. Theoretically I should be like Sophie, i.e., married men really should suit me. But the fact is that, to me, having an affair is no better than being married. In fact worse. None of the advantages, i.e., in-house sex and housekeeping money, just the disadvantages.

Because I look at Denis, pictured in the paper, standing beside his wife at some function or other, or with his kids at some school prize-giving, and I think in some way, however distant, however tenuous, Sophie's already a part of that, an outreach, a tentacle in this unacknowledged extended *family*.

'Look, you still have that thing of *belonging*.'

'No I don't.'

'Yes you do. Think about it. I mean, you're still a part of something. You're still *joining* something. Organising your life around a family diary.'

And I never wanted that, that's all. I never wanted to be a part of something, that's the point. I never was a *joiner*.

All of which is fine and dandy, or it would be if this was the truth, the whole truth and nothing but the truth about my dislike of Denis. Because there's another baser reason why I don't like Denis and I'm pretty sure Sophie knows it. It has to do with the first time she introduced us, the words that he said, in particular the way that he said them.

'So . . .' he said, 'Riley . . .' all knowing, ironical and morally neutral in that way that's a CID speciality. 'How is our good friend Lennie?'

*　　*　　*

At Cass and Fergie's party Archie stared over the top of his glass at me. He said, 'So how come you got to be so broke, Riley?'

I said, 'Oh, you know. Talent. Perseverance. A feeling for the subject.'

He said, 'Really? I heard you threw it all away on a waster, Riley.'

I had a dream about Lennie once. It was when I knew the thing was finally behind me. He was in a garage in my dream, in overalls working on a car, which just goes to show how ludicrous dreams can be. Because Lennie never worked on a car in his life. Lennie only just about knew where to put the petrol in, and wherever he is now, dead or alive, and whatever car he's driving, I can guarantee he hasn't a clue how to check the oil or the tyre pressure.

That was pretty much the only intriguing thing about Lennie. The way he played against type. How entirely useless he was at all things mechanical. Like the video he brought home, the most complicated and expensive one on the market. In the two years we were together, we never could go out when our favourite programme was on, this because he couldn't figure out how to work the video machine. (My first major triumph, awash with grief, my first step towards recovery, would be sitting down one day to teach myself how to set it.)

In my dream, I came behind Lennie with a cricket bat, which is also strange, bearing in mind that cricket also played no part in our relationship. In fact I'd say if Lennie had another saving grace it was that he had no interest in sport, either playing it or watching it on the television. In the dream I raised the bat high in the air with both hands and brought it down on the back of his head with a vengeance and a terrible crack that I can still hear echoing in my head all this time later. He went down when I hit him. Face forward, dropping like a stone, the way the name-less B actor does over the green baize table when De Niro hits him in *Casino*.

In the dream Lennie lay there on the floor perfectly still, the blood oozing out of his head over the grey concrete and I stood there looking down at him. I knew absolutely that he was dead. I dropped down on my haunches and put my head in my hands, feeling a sick sorrow and despair, the worse sickness and sorrow and despair I knew any human being could feel in their life, this because I'd taken a life, Lennie's life – not just because of the morality of it, not just because I knew it was wrong to kill, but because I knew I'd fucked my life up doing it; that because of this desire for revenge, it was over as well as Lennie's, and this, again, not just because I'd be going to gaol, although I knew that I would be, but more because I knew I'd never be free of it, this thing that I'd done, that I'd never be able to wash it away, turn the clock back to a time when it had never happened. I knew that in one terrible moment I'd thrown away all my hopes of peace and happiness in my one-and-only brief stay on the planet. And that's when I woke up shaking.

It's not possible to overestimate the relief I felt when my eyelids fluttered open that morning, when I saw my bedroom, all the familiar things, my clothes, books, CDs, the television, the smooth untroubled duvet beneath my fingers. But relief is a pitiful word that comes nowhere near it. Because in that moment of waking I felt the greatest joy I do believe it's possible for any human being to feel. What I felt in that moment of waking was that I'd been given my life back, a feeling so strong that all that day, the next too, even the day after that, it wouldn't go away. Instead it stayed with me, making everything I did, even the simplest things, washing the dishes, reading a book, seem that much richer and deeper.

And while I'm not a religious person, and while I don't really understand all that Christian stuff about resurrection, still I can tell you that the word that most approximates what I felt on waking from that dream, and looking round my bedroom and seeing all those familiar things just sitting there and recognising that none of it had happened is exactly that.

It felt like a Resurrection.[*]

---

[*] As a matter of fact when it happened, it wasn't a cricket bat at all, just a paper knife. A paperknife and a feeling that anything, anything, would be better than having Lennie walking around on the planet.

H is for ... Heroines

Right. Important this. So here we are: a few spinster heroines off the top of my head and in no particular order.

- **Florence Nightingale.** Formerly of the Establishment for Gentlewomen During Illness in Harley Street, latterly and in one massive leap the Crimea War: four miles of beds, 2,300 wounded men ('not an average of three limbs per man') and, more importantly, not a basin or a towel or a bar of soap between them; fighting dirt and disease but mostly the scandalous incompetence of the (male) chief medical officers content to sit out the war filling in requisition forms in the full and certain knowledge that nothing so requested was ever going to arrive. In Sebastopol she undertook feats of organisation that make mobilising the Gulf War look like an exercise for beginners. She totally reorganised the hospital, its kitchen and laundry, instituting major improvements including repaving corridors, reflooring wards and installing a new drainage system. In the process, she not only saved hundreds, probably thousands of lives, but revolutionised battlefield medicine. Arriving home at the end of the war, the same woman who had done all of this took to her bed where she stayed for the next thirty-odd years. Some say exhaustion was responsible but others disgust, that she took one look at what was on offer to her as a spinster in the society of the time and turned her back on it for ever. She died in 1910, still a tireless pamphleteer on behalf of military medicine ('whether the system or no-system . . . is to be . . . patched up temporarily, as you give a beggar half pence – or made equal to the wants . . .'). And all this in a time, let us not forget, when, as a spinster, her official status was that of a 'surplus and excess woman'.

- **The Brontës.** Emily and Anne, that is, spinsters both, but minus Charlotte, who went on to marry, which wasn't the worst of her crimes. First off little Anne, who while generally agreed to be the least talented of the trio, still manages a rivetingly truthful portrait of life before battered wives' homes in *The Tenant of Wildfell Hall*; then Emily who, as they say, needs no introduction, having written *Wuthering Heights*, one of the few books that you could actually slap the words *tour de force* across the top and not be embarrassed, a fact that unquestionably so stuck in Charlotte's craw she took a Judas-like revenge, writing a fawning apology for it after Emily's death, and this in the guise of loving sister. In the process she propounded one of the greatest literary calumnies of all time, saying Emily 'did not know what she had done', making her out to be some sort of a cartoon spinster with no more knowledge of the world 'than a nun has of the country people who sometimes pass her convent gates'. And this from a two-bit penny dreadful writer whose best effort was the simpering Reader-I-married-him *Jane Eyre*. (Synopsis: Oh Lord, aren't I just the plainest thing . . . how could anyone ever love me? . . . oh, you're blind with a scar, Mr R, so that's alright then . . .). Charlotte was the last of the three to go, dying in pregnancy a few months after marrying her father's curate. Serves her right, I say.

- **Louisa M. Alcott.** Whose Little Women became Good Wives, although she did not herself. The second of four daughters of Bronson Alcott, a Transcendentalist thinker and social reformer whose persona as All-Round Good Sport and Friend of Mankind was pretty much paid for by Louisa, since while he was out speechifying and receiving the praise and adoration of his admirers, she was at home teaching, writing and sewing and ruining her health to put food on the table. While everyone knows about the *Little Women* and *Good Wives*, few know about *Work*, something as can be seen by the above she clearly knew a hell of a lot about. It took her eleven years to write the novel, and while something less than sparky in parts, still it's a noble attempt to paint a faithful picture of the range of work available to spinsters at the time, i.e., servant, seamstress, governess or actress. The heroine, Christie, remains single throughout the novel until right at the end, when she marries, although Louisa shows what may well be her true inclinations, dispatching the husband from a fever a few months after the wedding, and leaving Christie free to pursue her true destiny as single parent, and reformer seeking to better the lives of working women. While Louisa's writing eventually brought her some financial reward, enabling her among other things to raise her dead sister's child, in the end financial security came too late. Often ill at the end of her life, certainly dispirited, she wrote: 'When I had the youth, I had not the money; now I have the money I have no time; and when I get the time, if I ever do, I shall have no health to enjoy life.' She died, almost certainly from exhaustion, the day her father was buried.

('God, this is miserable.' Sophie.)

Never mind. A few more names, all worthy of placing their handprints in the wet concrete of that spinster Pavement of Fame:

- **Emily Dickinson,** a woman who wrote poetry, as one critic put it, 'indefatigably as some women cook or knit' (Lord love the man, he was writing in 1959). **Flannery O'Connor,** who lived with her mother and raised chickens and peacocks, and who had lupus and never made it to forty yet still managed to write all those extraordinary stories. **Jacqueline Gold,** a.k.a. Ann Summers, for services to spinsters (work it out for yourself), **Beatrice,** of course, already mentioned, from *Much Ado,* so merrily grateful to God for not sending her a husband: 'for the which blessing I am at him upon my knees every morning and evening . . .' And last, but definitely not least . . .

- **Iaia of Cyzicus,** sometimes called Lalia, who gets a special mention in Pliny on two counts, first because she outsold all the male painters of her time and place (first century BC, Rome,) and secondly because she stayed unmarried. According to Gaius Plinius Secundus, scientist, historian, observer of the natural world and all-round garrulous geezer, Iaia 'painted with a brush . . . and also drew on ivory with an engraving tool.' She did mainly female portraits, including a large picture on wood, *Old Woman at Neapolis*, and a self-portrait done with the aid of a mirror. 'No one produced a picture faster than she did,' says Gaius the Geezer, 'and her artistic skill was so great that in the prices her pictures fetched she far exceeded the most famous portrait painters of the period, namely Sopolis and Dionysis, whose pictures fill the art galleries.' So there.

I wouldn't have known about Iaia if it wasn't for Magda, Iaia holding pride of place as one of her role models, Magda being a painter herself (also noted poet and play-wright, at least in her own estimation). Magda used to see her most days when they used the same deli round the corner from the temple where Magda was working as a vestal virgin. In fact, Magda once hinted to me that the aforementioned *Old Woman at Neapolis* picture, which Pliny mentions, was in fact her, Magda, in old age – 'I have a *distinct* recollection of being painted' – and this after telling me only a week or so earlier that she'd been cut off in her prime on account of being carted off to Alexandria and buried in some tomb or other.

'Phfff,' she said, waving a hand in the air, when I brought up the discrepancy. 'Sometimes it's just so *hard* to remember.'

It will have now become abundantly clear to you that

Magda is Queen Flake in our town, the High Priestess of Crazy. But like I said to Sophie just the other day, 'Really, does it matter? So what if she thinks she was carried off at the Siege of Thermopylae . . .' Besides which, where's the big deal in Magda's previous incarnations? Don't we all feel we've had them? What do old affairs seem like when we look back and don't understand why or how – mine with Lennie, for instance – but another life. As for marrying herself, why not? Like Sophie said, 'Well, it'll do a lot less damage than if she marries someone else.'

One thing's for sure, Hocus Pocus is the temple to New Age folly and excess in this town. For a start there's the sheer *extravagance* of the place, its prodigality. Compared to it, Aladdin's cave was well filed and orderly. Fifteen years ago when Magda first opened up her doors, it was possible to walk around the place. Not any more. Now you squeeze between the piles of merchandise, head and shoulders striking chains of bells, lanterns, scarves, mobiles and all manner of other tinsel and trumpery dangling from the ceiling. The back room is no longer negotiable at all. Instead it must be viewed, full of its mountains of goods, from the doorway like some piece of conceptual art. There's a belief in our town that Hocus Pocus is a front for drug-dealing but only because it appears that Magda never sells anything, that the piles of smocks, coats, blouses, belts, hats, bags, rugs, cushions, boxes, pictures, posters, bangles, necklaces, rings, earrings, candles (of all description), lamps, artificial flowers, crystals, Tibetan bells, oils, joss sticks, astrological charts, witchcraft starter kits, wildly expensive hand-crafted wooden toys and all manner of other bric-a-brac from A to Z never get any smaller. Which is true. They don't. But this is because Magda hates to part with anything. She runs the shop because she loves it, truly loves it and everything in it. Customers practically have to tear things from her grasp to buy them. To console herself when sales actually occur, she immediately re-orders, or better yet, shoots off to one or other of her suppliers in Turkey or Nepal or Morocco where she smokes a little high-quality hash to be polite and then gets down to the serious business of the day, ordering another bountiful selection. There's also the matter of her absurd generosity to her friends. At your peril do you admire a rug or try on an alpaca jacket.

'Perfect . . . perfect . . .'

'I can't afford it.'

'Take it, take it . . . pay me when you can . . .'

'This is not the way to do business, Magda.'

It has to be said that making a profit is not actually top of Magda's priorities and this is because it's not a strict necessity. She has a private income although the exact nature of it is something of a mystery. All I know is that it enables her to get a much larger overdraft than the rest of us, and that it derived way back when from several generations of Sri Lankan tea-planters. It's for this reason that Mad Magda MacBride of the wild Irish name has the look of an Indian princess about her.

For all these reasons I can forgive Mad Magda pretty much anything, but most of all for her God-given enthusiasm. She's always got some brand-new idea on the go (at the moment it's tantric drumming), some new idea, therapy, or self-help book that will change her life, or some new campaign to save something. Last year, for instance, she chained herself to a tree behind her house in the firm belief it had ancient spirits in it, this to stop Carpet World from uprooting it for their new car park. She's never floored by things. She never gives in either, always believing there is something to be done.

'Ummm . . . let's think,' I can remember her saying after the Lennie débâcle. 'What can we do?' which is when her face brightened. 'I know.' She waggled a finger in the air. 'I could put a spell on him. What do you think, Riley?'

Still, there's something else about Magda for me, something that forms the bedrock of our friendship although she'll never know it. It's that when I look at her I see writ large what I might have been. If it had happened to me. If I had taken that route.

I too might have been an utterly doting, supremely flaky New Age single mother.

At first I thought Magda was being slightly cavalier with the title 'spinster' that day she decided to marry herself.

'What do you mean?'

'Well, correct me if I'm wrong, but don't you have to be childless as well as unmarried to qualify?'

'Not at all. Check it out.' And I did. And I was wrong. And ten to one you'd have made the same mistake. But according to the definition,* the only qualification for being a spinster is to be an unmarried woman judged to be beyond the age of marriage. You can even have a marriage behind you if you like and still take the title since never having married is only part of the strict legal definition. One thing's for sure, in none of these categories is there any mention of children.

Magda was still working in television when she got pregnant. When she declined to name the father, many people

---

* **Spin-ster** (spinsta) *n.* **1.** an unmarried woman regarded as being beyond the age of marriage. **2.** *Law* (in legal documents) a woman who has never married.

assumed it was the presenter of the Friday night post-pub fodder chat show she was working on at the time as a researcher.* A married man with children, and mildly famous now, he had an early reputation as a philanderer. On the other hand, those more *au fait* with the situation maintained there were more practical reasons for Magda's discretion, in short that she neither knew nor cared about the identity of the father, his function being no more than sperm donor.

Certainly it would be true to say that Magda was sexually active that summer she got pregnant, making up for all those years as a vestal virgin is what I thought at the time. Now I see it was that old body clock chiming away like Big Ben inside her.

Magda was thirty-six when she had Rochelle. And if Rochelle is utterly pissed off at her daft name – the impression she always gives, rearing up at the sound of it when her mother calls fondly across the shop to her and making a faint spitting movement – well, all I can say is she should think herself bloody lucky. It's only surprising given Magda's resolutely New Age leanings that she didn't end up as Floating Lotus Blossom or Beloved Frangipani.

The meejah world of the mid-eighties was a cool time to become a single mother. It was entirely the right thing to do. And the role suited Magda well. Tall and extremely striking, with the look of some sixties folk singer about her, she appeared so positively *right* pushing that buggy. And she was capable too. She could change a nappy with a flick of the wrist. Better yet, she could demand in strident tones nappy-changing facilities in places that didn't

---

* 'That's it for paedophilia. After the break, used cars. Are they really worth it?'

possess them. A hard-liner when it came to breast-feeding in public, for a couple of years Magda's handsome raspberry nipples were out more than in, something that she confided to me (if you can call Magda's exclamatory form of address 'confiding') brought additional benefits.

According to Magda, her sex life was never as good as during those early years with Rochelle.

'Trust me, there are men in this world who get seriously turned on by the smell of Sudocrem and baby lotion.'

Neither did the presence of Rochelle in any way hamper Magda's social life. Never once did she suffer from the absence of a baby-sitter. Because 'Whither I go, thou shalt go' became Magda's motto, which is why at every party you went to in those days you could be sure to find Rochelle being passed from hand to hand, dandled upon knee or forced to goo-goo in the air as Magda held court among her envious circle of Baby Wannabees and Body-Clock Watchers.

Still, what the hell? Like I say, Magda looked the part pushing that buggy, and if there was the faintest suspicion as she strode along the High Street, head thrown back proudly, silver bracelets clinking on the handle of that sooper-dooper, top-of-the-range buggy, if there was the merest suggestion that both contraption and occupant were in some vague way – whisper the words – an adjunct, an accessory, a must-have to complete a life-style, like, say, a Habitat trolley, well, I can forgive it because it's Magda. Or at least I can for all but those odd, seriously irritating moments when she comes all over mumsy and patronising to those who don't have children.

'I do think there's something so wonderfully magical/mystical/elemental about the relationship between mother and daughter, don't you?' is one of her favourites, spoken as she gazes mistily over at Rochelle, who almost certainly at that moment is studiously ignoring her.

'Oh, I'm sorry.' She claps a hand theatrically over her mouth.

I sigh. 'For what?' I've played this scene a thousand times.

'I always forget.'

'What?'

The smile is wide and self-satisfied and only pretends to be apologetic. 'Well, I know not *everyone* wants children.'

Rochelle is seventeen now, with a multicoloured ponytail, and rings and studs in her face like she's using it as some sort of voodoo doll; that if she's really lucky, every time she gets a new piercing there'll be a mysterious, sudden sharp pain on the body of her mother.

Despite all this, Magda likes to insist, 'I think of her as my best friend,' always smiling serenely as she says it.

'For God's sake,' Cass said when I mentioned it to her. 'In what world are mothers supposed to be best friends with their daughters?'*

Still, there's something touching in all this, not least because, like I say, in Magda I see myself, what I might have become, the same totally obsessed and doting mother.

'You haven't . . . um . . . mentioned the wedding to Rochelle yet?' I said, after she'd buttonholed me in Hocus Pocus when I'd gone in for a birthday card for Sophie.

'No. No. I thought I'd wait till I'd finalised everything. Keep it as a surprise.'

---

* To put this into context, her own daughter had just stormed away up the stairs, hurling behind her words familiar to all good parents: 'It's not fair . . . *All* of my friends are going . . . *Their* parents say it's all right.' And all this on account of wishing to be allowed to camp out at the Glastonbury Festival.

Frankly I thought this a non-starter. I figured that since Rochelle has made it successfully through to seventeen with her mother there was now nothing on God's earth likely to surprise her.

It's going to be a 'traditional' wedding according to Magda (not an entirely appropriate word, I thought, it being short of a bridegroom).

'I hope you're not going to promise to obey.'

'No, no, no. I mean really traditional. With dozens of bridesmaids.'

In days of yore, apparently, the bride would be surrounded by many bridesmaids, to confuse the mercenaries but also any malign spirits.

'Are you expecting some then?'

'What?'

'You know. Malign spirits.'

Magda's bridesmaids will walk with her from her house up the Tor where the ceremony is to be held. They'll all be dressed in white, with flares (that's the torches, not the trousers).

'Do you think Sophie would like to be a bridesmaid?'

I was just pondering the simple unlikelihood of the words 'Sophie' and 'bridesmaid' appearing in the same sentence* when Rochelle broke in on my thoughts, crashing in through the front door of the shop and slamming it closed in the manner of someone Making A Statement.

'Darling,' her mother said with a wide and welcoming smile that indicated she hadn't noticed the foundations were

---

* I did ask Sophie.
   I said, 'Magda asked me to ask you, so I'm just doing it, OK?'
   I said,' Look, I will if you will.'
   She said: 'I'd rather take poison.'

still shaking. But Rochelle wasn't in the mood for talking. Her only acknowledgement as she flounced through was her customary curl of the lip and a look thrown at her mother that said that of all those who had ever been, or were, or could be in the world, this woman was the most contemptible.

That was the first time I noticed the tattoo on her upper arm. It glowed beneath the shop spotlights as she flounced through, purply-blue and bully-boyish. I caught sight of snakes crawling in and out of a skull, and matching daggers. Nowhere, as far as I could see, did it include the word 'mother'.

Magda saw it too, although clearly not for the first time.

As the door at the back of the shop to the living quarters banged closed and the place shook a second time her voice was wistful.

'I wanted her to have a little butterfly,' she said.

Thinking about all this, it seems to me that somewhere in here is what I wanted to say to David that night at Fergie's party. I think I wanted to tell him, 'Look . . . I know. If I'd done it . . . if it had happened, then I too would have ended up one of those besotted, resolutely flaky single mothers.'

One more heroine. A latecomer to that spinster Hall of Fame.

- **Cornelia Parker.** Not least because of her performance on *Desert Island Discs* this morning when she distinguished herself, etched herself for ever on my heart by choosing as her luxury, a solar-powered vibrator. Way to go, Cornelia. Cornelia Parker, who did *Cold Dark*

Matter: An Exploded View. Ten thousand glorious pieces of the former garden shed suspended in the air. Cass and I stood transfixed before it. I said, 'Oh, look, she got the army to blow it up.' I said, 'Maybe if you asked them nicely they'd do it to Fergie's.' Cornelia's married now and has a child, but still remains an honorary spinster as far as I'm concerned, and this because of the wedding ring she spun out into a thread of gold, and wound round a suburban sitting room. But better yet because of the way she bound Rodin's *The Kiss* with what one curmudgeonly male art critic called 'a mile of string'.

Which of course it wasn't.

Not string at all.

No, rope, stooopid.

Rope.

Thick glorious rope. Wicked rope.

Bonds.

Fetters.

Restraints.

All looped round that naked, kissing couple.

Which is what love is all about, isn't it? What love will always lead to in the end.

Nathan, for instance, standing there with the rain splattering down over his face, running in and out of his eye sockets. Nathan saying, 'I'm not trying to tie you down, Riley.' Nathan raising his head to heaven. Nathan raising that great bull head.

Nathan saying, 'If only I could make you understand how much I love you, Riley.'

I is for ... the Importance of Aunts

Dear Riley Gordon,

I have just finished your book *The Importance of Aunts* and I should like to point out several factual errors. You say that Alpha Chameleon from which the Aunts Aurora and Lavinia travel in their battered old spaceship is 60 light years away from earth whereas in fact it is 63.4 light years away. You also describe their star as glowing pale pink in the sky with candy floss edges whereas everyone knows it is actually a white star. Also you claim that the reason that they ended up on earth was that they took a wrong turn at Ursa Minor but, of course, this is not even in the same hemisphere. No doubt you will wish to ensure that your publishers correct these errors in the next edition.

Yours sincerely,

Philip Bridges, aged 11

PS: I enjoyed *The Importance of Aunts* although not as much as *Harry Potter*.

Dear Philip,

Thank you so much for your letter. It's so lovely to hear from my readers. I'm glad you enjoyed the book. I shall of course pass on your comments to my publishers and thank you again for spotting the errors and contacting me.

Yours sincerely,

Riley Gordon

Pompous little prick.

I guess you could say it was Jane Austen who really started me writing. I'd always written, of course. Don't writers *always* say that? But it's true of me as much as the rest. Recently, clearing out my mother's attic, I found a box containing souvenirs of my early girly years: Pond's cold cream, block mascara, that sort of thing. In it was an old exercise book with some early short stories (including one particularly plucky one in which the author attempts to turn an accountant into a romantic hero), this plus some suitably angst-ridden poetry.* I'd done a creative writing module as part of my English degree, something that had resulted in a couple of short stories, one of which made the college literary magazine. On the strength of this, and in the way of these things, I embarked on a novel.† It was grinding gently but inexorably to a halt when quite by chance, and browsing in a book of

---

* E.g.,
   I fold my memories of you
   Away
   In the tissue of my mind . . .
† About a mature student at university writing a novel . . .

Queen Jane's letters I came upon that glorious phrase 'the importance of aunts'.

'I have always maintained the importance of aunts as much as possible . . .'

It was written to her niece Caroline, who had recently become an aunt, and it struck an immediate chord with me, indeed one might almost call it a Road to Damascus moment.

Not the least of the reasons was that precisely the same thing had just happened to me.

I was appalled, I recall, when Cassie told me she was pregnant Not at all thrilled that the even tenor of our ways was about to be disrupted by some small and awkward being who almost certainly would not stop crying. Neither was I thrilled at the prospect of being an aunt, not least because I was quite sure I'd be lousy at it, a prediction that appeared to be true the first time Fergie and Cass went out and left me with Jonah.

In the end I rang my mother. I can't imagine why.

'Can you come round?'

'I'm sure that's not necessary, darling.'

'But he won't stop crying. What shall I do?'

'How should I know?'

'But you must know. You had me and Cassie. What did you do when we wouldn't stop crying?'

'I really don't know.' The silence at the end of the phone told me she was considering the matter. 'I can only think I must have handed you over to your father.'

As it turned out I wasn't lousy with Jonah and Elsa. On the other hand, I didn't discover any long-dead maternal streak either.

'We always liked you because you didn't treat us like children,' Elsa told me once, and for a while I wore it like a medal on my chest, until I realised it wasn't the truth, or rather not the whole truth. Because the secret of my success with Jonah and Elsa lay in the fact that I divined early on that neither of them was a child, that they were, in fact, from some alien species. With the advantage of having watched *Star Trek* for most of my adult life, I knew how to deal with aliens, which was to remain scrupulously polite to them to get them off their guard, all the while pretending not to notice that they had corrugated foreheads, or skin ruffles around their necks or shells and body parts in places where you might least expect them.

It's hard to remember now, looking at Jonah and Elsa, that once they didn't exist, that once they never were, and that our world, Cassie and Fergie's and mine, still managed to jog along from day to day without them. It's for this reason, I guess, that those who have kids can no longer discuss the concept of being without them, kids being so utterly and intrinsically *there* once they've arrived, so utterly blocking out the argument.

Elsa is seventeen now, Jonah two years older. Watching them grow up I became aware of a master plan thwarted.

'It's not fair,' I bawled at Jonah once, tears of relief pouring down my face. 'I did everything right. I didn't have kids. This wasn't supposed to happen.'

He must have been about eleven and all he'd done was to stay out late on his bike while under my protection. In the end I was reduced to lifting limp and begging eyes, screwing up a Kleenex like some Victorian heroine.

'Don't ever do that again, Jonah. Ever. Because the fact is, I can't stand it.'

I saw the knowledge dawn in his eyes, an understanding

of the utter frailty of women, in particular those whose names were preceded by the word 'Auntie'. He laid a brief compassionate hand on my shoulder and his chin gave an old man's nod.

'OK,' he said. 'I won't.' And actually, he didn't.

Once Jonah and Elsa entered my life, I began to see things about kids I'd never noticed before, things I guess that became useful in my writing. Like, for instance, how they live utterly in the present, which is why when you tell them that you're sorry, but you can't do X today like you promised, but you'll go tomorrow instead, they look at you like you're quite mad and/or burst into furious tears, or like Elsa, who never cried (I used to wish she would), favour you with a hard cold stare that says the trouble with adults is that they simply can't be trusted – this before turning on her heel, and stumping away in an abrupt and contemptuous manner because, like all kids, the future did not exist for her. I love the way, too, that kids pick up things – phrases, information. I saw Elsa do it when she was only three. She'd heard Fergie say something about our mother. I swear to God I saw her eyes brighten as she heard it; so did Cass, who said, 'Shhhhh,' but it was too late. I saw Elsa hug the wonderful words to herself, a few days later, judiciously considering the time was right, letting them out with a lip-smacking triumphant chuckle.

'You're from another planet, you, Aunt Riley.'

'You could be right,' I said.

The truth about Jonah and Elsa and I is that we have grown up together. Their rites of passage have also been mine, for instance the day that Jonah dropped that obligatory 'Auntie'.

'Riley,' he said, with only a small gulp but the grand air

of someone saying something *perfectly* natural. 'Where's my football boots?'

I scrabbled back in my mind through the *Parents' Manual*, Chapter 3, Lost Things (Appropriate Answers).

'I don't know,' I said. 'More than likely where you left them.'

The day I arrived to take him to the first morning of his work placement, some three or four years on, I put a hand to my mouth in the manner of one confronted by a work of art, new and shocking and moving. I simply didn't want him to be standing there, looking like that, in his first newly bought suit. What I felt in that moment was fear. No, not fear, white-hot terror, terror coupled with an awful resentment at the inflexible regime called growing up. I didn't want Jonah to be in that suit, no matter how good he looked (and he did look good). I didn't want him to be going out there into the world where he would meet other young men a couple of years older than himself who would take him out drinking. I didn't want him to meet some sharp young miss by the photocopier who would break his heart for the first time. Instead I wanted to lock him up, he and Elsa both, in a cupboard somewhere, or maybe in a tower like in a fairy tale, but most of all to keep them safe, to keep them away from that big bad world out there for ever.

Because when I think of anything happening to Jonah or Elsa, something happens to my heart. First of all it contracts. Which is just the good part. After that it curls up into a hard little ball and comes out through my back screaming. Which is why, when Cassie told me on the morning of Fergie's party that Jonah was talking about spending his summer holidays travelling in Asia, I reacted as any normal person would do.

'You can't be *SERIOUS*. You can't *POSSIBLY* let him go. He's *FAR* too young. It's FAR too dangerous.'

'Tell me about it,' she said with an old woman's look across the top of her spectacles.

Look. It's quite simple. The way I feel about Jonah and Elsa is this.

I don't want them to fly, or travel on trains. Certainly not coaches.

I don't want them to be even mildly friendly with anyone with a car or a motorcycle.

I don't want them to use their mobile phones in case they rot their brains (except, of course, to check in with me hourly).

I'd like them to be in by ten every night (at least until they're married).

I don't want them to take chances with strange diseases, eat anything even mildly carcinogenic.

I don't want them to run with a glass in their hands, or go up a ladder.

I don't want Jonah to go to pubs or clubs where other men get drunk or violent.

I don't want Elsa to walk alone, even to the corner shop, and I don't want her to go out with anyone I haven't first had checked out via the Police Computer.

I don't want them to drink alcohol or do drugs . . .

'. . . in fact, do any damn thing you did yourself . . .'

'Just mind your own frigging business, will you, Archie?'

'But it is my business. At least as much as it is yours.'

'I think not. I've been *here* all these years. I've been with them as they grew up.'

109

'And I haven't. Quite true. But then whose fault is that, Riley?'

Twice Archie and I have stood beside each other at the font. The first time, at Jonah's christening. This was my radical phase and I was particularly terse and bolshy.

'I thought we had an agreement.'

'For God's sake, Riley. Cass and Fergie asked me. Fergie's still my friend, you know. I was his best man, remember.'

'Hard to forget, Archie.'

Three years later, I merely sniffed when Cass and Fergie announced that Archie would again be sharing the godparental responsibilities, this time for Elsa.

'Fine. Although I would have thought renouncing the Devil and all his works would come a bit hard for a rank Thatcherite like Archie.'

Neither did I ever feel the need to abstain from chilly comment as Archie's generous cheques arrived each birthday and Christmas.

'If you feel you can take the money,' I said to Jonah, only half joking, one Christmas, 'knowing where it's come from. How it's been skimmed off the backs of all those Third World workers . . .'

'They make software. The firm's in Reading.'

'He's a *tax exile*,' I said only the other day to Cass, in the manner of one pronouncing on paedophilia.

She said, with a small air of irritation, 'Why can't you let it go?'

'What?'

'This thing you have with Archie.'

All of which was as nothing when I found out that it

110

was Archie's latest fat birthday cheque that was going to allow Jonah to take the year out from university and go travelling.

'Damn you, Archie,' I said, slapping my glass down on the buffet table at Fergie's retirement party. 'Why the hell did you have to encourage him?'

'He didn't need encouraging.' Archie looked down his long nose at me, took a swig of his wine. 'Anyway, I thought you'd approve.'

'It's not like when I did it. That's the point. Look around you. It's a bloody dangerous world now, Archie.'

Later Jonah caught me at the buffet table, tried to talk to me about it.

'I just want to get into other cultures,' he said.

'Why bother? Ours is the culture they all want to get into.'

He said, 'Come on, Riley. Travel. It broadens the mind, right?'

'Bollocks.' He was joshing me, trying gently to make a joke of it all and his face fell at the word. 'Anyway,' I said, 'it's all crap, Jonah. This wanting to get into other cultures. You'll just be like we were, Carrying your own around with you on your back.'

I saw his face fall then, all the enthusiasm depart, and I was sorry. He stammered a little, a habit he has when he's upset. It made me feel like someone had got hold of my heartstrings and was stretching them.

He said, 'I just want to see things. Learn about the world.'

'Why bother? I'm sure one internet café is much like another.'

He said, 'That's not fair,' and it wasn't, and his face was so full of hurt I didn't dare look at it.

He said, 'I thought you'd stand up for me. I thought you'd be on my side.'

He said, 'I'm only asking to do what you did, Riley.'

Who can say why some places pass you by, why others eat their way into your heart? I don't know. Maybe it was the heat that did it that day as I stepped down from the plane, the heavy seductive clamminess that dropped down over my head like a blanket. Or there again, perhaps it was the vulgarity of the place, the unashamed American-ness expressed in the vast neon sign flashing on and off as I came in from the airport. All this so different from the chill austerity of Nepal.

Bangkok. Bangkok.

Bang Makok originally. In translation, 'City of Olives', according to Jonah's *Lonely Planet Guide* lying incriminatingly open on the sofa, although not, as I recall, to Nathan, who maintained it was 'City of Plums'. Not Bangkok at all to the natives, instead Krung Thep, the name given by King Rama to the new city he founded the other side of the river in the eighteenth century, a shortened version, this being Krungthep mahankhon bowon rattanaskosin mahintara auythaya mahadilok popnopparat ratchanthani burirom-udomratchaniwet mahasanthan-amonpiman-avatansathir-sakkathatiya-visnukamprasit, not a snappy title, I'm sure you'd agree, but romantic, let me tell you, when Nathan wrote it out for me that first night we had dinner together, using a napkin, clicking the top of the pen he took from an inside pocket, pronouncing it afterwards mellifluously in his respectable Thai, making it sound like a love poem.

Krungthep mahankhon, etc, etc. In loose translation:

great city of angels, great land unconquerable, grand and prominent realm, highest royal dwelling and grand palace, divine shelter and living place of reincarnated spirits, royal and delightful capital city full of nine noble gems (ten counting Nathan).

There are many things to see and do in Bangkok, according to Jonah's guide book. Here is a small selection:

The Grand Palace
The Emerald Buddha
The Royal Barges
The Floating Market
Wat Arun
Jim Thompson's House
Thai Boxing
Khan Dancing

As for me, I saw and did none of these things.

Instead I just went to the Oasis each night and after that to bed with Nathan.

I arrived in Bangkok the day the last American ground troops were pulling out of Da Nang, something I wouldn't have known but for the headline on the *Bangkok Post* Zoe was reading in the foyer of the flea-bitten hostel where I booked in on my arrival.

There are always people like Zoe when you travel, people you touch lives with, and on the deepest level, but for only a short while, people you swear you'll keep in touch with but never do, so that one day you wake up to find yourself wondering what happened to them, how they ended up and who and how often they married. Like Zoe, for instance. Is she a comfortable matron, spreading of hip, the wife of a country solicitor? Is she even now doing the flowers for the church on Sunday? Is she a dominatrix in thigh-length boots, or sitting behind some big desk running some dot com introduction agency? Or is she where she always wanted to be, sipping gin on a terrace somewhere, moaning about where the amah doesn't dust, and married to a banker? Each and all of these things are possible with Zoe.

It's Zoe who tells me about the job at the Oasis.

'It's not Patpong,' she says, and it isn't, sandwiched between a bank and an office block, only the sign with its green neon palm tree, eternally swaying and its 'Girls' discreetly flashing on and off, marking it out it from the blameless premises around it.

'It's quite respectable,' she said with a grand Welsh wink. 'That's if you want it to be.' Which it turns out she doesn't. She's banking close on a thousand dollars a week from her extracurricular activites.

'I don't know why you don't do it,' she says, shaking her head in bemusement. 'You'll make a lot more money, girl, getting yourself booked out than sitting here talking to them.'

But I just stick to the talking. I've got £200 in travellers' cheques lodged in the safe in that flea-bitten hostel, plenty enough to get me to Hong Kong eventually, and a job on a paper.

'Never forget, you're playing at all this,' Nathan will say one day and I don't either.

Because it's words, in the end, always words. They call it 'nite life' now, in the guide books, on those sites on the Net, the new lite nightlife, which even now they still like to call 'naughty'. Only 'naughty' never worked for me. Not

114

even back then. Especially back then. A grubby pink nylon curtain of a word, frilled and flounced and pulled over a dark doorway. Back in Bangkok in '72, I'd hold that word up to the light, try to fit it into the thing like a piece in a jigsaw. I'd try to match it against Lee lying in the lap of her grizzled Australian engineer whose lechery after so long in the East had grown like a boil on his forehead. And I'd watch that word, that 'naughty', begin to shrivel and fall apart like a dead flower.

'Thai men no good,' Lee would say to me, and who could blame her, brought from her village at thirteen by one of those eponymous 'aunts' (ah the importance of aunts), brought to serve her countrymen in one of the thousands of backstreet brothels beyond the eyes of the tourists – the Lees of this world and their stories, the living, breathing lifeblood running in and out of Nathan's dry dusty prose, his graphs and statistics?

'It's just so . . .'

'What?'

In his hotel room, he's striding up and down behind me where I sit, pencil in hand, trying to make sense of his writing. I catch the jagged self-derisory smile in the mirror above the table.

'Say it. Go on. Dull.' He stops mid-stride, his hands pushed pugnaciously into his pockets.

'No.' But I mean Yes and his smile says he knows it.

'It's just . . . difficult. Hard-going. That's all.'

'It doesn't matter.' His shrug bears out the truth of the statement. 'It's an academic paper, Riley. It'll just be read by people as dull and boring as me.'

'Oh, well.' For a moment we stare at each other in the mirror. 'Just as long as it's not being written to be read by the rest of us.'

One night he calls the foreign sex trade 'a limpet, a barnacle, a carbuncle . . .'

I say, 'Why is it your best words never make it onto the paper?'

Meanwhile, once, it even looks like it might work for Lee. She hooks up with a blubbery red-faced Englishman new to the city and entranced by her waist-length wash of long hair and her ferocious dancing. Within the week she's leaving stuff in his apartment, standard bar girl fare – a faded T-shirt with a psychedelic motif, a bottle of nail polish, shoes with a heel broken.

'He virgin before he meet me,' she says. She rolls her eye, stabs a confident finger on her chest. 'He marry me. You see.'

But Mama San does see. Mama San's seen it all before. She shakes her head at Lee, turns a finger on her temple like a screwdriver to the rest of us.

She's right, of course. One night Blubbery Bill doesn't show and he doesn't show the next night either. That's when Lee breaks into his flat, finds someone else's T-shirt, someone else's bottle of nail polish.

She's waiting for him when he comes in. He's not alone. He has someone who looks exactly like her beside him.

He introduces her as his new 'girlfriend', an absurd vanity this, threatens to call the police when Lee won't go, in the end throws her belongings out of the window. In the street she picks them up, the T-shirt and the nail polish. She leaves the broken shoe where it landed.

'*Mai pen rai*,' she says the next day when she tells us. *Mai pen rai* – never mind.

Mai pen rai.

Most famous of all Thai sayings.

J is for . . . Jane

If anyone deserves a chapter to herself it's Jane. Which Jane? Oh, come on. *That* Jane, the one already mentioned, not just a spinster heroine, *the* spinster heroine, St Jane, patron saint of spinsters. Amiable Jane is what I call her and this because it's what she called herself. Jane, who also had a sister, Cassandra, one who was an artist too, although not a good one in my opinion, this on the strength of that awful portrait, the one they put in all the paperbacks, all thin lips, pointy nose and kiss curls. The very image of the spinster.

Those who dislike Jane, and there are plenty around, reach first for the cheapest, most banal and clichéd of insults, 'spinsterish'.

Spinsterish?

What exactly does this mean? More importantly, what could it possibly cover?

Even when Mary Tyler Moore waited with helmet hair and a freshly made martini for Dick to slam the front door and call, 'Honey, I'm home,' we didn't use 'married-ish' as an all-purpose, Gladstone bag of a description. We didn't

117

assume there was an all-purpose, archetypal, homogenous married state even then, so why, all these years on, are we doing it for the spinster? There's as many different forms of the spinster state scattered throughout the planet as there are spinsters so what price 'spinsterish'? More importantly, if it's meant to imply something slightly feeble, frail, spineless, delicate, something apprehensive, vulnerable and skittish, if it's supposed to mean 'whimsical', what the hell is it doing being applied to Jane Austen?

Because Jane could write a sentence as sharp as a stiletto, as deadly today as the day she wrote it. Take this little number for instance. It's the rich, vain Maria Bertram about to be wed in *Mansfield Park*.

In all the important preparations of the mind she was complete; being prepared for matrimony by an hatred of home, restraint, and tranquillity; by the misery of disappointed affection, and contempt of the man she was to marry.

Tell me there isn't someone you know, or have known, who that wouldn't apply to.

I call Jane the spinster patron saint for this reason: that any fool can see she was only hustling her heroines to the altar in the absence of any available option (it not being open to most to become, like her, a Giant of English Literature).

'Single women have a dreadful propensity for being poor,' she wrote in another of her letters. For it wasn't the spinster state she was against, far from it. It was the penury and the dreadful accompanying servility dictated by it.

As Emma Woodhouse says firmly to the vacuous Harriet:

'. . . It is poverty only which makes celibacy contemptible . . . A single woman, of good fortune, is always respectable, and may be as sensible and pleasant as anybody else.'*

And amen to that, sister.

In that same letter Jane wrote that money was indeed 'one very strong argument for marriage'. But it wasn't enough for her.

Little is known about Jane's marriage proposal and the man, Harris Biggs, who could have improved her financial position. Still a few facts remain. She was twenty-six at the time and staying with the Biggs Wither family. One night Harris, son of the house, proposed and she accepted. Perhaps it was the glow of the candlelight that did it, but whatever it was, it was gone by the time the grey light of dawn came creeping through her window.

She left on the early coach, before the family were up – an approach to be recommended to all like-minded spinsters.

As I said before, it was Queen Jane who started me writing, who provided me with that glorious phrase 'the importance of aunts', which broke like a clear white light over my head. In that same moment I knew that this would make a great title for a children's book. What was more amazing was that I knew I was going to write it.

---

* When planning Emma, Jane Austen said that she intended to create a heroine 'whom no one would like but myself'. Hold on to that thought throughout this volume, dear Reader.

I'd always liked sci-fi and, again, without really thinking about it, I knew that the aunts would be from some distant planet. Within a few months I had them: Lavinia, sensible and practical; Aurora, with her flamboyant good looks and talent for really bad driving, spinsters both, and from the planet Alpha Chameleon, a constellation, according to a book in the college library, 'faint and unremarkable and hidden from all but the most persistent telescopes', just the sort of place I felt spinsters should come from. I even had a plot, the pair of them crash-landing behind the shed in twelve-year-old Maddy Wilkins' back garden, going on to help her prevent her loving, domestically useless, widowed, mad scientist father marrying Entirely The Wrong Woman. (Oh, come on . . . doesn't it always happen?)

All this was during my last year at university. By the time I left I had a first draft. I'm a slow writer – more to the point I'm a slow learner. I got a job copywriting for an ad agency, and it took me another year of writing at nights and weekends before the novel was in sufficiently good shape to send it off to an agent. This I did and she took me on. And the rest, as they say, is history.

O for a Muse of fire now . . .

Imagine, if you will, à la the Chorus in *Henry Vee* not those vasty fields of France, those upreared and abutting fronts (and while we're on the subject, what exactly is an 'upreared and abutting front'?), not those proud horses printing their hooves or those thousand, thousand soldiers. No, no. Imagine instead if you will, but on the same scale, the sheer height and width and depth of my mother's joy when not only was *The Importance of Aunts* shortlisted for one of our major children's fiction prizes but, along with the rest of the shortlistees, I appeared on daytime television.

120

'Put *them* in their place, I can tell you.' 'Them' and 'their', as always, being short forms for anything and everything to do with The Other Side of the Family.

To say that my mother basked in reflected glory when this happened is totally untrue. My mother is congenitally incapable of basking in anything. She's far too hyper for that. Besides which, as far as she was concerned, said glory was not remotely reflected.

'Of course she gets it from me. You remember, Fran? When we were kids I was always scribbling.' Apparently Aunt Fran did not remember, something that paradoxically lends credence to my mother's claim, it being perfectly clear that any talent I have for making things up belongs entirely to Babs Gordon.

I was approaching forty by the time all this occurred. Despite my age, overnight I acquired a showbiz mother.

'You need someone.'

'Sorry?'

'To advise you.'

'On what exactly?'

'Your hair, for a start.'

'Oh, right.'

'And . . . really . . . darling. *Leggings.*' Her voice is hushed with a mixture of horror and adoration. 'On *Richard and Judy.*'

Ah, yes, heady days indeed.

Someone else won the prize in the end but it didn't matter. I was on my way and I knew what I wanted to do in life, not bad for someone previously without an iota of ambition. Beside this, the film rights of *I. o. A.* were bought, this by a production company with an impressive Los Angeles address and a supposed direct line to Steven Spielberg. To this day the film has not been made and I presume the resulting script remains mouldering away on a shelf somewhere. Still, I didn't much care. I had a cheque and an advance agreed on a new book and thanks to this, not too long afterwards, like I said, I was able to give up life in the city and move back to my home town and this cottage.

In the decade or so that has passed since then there have been three more 'Aunts' books (I'm still a slow worker), the last, *Day Trip to Corvus*. I was on my way back from the post office after packing it off to my publisher, edits completed, that very day I called in to see Magda and she told me about getting married.* Today, the advances for my books remain modest, but still I'm published, which is all that I care about. I don't make a stir, which is OK by me, not so my mother.

'See this,' she said, only this morning, slapping the paper down on her kitchen table. 'It says here they're camping out overnight for the new *Harry Potter*.'

My mother can be quite bitter, not to say spiteful, when it comes to my career. To understand why you have to picture her, year in, year out, growing steadily more pissed as she stays up with Tommy to watch the Oscars. She does this quite explicitly (drinking and watching) so she can weep and snuffle along with the stars when they do all that *without whom* stuff, blathering on about the debt they owe their mothers.

---

* Possibly the very reason why you're reading this. For the devil makes work for idle hands, particularly when it comes to writing. I see now that without a new Aunts plot coming – which it did not – I fell prey to this ABC for spinsters. It's a perverse and cussed notion if ever there was one. On the other hand, maybe that's precisely what it should be. Perverse and cussed. Just like the spinster.

'Ah, Tommy . . . what a nice thing to say. Oh, look at her crying. Isn't that lovely . . . ?' And all this spoken with the martyred air of a woman whose daughter utterly failed to acknowledge the debt she owed her on that occasion she was on *Richard and Judy*.

That I did not do so is entirely due to the fact that I've never been clear about the precise nature of my obligation.

'Listen. We went short for you, me and your father.'

'How? When? Where? Tell me.'

'We sent you to a good school . . .'

'I passed the eleven-plus. I got a scholarship.'

'Yes, well . . . Who do you think paid for the extras?'

'What extras?'

'Uniforms. *Hockey sticks*.'

'Stick. Stick. One stick in five years. I hated hockey.'

Still, bearing all this in mind, I believe I can do no better than conclude this chapter with a firm vow that in the unlikely event of this humble work being awarded some small token in order to denote its literary merit, and of my being thrust forward, protesting and tearful, to the microphone as a result, I shall indeed make a heart-warming speech in which I shall thank my mother for ABSOLUTELY EVERYTHING. It not being my way to push myself forward (indeed, such self-promotion is utterly abhorrent to me) I will only say that if it is the case that even now these words are being read by someone (you, sir, yes you, madam) whose onerous and thankless task it is to award such a token . . . Think, oh, only think, I beg of you.

You have it within your power to make a vain, batty, anorexic old woman deliriously happy.

*K is for . . . Kinder**

The reaction of Fleur to *The Importance of Aunts* was highly gratifying as far as my mother was concerned because Fleur gave all the signs of being mortally offended.

'Really. I'm amazed,' she said in a rather chilly tone of voice at the next family party.

'Why exactly?'

'Well, you . . .'

'Well me what?'

'Writing a book . . . for *children*.'

Let it be said, and this in her defence, that she wasn't the only one to feel her nose put out of joint in this respect. Looking through my press cuttings book, I see that I was questioned on more than one occasion about my spinster state.

'You don't have children of your own?' This I remember, in particular, from my own right on, left-leaning paper,

---

* As in *kinder, kirche, küche* children, church and kitchen, Herr and Frau Goebbels' receipe for success.

the smooth smile entirely failing to camouflage the air of accusation.

'No,' I said, smiling back, 'but then you don't have to *have* children to have children,' which is what I believe, and this thanks to Jonah and Elsa.

'Have you ever felt *broody*?' I said once to Sophie.

'No.'

'Me neither.'

Sophie comes from a large Catholic family. Besides her, there's a brace of brothers and three sisters. She's the eldest. By the time she was six, she could carry a toddler over one arm, jam food into a mouth in a high chair with the other.

'By the time I was thirteen, I knew I'd had all the child-care I wanted.'

It's never felt like a gap for me, not having children. I was going to say that not wanting them has been a conviction with me for as long as I can remember, something firm and fast and always present. But then I realised that it hasn't been like that at all, that not wanting children hasn't been a tangible desire not to have, instead it's been something else. A gap. An absolute *absence*. A component, just like ambition, missing.

'I guess I just never had it, that's all,' I said to Cass.

'So what?' Her hand flipped in the air, dismissing the argument. 'Neither do lots of woman. Neither did I. You're doing what you always do.'

'What's that?'

'Assuming you're different. That it's all cut and dried for everyone else.'

'Isn't it? At least for some people?'

'Maybe. For those who just always knew they wanted children. But for the rest of us, me for instance, you just fall into having children. Mostly it comes with the territory. I mean, if there'd been someone . . .'

'Oh, come on, Cass. There were always someones. If it had been what I wanted . . .' And I think I'm right. Because one thing's for sure, if my body clock ever ticked away, then it must have done so with such immaculate Swiss precision, with such a subdued clicking and whirring of its little cogs and wheels, that I never noticed. And maybe, like I say, my lack of maternal desire is all part of that ingrained laziness, or there again maybe it has to do with something else.

'Oh, well, I might have known.'

'What?'

'It would have to be my fault, wouldn't it?'

'I didn't say it was your fault. I just said it was interesting.'

According to research that had caught my eye, and which I made the mistake of mentioning to my mother, it appeared people who were the result of difficult births themselves were less likely to produce children.

'Yes, well, I can tell you, it was a difficult birth alright. You kept me hanging on for bloody hours.'

'Something I recall you mentioning on numerous occasions, Mother.'

My mother, always one for a colourful turn of phrase, likes to describe herself as 'shell-shocked' after my birth. Now it turns out, and against all the odds, she's entirely entitled to use the word.

'See . . . see.' She's waving the newspaper at me. 'What did I tell you?'

According to her paper on this particular morning (mine as well, so there's a chance it could be true) soldiers aren't the only ones to suffer from Post Traumatic Stress Disorder.

One in twenty mothers are apparently subject to the same symptoms – recurrent dreams of the event, excessive sweating and anxiety. Giving birth, it seems, can be as traumatic as going through a train smash or a bomb blast or being tortured, none of which comes as a surprise to me, merely a vindication.

Personally, I always thought Genesis said it all when it came to childbirth: 'In sorrow thou shalt bring forth children.' Childbirth, the punishment for eating the apple, a reminder, if one was needed, of that for which we were kicked out of Eden. More importantly an explanation by the early myth-makers for the inexplicable pain of childbirth. So that what I figured was, if a wandering Middle Eastern tribe circa 3000 BC, used to all the privations of desert life, thought giving birth was sufficiently painful to make up a myth about, that was good enough for me.

Squeezing out a six-pounder, legs akimbo, with some fool of a woman telling me to push, and the twerp whose fault it was doing bugger all but holding my hand and dabbing at my forehead never struck me as where I wanted to be in life. And since I found myself in the blessed position of being born in the Land of the Free where there was no Birth Police to ensure I kept the numbers up, well, frankly, I thought I'd give the whole thing a miss.

As it turns out, I'm increasingly less alone in this line of thinking than you might imagine. Take the matter of Caesarean births.

According to my friend Connie Cheung, who, being a doctor, and in gyny, is up with such figures, one in five babies are now born this way. Apparently, this is because the medical profession is much more likely to intervene these days, complication equalling the possibility of litigation. In private hospitals, according to Connie, where women get to choose how they'd like to give birth, the figure for Caesareans is even higher, one in two – that other big L, Life-style, thought to be largely responsible.[*]

All this is grist to the mill of the spinster. For hasn't she been given to understand from time immemorial that her life is irredeemably the poorer, and she so much less of a woman, for not having gone through the sweat and grind and good old-fashioned agony of traditional childbirth?

'Well . . . all I can say is I simply don't understand all this. I mean, for me the moment when I felt her THRUST herself out of me . . . well . . . it was . . . utterly ELEMENTAL . . . SPIRITUAL . . . I wouldn't have missed it for the WORLD.'

Yes, folks. No prize for guessing it. It's Mad Magda, president of the Miracle of Birth Party.

'I don't care what they say. For me, it was an *EXPLORATION* . . . a DISCOVERY.'[†]

If Magda could have got away with it, she'd have dropped Rochelle squatting down in the savannah and chewed through the umbilical cord before returning to the well to fetch water. Savannah being in short supply in Somerset, and, in addition, this particular form of childbirth being

---

[*] I won't go into details, it being ever my intention that this book be one you could lend at all times without fear to your servants.

[†] For more in this vein you need *Flesh of My Flesh, Poems on a Birth*, written and illustrated by Magda MacBride, Circean Press, £4.99; available from Hocus Pocus, Avalon Alternative Health and Therapy Centre and by mail order).

phallic mother
parthenogenitor
patchwork of blood and breast and bone

etc. etc . . .

128

frowned on by the local health authority, she had to make do with her tape of *Animal Calls from the Wild* and the surroundings of the local maternity hospital. Sticking to the spirit of the thing, however, she announced she would be refusing the pethidine et al., and instead would get by on Buddhist chanting. We might even have believed she'd pulled it off was it not for our good friend Connie, who was a junior doctor there at the time and almost got a black eye off Magda when she didn't get the gas and air in fast enough.

As a new mother Magda was, natch, radiant. Breast-feeding with six shows a day (doors open half an hour before performance).

'I feel so utterly *POWERFUL*.' I can see her now tracing a finger around the rosebud lips clamped to her breast and gratefully guzzling. 'It's so wonderful. To know that you can be loved by something so *utterly* unconditionally.'

I find it impossible to think of that moment now without seeing those rosebud lips the way they are today.*

Meanwhile, if spinsters have their heroines then I guess they have their *bêtes noires* as well, and top of my list would be that other Old Testament matriarch Rachel. Rachel, most famous of late mothers, clutching her fist and shaking it at her husband and at empty heaven too, I guess.

'Give me children or I die.'

I've never had much sympathy for Rachel. There's

---

* I smiled to myself when I first thought of this, which I now find unforgivable. Because now I see something grand in all that unflagging devotion, in that absolute refusal to acknowledge all Rochelle's snarling. I think my heart might have broken if it had happened to me. All of which confirms me in my opinion that it's an absurd, ludicrous, crazy thing to have children.

I wondered if that's what I wanted to say that night to David?

something so petulant, so goddamn *unhealthy* about that peevish blackmailing cry.

Maybe it cuts me out of the argument, not having that body clock ticking away. I don't know. On the other hand, from where I'm looking it seems like anyone who wants a baby so much they're willing to get pregnant past the bus pass age, or have it in someone's else womb, or clone it in a Petri dish, should probably be prevented by law from having one. What worries me more is that, as far as I can see, there's still a sort of unspoken but residual feeling that any or all this behaviour is marginally more sane, certainly more understandable and societally acceptable than deciding in a cool, calm level-headed way that you don't want children.

'Don't you want to be a *woman*?'

I remember the words from my spell in public relations, the one that propelled me into university, writing copy on everything from nappies to narrow boat holidays, and this for a brace of neanderthals (a nice touch of alliteration), one of whom, leaking ash down his lapels, over the restaurant table as we celebrated winning the bonny baby paddy puffy nappy contract, leant in at me, leering too (which is peculiar), and this after I'd disclosed how wildly unqualified I was to write about such products, never having wanted children.

Don't you want to be a woman?

Which is a good question, I'll give him that – one, I guess, that gets to the heart of the business, this by expressing the notion that the state of being a woman can be formalised, summed up and circumscribed in this way, i.e., by the production of a child. A further question being, why so? Because if *being a man* doesn't have procreation written into it by definition, doesn't require this for its legitimacy, why then should it dog the feet of women?

'It doesn't.'

'Yes it does. You don't see it, Cass. But that's because you're not single and childless.'

Within ten years, or so they say, infertility will be a thing of the past. It's big business and growing bigger by the day, this while whole areas of misery in terms of human health grub for funding – migraine, for instance, from which Danny's father has suffered viciously all his life, preaching his way through the pain; and lupus which Fergie's mother, Etty, now has, confining her to the sofa for half the day, depressing her beyond the reach of medication, conditions going to all intents and purposes unregarded while money pours into infertility treatment.

'As if we really are a brave new world,' as I said to Cass. 'As if we really are a throwaway society, and the not-yet-born have become more important than the living.'

Personally, I can't see how the whole infertility business is anything but a step backwards in the advancement of women. And maybe we have heaven to blame for this, that first judgement that set the precedent, that saw the justice of Rachel's case after she'd hurled up that outraged cry, so that when she gave birth, it was not just to a child but more ominously to her *right* to produce one. But if every woman has a right to have a child – the axis on which the whole baby business turns – then having a child must be at least part of what it *means* to be a woman, and my ash-covered friend was right. It becomes a defining feature, perhaps even – and this is the next step – *the* defining feature. And where does that leave women who don't want children? Because if not being able to have a child is deemed a sickness, something to be healed with all this money and effort, what does this say about those who deliberately infect themselves, those who inflict themselves with the disease of deciding to remain childless?

Fact of the matter is, I'm a hard-liner when it comes to all that babies-on-demand stuff.

'We don't get everything we want in life. I don't see babies should be any different.'

But Connie shakes her head. 'They're not on demand. You can't say that, Riley. A woman may go through the whole IVF thing three times and then not get pregnant.'

I guess Connie and I are bound to disagree. She sees the sorrowful side of the business, after all.

Apart from anything else, she was the one who had to break the bad news to Sandra.

When I think of what happened to Sandra, it makes me yearn for old certainties, for a heaven and a hell, the latter in which to consign Royston.

In any good Victorian saga, Cousin Royston would end up sinking slowly, cries unheard, in some boggy marsh, or drowned in a stone pit. In this regard I've looked longingly at many a rhine, I can tell you. A hundred and fifty years ago he'd be riding a two-hundred-guinea hunter he couldn't afford, beating it mercilessly with a whip. Now he does much the same thing but with forty grand's worth of metallic blue Audi Quattro. Only this morning he cut me up in it on the roundabout at the end of the ring road, giving me the finger – his most common form of communication – when I blasted the horn at him. The 'Baby on Board' sign swinging merrily in his back window as he disappeared over the horizon only added insult to injury.

A latecomer to the Fraser family, Royston was born a full ten years after Fleur. I guess he was something of a surprise to Aunt Fran, which is why she so hopelessly spoilt him. It gives me no pleasure to say it. She knows what she's done. From puberty onwards, when Royston's obnoxious personality began to seriously assert itself, it was possible to detect a sad little smile hovering about her lips when she looked at him. In Hugh this translated as an unhappy frown that drew in his eyebrows when his youngest was near him.

The worst thing that happened to Royston is that he was given the best of everything, including the statutory public school education, never a good move for someone not overbright but imbued with a vacuous sense of his own importance. His main problem is that he thinks of himself as Alpha Male whereas in fact he's way down the end of the hatchery.

Royston's job as sales manager at Frasers (a job mostly done by the minions beneath him), his name on the door, the smart suits he wears, his succession of flash cars still can't disguise the truth of the matter – that there's something of the spiv about Royston. He should be flogging black market nylons off the back of a wagon. Naturally my mother adores him.

'Royston. You wicked boy.'

'Babs. More beautiful than ever.'

When it comes to isms, Royston has the full house. Chauvinism, sexism and racism, they're all there positively vying for supremacy. He's grown up with the knowledge that being a Fraser gets him everywhere in this town so he uses the name unsparingly. 'Never pay full price for anything,' is his proud boast, and one that has earnt him a more-than-average degree of loathing among the purveyors of goods and services in the neighbourhood.

Few of us in the church among the pomp and ceremony,

the bouffant frocks and the garlanded pews ten years ago when Royston married Sandra, thought the hat we'd purchased specially for the occasion was anything else than a gross waste of money. And to this day I think every man jack of us there bears a responsibility. After all, to be legal in this country, the participants must be of a sound mind. Thus when the vicar asked if anyone knew any just cause why the two of them should not be wed, one of us should have raised our hand, stepped forward.

'Stop the marriage,' we should have said. 'The bride's quite mad. No one in their right mind could consider marrying Royston.'

Royston first saw Sandra on the front page of our paper, this when she made it into the early heats of the Miss England competition. Seeing her, he wanted her, more for his own vanity than anything else. Being what he was, i.e., a Fraser, he had little difficulty in enticing her away from her carpenter boyfriend.

Sandra had always wanted children. No. It's more than that. Sandra had *always* wanted children.

'Even when I was a kid myself I used to think about it,' she told me at her wedding. Her eyes shone innocently, like the teenager she still was. 'Six I want, six at least.'

'And Royston?' I remember I asked.

'Oh, yes. He wants a big family too.' This with a wide-eyed confidence that was heartbreaking.

Weddings don't mean much to me. They don't make me go choky. They don't make me coo or flutter either. Still, I'd say that however brides are supposed to look, then that was the way that Sandra looked that day. She was breath-taking, a corny word but I use it advisedly. She looked like something from an old Viennese fairytale, as exquisite in the flesh in her off-the-shoulder gown with wide crinoline skirt as she'd been in the spread in *Bride*, where she'd been featured a month earlier.

All this should have been enough for any man, shouldn't it? But they'd been together four years by the time they married so that the gilt was already off the gingerbread for Royston. He started in on that marriage the way he intended to continue, bonking one of the bridesmaids at the reception. This I know thanks to Fergie, who, wandering around the hotel grounds, caught them full at it through the gazebo window.

Royston led a rich and full sexual life during the marriage. The pity of it was that it wasn't with Sandra. All this was public knowledge in the town. Everyone knew his pick-up spots: local gym, the sleezebag country club, and Bristol, where he'd go ostensibly to watch the match from the directors' box, but actually to take full advantage of the R and R at various nightspots afterwards. When no children arrived, despite the stated aim, most thought it was because by now Royston was depositing his seed just about everywhere but Sandra. But then Sandra underwent tests, as a result of which it fell to Connie to tell her the terrible truth – that she suffered from endometriosis, a condition that would make pregnancy all but impossible. She let out a terrible cry, according to Connie, something that sounded like a wounded animal.

After this, Sandra became a wan and tragic figure at family parties, collapsing in floods of tears and disappearing into the bathroom at the most innocent mention of the word 'children'.

'It isn't fair . . . it isn't fair,' she wailed one night when I found her out on Hugh and Fran's terrace, and frankly I agreed with her. I didn't think it was fair, any of it, not least of fate to allow her fall in love with an arsehole like

135

Royston. But then, when did fairness ever have anything to do with the human condition?

I'd say she cried as if her heart would break that night, great heaving sobs that lifted her shoulders up to her ears, but how absurd that would be. Her heart was already broken. And it should go without saying that she received precious little comfort or tender loving care for any of this from Cousin Royston. I caught a glimpse of his face poking out through the French windows. He raised his eyes when he saw her, blew contemptuously out through his thin, mean lips, pulling back sharply.

'I don't usually say this,' I said that night, 'but you're a cunt, you know that, don't you, Royston?'

He raised his hands with one of his proud laddish grins. 'Hey,' he said, 'women's stuff. What can I do about it?'

In the end that night, Hugh ordered Royston to take Sandra home, this after Aunt Fran had failed with her pleading. Royston sighed as at some terrible imposition.

'Fetch her coat,' Hugh said sharply, and Royston did, but in the darkness of the hall, I saw him half throw it at her. Outside, she stumbled into the front seat of the car, still weeping. He got in the other side, turned the stereo full up with a flick of his wrist. Loud mindless music pumped out as he drove off, spraying the gravel.

The worst part about all of this is that Sandra – I think, I truly believe – was just beginning to get her shit together when Carlotta appeared on the scene. I'd seen her – Sandra – in Safeway one day. She'd grasped my hand, given me a shy look. She said, 'We're talking about adoption.' I doubted the 'we' even then, rumours already abounding about Carlotta.

Carlotta came for an interview for deputy marketing manager at Frasers. She turned up with a height of heel and a hardness of eye that had Royston's tongue lolling out and down over his chin within half an hour of their meeting. Naturally she got the job. Within a month or so she also had Royston.

It's my belief that nothing moves faster than a woman with her body clock ticking away – faster than the speed of light – which will give you some idea of how long it took Carlotta to whisk Royston away, tongue flapping, from the failed family home and into a newly constituted love nest at a safe distance in Bristol.

Being thirty-seven, and four years older than Royston, Carlotta was in no mood to hang about as regards procreation, so that when nothing happened after those first few months, she had not just herself but Royston as well down to the clinic, and this before you could say assisted conception. There the awful truth was revealed – that it wasn't just Sandra's fault they had not conceived.

'Poor boy . . . poor boy . . .'

'For God's sake, Mother. He's got a low sperm count. It's not cancer.'

In fact I breathed a sigh of relief when I heard about Royston's condition; so did Cass and Fergie.

'Good old Mother Nature,' I said, raising my glass in what turned out to be entirely premature celebration. Eighteen months later, thanks to the appliance of science, in particular six thousand quids' worth of IVF, Carlotta gave birth to Charlie.

'Great,' I said, when my mother passed on the news with delight. 'Just what the world needs. Another Royston.'

Meanwhile, as regards Sandra, it's my belief the word 'devastated' is overused, but in the case of her reaction to Royston's departure, it's entirely appropriate.

I'd say it was pretty lucky that a teacher friend of Cass'

was taking the air one night with her labrador. Walking past Royston and Sandra's house she was witness unwittingly to a most unhappy scene: Royston carrying a few prize possessions to the car, CDs, clothes, a yard of ale stick, Sandra trying to pull him back, falling on the gravel, holding on to his legs and being dragged across it, eventually spreadeagling herself across his bonnet, slipping off as he drove away. Knowing the family connection, the friend called Cass who went round, tried to sponge off Sandra's bloodied knees and phoned the doctor, because by now Sandra was hysterical.

She was in hospital a while after that. A private clinic. At Hugh and Fran's expense. And it was thanks to them, only thanks to them, for Royston didn't care, that when she came out eventually it was at least to a good divorce settlement.

They've continued to treat her as part of family, selling the house for her while she was in hospital, this being what she said she wanted, helping her move into the new place they bought for her in a development at the foot of the Tor near her mother.

Like a woman caught in a crazy hall of mirrors, Sandra turned from rake thin to pudgy in the hospital. When she came out her skin was doughy and her hair lank. Meeting her in the street she was scarcely recognisable as the lovely young thing who represented Miss West of England in the UK finals.

She's still this way, spending a fortune on all manner of wacky witch doctors and counsellors. They diagnose everything except the thing that counts, which is simply that she's desperately unhappy.

I guess she's tried just about everything in the Avalon Alternative Health and Therapy Centre. Every time I meet her it's something new.

'Reiki, Riley,' she said to me, stuffing down a vegetable samosa at the opening of the phobia clinic. 'It's wonderful. You should try it. You can't imagine how much better I feel.'

Only she didn't look any better, that's the trouble. She never does after all these new and wonderful therapies. At the same time she still spoke in the overbright voice, the one that seems intent on proving she's so much better.

'Peter thinks he might also try me on kinesiology,' she said, and then, after a small pause, making a miserable attempt at carelessness, 'How's Royston?'

She always says this and I always answer the same way.

'Just like he always was. A total arsehole. You're better off without him, Sandra.'

Like I say, in any good Victorian novel Royston would come to a bad end. But bad ends are hard to come by these days, certainly when it comes to producing children.

Charlie is three now, known to our side of the family as 'Chuckie', and for obvious reasons. There can't be any doubt about his parentage, that's for sure. He's a chip off the old block and already displaying the full range of his father's lager lout tendencies.

At the last Fraser Christmas party, for like it or not Hugh and Fran have had to accept Royston and Carlotta, we watched as Charlie smashed his pedal car with an obvious sense of delight into the backs of the legs of the guests as they stood talking.

'Makes you wonder if we haven't been too hasty over this whole business of eugenics,' I said to Fergie. 'I blame you.'

'Me?'

'You and your ilk.'

Because, like I said to him, Mother Nature did everything she could to ensure there'd be no more Roystons, coupling him with Sandra, who couldn't get pregnant, even lowering his sperm count to zero.

Across the room there was an agonised howl as yet another guest got mown down by Chuckie.

'It should have been foolproof,' I said 'A perfect plan.'

'You're right,' Fergie said, and he gave a sigh. 'And along came science to fuck up a beautiful system.'

L is for . . . that old Lost Love Story

1972 is history, I see that now.

In 1972 a man had not long since walked on the moon. How historical is that?

Brezhnev was still in the Kremlin, Nixon in the White House.

And the war was coming to an end in Vietnam.

In 1972, at the fag end of that year, at the fag end of the affair, I woke next to Nathan, broken from sleep by the dull heavy throb overhead.

'What is it?' I asked him drowsily.

For Nathan's eyes were already open. His hands at the back of his head as he leant back against the wall, the arms with their rich deep fur of hair, formed dark triangles against the institutional cream of the paint work. The neon light filtering through the blinds from the massage parlour opposite lit up his face in red flashes, making each new glimpse of him, the big bull head with its crew cut, the taut skin around his temples, the hardness of his mouth, all freshly unfamiliar, freshly compelling and erotic.

Nathan turned his eyes down from the ceiling at my

words but in the half-light they were no more than empty sockets. Without speaking, he lifted back the sheet, swung his long legs slowly out of the single bed, lowered them to the floor as he pushed himself upwards with his knuckles. He walked to the window, the familiar determined steps placing his feet hard and flat to the floor, straining and rucking the legs of the old-fashioned white undershorts, making them ride up on his haunches. His bull head was down, the way it always was, the fur-covered back slightly bent, as if all this hugeness, this weight of head and body was all just too much for him.

At the window he poked a finger through the blinds, the big bull head lifting up and back as he craned out to look as the heavy rumbling throb continued overhead.

'It's nothing,' he said without turning. 'Go back to sleep, Riley.'

Let me tell you, if I had a time machine now, if I had a choice of all the finest moments in history, if I was offered personal audiences with the most famous, the most gifted, the most holy and wise of men, still it would make no difference, still I would chose from everything to go back to that moment with Nathan, to take myself back to that room, to put myself in that bed, have myself say, 'Nathan,' very softly to his back, making him turn; still I would hold out my hand to him, hold it out in such a way, beckoning with such imperious yearning that he could not refuse; that he would take those long loping heavy steps back to the bed where I would take his hand, that Nathan hand, big with the long thick fingers, take the middle one, stroke it very slowly from the bottom right up to its tip, lay the hand flat against my face so I could feel it on my cheek. So I could feel that hand against my cheek, every last infinitesimal fraction of it . . .

142

'Hey . . . hey . . . hey . . .'

'What?'

'You've never talked about this before, Riley.'

And I hadn't. I'd never told anyone. Not Sophie. Not Cass. Not even Danny, who was staring at me now from the end of the sofa.

'So why now?'

'I don't know. Maybe with Jonah travelling and everything. Going to Bangkok. I guess it got me thinking.' I said, 'Just think. If it had worked out we could have been divorced by now.' I was trying – and I wasn't sure why – to make a joke of it.

'All of these years . . .' Danny has a hand over his heart.

'What?'

'Locked away inside you.'

I said, 'It's just something that happened, that's all. It's no big deal.'

'Yeah . . . right.' He's looking sceptical.

I said, 'Don't turn it into one of those Great Lost Love Stories, Danny.'

Because that's what everyone wants, isn't it? Maybe you too, dear Reader. An old lost love story. Another of those clichés. What the spinster is supposed to have (besides a cat), what makes her what she is, what lends her that enduring air of loss, the Lost Love Story, like some stole thrown around her shoulders, protecting her decency, her modesty, and not because she wants it, but because the world requires it of her, this faintly tragic *respectability*, making the world more comfortable with her, providing the necessary explanation, the justification for her state.

'Some people just seem happier if you can give them a good reason why you're single, Riley,' Olive Jepson said, and close on forty years ago too, and if that's not depressing

143

I don't know what is. And, surely she was right. Because in a world where people are worn down trying to make their relationships work, who needs the spinster standing by and smiling amiably and refusing to bother? All this makes the lost love not just the excuse, the defence, the *mitigation* for the presence of the spinster, it also makes it a panacea for those who need it, a camouflage for the horrible truth of the thing: that actually, as far as the spinster is concerned, her state has nothing to do with absence, or loss, or missed opportunity. It's not Second Best at all but First Choice. In fact the view up here on the shelf is pretty damn good from where she's looking.

'Hey,' I said to Danny, 'I'm not Miss Havisham. 'There's no wedding cake mouldering away in the middle of my table.'

I'd been two months at the Oasis when Nathan arrived and I guess you could say I was overprepared for him. But that was Angel's fault because she wouldn't stop talking about him.

'Nathan's coming,' she'd say, clapping her hands in delight like a child. 'Soon you see Nathan.'

You're taking a chance introducing a bar girl called Angel, I know that. And it doesn't help that this was her name, or at least what everyone called her. And I don't want to dress the thing up now. I don't want to make it more than it was. I want what comes through from this to be the truth, not some sentimental wish-wash. So that if I tell you that I can still feel a catch in my heart thinking of Angel's face, then you can believe it. And not because that face was beautiful. In fact, she wasn't especially beautiful, with a small pointed chin and large brown eyes that gave her face the look of some small, good-natured animal. But it was her smile that made her beautiful, a smile that seemed to stretch back to her ears when she bestowed it on you, which was most of the time, a smile that, just like Lee's, belied everything that had happened to her.

'She'll be dead by the time she's thirty.' I'm shocked at the weary, unsentimental way Nathan says it.

'But why? What of?'

But he just shrugs. 'Her heart. She has a weak heart.'

And anyway, what does anyone such as Angel die of in Thailand?

Nathan was a favourite of Angel. He'd known her since the beginning, which was five years before, when she'd met Barnie, then one of Nathan's Ph.D. students doing his research in Thailand. But then one night, in the way of these things, he'd met Angel in a bar, thrown up his studies and got a job as a barman.

'You and Nathan,' she would say, this before he arrived and with a knowing nod, her delicate fingers church-steepled over her mouth and her eyes shining. Once or twice when she did it I caught Barnie's brows drawing together and on one occasion, turning suddenly, I found his eyes on me with an expression I could not fathom. The day before Nathan arrived he finally cracked, her breath-less merriment undoing him. He banged a glass down hard on the bar top.

'For Pete's sake, shut up about Nathan,' he said.

She threw him a haughty look before turning back to me. 'You like Nathan,' she said, her small pointed chin giving a small nod as if everything was settled.

But I didn't. I didn't like Nathan at all.

'Come,' she said that night he arrived. 'You meet Nathan,' and she led me across the bar to him like a marriage prize to a wealthy potentate. Never was one more proudly born. And it comes to me now, all these years on, how much her innocent hopes must have been dashed that first night. For Angel would never be a matchmaker. She didn't have the stomach for it. She adored Nathan, and the disappointed hopes of that evening were plastered all over her face. She sat forward on the bamboo sofa, her hands clasped around her knees, gazing steadfastly at the pair of us. She was willing us to come together but, despite this urging, a cool unfriendly space persisted between us. His affection for her was strong but, even so, he refused point-blank even to acknowledge me.

'I'm sure I did not.'

'I'm sure you did.'

Safe in his arms a few days later, in a small wormhole of time, and sucked dry by his lovemaking, we were able to discuss it.

I sat there twenty minutes or so that first night while he ignored me. I smiled, but only for Angel. I didn't care. Not for Nathan or for the way he was treating me. All I cared about was the effect it was having on Angel, the way her characteristic calm was entirely disrupted. Her finger, interlocking on her lap, made small unhappy twisting movements as all that excitement and anticipation drained away. She sat on the edge of the sofa as if trying to urge the business forward, throwing small hopeful glances backwards and forwards between the two of us. She was like a benevolent spider, weaving a web, trying to draw us into it. But I was content with the way things were. I was twenty-two years old. I looked from the corner of my eye at this man with his tall, stooping body and his serious bearing and pronounced him an oddity – more, an irrelevancy, something and someone outside my desires or understanding. In the end I got up, carelessly, making my excuses, leaving him.

That was the way it was that night, and the next one and the one after that, and I don't recall in that time speaking to Nathan. I don't recall one look, one smile or one glance. Neither do I register at all his eyes upon me. Thus I have none of those traditional precursors of love that might serve to make what happened the more convincing or explicable. All I know is that on the fourth night everything changed between us.

And I want to go rushing on now. I want to get to the moment of our fingers entwining, Nathan's and mine, which is not right, not right at all, because I do not remember the moment of our fingers entwining. All I remember is the *being* entwined, the way we suddenly *were*, and the feel of our fingers caught in the space between the bamboo sofa's overstuffed cushions, locked fast between our thighs, mine bare in the short pink gingham dress, his in the conservative grey lecture-room trousers.

I think it must have been the stillness that did it that night, that made everything seem to spool down around us. It was early, with just a handful of customers. It was Zoe's night off and I sat at the bar talking to Priya, who worked behind it, and when she was busy just sat there silently. Barnie and Angel, who Nathan normally came in to see, had gone out to dinner, so that when he came in this night he sat down with a curt nod, leaving a vacant stool between us. For some minutes, I don't know how many, we sat there staring together straight ahead at Priya and the line of bottles behind the bar, the stillness mushrooming up between us. I seemed to see everything in great detail, the precise tone of the flecks of black on the fake marble bar, the way Priya's fingers in the mirror appeared to caress the tops of the bottles as she wiped them. It was

147

as if we sat, Nathan and I, in separate pools of silence, like spotlights, so that when the coin came it appeared like some third circle of light between us. His finger on it pushed it forward slowly and deliberately across the bar top, the thick black hair on the back of his hand reaching almost to the cuticle. The finger gave a tap, not once but twice, as if deliberating the wisdom of the movement. I can hear every last inflection of the way he said the words, the way he spoke them in that husky, embarrassed growl. And although they could not be more banal when repeated here on the page, still they come out to me now just the way they did then, bathed in glory.

For they were not said in any patronising way, neither as some cheap peace gesture. Instead they were said quietly and firmly as if this simple request was truly the thing he most wanted.

They say that time stands still when lovers meet, don't they? But it's not true, it's not true at all. It's so much better than that. Time doesn't stand still. It runs, it dances, it disappears down black holes.

As his long thin finger pushed that coin slowly along the bar towards me, it seemed like time collapsed, that everything we were or had been or ever could be was caught in that long lazy movement.

'Put something on the jukebox,' he said as Time bent and stretched and danced around us.

I put on 'Vincent'.

It was 1972.*

---

* I'd put it on again later, in a restaurant, a few months into the affair. I'd say, proudly, as if he couldn't know, it being pop music, my music, 'It's about Van Gogh.' He'd pass a sad, tired hand across his eyes as if something was too difficult to explain. He'd say, 'I think I guessed that, Riley.'

M is for ... Marriage

Pensioners Stan and Ada Vowles reckon their marriage fits like a glove.

The two, who met at Frasers factory when they were in their teens, have just celebrated 72 years of marriage

Stan worked all his life at Frasers, eventually retiring from the post room at 70. Two of the couple's three children followed him into the firm, along with three of their six grandchildren. One of their eleven great-grandchildren, Sharon (pictured with the couple), now works in the firm's dispatch department.

'The family has been very much part of Frasers and continues to be to this day,' said managing director, Freddy Fraser, at the party for the couple laid on by the firm at the Swan Hotel.

'We're very proud of Stan and Ada ...' blah de blah de blah.

I hate going to a Fraser function in my persona as reporter. Frankly, it makes me feel like a poor relation. I was hoping to get away with it, hiding behind the mass ranks of children, grandchildren and great-grandchildren as Cousin Freddy pontificated, tapping his little pinkie finger on his glass, and sticking out that Toad of Toad Hall chest.

'More than seventy years of marriage. Such a wonderful achievement . . .'

Later, though, as Danny clicked away at the family group, Freddy caught me.

'Bad business all together about Fleur and Martin.' He was trying to be conversational but there was a frown between his eyebrows. 'Mother's very upset. Can't accept it at all. Coming on top of the whole thing with Royston and Carlotta.'

I mmm-ed a bit, made a few consolatory noises, 'Well . . . you know . . . and 'These days . . . all the while staring over at Stan and Ada.

I said, 'Let me ask you something, Freddy. Can you imagine, honestly, being married seventy-two years?'

'Of course.' But he'd said it too quickly.

'No, come on, seriously . . . can you imagine it?'

He dropped his eyes, took another swig of his wine. The pompous chest seemed to dropped inwards and for a moment it was like there was another Freddy hiding there.

'No.' He was looking straight at me now and I knew it was a sudden moment of truth from Freddy. I found myself wondering about him, if he'd had an affair in all the – what must it be – thirty years he'd been married, cheated on Brenda with her loud horsy voice and her passion for corgies.

I think a lot about marriage. But then why wouldn't I? In its own way it makes me what I am, i.e., by virtue of my lack of participation in it. I think about it rather in the way that an anthropologist might, studying some rare tribe and faced with a puzzling ritual or ceremonies.

Look, as I understand it, in order to make something

work for you, I mean really work, as a concept, you have to be able to visualise it, to *imagine* it as a possibility.

'Maybe it's something to do with our new here today, gone tomorrow world. Maybe people just can't *imagine* being married for years any more.'

'God, even if they wanted to.' This drolly, eyes rolling, from Sophie.

I tried the argument out on Cass too, and to an even worse reception.

I said, 'Maybe that's why the Stan and Adas of this world are disappearing. Maybe that's why the divorce figures are going up.'

She said, 'Oh, for God's sake. People don't waste time *imagining* when they first meet. They don't *visualise*. They just get on with it. Then they turn round one day and thirty years have passed. And if they're lucky they're still together.'

Still, you'd have to wonder, these days, why in that grand moment in the wedding ceremony when the congregation is asked if anyone knows any reason why the two shouldn't be married, someone doesn't have the decency to raise a hand and step forward: 'Well, not exactly, but since you ask, have you seen the statistics . . . ?'

Hamlet might have been nearer the truth than he knew when he bellowed, 'We shall have no more marriages.' Sometimes that looks like the way that it's going. Four out of ten marriages in this country now end in divorce, news to no one except those whose job it is to produce my mother's daily paper, which only this morning did what it always does when the Office of National Statistics* release

---

* And if you do work in the ONS, and you are reading this, I'd like you to know just how much maternal ear-bashing I have to put up with every time you release those damn divorce statistics.

the figures, which is to announce it in seventy-two-point type on the front page and in the breathless manner of Joris springing to the stirrup and setting off for Aix from Ghent.[*]

I galloped, Dirck galloped, we galloped all three

In addition, doubting its readers would be able cope with the complicated arithmetical notion of four out of ten, and to add that extra End Of Civilisation As We Know It potential, it rounded up the awkward and uninspiring four out of ten to five, thus allowing it to proclaim an 'almost fifty per cent failure rate' for British marriage. Thus did it fulfil its prime objective in life, which is to provide a source of

---

[*] This is a cultural reference likely to be missed by younger readers. It's from the poem 'How They Brought the Good News From Ghent to Aix' by Robert Browning:

> I sprang to the stirrup, and Joris, and he;
> I galloped, Dirck galloped, we galloped all three;
> 'Good speed!' cried the watch, as the gate-bolts undrew;
> 'Speed!' echoed the wall to us galloping through;
> Behind shut the postern, the light sank to rest,
> And into the midnight we galloped abreast.

This plus the following six lines are embedded in my memory, thanks to the fact that I had to learn them as a punishment after Ronnie Gibson and I were discovered among the coats at the furthest end of the cloakroom poring over the dirty bits in *Lady Chatterley*. We received not one but three detentions for this, the severity of the sentence due in no small part to the fact that, following our discovery (this thanks to our ribald laughter), when asked by Miss Holderness, the English teacher, what exactly we were doing Ronnie answered 'Biology.'

Meanwhile, to my shame, and to this day, I'm not clear what exactly the good news was that Joris and Dirck and the other one had to carry to Aix at such speed.

However, for more about Ronnie Gibson, see the next chapter.

outrage and breast-beating each morning for that ever-Disgusted of Tunbridge Wells. And, for that matter, my mother.

'I don't know . . . I really don't know . . .' She might have been a novice playing with her rosary as she bent over the page on the kitchen table as I came in to give her a lift to the supermarket. She fingered her long fake gold chain of links and pearls, letting out a string of tut-tuts as she did it. 'I don't know. No one sticks at anything these days.'

My mother, you see, takes a revisionist approach to history, one that allows, nay enjoins her, to view the shocking increase in divorce figures from the standpoint of one who spent almost thirty years in a contented but tragically truncated union.

'Mind you, I'm not saying that we didn't have our difficulties . . .'

'One major difficulty being a complete inability, man and wife, to remain in the same room together.'

Yet another of those things I have never said to my mother.

More than hundred years ago, and this when divorce was only by a petition to Parliament, Samuel Johnson wrote:

> *Sir, it is so far from being natural for a man and woman to live in a state of marriage, that we find all the motives which they have for remaining in that connection, and the restraints which civilised society imposes to prevent separation, are hardly sufficient to keep them together.*

It was old Sammy, too, who came out with that famous thing about second marriages being 'the triumph of hope over experience', more relevant than ever today with some forty per cent in this country now in second, third (or more) unions.

'And why the hell not?' My good sister, Cass, hates all forms of cynicism. 'Why the hell shouldn't people go on hoping?'

And of course she's right. Besides which, as with Mark Twain, so with marriage. Reports of its death have been exaggerated.

Marriage is still the ambition of most, a fact backed up by a survey carried out by one of our leading building societies in which the participants rated it equal in the happiness it delivered to a £70,000 income.

'Well, as one who's had both . . .' Fleur's voice is severe as she flips the paper closed on the Hocus Pocus counter, also a tad tragic, 'I can tell you, *happiness* is much more important than money.' For good measure she glares at a couple of tourists whose crime is to attempt to pay for their Tibetan bells while she was talking.

Fleur is 'working' now – her word, not mine, since it covers three mornings a week draping herself elegantly on a stool behind the counter at Hocus Pocus, taking any money offered with an air of forbearance. None of which, I regret to say, prevents her acting like some Little Match Girl or Mimi minus the consumption and the arias.

'I have to work,' she says with the air of a woman fallen on hard times. 'I need the money.' Which, to put it bluntly, is total bollocks. Something I happen to know from a chance meeting with Martin in the Jolly Pilgrim several nights earlier.

'Got some shit-hot London divorce lawyer,' he said, shoving his beer glass in the air pugnaciously towards me. 'Says she wants half of everything.'

Martin was surrounded by his Rotary Club mates when

I saw him. He was acting blustery and cheerful in that way that separated men do when they're pretending they're doing well, whereas in actual fact they're doing extremely badly.

'We'll see,' he said, trying for defiance. 'Two can play at that game,' which is when I felt really sorry for him, wondering how he could possibly think that it was a game to Fleur and, more importantly, how he had a cat in hell's chance of winning it.

I couldn't resist telling Fleur I'd seen Martin, this because of all that crap she was giving me about happiness v. money. In particular I wanted her to know I was *au fait* with her plan to take a legal chain saw to everything Martin is and has in order to neatly divest him of half of it.

'And why shouldn't I?' Her eyes snapped defiantly over the counter at me. 'I've worked my fingers to the bone for Martin all these years. It was a full-time job.' By now her air of nobility had returned. Her hand was at her throat, although immaculately manicured and remarkably unbony from what I could see of it.

Now before we go any further let me say that as a good old-fashioned sixties feminist, I've always known that my views would be tested and possibly to destruction. I just never imagined it would be Fleur who did it.

'I mean, poetic licence or what?' as I said, reporting the facts of the case to Cassie.

Because while I accept that with three kids Fleur may have spent the last twenty years as a one-woman taxi service ferrying her offspring to football training, choir practice and ballet lessons, still the fact is that for all that time she's enjoyed: a) the services of an au pair (at least till the boys reached their teenage years and got frisky) and b) a four-times-a-week cleaner-cum-housekeeper. Neither of which, according to Fleur, now figure in the plot of the story.

'Martin had me there all those years to look after him and the kids. I've spent my life organising his life for him.' Her tone had become hectoring and one of those perfect *worked-to-the-bone* fingers was jamming down hard on the counter. 'I put my whole life into that marriage. I made him everything he is today. All the work I put in. All that entertaining . . .'

Now this was the last straw for me. 'La-La Land', as I said to Cassie.

Because while it's well known that Fleur did indeed do a lot of entertaining, it's equally well known that the nearest she ever got to slaving over the proverbial hot stove was to point the caters in the direction of it.

'Can you believe it?' as I said to Cass. 'Bloody woman's never even stuffed a mushroom.'*

---

* *Life is too short to stuff a mushroom* is a phrase that passed into the female language in the seventies thanks to Shirley Conran's book *Superwoman*. A woman who knew a good phrase when she heard it, Conran was also responsible for one of the great lines in late 20th century fiction: 'Which of you three bitches is my mother?' this from her best-selling *Lace*, a phrase which has a certain resonance for me and not just because my own mother picked the book up second-hand and took it on her coach trip to Austria with Tommy. She didn't read it, of course. She never actually reads books, particularly on holiday, just carries one big one around with her in her patent bag like a sort of totem.

'I don't know why you don't write one of these,' she said waving it at me as I dropped her off at the bus station.

Another question I ask myself frequently.

N is for ... Nature or Nurture?

The brain is an amazing thing. Come up with a memory, and before you know it, it'll start flipping over and over like one of those old-fashioned carousels of cards you occasionally still see in doctors' surgeries. And the next minute, hey presto, there it is, the name to fit the face as if plucked out by an invisible pair of receptionist's fingers.

Ronnie Gibson.

Ronnie Gibson had a blonde teen queen ponytail and eyes like blue glass marbles. She was the first of our class to get married. She kicked the dust of our ancient girls' grammar school off her feet at sixteen and was wed a year later. A year after that she was pushing a pramful of twins. She's probably thrice married and a grandmother of ten by now.

The day Ronnie announced she was leaving school, the door flew open and a Vision of Darkness appeared in our classroom. It strode to the platform, black gown billowing and pointed an apocalyptic finger at Ronnie Gibson.

'This girl,' it said, 'will do *nothing*.'

Miss Dawkins, first name Alicia, was the headmistress

of our school. Having the prettiest of Christian names, she was thus subject to the worst sort of irony. For Miss Dawkins was ugly. More than ugly. Ugliness was, in fact, Miss Dawkins' defining feature.

Miss Dawkins was the daughter of a missionary couple who carried the good news to India and were ill paid for their devotion. Once there, their only child developed smallpox, leaving her face cratered for ever like the surface of the moon and with a mouth swelled out like a boxer's.

It would have taken a human being with the disposition of an angel to rise above the hand that fate had dealt Miss Dawkins, and it's true to say that she did not feel called in this direction. As if to compound the horror, she filled those craters with a defiant mush of foundation and powder that hardened and cracked upon her face like a dried-up riverbed. And just in case anyone should fail to get the message she painted her mouth a violent spiteful red.

Miss Dawkins was a mean-spirited woman with a biting tongue and a penchant for favourites, which did not number Ronnie Gibson among them. Her bulbous lips dripped bile the day she raged at Ronnie. She pulled her out to the platform but all to no avail. For as she raged Ronnie just stood there, her arms across her chest, the diamond on the third finger of her left hand winking conspicuously. At the same time she cast a look of excruciating pity on the caricature that was Miss Dawkins.

Ronnie Gibson could spot a spinster at fifty yards, which I guess wasn't difficult with Miss Dawkins. Still, I was only thirteen when I was outed by Ronnie. She swivelled those blue glass marble eyes sideways at me behind her raised desk top and gave me a long cool look surprisingly free of blame or censure.

'Oh, no,' she said, her voice firm and matter of fact, as

if no one could think it. 'Not Riley . . . Riley will never get married.'

'How did she know?'

But Cass just clicks her tongue. 'She didn't. She couldn't. It was just something she said. You were just kids. Thirteen years old, for God's sake.' She shakes her head in mild exasperation. 'How many times do I have to tell you? It's all a matter of chance, Riley.'

Ronnie Gibson.

She who first showed me the dirty bits in *Lady Chatterley*.

I had my first quasi-sexual experiences double-dating with Ronnie, snogging on a park bench at lunch times with a couple of secondary modern school boys, eyes open as we twisted and turned and watched each other over the lads' shoulders. Later on sofas with parents safely at work, and after that the serious business – in the back seats of cars as we left the schoolboys behind and moved on to those with driving licences.

Sophie's jibe that day about the neanderthals I went out with in those days that we shared a flat together was not unwarranted, far from it. My favourites were always grease monkeys with fast cars (don't go there, Dr Freud, don't go there). I had a clear-sighted, not to say clinical, approach to sex at the time. Not knowing anything about it, i.e. how it was done (Babs told us nothing, but to be fair neither did ninety per cent of mothers) I learnt on the job and with serious application, unafraid of gaining a reputation, by contrast being determined to acquire one, Good In Bed being the label *du jour* among half-witted young women like myself at the time.

It seems odd now, of course, more like the custom of

another planet, having sex with someone you scarcely knew. But what does this go to prove except time moves on and if we're really lucky we get a bit older and wiser with it.

Some people count sheep when they can't sleep, others count lovers. My total is not grand in rock-and-roll terms, neither is it tiny. Mostly I can't remember about the sex, but then who can? The actual sex act, in my experience, is just about the hardest thing to recall, besides which, I was mostly under the influence. I could say that I'd been serially monogamous for most of my life, but this wouldn't mean fidelity, it not being that difficult for a one-night stand, or a two, or a week, or at most a month, by which time I'd generally be feeling edgy. Over the years I've experienced a wide variety of occupations – journalism, of course (print, radio and television), this being my trade, the visual arts (photography, painting, sculpture), the army and the navy (never did manage the air force), the natural world (several forestry workers, a zoo keeper, and a mad Scotsman with deer stalker on his passport), even the Church (Roman Catholic, but before he took his vows, which in my book makes it quite acceptable). With one obvious (early) exception, I never much went in for men of letters, more for men who had served their time, e.g., electricians, carpenters, painters and decorators, something that came in particularly handy back in the eighties when, thanks to *The Importance of Aunts*, I was able to move back here and buy what was then this tumbled-down wreck of a cottage. I also continued to retain that early affection for grease monkeys but then I never did much want a man to recite poetry to me or explain existentialism, or as happened once (oh, the horror, the horror), correct my feminist theory.

It may be that, looking back, I have been less aspirational than I might have been when it comes to lovers. My

160

excuse is that I never had the need to search out good partner/procreation material. I never had to worry about whether my liaisons were respectable (a freeing thing and one I thoroughly recommend, dear Reader), whether they had prospects (more often than not they did not) or if they had more than a touch of the rascal about them (an approach, in fairness, I tested to destruction with Lennie). Whether I should feel embarrassed about this I don't know, but one thing's for sure: I never stayed one more minute with a guy who bored me, cheated on me, or took his hand to my cheek, and I've experienced all three. And whereas I've had my famines as well as my feasts (and God knows those famines come more often and last longer as you get older), still I've never played the piranha, nosing round other people's partners. All of which has me wondering about Ronnie Gibson.

I'm not convinced that Cassie's right, you see, that it wasn't some weird prescience on Ronnie's part, that it was just the way it felt – hazard, luck, the Wheel of Fortune. Because the surprise when I look back on my life is not that I never got married, it's that I never ever got close to it. Never contemplated it. Never lived with anyone, not even arch-rascal Lennie. It's as if, like having children, it just never occurred to me, hence the need I feel to ask the question that heads this chapter.

Was it nature or nurture?

In short, in the manner of the late, great Carrie Bradshaw: Was I born dot dot dot or did I become a spinster?

Was it not for the presence of my disgracefully well-adjusted, well-married sister, we might come down on the side of nurture in this debate in my case, i.e., the experience of all

161

that marital bickering in my formative years that might have put me off the condition for ever.

'Oh, right, so it's my fault *again*, is it?'

'I didn't say that.'

'You might as well have done. You were always on his side but there's things you don't know.'

Which I believe. But God forbid you should ever tell me, Mother.

On the nature side, there's the obvious consideration that I might be gay, a suggestion from Archie, I recall, some years ago at Elsa's christening.* As usual, I wasn't pleased to see him.

'I thought we had an agreement.' This under my breath on the church steps.

'For heaven's sake . . . it's been ten years, Riley . . .'

I was in that radical phase at the time, at university as well as camping with Magda outside those military bases. Perhaps it was the butch flying jacket that did it, this plus the earrings (lots of them) and the multi-coloured hair, but more likely it was the presence of Sophie, who was going out with some (married) coke-head reporter (in a nice touch, from my mother's strait-laced morning newspaper). He'd given her some of the white stuff to make the weekend go with swing and it made her wildly affectionate. She kept slinging her arm around my neck, telling everyone how trusted and true was our friendship. Archie's eyes were bloodshot with drink when he swayed towards me.

---

* Also from my mother and quite recently.

    'If you want to come out of the cupboard, darling . . .' this after reading some 'Gay is the New Straight' piece in *Cosmopolitan* at her hairdresser's.

    I said, 'I rather think the word you're searching for is closet, Mother.'

'Tell me it's not true, Riley,' those eyes now nauseously sorrowful.

'What?'

'Tell me I didn't turn you into a lesbian.'

I stared at him in disgust. I said, 'No. But don't worry. You did your best, Archie.'

To be fair to him, I was experimenting, albeit mildly, with my sexuality at the time but then a lot of women were doing that. It came as a package with all those radical meetings, those courses and conferences. These seem like my Wilderness Years when I look back, and I don't mean that as any disrespect to those serious about the whole thing and not playing the dilettante. I was full of book learning in those years, not much more, and I could see all the arguments. I agreed with them, in part I still do. I can see what's wrong with the male/female sexuality but I can also see what's right about it.

It's like Sophie said once, throwing aside a magazine with another of those ten-thousand-word angst-ridden pieces, 'Jesus! Whoever said relationships were supposed to work? It's the fact that they don't that makes them interesting,' and I guess I agree with her.

Danny says he only feels 'comfortable' in the arms of a man. He says that's how he knew he was gay, when he tried sex with a man for the first time, this after several early courtships with women. And I can understand that too – that a woman too might feel this way, 'only comfortable' in the arms of another woman. Only for me what I learnt back in those Wilderness Years, on the couple of occasions when, emboldened by a joint and some powerful rhetoric, I put some of the book learning into practice, was that being comfortable was not what I wanted. That it was the sheer uncomfortableness, its ill-fitting quality, that I

163

missed, and this because it provided the bite of the thing, the sheer absurd impossible challenge.

When I asked Danny, 'How old were you? You know . . . when you first realised you were gay?' dragging him into my nature/nurture debate, he said, 'Gosh.'

'What?'

'In all the years we've known each other, you've never asked me that before, Riley.'

His back was turned at the time and he was holding up the silver sac from the wine box, in front of the window like some medical orderly about to attach it to a patient.

'Do you mind?'

'I guess not.' He began to squeeze the last of the wine into the two glasses. 'I was about eleven. When the boys around me were beginning to go bug-eyed over things like breasts. I guess I knew even then there was something different.'

'So when did you know? I mean properly . . .'

'Late teens. I'd had something I knew was a pretty serious crush on a guy in my class at school when I was about fourteen. But I never really realised what it was. Never identified it.' He threw the sac into the bin in one easy movement, sat down at the table with the glasses.

'What made you realise? In the end?'

'Going out with a girl. Liking her. A lot. Beginning to get serious but suddenly knowing that it wasn't right, wasn't what I wanted.'

Danny makes me nervous sometimes. Against all the odds. He can stare a little censoriously. He was doing it now but I plunged on anyway.

'I know it can be a dodgy subject. I mean political. But it's in the interests of my research.' I said the last words

164

hastily. 'Do you feel as though you were born gay or you became it?'

He shook his head. 'I don't think it's a tick-box situation. Born, I guess. I mean, I didn't have one of those *Angela's Ashes* home lives to push me into it.'

'Do you think it's better . . . if it's genetic?'

But now Danny's shoulders were giving a small irritated little movement as if shrugging off the question. 'I don't know. I don't really care to say. Tell you the truth, I don't spend that much time thinking about it, Riley.' He was looking at me over the rim of his glass at the time, a mocking look but with a steely little edge to it. 'But then I don't spend as much time staring fixedly down at my own navel as you do.'

It was a fair point, one that I acknowledged, but still not one I felt should be allowed to stand in the way of my scientific inquiry. Which is why I took the matter to the fount of all scientific knowledge in our family, i.e., Fergie.

He was planing a piece of wood when I arrived with his coffee. Something about the way he held it up to his eye, stared down it, made it look like an ancient inherited gesture.

Fergie's uncle was a master craftsman, a legend among those who knew him. He mended musical instruments. Yehudi Menuhin took his violins there. Paul McCartney brought a guitar in without his uncle recognising him. As a kid, Fergie would watch him work. He'd go with him, on a Saturday, if his uncle had a lot of work on, sit in the cramped little upstairs room in Soho.

'I've got a question to ask you. It's a serious question . . .'

'OK.' He put the wood back into the lathe again, twisted the handle and picked up the plane.

'Do you think there could be a spinster gene? You know, like a gay gene?'

'Who says there's a gay gene?'

Well, E. O. Wilson for one.

It's a cardinal sin to interrupt a scene with a long convoluted piece of reflection. But to hell with it. Rules are only there to be broken, beside which, this is not reflection, it's useful background information.

The idea of the 'gay gene' first appeared in E. O. Wilson's 1975 book *Sociobiology*, in which he speculated that genes might be doing their own bit for child-rearing by including a 'gay gene' in members of the extended family to produce childless uncles for the purposes of baby-sitting, visits to the cinema and art galleries and, in the case of Victorian fiction, taking in grubby and unpromising orphans and thereafter bequeathing them their entire fortunes.* The 'discovery' of the gene occurred some twenty years later, this thanks to Dean Hamer, described as part biologist, part psychologist, also as Big Gene Hunter. A gay man himself, he was trying to find out why some of his friends but not others were dying from Aids. Trawling through the DNA of forty pairs of gay brothers for statistical anomalies, i.e., stretches of DNA that were shared by more of

---

* A particularly interesting theory, this. After all, as with uncles, so with aunts. That Mother Nature should consider them of such consequence she decided to incorporate them genetically in the species clearly throws a new and fascinating light on the subject. We wait with interest further research on this. Meanwhile, special mention should be made here of the ground-breaking move by Liz Hurley, giving her son, Damian, six godfathers (i.e., 'uncles') to assist her with child-rearing. These include Elton John, to look after his musical education, and Hugh Grant, to take him to football.

Way to go, Hurley Burley.

them than could be expected by chance, he came across the same set of five markers – short, easily distinguished stretches of DNA – in the region of chromosome Xq28, which men inherit from their mothers. From this he concluded that somewhere in this region lay the gene or genes contributing to the homosexuality of the men concerned, a restrained and scholarly conclusion, which did not stop the world's media immediately dubbing Xq28 the 'gay gene' and it appearing on a million enthusiastic T-shirts along with the legend, 'IT'S TRUE. MY MOTHER *DID* MAKE ME A HOMOSEXUAL.'

All of which is far too simple, according to Fergie.

'Forget about genes *for* things, Riley.'

At best, according Fergie, genes might indicate tendencies, inclinations. 'Besides which, they're not fixed – that's the latest thinking, anyway. They're changing from the day we're born.'

I could see the genes as Fergie was describing them and I knew why he'd been such a good teacher. He was concentrating on pushing the plane across the edge of the wood, but still his voice went on painting the picture of them, 'pulsing, vital . . . picking up the data of everyday life, flicking on and off like switches'.

The movements along the wood had rhythm to them now as he bent over the lathe. Each clean, smooth and flowing sweep seemed more like a dance movement than carpentry.

'It's nature *and* nurture, Riley,' he said, putting the plane down, giving the lathe handle a turn and then a flick that sent it spinning. He pulled the wood out, held it up to his eye again. 'The two working together.'

All of which delighted me as an explanation, as I exclaimed a short while later.

'It explains it all,' I said, clattering the coffee cups triumphantly into the sink.

'All? All what, exactly?'

'Why all that marital bickering affected me but washed right over you.' I gave the tap a merry twist. Water jetted out. I turned, laughing. 'Why I turned out a spinster and you turned out wife and mother and so disgracefully well adjusted.'

'What makes you think I am?' There was that small note of controlled anger in Cass' voice. She went on carefully folding the laundry, putting it into the wicker laundry basket, not looking at me, which I took as a warning. 'What makes you think it washed right over me?'

'I always thought . . .'

But she went right on. 'I hated it as much as you did. To this day I can't bear a raised voice in this damn house. I can't have a proper argument with my kids or Fergie without a big lump coming to my throat.'

'I never knew.'

'No.' She looked up now, and whatever it was in her eyes made me feel small and mean and selfish. 'But then you wouldn't, would you?' She started to fold stuff again, like she wasn't that crazy about looking at me. 'I couldn't wait to get away to college. To get away from their bickering. But I worried about you, left behind. That's why I used to come home as often as possible.'

I felt the tears spring but she picked up the laundry basket briskly. She hates fuss like this and, like she said, any form of outburst.

I said, 'I'm sorry. So very sorry, Cass.'

I can see now, looking back, that things did get worse after Cass left, and this because, even as a child, she'd acted as peacemaker.

'Now, Mum . . .' I can hear the pacifying tone in her voice, and she no more than ten or eleven.

'Come on, Dad.' So full of sorrow. So cajoling.

I came to hate Christmas because of their sniping and I know Cass is the same. All that unseasonal spirit lying around house like a black cloud as they were forced, by virtue of the holidays, to be locked up together.

She'd buy him absurd expensive Christmas presents, cufflinks she liked but he'd never wear, expensive sweaters, once a silver hip flask. 'More use to you, Babs, than me,' he said, laughing coldly.

Each year Cass and I would prise money out of him to get something for her and pretend it was from him. Each year it grew harder. One year he refused altogether and Cass and I put some money together and bought her a brooch, pretending it was from him. She opened it in delight, pinned it on immediately. She even tried to kiss him but he turned away.

He said, 'The girls bought it. It's nothing to do with me,' and he walked out of the room, and into the hall and reached for his overalls.

She jumped up from her chair, followed him out, screaming at him, 'I'm leaving you. I'm getting a divorce.'

I remember how it went down my back like a jet of icy water. His voice was very cold but with a brusque, practical edge to it. There was something terribly knowing in it, some edge of premonition.

He said, 'No you're not. You don't want a divorce, Barbara. You just want me to die, nicely and neatly.'

Surely this was true. It's been said before, but it will bear saying again, that what she wanted to be was a married woman without the inconvenience of a husband. Or maybe she just wanted to be frozen in time, trapped forever in the pictures in her photograph album.

Because in the end, it wasn't just George Gordon who betrayed our mother. In the end she was sold out by those from whom she could have least expected such treachery and it was the photographs that caused the trouble, first of children, then grandchildren, of family holidays, weddings and christenings, all of these dropping out of Christmas cards, supplanting those grainy pictures of those laughing young faces around the smoke-filled table.

Some of the Buffies and Madges and Snowies have died, of course, but what's worse for my mother is that some just can't be bothered to visit. Only one turned up this Christmas – who but Buffy, the famous Buffy, late of Cairo, now of Devizes, she who once may or may not have thrown up over Larry Adler.

As always, she was with her husband, a miserable man from the first (I should know; I was that bridesmaid), one who's never lost the air over the years of making the trip under sufferance, his grumpiness making my mother's Chalet School merriment sound the more shrill and unseemly.

'The things we got up to, Stan, let me tell you. Isn't that right, Buffy?'

But after all these years of Stan's irascibility, Buffy has caught the habit. From the kitchen where I'd been dragooned by my mother into making tea for them after calling in with her dry-cleaning, I caught the sound of the key turning in the lock of the cabinet and I knew she was reaching for the photograph album. As the door squeaked open, Buffy's voice sliced through the air, not troubling to hide its irritation.

'For goodness' sake, Babs. Not that old thing again. We've had enough of all those old photos.'

When Buffy had gone, almost certainly for the last time, my mother sat with the album on her knee turning the pages slowly. I poured her a large gin and tonic, then another, one for myself too, sitting on the arm of the sofa, turning the pages with her.

'Nobody cares any more,' she said, despair in her voice.

'I care.'

'No you don't.'

'Yes I do. I kid you sometimes that I don't but I do.' I put an arm around her shoulders, something I seldom do, gave it a squeeze. 'Was it really so much fun?'

'Oh, yes . . . yes . . . yes . . .' She looked up at me, balling her handkerchief in her fist, and with the eyes of a child. 'Oh, it was so much *fun*, I can't tell you.' And her voice had that terrible yearning.

I wanted to ask her, 'Are you sure? Are you really so sure it was so much fun, or is it all just lodged in your memory this way, a mirage, golden-hazed, like an oasis?'

I wanted to ask her because I wanted to ask myself the same question.

After all, isn't this what I've been doing over the years with the memory of Nathan?

Nathan and I in my own private Oasis.

O is for . . . an Old Maid

Which I am, according to Roget's *Thesaurus*.

Dr Peter, for so he was, father of two, inventor of the pocket chess set, and a grand old man of ninety-one when he died in 1824, lists 'spinster' under celibacy, which I suppose they were then or at least supposed to be. He lumps us with bachelors, a nice touch, this, bearing in mind our heroine Beatrice's belief that in the end the Devil would refuse to take us, spinsters all, when we turned up at the gates of hell leading our apes, that instead he would point us upstairs where we would be met by St Peter, who would show us where the bachelors sit, there to live together 'as merry as the day is long'.*

The list of Roget's alternatives to 'spinster' is long and eclectic, from the slightly vulgar, fifties formica-topped 'bachelor girl', through the elegant 'debutante', the melancholy 'maid unwed', the fancy French '*feme sole*, 'maiden

---

* And if this view of heaven doesn't tear your heart out, oh, spinster, nothing will . . .

aunt', that stalwart of farce, vestal virgin (not *technically* mine to claim), with 'Amazon' and 'Artemis' – whoever they may be – bringing up the rear.

According to Roget, we are 'unmated' and 'unhusbanded', true by definition, also 'uncaught', which I like, carrying as it does an image of the sly, spry marriage-avoiding spinster. I must argue against 'unwooed' and 'unasked', however, this being something he could not possibly know, no more than yet another example of that old cliché-ridden argument that the spinster state could never be of her own choosing. For Jane is not the only one to have flagged down that early coach. There's many a one has done the same thing, taken that chilly, bumpy, early morning ride and more often than not, to spare the feelings of the person concerned, earning, for her generosity of spirit, nothing more than accusations of philophobia, or to be dismissed by Roget as women who 'have no offers', who 'receive no proposals'. A high-handed, unsubstantiated assumption. Erroneous too. Why, I myself have received even within the last month a firm quite unsolicited offer of marriage . . .*

'Heart-whole', Roget calls us, for which I can forgive him even though he's wrong. Who could get through life without losing at least some small part of this mysterious sometimes treacherous organ? 'Fancy-free'? Well, yes. Fancy is as fancy does, and if the shoe fits wear it. It does me – perfectly.

That I live 'in single blessedness', I certainly believe, and that my cottage can quite legitimately be termed 'bachelor hall'.

---

* See Z for Zing Zing Zing. But don't spoil it all and turn to it. Dammit all, this is a novel.

All of which only goes to show that Nathan was wrong in that bitter aside before we parted.

'What does it matter?' he said. 'Soon you'll be *married*.'

This is an old tale, I see that now, a tale preserved in the aspic of memory. For instance, if I close my eyes a quarter of a century on, I can still recapture the precise detail of Nathan's hotel room, the L shape dictated by the square box of the bathroom planted in one corner, the institutional cream of the walls – that grubby greying cream beloved of hospital and council offices and government departments the world over – the anonymous watery blue of the lino tiles, the trashy thin stained plywood of the bureau between the single beds, and the table in the alcove made by the bathroom wall with Nathan's books and papers spread across it, their corners lifting lightly in the draught from the air-conditioner that gave out that eternal shuddering hum; the Venetian blinds the same grey cream as the walls, but lined with dust, always closed against the heat so that the hubbub from the street below – the cries of the stall holders, the chain-saw scream of the tuk-tuks, the blare of the taxi horns and screech of the breakneck buses – all this seemed to filter into the cool institutional stillness that was so much a part of Nathan. And I remember too the precise note of the long melancholy squeak with which the plain featureless fire door to his room would open after I rapped on it softly each night, and how his face would appear in the crack, and precisely how he would pull the door open, very slowly, taking one step back, two, like some crazy gavotte; how he would let me in, wordlessly and without expression, as if all these things right down to the grubby grey cream of the walls, and the groaning air-conditioner and my silent entrance were part of some private rueful joke between us.

The first time Nathan and I made love I lay there afterwards entirely still, staring silently up at the ceiling. In the end, when I had recovered myself, when I had scraped all the pieces, so to speak, back together, I said, 'Where did you learn to do that?' He said, 'My grandfather. He was Romanian.' It seemed such an absurd answer, so entirely inappropriate that I laughed and in the half-light of the flashing neon I could see he was mildly offended.

He said, 'He told me I should learn to give a woman pleasure,' this rather stiffly, his voice full of an old-fashioned dignity.

Nathan, my old European with those fine hard European bones to his face and that big bull head. God knows, but when I think about it, this Old Maid was made for an old European like Nathan.

The surprise when I look back is how brief the affair was, scarcely more than a couple of months when I calculate it. And yet it seems so much longer. It stretches on and on in my memory, as if that Time that ran and danced and disappeared down a black hole that first night went on playing games with us from that first moment when he pushed the coin along the bar top towards me.

I've never been a hand-holder. It's just that it's never appealed to me. I'm a strider ahead, a pointer at things. *Come on, look at this.* My hand in that of another grows heavy and awkward. So that if I tell you, I had, *had* mark you, to have his hand in mine, I speak of something extraordinary, something I'd never felt before or have done since. It stands out as the thing I best remember about the affair, as if at that first moment when the coin began to travel along the bar it established some sort of gravitational pull between us, so that from then on it was merely a matter of course, as intractable as a law of physics, that we should proceed to one of the bamboo sofas (the one in the corner where from then on we would always sit) there to talk in low voices and to find, several nights on, to our own surprise, our hands clasped, locked fast together in the crack between the cushions, between my bare thigh and those sombre grey trousers.

If they were surprised at the Oasis to see what was happening to us, at the unseen gravitational pull that was drawing us together, keeping us every night staring out from behind the barricade of our clasped hands, at first they made no comment about it. Only Angel could not resist showing her pleasure.

'You . . . you and Nathan.' And her eyes were shining.

After three days or so, though, Barnie's brows began to draw together and Mama San's lips grew tight. I wasn't there, after all, to sit with my hand locked tightly into Nathan's. So, after that, Nathan and I merely came in together, this after we'd eaten an early dinner. He'd share a drink with Barnie and then return to his hotel to work while I sat on talking to the Chinese businessmen, the Japanese tourists, the Filipino embassy staff and to the poorly paid, high-spending Thai clerks whose wages would disappear behind the bar in a night, all of these forming the main bulk of our customers. I'd join Nathan later at his hotel. Just occasionally, though, and this to my embarrassment, he'd sit on for a while in the corner watching me.

I'd feel his eyes on me.

'What are doing when you sit there?'

'Listening.'

'Listening to what?'

'To you.' He said, 'You're very funny. You make me laugh, Riley.'

It was the worst thing he could have said. What I wanted to hear. Tiresome heroines from films of the time swam before my eyes as he said it.* I wanted to be one of them. I wanted to be *zany* (dear God, that terrible word) and *kooky* (there's another one) – and all this for my oh so serious professor.

One morning, in the bathroom, preparing to go down to breakfast, I stuck my head under his arm, made faces in the mirror, disturbing the peaceful, pedantic scrape of his old-fashioned cut-throat razor. The clowning had a forced feel to it, the uncomfortable air of a routine. He tried to smile but there was an embarrassed look in his eyes before he dropped them to rinse the razor in the water. It said, 'I know why you're doing this but it's not what I want from you, Riley.'

Later, in one of the sudden belligerent patches on my part that were a feature of the affair, I said, 'What is it you want from me anyway?'

He said, 'Nothing. I don't want anything from you.' He went on calmly twirling the angel hair noodles on his fork. Then he looked up suddenly and straight into my eye. He said, 'It's what I want *for* you, Riley.'

It's a pernicious thing, popular culture. I see that now. Novels, films and plays, how dangerous are they for a mind looking for role models? All those stereotypes lurked in my head as I tip-tapped along in those high-heeled sandals beside him. It's that incongruity, stock of screen and page,

---

* *Barefoot in the Park*, *There's a Girl in My Soup*, *Cactus Flower*, etc., etc.

177

that gives me so much pleasure. In particular I enjoy the sensation of him being from a time so much different from my own, a time that seems so much darker and heavier and more serious, of Korea, McCarthyism . . .

'It was a terrible time?'

'Yes. Yes. It changed the country. Overnight. It has still to recover.'

'I remember the Cuban Missile Crisis.'

He looked surprised. 'You do?'

'Yes. I made a list of all the things I'd miss.'

'What were they?'

'Stupid things. The sound of a tennis ball on a racquet. My favourite TV programme. My new Connie Francis record.'

'They're not stupid things, Riley. They're the stuff of life.' His look across the table was urgent and earnest.

'Were you frightened?'

'No, not exactly frightened. That's the strange thing. Just really sad, thinking I'd never get to do things . . .'

'Like what. Get married?' His lips were drawn into the thin mocking line.

'No. Not even then. Crazy things. Like playing at Wimbledon. Meeting Elvis Presley. What about you?'

'What?'

'Did you think it might really happen?'

'Yes. I still do.'

'Were you frightened?'

'More angry than frightened.'

'At who?'

'All of them. Khrushchev, Kennedy. Posturing. Playing games. Bringing us to the brink like that. I kept thinking of my son . . .'

And there it was. Nathan, like an iceberg, jagged, poking

178

up above the surface but with this whole other part lying beneath the surface.

'Your son?'

'Yes. How he might not have the chance to grow up.'

'You didn't tell me before.'

'What?'

'That you had a son. That you were married.'

'I'm divorced, Riley.'

'But how . . . ? When . . . ?'

'It was a long time ago. A brief marriage. She was . . . a student . . . We met when I was first teaching.'

Later I said, 'I'm trying to imagine it.'

'What?'

'You. As a father.'

'I haven't been.' He said it very gruffly and he didn't look at me.

'How old is he?'

'Sixteen.'

'Where is he?'

'Where should he be? With my wife. In New York.'

'Do you see him?'

'No.' He said it very brusquely, staring at the menu. 'Not . . . often.'

'Do you like him?'

He looked up sharply. 'Like him?'

'Do you get on with him?'

The stare had something else in it now. Surprise. At the question. He appeared to be pondering it and when he answered it was reluctantly.

'No. I suppose . . . not.'

Sudden he wasn't like Nathan any more, not like the severe, impenetrable Nathan. Suddenly he was leaning forward across the table, speaking earnestly. At first I was

179

going to say 'like any father', but of course he wasn't like a father at all. How could he be?

'I ask him what he wants to do when he leaves college, what he wants to do in life, and he tells me he wants to be *rock star*.' He said it searchingly, staring into my eyes.

I smiled, shaking my head, feeling, for once, wonderfully old compared to him. 'At sixteen he's entitled to want to be a rock star. That's what being sixteen is all about.'

He continued to stare at me, his eyes fixed on mine as if he was searching for something. He said, 'That's good. That's very good, Riley.'

More as a joke than anything I said, 'So you don't like rock and roll?'

He touched his lips with his napkin as if intent on giving a precise and fair reply. 'It's not my music, that's all.'

'What is your music?'

'The music I grew up with, jazz, classical.'

'I'd like to know more about jazz. I wish you'd introduce me to it.'

He gave a small shrug.

'What? You think it would be too *intelligent* for me?' My sarcasm betrayed the offence that had been taken.

He gave a sad sigh. His voice was patient. 'You know I don't think that. Or should do. I keep trying to tell you how smart I think you are. It's you who won't believe it.'

'Then what?'

'It's too complicated.'

'Oh . . . right . . .'

'No, look . . .' He laid his knife and fork down, clasped his hands across his plate, his elbows on the table as he leant towards me. 'In a relationship where there's an age difference . . . sometimes it happens that the younger person begins to try to take over the older person's taste. Absorb it. Make it their own. I don't like that, that's all. I don't like to see it happen. Stick to your own taste, Riley.'

'Do you like my taste?'

'It's nothing to do with me.' His voice had risen. 'It's your taste. Your age. Your era. That's what's important. Mine is different. I come from a different . . .' He hesitated and I knew he was loath to use the words. 'I come from a different time, that's all.'

And so he did. From such a different time. Nathan, old and classic, in black and white; Riley a brash, colourful blockbuster of a movie.

We only went to the cinema once together. I insisted we go and see *Summer of '42*. I'd seen it the year before with Sophie. At the time it seemed like the acme of sophistication. I was sure he would love it. But when we came out he strode wrathfully along the pavement away from me.

'You didn't like it.' I was almost in tears.

'It's rubbish. Sentimental. Utterly untruthful.'

Later that night, at dinner, he said, 'I'm sorry, Riley. It's too late. I'm too serious for you. I've lost the habit.'

'The habit of what?'

But he just made a terse gesture, went on staring determinedly at the menu. Eventually: 'Of . . . lightness . . . Of conversation.'

I laughed, thinking it absurd. 'What are you?' I said. 'Robinson Crusoe. The Man in the Iron Mask,' which, of course, is exactly what he was, when I think about it. Because he was right. He had lost the habit of easy conversation, if indeed he ever had it. So tight-lipped was he that sometimes when we were talking I'd feel as though he was having to force the words out. As a result I'd find myself gabbling, filling up the silence.

'I talk too much.'

181

'No.' He said, 'I like it, Riley.'

I tried to make a joke of it. 'It's my mother's fault. She has this thing. Silence should never fall on the dinner table.' I went on, gabbling, 'I'm like her. I just go on, talking, talking. All the time. About nothing.' I began to cry and his hand reached over sharply, grasping mine.

'It's not you, Riley. I told you, I've lost the habit. I've been too long in the laboratory, that's the trouble.'

I tried to smile. I said, 'You don't work in a laboratory, Nathan.'

Looking back I can see now how little I really got to know about Nathan in the time we were together, and how much this had do with that tight-lipped quality. So often when I would ask him something simple, for instance, 'What's it like . . . where you live?' the everyday stuff lovers ask when they're getting to know each other, his brow would furrow as if I'd presented him with some difficult philosophical question. He'd always answer the same way: 'What would you like to know?' and I was never sure whether he really was keen to help, whether he just lacked the knowledge of how to respond, or if he was trying to ward off the question. Either way the answer would be the same in the end – formal, bloodless, as lacking in any life or colour as his dry dusty prose.

'I live in the suburbs . . . it's quite pleasant . . . a one-storey house . . . a small garden . . .'

Once he said, 'I'm too old for you, Riley,' but he didn't say it any regretful way, not like people do when they're fishing for a denial or some sort of encouraging rejoinder. Instead he said it flatly as if it was a fact.

'For God's sake, Nathan. You're only forty.'

The answer came back quickly and sharply, 'An old forty,' and it was true.

We were in a taxi at the time, going back to his hotel from the Oasis. I said, 'I'm wet for you, Nathan,' but even as I said it I knew there was something false about it. I knew that I'd wanted to say it because it seemed sophisticated, part of what I wanted to be now, rather adventurous and extravagant and daring.

I said, 'Here, feel,' determined to take the thing further, putting my hand over his before he could pull it away and placing it between my thighs. He didn't look at me nor I him, but his hand rested there in some odd, sad, even companionable way. And that was how we sat, all the way back to his hotel, rigidly but curiously at ease, each one of us staring out of the window.

I was spending every night with him by now. We'd make love on one of the single beds in his room, most usually the one against the wall. Sometime afterwards, I'd crawl into the other bed, fall into a deep sweet sleep holding his hand over the divide. Sometime during the night our hands would fall apart, but I'd never feel it, and in the morning I'd wake to the sound of him through the bathroom door showering and shaving. After that we would breakfast together. He was a favourite in the hotel, this because he stayed there every year when he was researching, also because he spoke Thai and because of this we were always served by the head waitress, an exquisite creature who glided rather than walked. She'd place the flat of her hands over her belly with a small nod, watch us take our first spoonful of papaya.

I cannot buy papaya still without thinking of those Bangkok breakfasts. Each day we would start with it, not at all like the small shrivelled things I bring back these days from the supermarkets. Instead they glowed, rosy orange boats, each morning spoonful perfect on the tongue.

Papaya was so cheap in Bangkok back then, you could buy armfuls for a dollar.

'It's a rotten thing,' I said to Nathan one morning, 'to have something so beautiful in such plentiful supply that it loses all its value.' I paused with the spoonful of flesh almost on my tongue. 'There's a moral there somewhere.'

'I think you mean a metaphor,' he said quietly.

Looking back, those meals we ate together, breakfast and dinner most days, seem utterly central to the relationship, as important a part of it as the lovemaking. We ate in street stalls and restaurants, all the places where the tourists never went, these known from his days teaching at the university. On my nights off he would take me somewhere special.

'I can't let you do this,' I said one night.

'What?'

'Pay for me. Every night.' He made a sharp irritated gesture across the table. 'I like to do it. Don't make an issue of it, Riley.'

It should have been a special night when he took me to the Oriental. He'd booked a table on the terrace. I'd even borrowed a black evening dress from Zoe.

The city was lying in wait for a thunderstorm that night, with the air especially hot and heavy. Women in wide straw hats punted long thin boats full of fruit and vegetables and tourist gee-gaws along the river beside us. Not long after we arrived a pianist appeared and sat down at the white grand piano in the corner.

Nathan said, 'God, I love the sound of a piano in a bar.' And then, 'New York is full of piano bars.'

'You love New York?'

184

'Of course. I grew up there.'

'Tell me about it.'

'We lived with grandfather. In Brooklyn. A fourth-floor walk-up.' And that, as usual, was the end of it.

'Would you like to go back?'

'No.'

'Why not?'

'Because it's not the place that I want to be now.'

'New York?'

'America.'

That was when he took my hand across the table, began running one of his fingers up and down my own, staring at them.

'But I'd love to take you there.'

'New York?'

'Yes. Show you everything.'

I hear the words now just as he said them, slowly, carefully, with many layers, with a question in them, but with an air of regret too, as though they'd already been answered. As his finger went on travelling up and down mine, he seemed on the edge of saying something more but no words came so that we sat on there for a long moment like actors who have forgotten their lines. It seemed like a relief to us both when the waiter arrived, when we pulled our fingers away and leant back and the plates were put in front of us.

I drank a lot that night – Black Russians, my favourite drink of the time, a bottle of wine, then brandy. I was drunk by the end of the meal. I can see Nathan, exactly as I saw him then, leaning back in his seat the other side of the table, staring at me, his hands linked tight over the buckle of the belt of his old man's grey trousers. I feel the same tremor looking back at him as I felt then, and I know that part of me was always a little frightened of Nathan.

I can see him so perfectly, and yet I can't remember precisely how or quite when the chill set in between us. All I remember is that it was there in the heavy damp air when he called for the bill, and how he scarcely looked at the thing when it arrived, reaching for his wallet, and poking two thin fingers in, and throwing down the money carelessly and all of this in silence. He didn't wait for me to gather myself together, instead he got up sharply and strode across the lobby and out into the street. It seemed like all he wanted to do was to leave me behind. Outside, the rain had already started. It spattered down but he strode on up the street, seemingly oblivious of it, and so fast he left me many yards behind and I had to run after him, soaked sandals slip-slapping on my feet as I called his name, crying. And that was when he did that extraordinary thing, raising that great bull head upwards and turning his face to heaven as the rain spattered down it and letting out this cry of rage and sorrow.

He said, 'If only I could make you understand how much I love you, Riley.'

He shook his head with an air of weariness and turned his face back down to me. I was shocked at the open dislike in it.

I said, 'I love you too, Nathan,' and I gulped as I said it, because even then I knew that the words weren't true, but that I wanted them to be true and this more than anything else in the world.

The look he gave me in that moment, staring down at me, survives to this day, not least the look of pity, not for himself, but for me.

He spoke the words calmly and sadly, staring down at me as if the rain did not exist, as if it it did not spatter

186

down his face, as if it did not run in and out of his eye sockets like tears.

He said, 'No. I don't think so, Riley.'

Reading through all this now, it occurs to me that you may feel there is something missing in this chapter (can you spot what it is, dear Reader?). Yes, you're right. It's a sex scene, precise description of the pleasure, preferably with anatomical details. Well, I don't do sex scenes (it's one of the pleasures of being a children's author). As far as I'm concerned, sex scenes in books are either too clinical* or too flowery,† too athletic‡ or squeamishly embarrassing.§ The Victorians had the right idea, leading us up to the bedroom door, then closing it firmly in our faces, and I shall do the same (this despite the enormous attraction of gaining the opportunity to make that public thank-you speech to my mother while picking up the Bad Sex Award).

Thus I shall only tell you that the first time Nathan made love to me I thought I'd fallen asleep without noticing, woken up on a different planet. Because what happened then, and all those subsequent nights, on that single bed, with the light flashing on and off through the blinds had, theoretically, been practised on my person before but with

---

* All those anatomical terms, so often favoured by male writers, you feel belong on a chart to be pointed out by a man in a lab coat.

† I.e., rivers flowing, lakes becoming seas, woman becoming earth becoming man becoming mountain becoming ONE; visions of the Eternal, the Ineffable, etc., etc.

‡ Pumping, thrusting, arching, plunging, piercing, prodding, probing, spurting, spattering, that sort of thing.

§ See all those dirty words and the daisy chain stuff in *Lady Chatterley's Lover*.

Nathan there was not one scrap of recognition. With Nathan there was none of that *reticence*, that air of duty, of derring-do. Neither, as can happen, was there the faintest sense of embarrassment. And all, on the face of it, so utterly unexpected, from a man who said, 'I'm too old for you, Riley,' who wore strange, unfashionable old man's clothes, and yet who seemed possessed of a sort of magic.

I came, each night, with a last shuddering cry, whereupon, almost immediately, I would find him beside me again with his arms around me. Gathering myself together, I would try at least in those first days to move down his body. But he would hold me tightly, preventing me.

'It's OK. Just relax.'

'But . . . I want to do the same . . . I want to make you . . . happy . . . too.'

'I'm happy. Go to sleep, Riley.'

'To tell you the truth, Danny,' I said, telling him all this, 'I think he was the best lover I ever had.'

His lips pursed in a small expression of disapproval.

He said, 'It might have been good to tell him that some time over the years, Riley.'

P is for ... Philophobia

Philophobia.

A fear of falling in love.

Courtesy – as with so many things – of Bad Ponytail Peter.

Philophobia was Peter's parting shot. He fixed me with his traditional accusative look, the one that said, if the cap fits wear it. He said, 'Some people are terrified of falling in love.'

I said, 'Really?' this in the shocked and horrified tones of a woman who couldn't believe such a thing could be happening within the borders of her own country. I said, 'Can you believe it?' and afterwards, 'Yeah ... yeah ... yeah ...' to Danny.

Because this is not a new one on me. I've heard this before – not a thousand times, it's true, but still enough to know when it's about to happen. It's the last refuge of the belligerent male and this when you're doing your damnedest to dump him with the maximum degree of tact and decency.

You're afraid of falling in love, that's your trouble ...

No, no. No.

Wrong, wrong, wrong.

I'm just afraid of wasting one more precious hour of my life in your company.

In my experience you don't get any thanks for all that tact and decency, just a barrel-load of barrack-room psychology.

You just won't let yourself feel . . .

I know, I know . . .

(Trust me I do, I will. Just not with you, baby.)

I always let them get away with it. It seems only fair. I stand there, head bowed, hands folded dutifully. After all, they're not wrong. Entirely. There is a fear of falling in love, just not one that they know anything about or that Peter needs to worry about curing. Because it's a decent fear, this one, a responsible fear, not some pathetic neurotic shirking. It's a terrible fear, the fear of hurting others. It's born of self-knowledge, and your desires and limitations. It comes from knowing that no matter how much you want to want something, it won't be the same – even if you manage it – as truly wanting it. And it comes from knowing that what someone else is willing to offer in the absence of what you are able to give, generous as this is, simply won't solve the problem.

If only I could make you understand how much I love you, Riley.

I slipped away from Nathan in the end, did what I wanted to do – what I've always done – which is to untether myself, set myself free, this is order to minimise the pain of parting.

'It's not as if we won't see each other again. I'll visit you . . . in Australia.'

But the words were an excuse, a pretence. He didn't lift his head from his papers and his reply was heavy with irony.

'I look forward to it, Riley.'

'Look, he didn't say, "I'd love to take you to New York,"' this to Danny defensively. 'He didn't say, "I *will* take you to New York," or, "Come back home with me now, Riley."'

'Would it have made any difference if he had?'

But a quarter of a century on it still wasn't a question I wanted to answer.

It came as a relief the day Barnie ran a finger down the calendar behind the bar.

'We need to extend your visa again, Riley.'

Three times we'd been down to the grubby breeze block immigration building to extend my visa. There the pair of us would sit on hard little chairs in the waiting room with a dozen others, a mixed bag, Europeans and Asians of all persuasions. Eventually an official would come out and call our name, and we'd go into a little plywood box of an office where he and Barnie would conduct a set-piece conversation like a ragged gavotte, Barnie in stuttering Thai, the official in occasional broken English.

'Look humble,' Barnie would say. 'Smile a lot,' and I would. The officer would play the game, pursing his lips like this really was a decision of major importance. He'd hum and hah and bounce his biro up and down on his blotter. Eventually he'd leave the room with the air of man who needed some important piece of paper. As the door closed Barnie would reach into his pocket, and take out the wad of notes and slip it under the blotter. A short while later the official would return and then before you knew it, we'd be out on the street with a fresh stamp on my passport.

Barnie said, 'They might not buy it this time, Riley. You might need to take a trip out.'

I said, 'Probably time to move on anyway,' and I didn't look at him when I said it.

Because something was happening to the affair by then. For the last month and a half, I'd leapt into a tuk-tuk each night outside the Oasis, raced across the city in a white heat of passion and longing to be with him. In my haste I'd stamp at the lift buttons in the lobby of his hotel, jump out before the doors were properly open, run along his corridor to his door. At first the changes to all this were scarcely perceptible, no more than a less feverish touch on the lift buttons, a more stately tread along the corridor, something natural, something desirable, I know that now even if I didn't know it then. The point where the affair passes into its second stage, the less frantic stage that heralds the future. But I didn't want the future heralded. I guess I still don't. Close on the feel of that gentle slowing-down of my footsteps along that hotel corridor in Bangkok came something else, a listless quality, faint at first, coupled with a vague feeling on my part that things were not as fresh as they once were. Following on from that came something worse, the most wicked feeling of all, the destructive feeling of restraint and then something else too early to call resentment, but sitting like a chill on the back of my neck and unignorable, making me want to shake my shoulders.

One night, I didn't go to Nathan's hotel at the end of the evening. It was as simple as that. Instead I went out with Zoe. It was December by then. We sat in the foyer of one of the five-star hotels beneath the shadow of a large imported Christmas tree winking with lights and coloured balls and tinsel, and standing out like an ungainly intruder

192

among the delicate sandalwood and silk wall hangings of the touristy Siameserie.

Errol came across to us first. He gave a deep bow from the waist in front of us, and said, 'May I introduce myself?' in a Southern voice both courteous and musical.

'Why, certainly you may,' said Zoe.

They were off a carrier, Errol, all corn-coloured hair and blue eyes; Quincy, dark and dangerous, stagehands from New York in a different life. They'd joined up to beat the draft. Now they settled down into one of the foyer's pouchy leather sofas opposite us and drank a toast to going home.

'You think you will be?' I held out my glass.

'Why, sure. Everybody knows it.' Errol sluiced the champagne into it joyfully. 'Of course. The war's over.'

They wanted to go somewhere good to eat, somewhere the tourists didn't go, so I took them to a place Nathan had taken me. I walked in feeling disloyal and guilty. Afterwards we went to a cabaret where the band played loud and brassy, and the stage turned, and the lady-boys strutted and kicked and dipped their feathers.

We were on our way back to their hotel when it happened. The tape in the taxi was playing Santana loud and tinny. I was sitting in the back, against the window with Quincy next to me, an arm around my shoulder. Zoe was the other side of him. She'd pulled a joint from her bag, lit it up. Now it passed around, even the driver taking a toke, seeing a big tip coming and thumping on the wheel in time to the music. The windows were wound right down and Zoe was leaning out, whooping. The whole vehicle seemed to reverberate to the sound of it, all the *youthfulness* in it, the craziness, the gaiety and laughter. I was laughing too, feeling like I was recapturing something I didn't want to identify, or how or when or why I'd lost it. I threw my head back with the joy of it as we pulled up at some lights, turned to look out the window. And that was when I came face to face with Nathan.

The first thing I said when he opened his door that night was, 'Nothing happened,' but there was a belligerence, a dark, mutinous feeling of rebellion to the words.

He said, 'If only you knew how much I don't want to be having this conversation, Riley.'

He'd dropped his eyes as soon as they met mine through the taxi window. In an unhurried, curiously dignified and courteous gesture he'd swung his shoulders away from me. I didn't get out with the rest when our taxi pulled up outside the boys' hotel. I made excuses. I said, 'I have to go somewhere.' Errol said, 'What? C'mon . . .' and I almost changed my mind but then and Zoe said, 'Leave her,' mockingly, 'the girl's in luuurve,' cutting off my exit and reminding me.

Because it didn't feel like love, walking into Nathan's hotel that night. It felt like duty and, of course, he knew it. That thin line of derision was there on his lips at the door as he let me in.

'Riley,' he said. 'What a pleasure. I wasn't expecting you,' and he sat down almost immediately at the table, made a play of being engrossed in his papers.

I said, 'Don't stay angry at me,' touching his shoulder. I felt him freeze beneath my fingertips.

'Don't flatter yourself, Riley,' he said. 'I'm not angry.' His voice was very cold and he looked up but only at the wall ahead of him. 'You looked like you were having a good time. You looked like you were where you belonged,'

194

this said thoughtfully. But then his head bent again to his papers and the next words were harsh. 'It's none of my business, Riley.'

I dropped down on to the floor then. I was kneeling beside him. 'Don't talk like that.' I looked up into his face. 'I want to make it right, Nathan,' and I think I did too, in some awful impossible yearning way – in a selfish way too, not wanting the pain shooting in small darts across my heart. I said, 'Can we forget it?'

He turned to me, staring down, and there was that same look of pity on his face I'd seen outside the Oriental.

'There's nothing to forget. I've told you, you don't have anything to apologise for. You can do what you like. It's your business, Riley.'

'I've hurt you.'

'Damn you, damn you. Damn you.' He was up on his feet, the movement throwing me away from him, striding up and down. He stopped abruptly in front of the blind, looked out through the slats at the flashing neon. 'How dare you?'

'I'm sorry. I'm sorry.' I had my hands over my face. I was beginning to cry. 'Tell me what I can do, Nathan.'

He put a hand to his forehead as if all this was too much for him, took a deep breath, closed his eyes and threw his head backwards. When he spoke his voice was low and calm.

'There's nothing you can do, Riley, that's the trouble.'

He walked back towards me where I knelt on the ground, held out a hand, but instead of getting to my feet I grabbed at it, pulled him back down on the chair beside me.

'Please, Nathan, please. Say it's OK.' I was whispering the words, pulling at him, putting my arms around his waist, burying my face into him.

I was crying now, sobs shaking my shoulders. At first he was rigid but then I felt his body soften in my arms. His hand began to stroke my hair, tentatively at first and then more firmly. There was something kind and comforting in the strokes but also something deeply regretful.

He tried to lift me up but I wouldn't let him. Instead I burrowed my face deeper and deeper into him, which was when I felt him stir beneath my forehead.

I lifted my face and began stroking him with the flat of my hand. I didn't look up, but the stroking stopped and I could feel him staring straight at the wall.

I pulled at his belt, unzipping him, taking him in my mouth, at the same time pulling at his trousers.

He was still there, rising, harder than I had ever known him as I pulled him to the bed, tearing off my own dress and underwear. I was on top of him in a moment, reaching for him, grabbing at him, trying to jam him into me. But it was too late. Already I could feel him softening.

I cried out, a greater cry than any of those great ones I had cried before when I came. I flung myself off him and down beside him, began to weep again.

He said, 'Don't. Please don't, Riley.'

Some time later, staring into the darkness, for he had put out the light as we lay there, side by side, I said, 'Is it me?'

'No.' And now he turned, drawing me into him, saying it into my hair.

'Is there anything I can do? Something I'm not doing?'

'No.' The room was very still, as if nothing moved, anywhere, here in the world, as if everything waited.

I said, hesitantly, afraid of the words, 'Would it . . . come back?'

But Nathan was not a man to compromise and, unlike

me, not given to lying. He said, 'I don't know. I can't say, Riley.'

That was the night we heard it. I'd fallen into one of those deep, satisfied selfish sleeps as I always did after he'd made love to me, when somewhere at the bottom of my dreams came that long low continuous rumbling.

'What is it?'

I don't know how long he'd been awake, leaning back against the wall like that, his hands at the back of his head. Perhaps he'd been watching me.

'It's nothing,' he said, this after he'd gone to the window, poked the blinds and stared out. He said, 'Go back to sleep, Riley.' But there was no chance of sleep with that dull heavy throb passing in wave after wave overhead, so eventually he got up, pulled on his pants, padded down the corridor to fetch tea from the night porter.

I crawled into his bed again after we had drunk our tea, clung to him very tightly. I was three parts asleep, my head against his neck when he said the words into the darkness.

Many times over the years I've thought about what he said then, particularly about the way that he said it. I've tried to pin down every last nuance in his voice, tried to decide what gave the words their peculiar emphasis, the resonance that has carried them so forcibly over the years, that makes them still the words for which I best remember him.

There was contempt in there, disgust, but not for me, but more for the state itself as if it was on this that he lavished all that bitter hopeless fury.

'What does it matter?' he said, his arms tightening like a band around my shoulders. Then came the words:

'Soon you'll be *married*.'

*   *   *

197

I left a week later. The day before I flew out, he took me shopping. He wanted to buy me a present. 'Call it a Christmas present.' A coat.

'A *coat*?'

'Trust me, Riley. People are always prepared for how hot Hong Kong gets but never how cold.'

In the end I settled for earrings, simple gold hoops. I lost one early on in Hong Kong but still have the other down the bottom of my jewellery basket.

After the shopping we stood for a moment at the entrance to the mall, shifting from foot to foot and making desultory conversation.

'You have to go . . .'

'Yes . . .'

'You have an appointment . . .'

'Yes.'

'The university.'

He took my hand, stared down at the fingers. For a moment he looked like he was about to say something. But then he dropped it, wheeled about abruptly and the next minute was lost among a crowd of arriving tourists.

'And that's *it*?' Danny was looking at me.

'Yes.'

He shook his head. 'That was the *end* of it? But why?'

'I was afraid. I didn't love him enough. I couldn't love him enough. Also . . .'

'Yeah?'

Something else, something that has to do with the passion of that cry spiralling up to heaven: *If only I could make you understand how much I love you, Riley.*

'I was . . . afraid for him. Afraid that he'd take anything I had to offer. And I think he would have done. I think if I'd stayed longer we might have got to some terrible moment

198

where he asked me to go with him and, who knows, I might have gone.'

'And that would have been so bad?'

'Yes.'

'Why?'

'Because it couldn't have worked out. Our lives together.'

'How could you know that?'

'Because I knew myself. What I was. What I wanted.'

He'd talked little about his life, it's true, and yet, even in the absence of facts, I believed, still believe, I could form a picture of it. Such a *serious* existence, far away from the lightness, the gaiety that suited me, and which he'd seen too through that taxi window.

I saw a low, dark house with heavy furniture, heavy rugs, heavy classical music, Wagner say, Beethoven, or that modern jazz, all the stuff that belonged to his life and not mine, playing low, scarcely disturbing the silence. I saw books, shelf after shelf of them, and I heard a clock ticking, that heavy tick that measures the minutes one by one and falls solemn and heavy into the silence. I saw myself trying to be a part of this life and I saw what would happen – boredom first, then disillusionment, bitter sniping, anger, and worse, tawdry, soul-sapping affairs. Afternoon sex perhaps with one of his colleagues, even a student.

I think he saw it all too.

'I don't believe he ever truly thought it could work between us.'

Because, looking back on all this, I think that Nathan knew me better than anyone has ever known me. Certainly, as far as the affair is concerned, I think he knew what would happen from the beginning, that he saw it all spread out before him like a map. And yet still he threw himself into the thing, wholeheartedly, holding nothing back. More than a quarter of a century on, such courage, such utter generosity of spirit still takes my breath away.

At the airport all the papers were full of the bombing.* Their front pages all carried pictures of Hanoi and Haiphong, both looking like Hiroshima. One called the bombing 'a stone-aged tactic', Nixon 'a maddened tyrant', another 'a senseless terror which stains the good name of America'. I read them in a deserted corner in the basement where I lit up the joint of sweet Thai grass Zoe had given me the night before as a farewell present.

Zoe had arranged a party for me that night. She strung lanterns and gaudy Chinese decorations around her room in our hotel, swelled the guest list with freaks I didn't know and who had no idea who I was either. Sometime in the early hours of the morning, when there was just a handful of people left, and both she and I were very stoned, she dragged me to my feet, made me dance with her.

She said, 'What are you doing, oh, what are you doing, Riley?'

---

* The Christmas bombing of Hanoi and Haiphong lasted from 17–29 December. Instituted by Nixon with Kissinger's agreement, it was designed to kick-start the mouldering Paris peace talks, a piece of diplomacy hereafter famously referred to as 'bombing the enemy to the conference table'. It worked, and on 27 January 1973 the infamous 'peace with honour' was officially declared. The Vietnam War cost the lives of some 57,000 American servicemen. The number of Vietnamese casualties, plus those in Laos and Cambodia, runs into millions. As regards the US total, it's worth mentioning that it's reckoned that more Vietnam veterans have committed suicide since the end of the war than actually died fighting it.

'It'll haunt us for generations,' Nathan said that night as the rumble continued overhead. 'It'll take years for us to get rid of it.'

There was such a terrible edge of tragedy in her voice that we both burst into laughter. She draped herself over me, arms over my shoulders, howling with it and taking deep tokes from the joint in her hand. With each toke her laughter became more hysterical. She said, 'You're making a terrible mistake. You know that, don't you, Riley?'

She could hardly get the words out now for the awful cackles of laughter. At the same time she had begun to weep, using the thumb of her right hand, which held the joint to wipe away the tears of combined sorrow and laughter. She kept trying to compose herself, to say something serious again, but each time she did, both she and I broke into further hysterical laughter. We rocked and swayed as the few remaining guests began to laugh with us. Their laughter added to the great gale of the stuff that rose up with the dope smoke and hung on the ceiling.

At last she got the words out.

She said, 'You love him. Why won't you see it? Don't you see that you love him, Riley?'

He was right about the weather in Hong Kong. The rich of the colony were celebrating when I arrived, it being one of those rare, sought-after opportunities to bring the fox fur out of cold storage. There'd be frost in the New Territories, something that happened one or two days a year and which always made the morning papers.

The biting wind, as I walked across the tarmac at Kai Tak, felt like it was sweeping straight down from the Steppes. Scornful of Nathan's offer of a coat, I was wearing no more than a T-shirt.

The chill in the evening air seemed more than physical, I remember. It seemed to bring with it a blast of pure misery and loneliness that blew right through me, telling me that Zoe was right. I was making a terrible mistake and I did indeed love Nathan. Inside the building I halted before the check-in desk of the airline I'd just left, stood looking at it so long I caught the attention of the girl behind it, who stared back at me suspiciously as I fought for and against the desire to walk up, throw my last traveller's cheques down in front of her in a grand gesture, get back on the plane to Bangkok. I imagined myself going straight to his hotel, tapping again on his door, seeing it open that crack and then more, as he saw who it was. Flinging myself his arms, feeling them. All that *solace*.

I've made a mistake, Nathan.

I love you, Nathan . . .

A grand gesture indeed. Because I still couldn't say it. Not with the truth required. Not so he'd believe it. No more so than he'd been able to do that night outside the Oriental.

I knew all this and I knew something else too, something more wicked and deadly. I knew that lying beneath all the dark, cold misery and loneliness I was feeling now, all but hidden between all those layers, was the smallest, the most minute gleam of something – nothing but a shard, but still shining. It was excitement, a clean, sweet sense of new beginning. Of *freedom*.

'Do you think that's terrible? Do you think that's awful?' I said to Danny. I mocked because the moment was so serious. I said, 'Do you think it makes me a bad purrrrrrson?'

He answered in a Danny way, kind of cool, like he does sometimes so that you don't quite know what he's thinking.

He said, 'No. Probably just seriously emotionally stunted.'

On the other hand he also said, 'Let he or she who is without sin, et cetera, et cetera . . . I guess there's plenty of us not entitled to reach down and pick up that first stone, Riley.'

Q is for ... A Question of Sex

No. Wrong.

Not *a* question of sex, *the* question.

The only question.

The question that has troubled mankind since time immemorial and possibly even before that; the one that has been mulled over by the great minds, Plato, Descartes, Lao Tzu ...

How often do single people, spinsters in particular, have sex?*

And when all is said and done, and at the end of the day (which, after all, is still when it's most likely to happen), do they have it more or less than their married sisters?

My married sister, for instance.

'Mind your own bloody business.'

'Look, it's not idle curiosity. It's a purely scientific enquiry.'

---

* Lao Tzu's answer: *'The dragon who swims is not a dragon'* and *'He who sits beneath the cherry tree will still see the tiger'* being particularly unhelpful.

According to the Office of National Statistics, forty per cent of married couples have sex at least twice a week.* Or at least they claim they do.

'Well, I'm sure.' Sophie raises a deeply sceptical eyebrow. 'I mean. You're married, right? And someone comes along with a clipboard and asks you if you're having sex. You're not going to say No, are you?'

'The singles did.'

Because indeed they did. In the same survey three-quarters of unmarried men owned up to falling short of the twice-weekly marrieds' figure, while spinsters let the single side down even further. Only a bare one-fifth were able to lay claim to the married total.

Now, I'll warrant you, there'll be more than a few of you married people out there surprised at this. You, sir, for instance, yes, you. Or you, madam, stuck there in the middle of those first fine glorious years of child-rearing, reading this at two in the morning, book in one hand, rocking cradle in the other, you who have learnt to live not just without sleep but without other things too – health, for instance, humour, all those other common decencies of human existence. And, of course, sex, which has become so vague a memory you couldn't even swear any more that you know how to do it. Listen. No victory more sweet than the unexpected one. No laurels more welcome than those placed unforeseen upon the brow.

Next time your party-going, dirty stop-out, single, next-door neighbour wakes you up by banging the front door

---

* Just kidding. The ONS may be burrowing down into our lives but they haven't got that far down yet. Actually it was a survey in *Cosmopolitan*.

at three in the morning and clumping heavily up the stairs, don't get mad, get even.

Remind yourself you're statistically more likely to have had sex than she has.

None of this surprises me. Because it stands to reason, as far as I can see, that by and large, and all things being equal, anyone who lives as part of a twosome under the same roof with another person is bound to have more chance of having sex than someone living alone. Because the most obvious advantage of a live-in relationship is that, theoretically at least, sex is on hand. There. At home. In the freezer.

'Yeah, well. We all know about freezers.' Sophie ticks her argument off on her fingers. 'One, the stuff has to be defrosted before you can use it. Two, half the time when you've done that you don't want it. And as for the sell-by date . . .'

'Right.'

'Don't even go there.'

One thing's for sure. The news that marrieds have more sex than singles comes as no surprise to the spinster, neither is it going to swing any red-blooded of her species the married way. Because only a fool would try to sell the single life on the grounds of sex. Because being single is like being on an expedition to the North Pole, or climbing Mount Everest, or sailing single-handedly around the world. In all these instances you'd be pretty sure of being short of sex. But it wouldn't matter because sex wouldn't be the reason you were there. Sex wouldn't be why you were doing it.

For years I kept the faith, believing in the mythical little black book, believing that somewhere there existed a society, a utopia, inhabited by like-minded singles keen to combine sex and friendship in occasional, uncomplicated couplings. All I had to do was find it. But what I can say all these years on, is that if such a Shangri-la exists, if there is such a community, fraternity or fellowship, if somewhere on this planet there are men and women with the names and numbers of purveyors of cordial and unconditional sex pinned up on their notice boards next to the plumber and the electrician, well, I have yet to come upon them.

'That's because you're straight.'

Oh, yeah. Sorry. My mistake.

I was forgetting Danny and Hanrahan.

Our cottage walls are thick and built to last. Still sometimes I hear Danny and Han making love. Normally it's that last cry of joy and abandonment. It wakes me from sleep. Hangs on the air a moment. Then it falls away into the night like the call of some forgotten bird.

Danny and Han have known each other for five years, since Han opened Hanrahan's Books at the bottom of the High Street. Still, according to Danny, they only meet for sex.

'"According to . . ." And that means what, precisely?'

It means I don't quite believe him. Because I can't help noticing that other things have crept in now as part of this 'only for sex' relationship. Meals out together, for instance, visits to the cinema and art galleries. A while back they even spent a long weekend in Prague together.

'I think you get on better with Han than you're willing to admit, that's all. In fact, if you were up for settling down—'

'Which I'm not.'

'Which you say you're not.'

Well then, as far as I can see, Han would do quite as well as the next man.

Dr Johnson said all of us could be happy with one of fifty or fifty thousand people. The only trick is you have to want to be happy *with* someone. Which is more than a trick; actually, it's the crux of the matter. And therein lies the difference between me and Danny. Because Danny's ten years younger than me and still looking for a relationship, even though more often than not he won't admit it.

'It's not a love thing,' he says about Han.

I say, 'Tell me, what does a love thing look like, Danny?'

It's an old argument, this, but one good and true. Be absolutely sure when you're yearning for something you know what it looks like. Be sure you'd recognise it if it turned up.

Last time I was in Han's shop he said, too casually, too carefully, 'So how's Danny? Haven't seen him for a while.' I said, 'He's fine. He was coming in with me but then he got a call to go back to the office.' Which was a lie. I only said it to make Han feel better and more than likely he knew it.

Because it turns out the pursuit of the easy, uncomplicated sex is a difficult business inasmuch as it's hard to keep up the reciprocal aspect of the arrangement. Before you know it, one's up and one's down. The givers and the takers have asserted their positions, and this because sex has a way of sorting out the winners and the losers.

In short, in my experience you can go to bed with someone so confident of the lightness of the thing, its lack of importance in your life, in fact you'd be willing to take bets on it. Six months later you can be down on the ground and scrabbling at his feet, not knowing how you got there.

All of which I know from Lennie.

*   *   *

Sometimes I think Lennie is a bit like God. If he hadn't existed, I'd have had to make him up, which is actually what I did. I made him up. I assembled him like one of those paper dolls. Took the outline and coloured it in to my own specifications. Which is why I'd never be able to come out of the undergrowth with my hands up as regards Lennie, never be able to wave a white flag like some innocent bystander. When I think of Lennie, I think of *A Midsummer Night's Dream*. I wonder how I fell asleep on that bank but, more importantly, who dropped the potion in my eyes. And then I realise it could only have been me who did it.

Because I *knew* Lennie, you see. That day, for instance, when the phone went in his office as I was signing the forms for my new sound system, the way he said, 'Currys, can I help you?' cheerily, and then the change in his voice, instantly, hearing it become hard, inflexible, like that. As if there was granite in it. No, not granite, marble. Because it was still a salesman's voice, bright and white and even.

'I told you not to call me here.'

Somewhere down the line, even from where I stood outside the little glass box of an office, I could hear the female voice squawking, just the way mine would squawk sometime in the future, all this like a warning, a message from the gods.

'So what? It's none of your business what I do.'

And then the words that would forever sum Lennie up, that should have been tattooed on his forehead the way they were engraved on his soul.

'I don't care.'

And I could tell that he didn't. And that it wasn't one of those, *I don't care*s that ordinary mortals use in moments of heat, said for effect and retracted afterwards.

Lennie's *don't care* was ice cold and truthful.

Ah yes, everyone knew Lennie.

Lennie, in and out of the White Swan, the Queen's Arms, the Jolly Pilgrim.

'Hey, Lennie.'

'Hey, Riley.'

Lennie here today and gone tomorrow. Lennie's postcards behind the bar from exotic locations. Lennie part of the scenery.

When I got around to admitting Lennie and I were an item, I saw the truth of the thing reflected in other people's eyes: Connie, Sophie, my sister Cassie.

'Lennie . . .' they all said, of one accord. 'You don't mean Lennie *O'Halloran*?'

Living in a small town is not like living in a city. You can't leave your sexual blunders behind you. They follow you up the High Street, accost you in the post office, in the shape of Fleur, for instance, still married to Martin then, and with a smooth smile that pretended commiseration but was lit with an unmistakable touch of pleasure.

'Of course we knew what he was from the start.'

'Did we? How's that?'

'Well . . . you know.'

'No. I don't.'

'Oh, come on. You know. Even when he was working with Daddy.'

'Well now, that's strange because as I recall your daddy told me once Lennie was the best salesman he ever had.'

It was only a week or so after Lennie had left so I was in what you might call an excitable condition that day in the post office. A couple of heads turned in the queue as my voice rose above the hubbub.

I said, 'In fact, your daddy said if Lennie had stayed, he'd have ended up sales manager.'

Fleur said, 'Shhh,' casting a nervous look over her shoulder. She reached a hand out to my arm like some nurse trying to lead out a patient.

I shook it off angrily. 'Don't shush me.'

That was where the point of an umbrella suddenly appeared in our midst.

'Stirring the shit as usual, Fleur?' my mother said briskly.

I tell you, that woman was like some latter-day Mrs Bennet in the post office that morning. She rested her two hands on the crook of her umbrella for all the world like it was a parasol. She might have been staring at Fleur from beneath a fur-trimmed bonnet.

'Whatever has happened between my daughter and her *fiancé* –' (Oh God, I love that. What Lennie would have said if he'd heard it) – 'is exactly that: her business and his business, and we'll all thank you to keep that poky little nose of yours out of it.'

I know. It's hard. I've just utterly transformed your view of my mother.

One thing's for sure, Uncle Hugh was right about Lennie being a great salesman. Over the years Lennie sold just about everything. Office equipment, agricultural implements, kitchens, cars, carpets, clothes, jewellery, furniture, insurance policies, holiday homes, and plots of building land in Florida, which may or may not have been under water.

I asked him once. 'Is there anything you haven't sold?'

'Probably not,' he said.

'What about your soul?' I was joking but he answered it quite seriously.

'Oh, that went early,' said Lennie O'Halloran.

Lennie said it didn't matter what you sold. Big or little, cheap or scarily expensive, it was all the same process. And let's face it, he was the man to know. Watching Lennie sell was to watch an artist at work, a maestro. Any number of disparate pieces of imagery spring to mind to describe his *modus operandi*. An animal carefully circling its prey, a dancer blocking out his moves, an actor. When selling he appeared to make no effort at all. He'd approach any customer as if by default, with an air of apology for disturbing them. The next minute he'd be sliding away, begging them not to be embarrassed or impeded by his presence. On the other hand if he could help them in any way . . . And twenty minutes later they'd be signing on the dotted line and for something twice the price they came in for.

Lennie's job at Frasers was his first in our town. He was there four years, leaving to work for a Triumph dealership in Bristol. He'd come down weekends in a good suit and a TR6.* The next thing he's in London, selling office equipment, then seriously upmarket kitchens. After that it's Seattle, where the firm sends him, so that behind the bar at the White Swan or the Jolly Pilgrim, the postcards and

---

* A word here about the TR6, which anyone not possessed of a heart of steel could not help but love and desire from the bottom of their being. Straight six engine, four speed with optional overdrive, independent rear suspension steering and an all-synchromesh gear box, the last two both innovations. Top speed 120 m.p.h., but never mind that. Oh, the styling, the styling. A revamp of the Michelotti 4 and 5 version by Kartmann of Germany gave the body of the 6 even crisper, cleaner lines (dear God, that this thing of beauty should have been supplanted by the wedge-shaped monstrosity that was the 7). And the downside to all this, given that as with all the great things in life, there has to be a downside? Well, I'll merely mention the words

the pictures are stacking up. An apartment with a pool, a shop with his name on the fascia and a Porsche parked outside it. But then just when you think nothing can go wrong he's back home with nothing but one bag, and a shrug and a careless, 'It didn't work out.' And all this because he doesn't care, he truly doesn't care. He's not like ordinary folk. He's older than that. A million years older. He's careless, absolutely careless – careless of himself, of life, of everything, the good times as well as the bad, and there's a reason for this and it turns out it's not a good one.

I don't know if there's a descending order of wickedness in this world, if there's a tariff, a list of crimes and their charges you might be taxed with up there when you get to those pearly gates. Still, I think adopting a child, an innocent, and then abusing him has to rank pretty high up on the list.

I love to think of Lennie's parents reading this. I'd like to think of them playing the part of cuddly old innocents somewhere in some care home, and being confronted with their crime, having it read out to them, and all the half-decent people turning away, and this because I never could see simply growing old as an excuse or mitigation, and certainly not as some form of final redemption.

---

fuel injection. This a phrase which, even years on, will strike fear into the hearts of anyone lucky enough to have owned a 6. Truth to tell, you pushed a TR6 more than you drove it, and this thanks to the 'notoriously troublesome' Lucas system as one (highly restrained) classic car book has it. I can think of several occasions where, weighed down with shopping, I bumped into Lennie and he offered me a lift. Each time, when we got to the car park, the TR wouldn't start.

Each time, Lennie would say, 'OK. We'll see if we can get her going again . . . You push, and I'll steer.'

God knows why that didn't tell me something.

I don't know who Lennie's real parents were; neither did he. If he'd wanted to trace them, or at least his mother, because it's unlikely any father's name would have appeared on the birth certificate, it would have been possible. These things were just beginning to happen. I showed him an article one day in the newspaper, exactly about that. Showed you how to do it. But he didn't want to know.

'Forget it, Riley. I'm not interested.'

And I guess he wasn't interested because he'd written the story himself. Because he already knew, because he'd put the pieces together and therefore didn't need to make the enquiries.

Lennie was born in Liverpool, a place of ships and, like all such places, with a lot of dockside activity. A local Catholic orphanage dealt with the result.

You could figure by Lennie's looks that this was his likely lineage. In old novels, they'll talk about lascars, who were sailors from the East Indies, or possibly old Persia. One of those might have been Lennie's father. And there's no point from here on in fooling around with phrases like 'dark good looks' because they come nowhere near it. Lennie's face was extraordinary. It could have looked down at you from a mizzen mast any time over the past centuries. Something about it seemed not quite human. You looked at it and you thought that it must have been the face Emily caught sight of and created Heathcliff from, the one Robert Louis Stevenson saw halfway between Jekyll turning into Hyde or back again. I don't do descriptions much (you'll have noticed that, a succession of editors have pointed it out as my weakness), but I could go on all day trying to capture for you the enigma that was Lennie. First, the hair that he wore thick and long to his collar, whatever the fashion, that tucked behind his ears, and lay around his face and around the smooth delicately lined forehead in black and silver-grey curves. Didn't some poet say he could write a sonnet to some woman's eyebrow? If I wrote sonnets I could do it to Lennie's, the thickness of them, the blackness, the way they winged out instead of arched, but were always drawn in together, causing that small furrow over the bridge of his nose and giving him that air of slight menace. Add to this the skin that a dark designer stubble would grow on in hours, and the eyes, the darkest brown I've ever seen in my life, a liquid iris-less brown; and finally the lips, dark lips, smooth and wide and always a little open. Utterly incapable of looking innocent or unsensuous.

A dull swirling anger can still settle on me when I think of what happened to Lennie, one he'd always be intent on diffusing.

'So what?' he'd say. 'How many other kids do you think it happens to?'

A Manchester couple adopted Lennie. Catholics. Good living (and doesn't that cover a multitude of sins). His mother was Polish, his father Irish, a believer in discipline. Pretty much anything, by the time he passed the age of ten, could earn Lennie a thrashing. Which wasn't as bad as what came afterwards, when his beauty began to show and his sex-deprived mother began to take an interest in him best described as unholy.

'I don't know why you keep it,' I said to him, full of fury, one day reaching up to tear at the framed photo, the only picture on his walls. He grabbed my hand. Said, 'Leave it, Riley.'

They must have handed the camera to a passer-by.

Take a picture of us. Would you mind? Yes, us and our son . . .

And so there they were, gargoyles in their long, dark

fifties macs, clutching his hand on that trip to London. Six or seven he was then, and still with that sweet trusting smile on his face and – a nice irony this – the mother of parliaments behind him.

'It's awful,' I said. 'I don't understand why the hell you keep it.'

He said, 'It's the last time I can remember being really happy.'

Several times I said, 'You should do something about this, Lennie.'

He said, 'What? Talk to someone?' and his face and his voice were scornful.

Once he almost did . . . something. We were in Manchester, checking out mobile phones at an exhibition, this for the shop he was thinking of opening. On the edge of the city, on our way home, he suddenly turned off the main road, took a detour round a backstreet, parked in a street of grey run-down houses looking that much worse with the grey November mist curling all around them.

I didn't have to ask why we were there. I guessed immediately, not least because of the way he was sitting there not saying anything, but just staring at the house with its sagging, dripping eaves and a weak grey light escaping through the curtains.

'Come on.' I grabbed his hand. 'Let's do it. Let's face them,' but he pulled his hand away sharply. Instead he just went on sitting there in silence, not moving.

Lennie wasn't a tall man, around five-five. He had a small frame too, small hips and shoulders. Sitting there that day, he seemed to get lower and lower in his seat and that much smaller as if, I guess, he was turning into a little boy again.

216

In the end he'd flicked the ignition key and put in the clutch and we began to pull away.

He didn't look back as we drove down the street. Still in darkness, still in silence.

There's a lot of different things you need to feed into the equation to make sense of what happened with Lennie, and one of them would have to be – and this the one with at least a shred of credit – that I wanted to make him happy. I wanted to do what plenty of woman had wanted to do before me – and there had been plenty. I wanted to make up for all the bad stuff that had happened to him. He was not a large man. There was something delicate about those lascar good looks, and sometimes in my arms he would feel remarkably frail. I'd get the feeling, holding him, that I was touching a different Lennie, as if I was getting to some decent heart of him. But then all the women of the world who go out with the Lennies of this world will say that. Check the agony columns if you don't believe me. And who could tell if any of this was real, with that cloud of Afghan black hanging over us?

We were together about eighteen months, Lennie and I. I guess the thing that sticks out, looking back, is how little we had to show for it in terms of a relationship. What I mean is there was just so little damn enjoyment in the thing. Instead, in the way of such affairs, it was a paltry, diminished existence. The mail bags of agony aunts as I say are full of such affairs. People, women, accepting so very little. I'm ashamed that it happened to me.

We had nothing in common the pair of us, that was the thing, and I was proud of that, perversely, foolishly proud. I'll be honest now, I never was the sort to search for brain over brawn, this being partly the result of my calling. I wasn't looking for a long-term-partner, for a father to my children, and this affected my choice. I could afford to be cavalier about it.

Because we had nothing in common, we did so damn little together – rented videos, mostly, got takeaway meals, went to the odd rock concert, Springsteen, Ry Cooder, but never to the cinema, seldom even out to dinner.

We did take the odd weekend away to expensive hotels, where we'd take cursory walks around the grounds, then retire to our room to watch films on the TV, order up room service. And mostly, because he didn't have his credit cards, or for some other convoluted reason I couldn't figure, I'd end up paying.

'Remind me, Riley. I'll pay you back next month.' But somehow he never did and I never got around, from sheer shame, to forcing the issue.

We did go to the theatre once, I remember that. It was by way of an experiment on my part, an attempt as always to give the affair some *legitimacy*. I took him see *Death of a Salesman*, and he came out stunned, almost entranced, you might say, exhilarated too and thoughtful the way I'd never seen him.

He said, 'He got it, Riley. That guy ... Miller ... he got it right.'

But we never went again. There never was anything he wanted to see. That was the end of it.

There was the sex, of course. And this is important. Ah, yes. The sex.

The first time I went to bed with Lennie it struck me in a blinding flash that this is what I'd wanted to do for years, all through those *Hi Lennie in and out of the White Swan* years, when I could have sworn I had no interest in Lennie O'Halloran whatsoever.

218

Sex with Lennie was good, very, very good, there's no question about that. Lennie had been around and knew his way around. A good combination. He knew the moves and how to make them, besides which – and this against all the odds – he was a generous lover. Most surprising about him was the way he kissed, which was warm and full-blooded, as if from this at least in life he gained enjoyment. In sex he always gave an impression of tenderness, and I put it that way because with Lennie you could never be sure what was real and felt, and what was just an impression that he was able to give for whatever reason. Still, it was as if any warmth and responsiveness that he was unable to demonstrate in everyday life he could at least show in bed.

Besides all this there's something else that has to be factored in, that potion like the one in *A Midsummer Night's Dream*, only in this case that I poured into my eyes, and that Lennie poured into his own too, and that, at the very least, helped to generate the warmth and ease of the love-making, to knock off – the way it will – all the rough edges.

In short, the very best Afghan black was never far from Lennie's person, never far from mine either during that time we went out together. I don't intend to do one of those *Just Say No* lectures here; frankly it's not my thing. Instead I'll just say I had a taste for it that had developed on my travels, and which had stayed with me, which, in the main, had always a) wasted my time and b) wildly skewed my judgement. And there's no question, it did both of these things with Lennie.

'I'll take care of this customer, Barry,' he said that day I went into Currys, looking for a new sound system, pushing a pimply youth aside. He'd only been back from one of those mysterious foreign forays a matter of months; still he'd managed to jump up from common or garden salesman to sales manager.

'Hey, Riley.'

'Hey, Lennie.'

'Saw you in the paper. Written a book or something. Is that right, Riley?'

Ten years or so on, opinions are still divided as to whether the change in my financial circumstances was a factor in Lennie's new and previously unrevealed interest in me. Basically they divide up like this:

All of my friends and loved ones: Yes, no question.

Me: No, but only because as far as I'm concerned the only way to come out of this whole thing with a shred of dignity is not to shift the blame but to take it at least where it largely belongs, fair and square on my own shoulders.

Because if there is one thing I despise more than all else it's those dumb letters you get on the agony pages. You know the sort of thing:

Dear Abbey,
     The last three dozen men I've been out with have
     all been bastards. Why am I so unlucky?

Like they really do believe it. That it's all a matter of luck. That they just had the misfortune to hit an arsehole cluster.

Just about the only thing I've got going for me as far as the whole episode is concerned, is that at least I learnt from my mistake, that it only took one Lennie for me to learn my lesson. Besides this, in the main, I'm a cock-up rather than conspiracy theorist. Like I said, Lennie's one defining feature was that overwhelming carelessness, so

220

that if I fell into his lap, I figure he thought that was just fine. But do I think he planned it all ahead of time? Frankly, no. He was just too lazy.

Because that was the thing about Lennie and me. In some ways we were alike, frighteningly so. That's what he'd say that last day, in the doorway, smoothing his hair back like nothing had happened, staring down at me where I still lay on the floor.

'We're alike, you and me, Riley,' this with a touch of regret in his voice. 'We could probably have made a go of it if you'd have only accepted that.'

And I know now what he meant. But it wasn't the truth, or at least – as always – not the whole truth.

Because while confronting Lennie was like confronting my own image in the mirror, his was that image magnified, blown up out of all proportion – my *doppelgänger* walking the earth, yes, but imbued with everything I was, my inclinations, leanings multiplied a thousand times over, a sort of Über-Single dedicated to himself, to his own ambitions and desires, the centre and span of his universe. In the world of the self-absorbed, the self-sufficient, the self-interested, all those other selfs (and for which I make no apology), he was a professional among amateurs, a giant among the pygmies.

Meanwhile, it should go without saying that my mother, like some Little Minstrel Boy, remains one lone and faithful heart as regards Lennie O'Halloran. Despite everything, he's still up there with the heroes, as far as she's concerned. Doing that flicking thing in the sink with her Marigolded hands, she'll still occasionally stare mistily out of the kitchen window as she remembers him.

'I don't know why you didn't marry Lennie,' she'll say.

'Um, let me think. There must be a reason. Oh, I

remember. Because he cheated on me and left me with twenty grand's worth of debts . . .'

Oh, you.

You're so picky, Riley.

R *is for* . . . Regret

There's one thing you need to know before we go any further.

I don't do regret.

I don't do regret like I don't do poker-work, or petit point or any of that other hokey-pokey, pointy-nosed patronising crap that's supposed to attach to the single, childless older woman.

I'm heavy on regret and this is why. Because regret is another of those clichés dogging the feet of the spinster. It translates into that 'air of sadness, of loss' wished upon us by the likes of that celebrity interviewer.[*]

It's a popular view of the spinster, this, and not least because it keeps her safely and firmly in her place, in post-World War One mode, victim of missed opportunity, of dispossession and skewed demography, an enduring image too, positively iconographic, but unborn out by the very statistics that claim to substantiate it. For how do we know how many of those spinsters 'left' by the war might have

---

[*] See A for Attitude.

had ample opportunity to become wives and mothers later on in life, but decided against it, their spinsterhood therefore not due in the end to the tragedy of the trenches but to a liking for their single state?

There's a terrible whiff of the Madonna about the spinster left by the war. It turns her into what some would like her to be, sexless, the eternal virgin, her spinsterhood equally and eminently suitable for grubby jokes and sickly worship, and this with the added advantage that she can be patronised and in the classic fashion, any dignity and honour that she's granted only as much as others will allow. And then there's the safeness of it all, which Olive Jepson had discovered and which kept that picture on top of the piano.

Sometimes it's really useful to have a dead fiancé, Riley ... I don't know why but some people just seem happier if you can give them a good reason why you're single.

She knew why. The knowing satirical smile said that. She knew, although doubtless didn't care, that this long-gone fiancé bought her a place in our town, that with him she slotted neatly into its scheme of things.

For what better justification or mitigation can there be, will there ever be, for those too scared or just too downright lazy to get out of an unsuitable and/or unrewarding relationship than this ever-present picture of the Grim Alternative, this Warning of a Worse Fate, the Spectre of the Solitary Spinster, complete with obligatory 'air of sadness' lying like a cobwebby shawl about her shoulders. Regret like Miss Havisham's unused bridal wreath, wilting on her brow.

'It's not about regret.' That's what I said to Danny.

'What's it about then, girlfriend?'

'Roads you didn't take, doors you didn't open. That sort of thing.'

'And that's not regret?'

'No.'

Something else, something more subtle. A grey area. Pearl grey. Translucent. Shimmering. Like the early morning mist I'd see, a wicked mix of heat and pollution, from Nathan's hotel window . . .

I slightly bastardised the quote that day to Danny. It's actually the 'passage' we did not take, not road. It's from T. S. Eliot's *Four Quartets*, from the first of the four, 'Burnt Norton', and it's been a lamp to my feet over the last few months, thinking of all that's happened.

Smart alecks among you probably recognised the quote straight away. More to my shame, then, that I so recently discovered it.

More reason to offer up my grateful thanks, albeit posthumously, to Mervyn.

Mervyn was the first of us to join this paper. Except, of course, it wasn't *this* paper then. Then the *Free Press* was a bona fide weekly people cared about enough to buy, its name a proud boast, advertising its credentials. Now that name says it all, spelling out exactly what it is, a two-bit give-away, which comes through the door regardless.

'Once they rang to complain when they didn't get it,' Mervyn said gloomily one day, banging down the phone on a complainant. 'Now they only ring to say they do,' 'they' being the second home owners who visit their cottages so rarely that by the time they arrive, bearing their rocket and their Parmesan shavings, nerves equally shredded by the queues on the M4, there's a wall of *Free Press*es so high and so wide behind their front door they can't actually get it open.

'Like I care,' Mervyn said, screwing up the paper on which he'd noted the name and address, hurling it in the bin. 'They're the bastards who've pushed the price of a dog kennel beyond the reach of the rest of us.'

The more I think about Mervyn's life and career, the more I think of the rings on the trunk of a tree, or layers of strata in rock, each one representing an age: the Jurassic, the Palaeolithic, the Neolithic.

The Jurassic was the mid-sixties (for surely dinosaurs ruled the earth at this time and none more so than Mervyn). He had a column on the paper then, 'Pop Sounds', which was Harry Oates' rather touching response to the seismic shift that had replaced the likes of Alma Cogan with the Beatles. At the time, Mervyn 'managed' bands for whom great things were always predicted.

'*Ready Steady Go!*' he'd say with a nod and a tap to his nose. 'Just watch. Any time now.' You can still see those same band members today. Unfortunately they're working in the local butcher's shop or the filling station, or driving a bus up the High Street.

The seventies was Mervyn's punk period. A photo still graces the wall proudly next to his old desk, no one having had the heart to take it down: Mervyn with a safety pin where no safety pin should be, particularly on a man already too old for it.

Cometh the eighties, cometh the man. He moved into politics, standing for the Green Party, unsuccessfully, but – this to his credit – taking 836 votes off the Tory incumbent. As the eighties gave way to the nineties he metamorphosed into Serious Intellectual and Man of Letters. In this capacity he ran the Writers' Circle, which met weekly in the local library. Invited by him to give my first public appearance there in my own new persona as author,

I never actually got round to reading my carefully selected extracts from *The Importance of Aunts*, thanks to him using the time available to declaim the latest chapter of *Priapus Unbound*, his own as yet unpublished novel.[*]

Lunch times during this period were spent browsing Hanrahan's for obscure Latin American novels and/or collections of Eastern European poetry or sitting over several espressos in Hocus Pocus (he only drank espressos now) where he would drag me to debate the burning topics of the day such as Whither The Novel, or more commonly, Why Won't Some Bastard Publish Me?

'Ahead of my time, Riley, that's the problem. Always the same for a writer who wants to take chances . . .'

In all this he liked to imply that he and I represented an island of intellect and culture in a sea of Philistinism, this last being a direct reference to what he liked to term 'wet-behind-the-ears young whippersnappers off media courses', these being the trainee reporters who, since we were taken over by the conglomerate that gave us Sophie, now pass through our office in a steady stream, and so quickly we scarcely get to know their names before forking out for a farewell present.

Mervyn's death shocked us all, no question, and not least Magda, in the middle of planning her wedding.

'I shall postpone it, of course,' she said. 'It's the least I can do. As a mark of respect.'[†]

I guess the only consolation in Mervyn's death, if

---

[*] Still, regrettably, unavailable.

[†] Magda and Mervyn were an item for a while back in those CND days, something I discovered coming upon them one day amongst some bushes around the perimeter of one of our better-known American bases.

consolation there be, is that at least he went the way he would have wanted to go, pitching forward in the press box of the magistrates' court, knocking his trademark black fedora on to the floor where it rolled in a full slow dignified circle like a last lap of honour.

On the face of it, it might seem to be pushing the bounds of credibility to have Royston's court case the very one in progress when Mervyn keeled over. On the other hand, the thing becomes considerably less coincidental bearing in mind Mervyn's position as court reporter and the sheer regularity with which Royston appears at the magistrates' court on account of his careless/dangerous driving.

Just how Royston has managed to hang on to his licence over the years, given the number of his convictions, is a mystery to us all. It can only be thanks to the Fraser name, which, as we know, he drops on every conceivable occasion, a habit his solicitor was slavishly copying ('Now, Mr *Fraser*, you are, of course, marketing manager at *Frasers*, and you had just pulled out of the *Fraser* car park . . .') when Mervyn made that queer guttural noise in his throat and slumped forward over his notebook.

'Poor boy. He was quite traumatised.'

This from our mother, and the subject of a great deal of hollow laughter from the rest of us, i.e., Cass and Fergie and me, believing as we do that maybe, just maybe, the Texas Chain Saw Massacre staged live in front of Royston would bring on symptoms of trauma, but even then it wouldn't be a pushover.[*]

---

[*] In fact so traumatised did Royston declare himself to be that the case had to be adjourned. Further, when it was reconvened a week later he discovered that the shock of Mervyn's collapse and death had completely erased from his mind any recollection of the incident for which he was

Meanwhile, by the time of his death Mervyn had been through several marriages and liaisons, the last and most important of these being with Irena, with whom he took up a decade or so ago, in his own glum words, 'like some old train shunted into a siding', a rather touching and lyrical phrase, I always thought, and certainly one considerably more resonant than any of those he force-fed me during lunch time from his *magnum opus*.

How Mervyn and Irena met has remained a mystery to all. Since she's Russian, and since she appeared in his life around the end of the Cold War, most of us assumed she was some sort of mail-order acquisition. Not that there was ever the slightest indication of *détente* between them. A further mystery to us is how they managed to remain together during the last decade, or more especially, how they failed to murder each other. Personally, I've always believed that they were cemented by a sort of affection-ately mutual loathing. This I judge from the way he always referred to her, which was generally as 'that mad bitch', but always with a certain air of admiration. In the same vein, he appeared to take a sort of patriarchal pride in the colourful insults she would hurl at him in foaming Russian, her favourite, which I can neither spell nor pronounce, loosely translating as *mean bastard whose mother does unmentionable things with soldiers*.

It came as no surprise to anyone that Irena had Mervyn cremated.

'Not taking any chances,' said Sophie, as we stood together on the steps of the crematorium.

---

being tried, in which he had almost run over the pensioner on the zebra crossing. Thus, yet again and by the due, although in this case, remarkably murky process of law did Royston save his licence.

The funeral service was a grim affair, not enhanced by a number of self-penned pieces by members of the Writers' Circle, including Magda:

'priapus
unbound
and for ever now . . .'

Irena sat through the whole thing with a bad-tempered look on her face, this being her normal expression. The only time she smiled was at the end, when she pulled off the final indignity by using the excuse of his punk years to send him out through the red curtains into the hereafter to the sound of Sid Vicious singing 'My Way'.

Being editor, and with the excuse of a paper to bring out, Sophie was able to slide off after offering her condolences to the widow at the crematorium door. Not so Riley Gordon, her arm being caught in a claw-like grip by Irena.

'You vill come to the house,' she said in the manner of a woman who may indeed have worked as a guard in the Gulag, this being among Mervyn's favourite insults and the one that more usually followed her allegation about his mother and the soldiers.

Half an hour later, doing that traditional funeral thing of trying to balance a piece of Battenburg on the side of a saucer while sipping my tea, I felt the claw catch my arm a second time. The words, 'Heeeee liked you,' hissed into my ear in a manner that made it sound like an accusation. I was still scrabbling around for an alibi when I found myself being marched down the corridor to what turned out to be Mervyn's study, although judging by the amount of wine bottles still lying in the waste bin it was less reserved for late night addition to his novel than the drinking that almost certainly helped to kill him. She flung wide the door with a grand gesture that sent the several dozen gold bracelets shooting down her arm, and said in a throbbing 'Song of the Volga' voice, 'Hisss books. You take them.'

Now Mervyn's books rose in shelves to the ceiling. They also teetered in piles on the floor. Happily, however, Han was at the funeral, Mervyn being one of his customers. Thus I was able to persuade Irena that not only would my cottage not take Mervyn's library, but returning the books from whence they came, i.e., to Han, would be a much better deal since he would pay her for the ones he wanted. This cheered her up considerably, but she still insisted, although tearfully now, since she was two-thirds of the way down a bottle of vodka, that I take a book to remember Mervyn by.

'He vould like it. Yessss. Yessss.'

Thus it was that I grabbed the nearest thing lying on his desk, which turned out to be *Four Quartets*.

'Gosh. Just imagine. It was probably the last thing he was reading,' said Magda, tenderly stroking its cover. The wake had moved on to the Queen's Arms by then, this mainly on account of Irena passed out on her sofa. 'It's as though it's still warm, isn't it, as though he's still with us?' this with the faintly tragic air of a woman who would have us all remember that she and Mervyn had, after all, once been lovers.

'Oh, look.' She'd opened it up. 'He's underscored some lines, made notes in the margin.' She began intoning the words as indeed I knew she would. When she'd finished, her mouth fell open in a long aaah of grief and she raised her eyes like some praying saint, clasping the book to her bosom.

'Imagine . . .' she said. 'It's just like a message, isn't it? A message from the other side. From Mervyn.'

I said, 'Oh, for God's sake, give it a rest, Magda.'

Still, when I got home I couldn't help looking at those underscored lines again and Mervyn's 'Yess' scribbled next to them. And I had to admit there did seem to be something reaching out from the ether about them. Maybe it was the firm, even triumphant nature of the 'Yess'. Who could tell why Mervyn had scrawled it? Still, it seemed to make the lines resound in some peculiar way, like the voice of Hamlet's father coming from beneath the stage: *Swear . . . swear . . .*

Perhaps it was just that old intimation of mortality we all get at funerals, each man's death, etc, etc. There again, perhaps it was the memory of Mervyn himself. He'd followed me pretty much through my life when I thought about it. And while he was as mad as a hatter in some respects, still there was something rather magnificent about all those different incarnations, those different rings on the trunk of his tree.

'Here's to you, Mervyn,' I said, raising my glass, toasting him, seeing him stalking through the newsroom in that big black hat, his voice booming from behind the computer at those young whippersnappers.

'Read and learn . . . read and learn,' he'd tell them, summoning them to his screen to read his copy over his shoulder.

'Read and learn,' he'd said. And so I did, pouring myself another glass of wine, opening up his *Four Quartets* again, staring at the lines he'd underscored and his 'Yess' beside them

> Down the passage which we did not take
> Towards the door we never opened*

I read them over and over.

And before I knew where I was, I was thinking of Nathan.

When I think of how Nathan appeared to me over the years, I seem to see him as one of those small garishly painted figures in a little alpine chalet barometer, the sort my mother brought back from one of her coach trips with Tommy to Austria, and hung in the hall, a little figure in a green feather-cocked hat, sometimes in, sometimes out, but always *there*. Always present, which is how he seemed to me, even when I didn't realise it, waiting at the back of my head.

Nathan, Nathan. In direct translation, *Given of God*. A scary thought.

'If I believed it. Which I don't.' This to Danny.

Over the years, thinking of Nathan, I'd daydream sometimes, imagine myself jumping on a plane (this before I'd discovered I couldn't fly), crossing to the other side of the planet, checking into some hotel near the university, playing the detective and finding out when and where he was teaching. I'd imagine myself going to one of his lectures, see myself sitting at the back behind my dark glasses,

---

* Here are the lines in their entirety that Mervyn underscored:

> Footfalls echo in the memory
> Down the passage which we did not take
> Towards the door we never opened
> Into the rose-garden.

watching as he put up his dry dusty slides with those dry dusty statistics, made his dry dusty asides.

'Do they like you? Your students?' I asked him that once.

'I guess.'

'No. Do they?'

'Yeah. Maybe. I make them laugh . . . sometimes.' This said with that old determination never to show the slightest hint of vanity or self-favour.

I'd imagine then, how it would be at the end of the lecture, how I'd wait until the last student had departed. How I'd walk down those steps, very quietly, very slowly, how he'd see me out of the corner of his eye as he collected up his slides and his notes, how he'd ignore me, refusing to raise his head, thinking it no more than a pitiful excuse for a late essay. How I'd stand there for a moment, just staring at him and then how I'd say his name so very quietly.

'*Nathan* . . .'

'Jesus. And all this time you've never contacted him.'

'Did I say that?'

Oh, did I say that, Danny?

Because every so often, for no reason, out of the blue, something like an alarm would go off in the back of my head. I'd awake with the desire, the need to phone him.

'Right. So you have been in touch?'

'No.'

Not exactly, Danny.

'Because when I phoned him, it was always out of hours. I'd always get the night porter and I'd make up a story. I'd tell him I was phoning Nathan about some conference. That Nathan had told me to ring because he knew he needed to be in his room overnight finishing a paper. And the porter would try Nathan's number for me, and the phone would ring on and on, and as it rang, as I waited, the receiver would grow wet in my hand, so wet that sweat would run down my hand into the receiver. And all the time my heart would hammer hard against my chest, and I'd have my eyes closed, both of these against the possibility of Nathan actually picking up the phone, and me *hearing his voice*, actually hearing it, so that all the time I'd sit there lost in the contemplation of it, the sheer honest-to-God fear and wonder of it, that amazing, unmanageable moment. And all the time I was thinking this, the phone would ring on and on with that one long weird empty tone they have over there. And in the end the porter would come back on and say that there didn't seem to be an answer, that Nathan didn't seem to be there. And he'd apologise, like it was his fault and not mine. And I'd say that was OK, and it didn't matter. That I'd try again later . . .'

'So let's get this straight . . . You knew the time difference.'

'Yes.'

'But even so you still rang at those times?'

'Yes.'

'How many times?'

'What?'

'How many times did you ring?'

'You mean over the years?'

'Yes.'

'I don't know.'

'Yes you do.'

'What is this? An interrogation? I don't know. OK, maybe half a dozen.'

'Even though each time you knew he wouldn't be there?'

'Yes. Except he was.'

'What?'

'There. Once.'

It was early in the morning. Earlier than I could have expected him to be in. The phone rang out a couple of times and then the tone broke and it was lifted.

'Well, what happened? What did he say?'

'I don't know.'

'You don't *know*?'

'I put the phone down.'

'Look, I know how crazy it all sounds . . .'

'You bet.'

'But the fact is I always believed, I mean *really* believed, from the bottom of my heart, that we'd meet again and it seemed *wrong*, that's all.'

'Wrong?'

'Phoning him and stuff. It seemed like . . . I don't know . . . like I was trying to engineer the thing. Trying to push the plot forward.'

'So you thought it was better to leave it to *chance*, to sheer *luck*?' Danny's eyes were fixed on mine, like he was trying to see something, trying to discern it.

'Yeah. I guess so.'

There was silence. Danny leant back on the sofa, crossed his arms over his chest and then uncrossed them. After that he pursed his lips, shook his head and gave a long low whistle of what sounded like appalled admiration.

He said, 'I'll tell you something, this is one weird town. But sometimes I think you're the weirdest thing in it, Riley.'

S is for . . . Solitude
(or Sunday in the Park with Riley)

The question is, what will they find when they comb through all that DNA searching for the little bundle that binds us, spinsters all, together? What will be the predispositions, the tendencies they discover? An overaffection for freedom? I guess. A wariness as regards love and marriage? That too. But something else. Because I'll warrant that when they get in there, start pulling all those strands apart to find those genes that predispose us to what we are they'll find one Big Bad Mother labelled 'Solitude'.

Once upon a time, I'd have gone to my grave trying to explain to Fleur the difference between being alone and being lonely. But as we know, times change.

I'm just so looking forward to being on my own, Riley.

I learnt early on in this business what a complete waste of time it is trying to explain the difference to those who can't or won't grasp it. He that hath ears to hear, is my motto. If not, why bother?

Trying to explain the attraction, nay necessity, of solitude, is kind of like being stuck in the middle of that old joke about asking the way in Ireland. The guy giving directions says, 'But I wouldn't start from here,' which is how it is with the debate over loneliness and being alone. Where I start from is the presupposition that being alone is a physical state, simply that, no more and no less, yours to cherish and enjoy, worship like a god, hoard like a miser or spend wisely as best suits you. Being lonely, by contrast, is a state of mind and one which more than likely won't be cured by any amount of company. But if you don't start from there, then it's a waste of time trying to explain or even discuss the thing.

One thing's for sure, though. When they come across that strand of solitude in my DNA, it'll have come straight from my father. He loved to be on his own. Evenings, weekends even, he'd be there in his garage alone until ten or eleven at night.

'I know you blame me for that,' my mother said once, the mask of the happy but tragically truncated union slipping drunkenly sideways. 'But he wanted it that way. He was a loner. Me, I need people.' And it's true. And actually I didn't blame her.

'She doesn't understand,' my father said, his head bent beneath a bonnet one night, the long peaceful summer twilight disturbed only by the clink of his spanners. 'I don't *want* to spend nights sitting drinking with her cronies. I like a bit of peace and quiet, a bit of solitude . . .'

I used to try and cover up how important solitude was to me. I treated it like a dirty habit, like an alcoholic hiding the bottle in the laundry basket. Now I don't care who knows. Neither am I interested in any form of therapy or rehabilitation. The fact is, I get withdrawal symptoms if I don't get enough time on my own. That's the way it is and that's the way it suits me. As far as I'm concerned, the main problem with relationships, the thing that gets me down about them, is the time they take up, the way they eat into your life, and in particular Saturdays and Sundays when you could be on your own. A night in bed with someone (sometimes no more than satisfactory, which always adds to the chagrin) and the next thing you know, instead of doing what you should do, which is call it a day, wave him off on the doorstep, you're trying to figure something incredibly boring to do together, taking part in physical activities that don't suit you, quite possibly requiring you to buy special clothing, or walking, in parks, on waterfronts where you don't really want to be, or round museums of dubious interest, or art galleries or, *quelle horreur*, country houses, so that in the middle of some drizzly English Sunday afternoon you find yourself drinking cold, overfrothy cappuccino surrounded by pushchairs in the steamed-up coffee shop of some stately home.*

Alternatively (and just as bad in my opinion) you spend far too long in bed, cooing over croissants and coffee like they've just been invented, *sharing*, God forbid, the Sunday papers, finding yourself left with travel and business, and this because he's snaffled the culture section, all of this like you're already in training to become some old married couple. As the afternoon progresses you make love again, usually unnecessarily, so that it acquires an overblown, used-up edge, leaving you in the late afternoon with a feeling of ennui and faint nausea. Before you know it you've hit rock-bottom, so bored and unable to function

---

* I once found myself at a car boot sale on a Sunday afternoon as a result of sex the night before (Alan). I'm still receiving counselling.

you're sitting beside him on the sofa watching the God slot or the kids' serial on Sunday tea-time television.

And all this, dear Reader – and tell me it's not true – because you felt that terrible responsibility to *do* things together.

Look, the fact is, I never was a Sunday-in-the-Park sort of girl. My fondest memories in recent years of that first fine careless rapture of sex comes from those days spent working on this cottage, helping (well, watching) a man take a sledgehammer to a chimney breast to find the original fireplace, thereafter pouring him a large glass of good red wine, cooking him a spaghetti, and retiring to bed with him.

See, I like what might be termed the economical approach to relationships. Time is not money for me, it's something even more precious. For this reason I like to merge my work and play. I like to have my business and pleasure conveniently bound up together.* I realise that this is an unorthodox approach. Some might even call it reprehensible. Relationships are supposed to be about give and take, I know that, I've read the advice columns. They're supposed to be about sharing your life, and if I needed a first-class example of that (which I don't) I've got Cass and Fergie to show me.

'You have to understand,' Fergie said with tears in his eyes, when we were coming to terms with Cass having cancer, 'there's no one else in the world I want to be with.' And I know it's true. And I know she feels the same because

---

* Although again, I'm forced to admit, it was this sort of thinking through which I came to grief with Lennie.

I see it in the way they are together. Even dumb ordinary things, going to the supermarket, taking the car to the garage, they actually *prefer* to do together. They would just rather, given a choice, be in each other's company, and I know this because I can see it in their faces. But it's not for me, that's all. Life's too short to share, as far as I'm concerned. Just too damn short. And I don't care if that sounds selfish. I don't want to merge my life, my past-times, my passions with someone else. I don't want to cheer him on at football, lay out the cucumber sandwiches in his cricket pavilion, or sit in some folk club (God forbid) while he sings some thirty-eight-verse songs about shipwrecks and mining disasters.[*] I don't want to trail round his exhibitions (Norris, a painter), and since I don't want him to read my books, I don't see why he should expect me to read his either. (Richard. And, by the way, I never did like your novel.) I don't want to go to his firm's dinner (Harris, a solicitor) or drinking with him and his friends (Mark), and I certainly don't want to meet his parents.[†] I don't want to spend a weekend with someone, book a holiday together. In fact, I don't want to do anything normally thought to constitute a relationship, all of which, as I said to Sophie, serves to convince me that there's a gap in the market.

'We pay people to mind our children, after all, to walk our dogs and clean our houses. Why not pay them to go out with our lovers? To take care of the boring bits.'

---

[*] Even worse are the ones who want to co-opt your hobbies, want to go swimming just because you do (Michael), buy a mountain bike so you can go out together (hope you managed to get rid of the bike, Neil). Want to accompany you to the cinema or the theatre when really you'd much rather go with the Greek Chorus.

[†] Eric. Jesus. Like I didn't have enough problems with my own aged parent?

'What sort of boring bits?'

'Oh, you know. Drinks after work. Firm's do's. *Dinner parties.*'

'So do you have sex?'

'Of course. But then it's quality time. You meet once a month or something.'

'*Once a month?*'

'OK. Twice.'

Sophie is shaking her head. 'I tell you, there should be an organisation for people like you, Riley.'

'There will be. I'm forming one. It'll be like Outrage except it'll be called Faintly Annoyed. We'll march for the rights of the sexually lazy beneath a banner that says, "SORRY, CAN'T BE BOTHERED".'

Sophie is hard on my sex life, or rather my lack of it. Like I said before, I've been through feasts and famines in my sex life and what bothers Sophie is that one bothers me no more than the other.

'Remind me again. When did you last have sex?'

'I don't know. I can't remember. When was the Coronation?'

'If you don't get it soon, you'll start doing weird things.'

'Like what?'

'Shoplifting. Writing salacious letters to weathermen and news readers.'

'Oh, I'm doing that already.'

I'm not like Sophie, you see. Sophie is never without sex, but that's because she puts time and effort into acquiring it. She treats it as a hobby, approaching it the same way, trawling the personal adverts, clicking around the on-line dating.

On a Saturday night, with a glass of wine in her hand and nothing better to do, she'll say, 'Come on, give it go

. . . oh, look . . . "Bookish Bohemian, forty-seven" . . . that would suit you . . .'

But it wouldn't, you see. Because the way I feel about it is this. I'm pretty much up for anything people want to do in life – morris dancing, stamp collecting, trainspotting – I'll march to the death for their right to do it. It's just not for me, that's all. And I feel the same way about personal ads and on-line dating. And it's not just laziness, although that's what Sophie normally accuses me of. But as I tried to explain last time we had the argument, it's more complicated than that.

'Look, I'd like to believe, I mean, I'd *truly* like to believe that a relationship is the answer.'

'The answer to what?'

'I don't know. That's the problem.'

Because when I look at my life, this Life of Riley, I feel, like I said right at the beginning, that it is a pretty good one. I don't live Thoreau's life of 'quiet desperation', far from it. In fact, in the main I'd say that I've got pretty much everything I want in life.

'Obviously I could do with a bit more money, but then who couldn't?'

'Umm . . . let me think . . . Oh, I know, Archie.'

Still, all that said, I'd be dishonest if I didn't hold up my hands and admit that there does sometimes seem to be . . . well . . . a gap in my life.

'Not a major gap, you understand.'

'Of course not.'

'I mean, not a yawning chasm.'

Not even a gap I can pin down, if you want to know the truth of it; put a name to. But a gap none the less. And the problem is that I can't imagine a relationship plugging that gap, at least not any sort of relationship known to

243

me, not one I could even *imagine* knowing, as I said to Sophie.

'I mean, when you get to our time in life, you pretty much know what's on offer, don't you? How it all works?'

'How all what works?'

'Everything. Men, women, sex. *Relationships*. I mean, there's no surprises any more, are there?' And I think that's true. So all you really yearn for is some sort of alternative. Some entirely new option.

'Like what?'

'I don't know. Little green men with a completely different take on life. With entirely different appendages and orifices.'

Meanwhile Sophie says. 'I like a man with his own bed to go to,' and I agree with her. I like a man who knows how to say farewell, to observe the traditional courtesies.

Gosh . . . two a.m.

Well, there, doesn't time fly when you're enjoying yourself?

Still, if you must go . . .

After all, we both have to get up in the morning . . .

The fact is that I get choked up when I lose out on my solitude. I get a feeling of being strangled. It works on me like torture, the way sleep deprivation works on other people. I get fractious, short-tempered. I begin to see the world in a different way. Stay after breakfast and I'll name names. And truth to tell, I feel the same way about relationships. I get the same cramped feeling, the same feeling of mild strangulation.

Because what I hate is the way, all of a sudden, they turn you into a couple, the way, all of a sudden, people are inviting you Together. But I don't mind showing up everywhere on my own – in fact, I've come to like it. For a start I can arrive when I like; even better, depart when I choose to.

'No doubt you're going to do that old *methinks the lady doth protest too much* thing now,' I said, sitting on the wall in the darkness as the sounds of Fergie's retirement party came out through the pub window. 'Well, let me tell you, I've had that from other people, and as far as I'm concerned it's just about as patronising, condescending and self-satisfied as it gets.'

In the darkness, Archie's mouth opened and closed again. He folded his arms across his chest.

He said, 'Actually, it wouldn't have occurred to me, Riley.'

T *is for* . . . *Titles*

An important subject. You may wish to take notes.

But first a short anecdote by way of illustration.

I'm upstairs when the phone rings. I'm expecting Sophie to call so when it does I dash out of the bedroom and down the stairs. Three steps from the bottom I catch my foot in one of many holes in the stair carpet and at the same time on a tack holding it only mildly in place. It catches the soft flesh of the large toe on my left foot like it's personal, like it's seriously enjoying the experience. By the time I get to phone and grab the receiver the toe is bleeding profusely all over my pale Chinese washed silk rug – just about the smartest thing in my house and a present from Cass for my last birthday.

'*Mrs* Gordon?'

I know immediately the nature of this call. So would you had you heard it, and this because of the nature of the voice, which is always the same, a mixture of jauntiness and wheedling, the whole overlaid with a faint tinge of melancholy. But then you'd be melancholy too if you were working for a tenth of what you'd get doing the same job here, and furthermore had to do night school in *Coronation Street* and *EastEnders* just so you could convince your cold callees you were ringing from the West Midlands rather than New Delhi.

'Mrs Gordon?'

'No.'

Because I'm not. I am, as we know, *Miss* Gordon.

Which actually she knows, and this because she is familiar with everything about me. It's all there down in front of her, which is why she's calling me.

She has:

- my full name
- my address
- my marital status
- my income
- quite possibly my spelling test results when I was ten, and for all I know the precise contents (number, colour and condition) of my knicker drawer.

In short, whatever else she knows or does not know about me, she is perfectly well aware that this is indubitably, irrevocably, inextricably a spinster household.

Yet still she asks . . .

'*Mrs* Gordon?'

Mrs Gordon, do you have:

- double glazing
- plumbing insurance

247

- electrical insurance
- life insurance
- loft lagging
- cavity-wall insulation
- broadband

Or in this case:

- windows

'Mrs Gordon, can I ask you? Do you have Windows?'

For a moment I'm bemused. In fact I'm so bemused I do what I did above. I put a capital W on the windows, thinking it must mean Bill Gates' Windows. And I'm about to answer in the negative (like Eve I'm an Apple girl) when it comes to me.

It's not Bill Gates' Windows at all she's interested in.

It is. It really is . . .

'You mean the square things made of glass, front and back, I look out of.'

Look, here's the way it goes (and check it out if you don't believe me). When dealing with new female customers sales people always use the term 'Mrs', and they do this thanks to an error that occurred several million years ago when dinosaurs ruled the earth and a few of them went into marketing. Armed only with a flip chart and a slide rule they worked out that when cold calling, 'Mrs' was by far the safest option. As a one-size-fits-all courtesy title, its use would gratify those legitimately able to claim this form of address while at that same time flattering and gladdening the heart of those not so lucky.

Ah, bless.

In short, address *Mrs* Bun the Baker's Wife as *Miss* Bunn and you'll be down a snake before you start, without a hope in hell of flogging her that extremely dubious additional plumbing insurance. For what married woman wants to be considered a spinster? By contrast, compliment *Miss* Bunn the spinster daughter by addressing her as *Mrs*, and you'll be up a ladder and signing her up before you can say Not Covered By The Policy.

Now there's a surprising thing about all this, and one I wouldn't have learnt was it not for the windows episode, and in particular the torn toe, which took me into my health centre for a couple of stitches and afterwards into Hocus Pocus for some consolatory chocolate cake and coffee. And which is where Magda revealed she wished to be referred to as 'Mrs' following her marriage.

'I've decided to take the title,' this like it came with a castle and fishing rights and several thousand acres of prime Scottish upland.

'Really. Can you do that?'

'Yes. Absolutely.'

'But . . .'

'What?'

'Well . . . isn't it a bit . . . you know . . . unliberated?'

'Not at all. I'm using it in its *traditional* form.' (Magda always says the word 'traditional' in a hushed tone.)

Because it turns out that all those cold callers have history on their side. Their blanket use of the term 'Mrs' does no more than bring the whole thing full circle. For pre-twentieth century, 'Mrs' was merely a title of respect, used by married and single alike. To differentiate between the two – this being an important matter for many a married women – the husband's Christian name was adopted as well as his surname in formal address.

It's a habit that continues to this day among the older generation. You may have noticed it. I remember it particularly from my junior reporter years when Sophie and I would stand shivering at the church gate, collecting the names of the mourners at the funeral of some town worthy (Mervyn *always* somehow tied up writing his column), there, as likely as not, to be fixed by two pairs of steely eyes from each woman, a pair of their own and another of the dead fox complete with face and paws clasped about their shoulders. Their very expressions beneath their large black hats, and the way they gave their large bosoms an accusatory heave implied that the country was going to the dogs and a mere glance at Sophie and me would show why. They pronounced their names in severe, dictatorial tones, this in the manner of those who knew beyond a shadow of doubt that they were single-handedly holding back the wicked sweep of fashion:

'Mrs *John* Smith . . .'

'Mrs *Harry* Jones . . .'

'Mrs *Ernest* Wilkins . . .'

Indeed, my own dear mother still abides by the same old rule. In yet another swipe at all those damn spinsters, all letters that drop onto her mat come firmly addressed to 'Mrs George Gordon'.

'It's the co-rr-ect form of address,' she insists when I remark upon it, rolling out the r's as she always does when co-rr-ecting me on matters of etiquette.

'Anyway, it helps to keep his dear name alive,' this

last said with a dab at her eyes, adding yet another irony to that sum of all ironies, which I sometimes see in the form of a cone-shaped pile in that pine-fresh front room, rather in the manner of the one that Richard Dreyfuss built as he went steadily bonkers at the end of *Close Encounters*.

Interestingly enough, however, there is one thing upon which my mother and I agree when it comes to titles. The utter absurdity on all fronts of the title 'Ms'.

'Like some bluebottle trying to get out of a window,' according to Sophie.

These days I'm more than happy to use 'Miss'. Much, much more than happy – in fact I'm delighted. I love the soft sweet sibilant hiss of the thing, besides which I think it suits me. If I thought it would help, I'd pin my hair in a bun, this to fit in with the image, only, of course, I have no hair now, it being half an inch all over.

Meanwhile, the interesting thing about the old Ms thing is that while this piece of feminist flummery never could have worked without the participation of the spinster, it never was of the slightest interest or use to her, she having no call to disguise her status. In retrospect it can be seen to have been coined merely for the benefit of her married sister, she for whom getting wed was still the ultimate ambition, and this so that she could use it to pretend that she might not be.

'Go figure,' as Sophie says, and I never heard it put better.

It annoys me now, thinking about this, how we spinsters played along with all this, ignoring the distinguished and noble title already in our possession.

Miss.

251

A *nom de guerre* that could be worn with pride and which, this to my shame, sometime in the early seventies I began striking out along with everyone else, ticking that damn Ms box on every form put in front of me.

'Not everyone.'

This is true.

Alone among our peers, and this I remember, Sophie would have no truck with 'Ms'. But then Sophie would have no truck with any sort of title. Asked whether she was Miss or Mrs, even in the days of her youth she'd reply curtly, 'Neither. Just Sophie. Sophie Aitchison.'

Apart from anything else, there was the awkward ugly nature of Ms when we attempted to pronounce it.

Mizzzzz. Exactly like the demented bluebottle identified by Sophie, those harsh zzz's contrasting so sharply to the sweet sibilant sss's of the Missss we'd surrendered.

Another disadvantage was the way it laid itself open to mockery and insinuation, particularly with those zzz's. I remember how Lennie would say it – '*Mizzzz* Gordon' – lingering over it, those brown eyes full of scornful pleasure. Proving every time he said it the terrible irony of the thing: that the supposedly liberated Mizzzz Gordon was becoming more enslaved by him by the minute.

One day, arriving unseen in the bar to pick him up, the sort of bar where I should never have been, where I *would* never have been had I not let my life descend to that level, I caught him, elbows on the bar, boasting to the men around him.

'Yeah,' blowing out a satisfied plume of smoke, 'I reckon I've just about knocked her into shape.'

A chill of shame went down my spine at the words, knowing who the 'her' was and just why all those men around him were laughing admiringly.

Oh, yes, I got into some bad ways with Lennie, no question about it.

But at least thanks to him I kicked the habit of Mizzzz Gordon.*

---

* It's an interesting fact that men have never shown the same interest in evolving a title system as women have. I suppose you could say that the now scarcely used Esquire was the equivalent of the generic Mrs in as much as it was used to denote social status. Master, now used only for boys, was once a title for a young man not yet married but would never have been used for an older bachelor (e.g., Farmer Boldwood in *Far from the Madding Crowd*). Thus, despite the presence of the bachelor, there has never really been a male equivalent of the spinster's Miss. What is clear (and not to the credit of our sex) is that men have never shown the same need as women have to signal their marital status by means of title and/or form of address.

'Oh, pleeeease. Get real.' Sophie's look is scathing when I mention it. 'The average man's interested in concealing his married status, not advertising it.'

U *is for . . . The Unsuitable Liaison*

If every spinster should have a lost love, according to legend, then for sure she should have an unwise liaison. It's another staple of stage and screen and novel, the fey lonely spinster trying to recover her lost years by succumbing to the charms of the odd-job man, or the pool boy or some penniless old roué pretending to be a minor member of the Habsburgs she meets on a walking holiday. The vision is one of some hankie-clasping, sal volatile hysteric, ever at risk from the emotional effects of her unfulfilled state, in particular her empty womb (and thanks a bundle for that, Sigmund). All of which could be dismissed as an anachronism, a hoary old chestnut way past its prime if that vision didn't continue to exert its influence, albeit in a watered-down version, even to this day.

Take my mother's paper (oh, if you would, if you only would, dear Reader). Only this morning it positively exulted in the news that a survey in the states showed the mental health of wives to be twice as good as that of spinsters (my mother's paper, natch, being firmly of the Married Party). According to the figures, fifty per cent of wives interviewed claimed their general state of emotional health was *good* or *excellent*, as opposed to only twenty-five per cent of single women.* And I could mock all this. And indeed I do. Trust me. I've got that old Sword of Truth right here by my desk and even now my palm is itching to swing it in the air. I could say, and so I do, that to claim the spinster is at risk from every roving-eyed pool boy or renegade member of the Habsburg household is no more than an old wives' tale (taking particular delight in that expression). I could say all that hysteria stuff is just another example of that enduring cliché-ridden thinking; that the spinster is as emotionally well-adjusted and as level-headed as the next woman. And indeed I do say that. I do. I do.

However, in saying all this, constrained as I am, as always, by the need for absolute honesty, I none the less feel obliged to add a small caveat.

Unfortunately the caveat goes by the name of Lennie.

*   *   *

* *Mental Health and the Single Woman*, G. Edwards and R. Eisenbrowsky, Woolford University, 2001. Closer inspection of the survey (via the university website) throws up serious questions about Edwards and Eisenbrowsky's pre-established agenda, and in particular their cavalier approach to the category of 'single woman', which in the case of the survey includes not only spinsters but separated, divorced women and windows. In addition, the survey also does not differentiate between those recently separated, divorced or widowed, i.e., those who quite understandably might be feeling bad about the state of being single, and those who had been on their own a long time. Thus because Edwards and Eisenbrowsky chose not to break the categories down, we shall never know how the spinster fared as regards emotional health compared with, say, previously married women. In fact, all in all, as Sophie pointed out, some might think that the figure for contented wives didn't exactly shape up as an endorsement for the state of marriage.

    'Bloody hell. Only a fifty-fifty chance of feeling good. Wouldn't make me want to do it, I can tell you.'

'Of all the gin joints in all the towns,' I hissed at Sophie, that first night she introduced me to Denis. Because it didn't quite seem fair of fate that she should hand Denis a promotion that would bring him from the city to our small country town, and that having got him there she should then ensure he was thrown together with Sophie.

'Never forget a face,' he said, stroking his chin as Sophie was at the bar. 'Remind me.' But I never got the chance.

'Oh, yeah,' he said, and now he was smiling broadly in that utterly amoral, *we're all friends together here/I smoke the odd joint myself* way that CID men do.

'So . . . whatever did happen to our good friend Lennie?'

I read something once in *Anna Karenina*, never a favourite book of mine but still it struck a chord. It's after she goes off with Vronsky. She begins to feel herself slipping down through society, through the strata and the layers she'd never noticed before. Which is how I began to feel, increasingly, during those two years with Lennie.

It's a scary thing the first time a law-abiding citizen comes face to face with the strong arm of the Law, particularly when it arrives in a police helicopter and half a dozen panda cars. I was working at my desk when I first heard the awful clatter, so loud it seemed to be landing on the roof, and the next thing I knew I was looking into the bright white beam of light coming in through my window. It seemed to cut through my life, dividing it up between that previous, unctuous law-abiding existence and what my life had become with Lennie.

'Crap. You break the law all the time. Everyone does. What's that in your hand, for a start?' And, of course, he was right. Between my fingers as I discussed it was one of the long, thin, elegant joints he rolled with matchless dexterity.

'And what about your *accounts*?' Another man might

have sneered but Lennie never sneered; instead there was that cool carelessness. 'What about all those "expenses" you get as a writer? All those weekends in expensive hotels and health clubs you pretended was "research".'

'You came with me.' But my voice was that of a mutinous child and I could hear it.

I can still feel my stomach falling away at the thought of what my life became with Lennie. There were so few good times in the two years we were together, so little damn pleasure. A few dinners out, a night at the theatre, a few luxury weekends away, all of which I paid for. And all of this, on my part, in a sort of dream, as if I was being taught to make do with so little.

One night, sad, stoned and full of careless courage, I said, 'Sometimes I think you don't even like me that much, do you?'

He said, 'It doesn't matter. I don't like anybody that much, Riley.'

It's when I look back on a night like that, one of so many nights, wasted nights spent smoking, drinking, wrangling spikily, making love afterwards, that the whole affair seems more than anything else like one of Magda's incarnations, as if that person curled up there on the sofa with that joint in her hand, trying to convince herself with every drag that this is a bona fide relationship, was someone else entirely.

I find it hard too to plot the progress of the affair with Lennie, how in particular it came about that I moved so seamlessly from that first night when he represented no more than a source of that easy uncomplicated sex, to the moment where I found myself crawling on the ground at his feet amid the wreckage. Of all the characters in this drama, he's been the hardest to pin down. One minute I think I've got him and then he's slipped away from me.

'I never really knew you at all, did I?' I said on that last day. He looked up from snapping his briefcase closed. Gave me a long look.

He said, 'There's nothing to know, Riley.'

I guess he was right about that. There was a *vacancy* about Lennie, an emptiness where the real person should have been, which is how I came to create him, colour him in. Which is why I guess it's so hard for me now to paint the 'real' Lennie, why his portrait seems to change from day to day, why, for instance when I use those broad brushstrokes, turning him into no more than the archetypal con man, I know that it's too simple, and this because actually he wasn't that good at it. In the old days, still angry about the loss of the money, I'd talk loosely about Lennie 'ripping me off' but all these years on, and with that old benefit of hindsight, I'm not even sure it's the right term.

'Trust me, Riley. If you go down, I go down.'

Maybe he really believed that.

'It's an investment, Riley.'

Maybe he believed that too, that the business really was going to work, in all of this forgetting to factor in that while he was a good salesman, he was actually a lousy businessman – something he'd proved with past failures – any sort of detail, any small print, any everyday stuff of business life boring him. Working in the shop bored him too, which is why it lasted less than nine months, and this not least because most days he wouldn't be in it. Instead it was in the hands of a succession of those pimply youths, the Barrys of this world, who really didn't care, who'd wander up and down aimlessly, or sit behind the beech sales counter picking at their nails and shuffling the paperwork from non-existent sales, all this while Lennie was, allegedly, out scouting for contracts, which fitted in with the vision he had of himself, of some flamboyant entrepreneur about to make a fortune.

'Mobile phones?' I remember I said when he announced the plan a few months into the affair, inviting me to invest although somehow not directly saying so. 'Maybe for people on the road who have to keep in contact with their offices. But don't tell me the ordinary Joe is going to want to carry one around.'

Not much of a clairvoyant, you might think, but still not the worst mistake I'd make forecasting the future with Lennie.

Against all the odds – this to borrow from another of those portraits – I think there was a touch of the Micawber about Lennie. He was always waiting, not for something to turn up but for something to work out. What he was good at was groundwork, setting up situations, putting on a good suit and going into banks, business organisations, suppliers, etc., convincing them to part with their goods and their money. His talent lay not just in being a great salesman, but also in survival, in being able to sustain a situation, fight off his creditors, convince them everything was OK long after the thing was collapsing, and this most likely through his own hand, through that carelessness, which in the end wouldn't let him attach himself to anything or anybody seriously.

'Who is she?' I said that day the photograph fell from a pile of papers on a shelf in the flat. He picked it up, gave it a cursory, cool glance of absolute indifference before tossing it back on the shelf.

'My ex-wife.'

She was sitting in the Porsche in the picture. Dark and pretty, and in front of a shop with Lennie's name across the fascia.

'I married for my Green Card,' he said later, speaking flatly, without either arrogance or apology, and I had no doubt it was true, this because I was learning by now that Lennie had no interest in lying.

That was something else about Lennie, something to pull out, mark about him, the way he had no interest at all in any form of prevarication.

'Don't ask me,' he said the night before the shop opening. 'Don't ask me unless you really want to know,' this with all the new bright shiny phones winking derisively on their display shelves around us, with the bottles of good wine, white and red, standing to attention on the white damask tablecloth besides the wine glasses, with the crisps, and the nuts, and the cheese straws, all of which I was paying for, and all in the same determined effort to demonstrate to those who would be there the next day that this was a serious business exercise, not just some accompaniment to licentious pleasure, to all those people whose names in their little plastic containers lay beside the bottles – the Mayor and Mayoress; the representative from the local development agency; the bank manager who gave Lennie a loan, and who would call it back later in so much less friendly a fashion; the accountant whose biggest earner in the whole affair would be its bankruptcy; Sophie, invited as editor of the local paper, who'd just stick her head in because she was new to the job still and very busy; the reporter she sent called May (long since departed and now the traffic girl on local radio); the photographer who came with her, a newcomer to the paper called Danny; Peter, still with his long thin ponytail in those days, invited as the owner of Mumbo Jumbo on one side of the shop; Magda, from Hocus Pocus on the other side; my mother, who, being Banquo's ghost, as previously mentioned, if not invited would have turned up anyway; Tommy, who came with her; Cass and Fergie, who slipped out in their lunch time in a show of solidarity despite their huge reservations about a) the shop itself, and b) the whole relationship with Lennie; the boss of the firm that fitted out the shop rather more luxuriously (i.e., boutique style, stripped floor, fitted beech counter, subtle spotlighting) and at considerably more expense than I thought we'd agreed on; some 'suppliers' (several of whom I thought, even at the time, distinctly . . . well, *rakish*); Martin, he being the estate agent through whom Lennie got the premises (a connection that would come to haunt me); Fleur, who came with Martin even though I didn't ask her; my cousin Freddy, who by sheer bad luck was that year's president of the town's Chamber of Commerce – all of the last three, you might say, adding particular insult to injury as I acted the waitress, filling glasses, passing canapés, posing outside the shop with a glass of champagne in my hand next to Lennie, and all this with a fixed smile on my face, pretending everything was OK when there was a pain through my heart like an arrow.

'Don't ask me unless you really want to know,' he warned me after I'd come storming back into the shop late at night.

'I want to know,' but of course I didn't. I knew the answer. It glinted there, like Macbeth's dagger in the air.

'OK then. Right. I slept with her.'

She wasn't the first. I doubt she was the last. She was called Donna and she worked in office supplies. On my way over to Sophie's that night I'd seen her car with the firm's logo parked alongside Lennie's in the car park of a pub down on the moors. I probably knew what to expect when I parked, looked in the window. I'd seen her in the shop more times than I'd thought strictly necessary. Her handshake was limp when she was introduced to me and she slid her eyes away, making me suspicious.

I held out for a while after Donna. I said, 'As far as I'm concerned, we're just business partners now,' and he said, 'Sure. Whatever,' this with a shrug and a careless smile that said it didn't matter because we'd be back together before long, which is exactly what happened

All of this is why I'm not about to blame anyone but myself for the affair with Lennie, certainly not for the loss of the money. I conspired in my own fate. The gods couldn't have done more, after all, than toss that picture of his previous business failure off that shelf, or piled up the bills behind the door of his flat, which I'd watch him kick away carelessly every time we entered.

'But you have to pay your rates/tax the car/pay your credit card bills . . .' But he'd just give me that pitying look, which is the way the likes of Lennie will always look at rest of us, this to say that rules are for other people.

I paid his rates in the end, also some of his credit card bills, and this because it's a small town and I didn't want people talking. He didn't thank me for it when he found out. Instead he just gave me another of those mild pitying looks.

He said, 'Don't forget I didn't ask you to do it, Riley.'

It was beginning to dawn on me now – a dull grey dawn – that Lennie was a man willing to skirt around the law, not least from the things that seemed to 'appear' and logically were incompatible with his income: the designer suits and shirts and ties he wore, the BMW, the exceedingly upmarket apartment block where he lived and the Italian furniture scattered around it.

Then there were the incidentals, the ones that kept turning up: the mountain bike, the wide-screen TV and VCR and the Tag Heuer he threw carelessly at me one night, a beautiful thing, 18 carat gold, with a black lizard strap.

'I don't want it.'

'You said you needed a new watch.'

'Where did it come from?' I looked him square in the eye, saw the cold hard little shutter drop down in his own. The silence held as if neither of us wanted to give in and break it. He reached for the thing, tossed it in the air.

'I've got a friend.'

I've got a friend. Another of Lennie's favourite phrases.

Lennie had many friends, as it turned out. Mostly he met them, these *friends*, at pubs and clubs in the city. Sometimes we'd drive up together. I'd go shopping and then I'd meet him, finding myself in places I didn't want to be, in the company of people – mostly men – I didn't want to be with. They'd always treat me with exaggerated politeness, which was the worst of it, because I knew that behind their queasy smiles lay the truth of the thing: that being what they were they knew that Lennie was on to a good thing, that the affair was a boat that should not be rocked so the least they could do was play along with it.

The night Lennie tried to outrun the police I presumed it was because he was over the limit as he so often was when he drove back from meeting his friends. I heard the screech of his car first in the back lane and then the clatter of the helicopter. The next minute the back door banged and Lennie was beside me, pulling his shirt and sweater off in one over his head.

'We've been in all night,' he said, grabbing my hand.

Outside there was the sound of sirens, of braking. Behind the beam of light from the helicopter I could see the other flashing lights, the running figures, the panda cars with their doors open.

'We've been here together,' Lennie said, trying to pull me up the stairs, but I yanked my hand away sharply.

'That's the trouble,' I said. 'We haven't, Lennie.'

Because it was pretty much over by then anyway. The swan song had been a couple of days before, when I'd paid a surprise visit to his flat, an expensive thing in a barn conversion in the Mendips, with a grand view, halfway between us and the city. It was his birthday. I'd been intending to cook a meal, lay out his presents. I'd gone round to the shop to tell him, but only pimply Barry was there and, as usual, he had no knowledge of Lennie.

I still don't know who was in his bedroom that day. Maybe it was Donna or maybe it was a woman called Bryony, whose faintly insinuating message I once caught on the shop answer machine. As I let myself in, my hands full of bags, he appeared at the bedroom door in his bathrobe.

'Oh, good,' I said, dropping the bags of food in the hall, walking towards him, extending a hand, ready to curve it through the gap in the bathrobe around his waist. What a fool. Not even suspecting.

He caught me as I walked into him but it wasn't an embrace. He grasped at my hand too, as I made to push the bedroom door open. Still I didn't get it. His hand holding mine, I twirled in a circle as if we were jiving but he dropped my hand and raised it to the lintel of the door barring my way.

His voice was not unkind, I remember, just devoid of all identifiable feeling. He said, 'I wouldn't if I was you, Riley.'

Looking back now, I see how frail the affair was, how it was just a shadow of what an affair is supposed to be, how it was never more than a house of cards, held together more than anything else by the dope and the wine, the only miracle that it tottered on for the eighteen months it did. I felt it collapsing all around me as I watched the helicopter swoop away, and Lennie walk down the front path with the relaxed and amiable gait of those who operate on the edge of the law, the hand of the young policeman on his arm more of a formality than anything else and not remotely unfriendly.

That night, I rang Lennie at home any number of times but there was no reply. The next day at the shop the number just rang out without the answer machine firing. When I drove round I found it closed up with the iron security shutter down and bolted. There was no sign of Barry and a couple of days later I got the call from the bank manager.

In any half-decent novel he'd have been grave and elderly, that bank manager. He'd have stared at me severely over half-moon spectacles, but with a touch of pity in his eyes, this as I scrunched my reticule in my lap, preparing for a new and reduced life as a governess. Even at the time I knew how much better this would be than this thirty-something, with the picture of his family on the shelf behind him, and his squash racquet and bag beside him.

He said, 'It appears Mr O'Halloran has ceased trading,' and he gave me a firm false smile, one clearly designed to say that he hoped I saw that we were both sophisticated adults, that whereas certain things would need to be said they were merely formalities, and as long as I played my part it did not mean we could not be friends hereafter.

It had seemed such a small amount when I had first agreed to coguarantee the loan with Lennie. I could scarcely believe the figure when Mr Shower Fresh pushed the piece of paper towards me.

'Thank God, I'm only liable for half of it,' I said, which

was when he cleared his throat. Never a good sign, in my experience.

They couldn't get hold of Lennie, apparently, but it didn't matter. They weren't really looking.

'No assets. No assets at all?' (I think the phrase is 'echoed faintly'.) 'But his flat . . . the BMW . . . the shop . . . the stock . . .' About to be repossessed. The lot of it.

I went in search of Lennie after that. It was about all that was open to me. The shop was still locked up. It gave off a cold air of abandonment and when I phoned the number it just rang out unobtainable. There was no answer at his home and when I tried my key, I found the locks had been changed. I drove up to the city, faced out those men in those bars. They shook their heads when I asked for Lennie, and when the doors clashed behind me, I knew he could easily be there, hiding in the gents, and that he and they were probably laughing at me.

It was late one night at the shop that I finally caught him. The security blind was still down but when I biked along the lane I saw the ghost of small thin light beneath the back door. Further along, between some sheds, half-hidden, I saw the BMW. The back door of the shop was bolted from the inside, but there was a toilet at the back, and the window which I'd once climbed through when we'd left the shop keys inside was open. Now I did the same, hoisting myself up in my Ron Hills from the seat of the Hopper.

Lennie was standing behind his desk when I pushed open the door to the showroom. He was pulling out drawers, taking things out, papers, a calculator, pens, throwing them into his briefcase. He looked up briefly as I entered, stopped for a moment, before resuming.

Staring down into the briefcase, he said, 'So, Riley.'

I said, 'What are you doing?'

He said, 'I'm leaving, Riley.'

I put a hand to my head then. It was like the words didn't make sense.

'Leaving? But where are you going?'

'You don't want to know, Riley.'

'But you can't just . . . be going.' I could hear the desperation in my voice. 'You can't walk out on me. Leave me to pay everything.'

'I can't help you.' He said it sharply and now he looked at me. 'I'm sorry, Riley.'

The word didn't seem to make sense to me. I repeated like I was trying to learn a new and difficult language, '*Sorry?*'

'I've got no assets. The bank will have told you.'

'Sure, but the business . . . the lease . . . the stock . . .' And that's when I looked around, saw there was no stock, just empty boxes.

'Where's the stock? Where's all the stock?' But now it was dawning on me.

'The suppliers. They took it back.' It was a joke, a wicked joke, and we both knew it.

'You've cleaned it out. You've cleaned the place out.' I advanced on him, fists in the air. I was crying. 'You bastard. You wouldn't even allow me that. You selfish bastard . . .'

I flung myself at him then, pummelling his chest with my fists. He grabbed hold of them, hurling me violently aside where I went limp, slumping against the desk and on to the floor where I sat for a moment getting my breath back.

'Have . . . you . . . no . . . *shame?*' I said very slowly. The word 'shame' seemed to catch him unawares. A frown creased his brow as he stared into the air.

'No. I guess not, Riley.' He paused as if further considering it. 'Guess I've never had any use for it.'

He picked up his filofax, tossed it into the briefcase, snapped it closed.

'Look It's a lot of money. I'm sorry,' but his voice had taken on a faintly bored tone. Perhaps that's what did it.

I guess if it had succeeded they'd have called what followed a crime of passion, except that it didn't feel like that. It didn't feel remotely passionate. Instead it felt ice cold, like what was done was done in cold blood, in blood as cold as his own. It seemed like there never was a clearer calmer moment in my head. Ten years on I can still feel it and it scares me. All I knew was that more than anything else in the world, and this quite regardless of the consequences, I didn't want this man walking around on the planet.

From where I sat, slumped on the floor, I could see the paper knife on the desk, another birthday present, steel, with a blade like a stiletto, which glinted beneath the spotlights.

'Where you going?'

'I've already told you. It wouldn't help to know, Riley.'

That was when I jumped up, grabbed the paper knife, leapt at him a second time. I remember the action of my arm, the way I jabbed at him. Stab, stab, stab. Like Anthony Perkins in the shower scene in *Psycho*. He was wearing a leather jacket, antique leather. I'd bought it for his birthday. I hacked away at it, first the sleeve, then the front of it, but the leather was hard and it wouldn't penetrate. He managed to grab my wrist, began pushing me back. Wrestling, we got free of the desk, crashed against a filing cabinet and then fell to the floor where we rolled around for what seemed a long time, heaving and grunting.

I could never have won. Frail he might be but he was still larger than me. I thought maybe his lifestyle would have weakened him, all that smoking and drinking. But

I'd forgotten that he was wiry too. He won easily in the end, getting on top of me, forcing my hands back on to the floor either side of my head, prising the paperknife from my grasp and hurling it across the floor, where it bounced and skittered, ending up under a display cabinet. For a moment he stared down at me still holding my wrists back on the floor.

He said, 'I know what I am, but so did you. If you wanted to make me something else, that's your business.'

He got up from the floor, brushed his hands together as if dusting off the argument. As I lay there, too exhausted to move, he lifted his briefcase from across the desk and walked to the door. There he stopped, stood still for a moment.

He said, 'You can't say I lied to you, Riley.'

He turned, glanced at me one last time and I remember thinking that he had never looked better. He looked so good, goddamit; like an actor playing the scene. Although as far as I could see he wasn't playing it quite right, because there wasn't a shadow of shame or guilt in those liquid brown eyes, and that familiar slight frown that pulled in his eyebrows was only of irritation. The full dark lips curled a little in a purse of dismissal as he shrugged his shoulders.

He said, 'I never made any secret of anything. You had what you had. You knew what I was, Riley.'

I found out about the mobile phone scam from Denis, about the way Lennie's boot had been full of them when he'd tried to outrun the helicopter.

I'd been out for a ride on the bike and I came back to find Denis standing on the doorstep. He was perfectly polite. He said, 'We think Lennie may have been receiving stolen goods. Nice bike, by the way. Not by any chance a Hopper?'

As he left he said, 'You'll let us know if you hear from him?'

I said, 'Trust me. It isn't likely.'

At the Fraser family party, a few weeks later, Martin buttonholed me in a corner, complained because Lennie had left owing three months' rent.

He said, 'I'm not very happy about that, Riley, I mean, I wouldn't have rented to him if there hadn't been a family connection.'

I said, 'Oh, please. You're an estate agent, Martin. You'd have rented to Hitler if it'd suited you.'

Later Fleur's pearly little teeth did one of those sharp little tch-tch-tching sounds, jumping up and down like a plastic joke pair on a table. She said, 'I don't know, Riley. Fancy signing something without reading the small print.' This from a woman whose only experience of anything less than twelve point was on the back of her Christian Dior moisturiser.

I said, 'That's why it's small, so you won't read it. Geddit?'

It was a bummer losing all that money, that's for sure. I ended up remortgaging the cottage to pay off the bank. Ten years on, the ripples can still be felt in my finances.

It's been a learning curve, though, going over the whole thing. I think I can see now why it happened – that wham bam sexual attraction, for a start, something I guess I haven't liked to acknowledge. There's also the fact of wanting to make him happy. More than that, though, more than both of these things, I think I was caught unawares by Lennie. I think he sneaked through the net of my philo-phobia. Because I think I was afraid of falling in love. I had that honourable fear of hurting people. I knew I never could hurt Lennie, I knew that from the start. I relaxed my guard. I thought I was safe. And I fell, hook, line and sinker.

Still one question remains, the most important one, spinster that I am: does Lennie O'Halloran qualify as an Unsuitable Liaison? I'd say that depends on the way you look at it. If I'd been in search of long-term relationship material, then the answer would be yes, no question. But for an old dyed-in-the-wool spinster with a severe case of gamophobia, I'd say he was entirely appropriate.

One thing's for sure, I got my comeuppance with Lennie. In terms of pure self-interest (always a danger for a self-centred spinster like myself) I got to work with a true professional. And in those moments when I'm ranting about how I hate finding things to do in relationships (yes, yes, folks, I know that I do), it's good to remember that once upon a time in that narrow, circumscribed *curry and video* existence, I'd have loved to have taken off one Sunday afternoon to some stately home, sat in the coffee shop over a bad cappuccino.

Looking back on it all now, I'd say the only thing I regret (OK so, big deal, I've used the word 'regret') is the good time I wasted back in my forties getting over Lennie (forties are good; moral, don't waste them). Still it's a sound lesson to learn. The big rule in this regard. Whatever it is, move On. Get Over It.

'I don't know where Lennie is,' I said to Denis that first night we met, 'and, trust me, that's the way I like it.'

Later, after he got called away, and Sophie and I were alone, I said, 'You know I see now, it was only pride. That's what took me so long to get over Lennie.'

She shook her head. She said, 'There's no such thing as *only* pride, Riley.'

271

V is for . . . Values (i.e., Family)

OK. First the facts of the case.

In order to keep a population static, i.e., prevent it from decreasing, it requires a procreation figure of 2.1 children per woman.

Across Europe at the moment the figure is a mere 1.5.*

A hearty hollow laugh it would appear is due to those olive oil and pasta ads featuring football-pitch-length dining tables with bambinos crawling all over them. In fact Mama Italy is only procreating at the rate of 1.25, neck and necking with Germany on the same figure (the sound you hear is the crumbling remains of Joe Goebbels turning in his grave). Spain is even lower at 1.22. Greece nudges slightly ahead but only just at 1.30. The UK comes in at 1.63, with Denmark, the only country with a figure on the rise, at 1.74. Long-time leader, Catholic Mother Ireland, is now in second place with 1.88 (and you might like to compare this with her sixties figure of 3.5) while Top of the Moms and Pops is France at 1.89, a slender victory certainly, but still

---

* Figures from Eurostat.

a cause for great jubilation when the figures were released.

Neither is the problem confined to Europe. In countries as diverse as North Korea, the Czech Republic, Singapore, Colombia, Bangladesh and Australia women appear to be refusing to lie back and think of population replacement.*

With regard to the scenario that started this chapter, the upshot of all the above is that, theoretically, if things continue as they're going, within a couple of hundred years the population of the European Union will have dropped from 375 million to 75 million, while come the third millennium a scant 50,000 of us will be scattered across the continent.

Still, as I say to my mother, at least parking will be a lot easier.

'And hey, you'll have a much better chance of winning the lottery.'

But my mother is not listening. I know the look on her face. The eyes glazed with fake memory as she stares at me over the top of the paper with its traditional End of the World As We Know It in 72 point, this time proclaiming:

THE END OF THE FAMILY

Around her mouth, which is skewed sideways as she clicks her teeth, there's a look of what I can only describe as utterly satisfied dissatisfaction, one that would please the powers that be who produce the paper, could they but see how they've hit pay dirt with my mother this morning.

'If I'd been like that.'

---

* Clearly, in the case of Australia, an opportunity to revive that old spinster deportation plan.

'Like what, Mother?'

'I could have been happy with just your sister, you know?'

This is a rhetorical question. It does not require an answer. For now Babs Gordon has her saintly Mother Theresa look about her. Were her hands not at this very moment folding up that newspaper and laying it aside with customary reverence on the kitchen table, they would almost certainly be folded nun-like in her lap.

'But then, of course, in those days it was different. In those days you were *supposed* to have two. In those days they said having just the one was bad for them.'

The most surprising thing is the bile in my mother's voice. It glugs up like dirty water in a blocked sink. The suppressed snarl plumps out her cheekbones. But then we've heard it before.

'Hey . . .' because Cass has just slid in the back door with my mother's dry cleaning, 'Mommy Dearest is about to rewrite history.'

'Oh, good.'

'You can laugh but I was always *there* for the pair of you.'

'*There* for us?' I hoot over the words. 'Jesus, Mother, you've been watching too much daytime television.'

It's at this point I always think it might be true what my mother says about me. Maybe I do get any talent for fiction I possess from her because for certain she has a rich imagination. Like now, for instance, when I can see by the look on her face that she has a vision of herself, the perfect hausfrau in a mythical world, with gingham curtains at the windows and a pan on the boil and a scrubbed pine table covered with bottles as she makes jams and chutneys for the family.

'I always had a proper meal on the table for you.'

'You're kidding. You turned me into a Vesta Paella junkie.'*

'You said you liked it.'

'Not five times a week.'

See, you have to understand my mother doesn't lie. It's like I said: she simply redraws history and, make no mistake, she believes it.

'There's a lot you wouldn't have had if it wasn't for me.'

She's by the fireside now. In her mind, she's rocking in a chair, grey-haired and with a sock and one of those mushroom things. Dear God, she's *darning*.

'I made all your clothes.'

Not true. Thank God. Although she did try. And there wasn't an armhole that didn't sag, or a buttonhole that closed or a skirt without a hem that waved like the ocean.

'What did she do, actually?' I look around from the wheel with furrowed brow at Cass as we pull away from my mother's front gate. 'Can you remember? I mean, what did she do with her time?'

'She shopped.'

'Oh, yeah. Of course. How soon do we forget?'

Even in the early days, in the fifties, in our one-horse town where it was like the Marshall Plan never happened, still our mother managed to come home with carrier bags of all shapes and sizes. Gloves she didn't need. Scarves she'd never wear. She was forever buying bric-a-brac, vases, pictures, obscure kitchen implements.

'And handicrafts.'

'Oh God, yes.'

'Rug making.'

'Tufts of wool all over the house.'

---

* This is true. Sometimes, still, I wake up in the middle of the night and have to get up and drive out to the all-night garage to score one.

'And ikebana.'

'Bits of branches everywhere.'

'Oh, that stuff with nails and pieces of wire she made into pictures we had to hang in our bedrooms.'

Once – I must have been about twelve – in the middle of one of their rows, I saw my father sweep an arm across the surface of the sideboard. There was the sound of tinkling clinking china as a dozen tiny ornaments and knick-knacks fell to the floor.

'All this *junk*,' he shouted.

The action, the voice, were full of such viciousness that I cowered behind the kitchen door. Through the crack where the door joined the wall I saw my mother's face pucker up – the only time I ever remember seeing her cry. All the hopelessness was in it, all the misery of what they were. I saw my father's shoulders, which had risen high up to his ears with his fury, drop. He seemed to deflate. When he spoke again it was not tender exactly, but weary and sorrowful.

He said, 'It's all right. Don't worry. I'm sorry.' He said, 'It doesn't matter. Don't cry, Barbara . . .'

Declaring his (reluctant) love for Beatrice, Benedick (thinking woman's tottie, if ever one existed) proclaimed: 'The world must be peopled.' However, as is clear from the figures in my mother's morning newspaper, in certain parts of the world, most notably our own, it isn't being.

'I'm not a bit surprised.' This from Cass as she scrabbles in the medicine cabinet after yet another argument with her daughter over the matter of her attending an all-night party. 'Have you any idea how the sales of Neurofen would plummet if people stopped having children?'

In fact, that's exactly what's happening. Not only are

couples choosing to make do with one child, a number of them – the Dinkies and Thinkers* of this world – are dispensing with the idea altogether.

'Shallow and hedonistic' my mother's leader writer calls them, singling out for particular reprobation the one in four women now prepared to say outright that they don't want children. 'Playing games with their fertility', 'Defying their biological destiny', 'Condemning themselves to remain unfulfilled as women . . .'

'Very sensible,' according to the wife and mother now lying on the sofa, hand to her forehead in a vain attempt to counteract the sound of Elsa's music thumping accusingly down through the ceiling.

We thought we were trailblazers, didn't we, we, the peace-and-love generation? We thought we were turning the world upside down but as it turns out, in terms of procreation, we were wildly conventional (clearly I'm using the generic *we* here). A full ninety per cent of us had become parents by thirty, this as opposed to the 1970 generation coming along behind us and turning thirty at the millennium, only fifty-two per cent of whom have so far done the decent thing and continued the species.

To the leader writer's obvious delight, the outlook for these women isn't that good in terms of procreation. Two-thirds of those who leave it until forty to become pregnant won't be able to do so naturally, and the odds drop right down to a three to five per cent chance for those who postpone it few years further.

'Thinking science can solve everything . . .'

What's clear from all this – and hence the wrath of my

---

* Dinkies – Double Income No Kids; Thinkers – Two Healthy Incomes No Kids. Early Retirement.

mother's paper – is that the establishment of the nuclear family (or the 'normal' family, as the paper prefers to call it) is no longer the aim of an increasing section of society, something that begs the question, why, since this is the case, should the words 'the Family' continue to be repeated in hushed tones, and in the manner of received wisdom, by Left and Right alike along with the concomitant mantra 'family values'. Why, to put it more bluntly, when forty per cent of households in this country will soon be made up of single people, should the 'the family' continue to be referred to unceasingly as 'the backbone of the country?'*

In the not-too-distant future, half the households in the country will be single ones. And when they are, will we still be attracting that same palpable lack of interest from the politicians? Will it still be the case, as it is today, that only the mythical, iconographic 'Family' will be courted, that not one of these politicians will be considering us worthy of targeting or even tailoring his or her language to. And if it is, will it just be our own fault?

Because according to a recent voting survey in the States – where, incidentally, the fifty per cent single household figure has already arrived – single women are some twenty per cent less likely to vote than their married sisters.† They don't vote, according to the survey, because without children in school, or such things like joint retirement plans

---

* And a memo to the Labour Party here: waffling on about 'new family structures' disguises the same old prejudices not one iota.

† Not only do married women vote more, according to the poll, but they also vote the way their husbands do, which is likely to be Republican. Single women, by contrast, are more likely to vote Democrat, thus had the twenty per cent or so of single women who didn't vote in the 2000 election done so, George Bush would not have 'won' the presidency.

to consider, they see themselves as having a much less vested interest in society.

Which is crazy. Utterly paradoxical. Because the fact that single people use less of society's resources, e.g., schools, health service, etc., and pay proportionately more for everything, should be the very reason *why* they need to make their voice heard, *why* they should be voting.

While this may as yet not have got through to the singles across the water, it certainly has to all those Dinkies and Thinkers. Pressure groups are already up and running in the States and Canada to fight for tax breaks for child-free couples, plus the right not to be forced to admire little Johnny's painting or listen to Miranda piping 'Frère Jacques' on the recorder.

'There is something inextricably selfish about the decision not to have children,' according to the leader writer in my mother's paper.

'Quite right,' according to my mother, as she slapped down her paper. 'Supposing I'd been that selfish. Put it off. Had just the one. Maybe not even bothered at all . . .' She looked at me triumphantly with the face of a woman who'd won the argument. 'Well . . .'

'Well, what?'

'Well . . . you wouldn't even be here, would you?'

Now, no argument with my mother is easy. It's like playing tennis with someone so bad they keep hitting off the wood, or else they do those little shots that crawl over the net, quite by accident and always when you've already turned your back and are walking back to the base line. Even a relatively simple question, for instance, whether the monarchy should be abolished, can lead you into uncharted waters.

'You should be glad we're lucky enough to have all this

279

tradition. I mean the Queen . . .'

'Gawd bless her . . .'

'Yes, you may mock, *Adeline*. But remember, the Queen *still wears gloves*.'

Imagine, then, trying to debate with her the metaphysical question of my not actually existing.

Because it's an interesting argument, this one, whether those who don't have children can be accused of being selfish. It's one I've never quite got my head round although I've developed a permanent crick in my neck from trying.

The definition of selfish is 'chiefly concerned with one's own interest, advantage, etc., especially to the total exclusion of the interests of others'. Thus logically you can't be selfish in a vacuum. You have to be selfish towards someone, and in broad terms (always a good phrase) you'd think the child-free were home and dry on this one. I mean, how can those who don't claim maternity and paternity leave or child benefits, only use the education system themselves and one seat in the doctor's surgery be deemed selfish towards others in society?

In fact, that old leader writer is on pretty shaky ground with the argument that we, the childfree, are selfish. In a recent survey carried out by a couple of psychologists[*] to determine the most common reasons for having and not having children (reported in my decent, even-handed liberal-leaning paper, but surprise, surprise not in my mothers), those who decided against came up smelling of roses compared to those who went ahead, this in terms of sheer egocentricity. Against all the odds, of the thirteen reasons given for not having children, only *five* were judged to be selfish: for example, financial and career considerations,

---

[*] Rathus and Nevid, 1992.

the desire to have time and freedom to spend with a partner; the rest – worries about the world, the community and the child who would be born into it – were deemed positively altruistic. By contrast, *eight* of the nine reasons given for having children were considered selfish, all of them being concerned with the personal pleasure to be gained from having children, the fun and joy of raising them, the close bond they would provide and the status and power opportunity they would bring with them.

I suppose you could say that those who don't procreate are selfish in terms of the species, but this'll only stick if you can show that concern about the future of the species is the reason most people have children, which frankly I doubt. Merely wanting to pass on your genes – Number 3 in the list of Most Common Reason For Wanting To Have Children – doesn't qualify, certainly not when it comes from Cousin Royston.

'Couldn't think of going to my grave without leaving a little chip off the old block,' he said at the last Fraser party.

As if on cue, Charlie, riding high on his shoulders, poked his tongue out at me and, lifting his pudgy little hands from his father's forehead, made what I deduced to be an early attempt at a V sign.

'Oh, I think I could have learnt to live with it,' I said.

So what are we left with here as regards the argument for selfishness? As far as I can make out, only the unborn child. Can he or she be the victim of the desire not to give birth? It's hard to see how. For instance, if my mother had not had me, why or how could she be accused of selfishness? The only person to so accuse her would be me. But I wouldn't *be*. So how could I do it? How could I so accuse her? On grounds of logic or any other? How could she possibly be guilty of selfishness towards something that didn't exist? In any sense of the word. That was simply . . . well . . . *not*. Not merely unconceived, but never going to be. Not even a glint in her eye.

'It was your father.'

'Sorry?' She'd broken in on my metaphysical musings.

'Your father. He wanted you. The both of you. He said I'd be "selfish" not to do it.'

And so it happens. The sins of the father. Or is it the non-mothers? What goes around, comes around and all other assorted clichés.

'Don't be so fucking *selfish*.' I remember how he said it. One last desperate throw.

'Selfish? Jesus! How dare you? Selfish.' I was outraged. 'The last refuge . . .'

'The last refuge of what?' He snapped it back at me but I couldn't think of *what*. I had no answer for him.

He said, 'Look. Please . . .' staring fixedly into his hands linked between his knees. 'Please. I'm asking you. For both our sakes . . . Just think about it, Riley.'*

---

* Was this, the whole thing about selfishness, what I wanted to discuss with David?

W *is for ... Weddings*

I had a dream once I was getting married.

It was one of those frantic ones, you know the sort, where you run around in a terrible state trying to get people's attention but no one will help or even notice you. I was in London, I don't know why. I don't even know London. I was dressed in one of those big white candyfloss wedding dresses, trying to get to the ceremony, but I didn't know where it was being held, probably the reason why taxi drivers kept refusing to take me. In the end I decided to go by tube. I ran to the station hoicking up my skirts as I went. There were a lot of people jostling and pushing around the entrance. I picked up the skirt to go down the steps, which is when I noticed the state of it – not white any longer but with a wide band of dirt around the hem.

'And . . . ?'

'And what?'

'What happened?'

'I woke up.'

'Oh, right.' Danny got up from the chair beside my desk.

'Probably no need to check with Sigmund about that one then.'

In fact, according to Freud, dreaming about weddings doesn't have much to do with getting married. It's more likely to presage money or health worries.[*] Meanwhile, Magda, who tells dreams on the strength of a Romany grandmother[†] claims it's bad news to dream about a wedding although only if you're the bride or the groom. Dream you're a guest and there's good news in store, which just goes to show that in dreams, as in real life, the only safe way to attend a wedding is when other people are getting married.

Wednesdays is Weddings Day at the *Free Press*. And it's a nice irony, all things considered, that it's this confirmed spinster who on Wednesdays becomes the very patron saint of weddings. On Wednesdays I take the pile of wedding forms from the tray, dump them on my desk and thereafter attempt to winkle out the odd original feature from the homogeneous accounts of strapless gowns and hand-tied bouquets and white Rolls Royces. As in: 'Bride Arrives in Horse Drawn Carriage ...', 'Couple Met at School ...', 'Best Man Flew from Canada ...'.

On Wednesdays I think I understand weddings. I think I know the reason why people do it.

'It's the Andy Warhol thing, isn't it?' I said to Danny

---

[*] He does mention in passing the possibility of it indicating a source of resentment or friction surrounding a relationship, something that might be worth considering if you do actually dream it the night before your wedding.

[†] In the event of you being lured into Hocus Pocus by the 'Dreams Told' postcard in the window, it is worth noting that one of Magda's grandmothers was married to a plumber in Acton while the other worked her entire life here in our Woolworths. Neither, to my certain knowledge, ever even saw the inside of a gypsy caravan.

one day. 'The fifteen minutes of fame. A day when you're the most important person.'

Once upon a time, back in the mid-sixties when I started on this paper, ninety-five per cent of weddings were in church – Catholic, Anglican, Congregational, Methodist, Baptist. Register office weddings were rare then, even had a whiff of the risqué about them. Now less than half are in churches, the rest in the register office, or in other, more exotic, locations – a palm-fringed beach, the grounds of a grand country house, or in a glittery Las Vegas wedding chapel.

'See, now that would be good for you, Magda,' I said, holding up last week's paper with the picture of the local couple smiling either side of the 'minister' – in this case a white-suited, jewel-encrusted Elvis impersonator. I mean, why have some boring old wedding? Come to think of it,' for then it struck me, 'why bother at all? Why not just elope? How romantic. Just the one of you . . .'

Magda sighed. 'I see you're *ab-so-lut-ely* determined to go on mocking, Riley.'

There are a number of basic legal requirements as regards getting married in England. (Our aim with this book, as previously mentioned, is ever to inform. Thus what follows could be useful if you're thinking of doing it.) Both partners must be of a sound mind (a law more honoured in the breach than the observance, and not just all those years ago with Royston and Sandra). Both partners must be acting by their own consent and one – still – must be born male and one female. (Despite Magda's groundbreaking work, those dreary old traditionalists up there in the Ministry of Marriage are still insisting there should be two of you.) If you marry in any place other than a church where the officiating clergyman is entitled to register your marriage, which means pretty much anywhere outside the Church of England, you'll need an official to register the marriage and it'll cost you, all of which goes to show that marriage is essentially the business of the state, a relatively modern interpretation. Up until the Middle Ages, for instance, marriages were considered merely family affairs, of little concern to anyone but the couple involved and/or their nearest and dearest. More often than not, in the case of the wealthy, it was the families who got together to draw up the nuptial arrangements; the bride didn't even need to be there.

'That would have suited you,' Danny said, dusting the crumbs of Magda's prize-winning chocolate cake off his fingers.

So true . . . so true.

So many things I could have done in life – marriage . . . childbirth . . . if only I didn't have to be present.

Magda was studying the stuff she'd pulled from the Internet the day Danny and I went in for our chocolate cake. Scattered around the Hocus Pocus table were sheets on Celtic weddings, medieval weddings, Victorian, Edwardian, thirties, forties, Greek, Inca, Egyptian, etc., etc.

'What do you think? Roman?'

'Good choice. Going back to your roots.'

She gave me a sharp look. 'It's a big day for me, Riley. I want to get it right. It's not every day you get married.'

'Particularly to yourself.' But luckily she'd gone off to serve a customer.

The official mourning period now being over for Mervyn – 'I think he'd understand. I think he'd want it' – Magda had now got around to planning the wedding.

According to the plan, the bridesmaids will form up outside the house with their flares.

Meanwhile, Magda will perform the ancient ceremony of laying her toys on the family shrine before the house god.

'Umm . . . toys . . . family shrine . . . house god?'

'It's just symbolic, Riley.'

'Still, it's a while since you cleared out your toy cupboard.'

'What about a sex toy?' Danny's face is bright with innocent suggestion.

'Good thinking, Danny. Or . . . I know . . . how about a packet of condoms? That would be symbolic.'

'Specially if they were past their use-by date.'

'Thank *you*.' Magda's look was severe. 'It's supposed to be a pagan rite, not a bloody Harvest Festival.'

For the ceremony the bride will wear a long white gown and saffron veil . . .

'With, I thought, a narrow plain silver band across my forehead.'

'Matching silver sandals?' (I've been doing the wedding pages too long.)

'No, barefoot.'

'Barefoot? Walking up the Tor. With all the glass around. Are you mad?'

But Magda's leaning forward in the manner of a woman conveying a terrible secret. 'Shoes,' she says, looking over her shoulder,' are *patriarchal*.'

OK, a few more things you probably don't know about weddings. First, that old tradition of tying old shoes on the bumpers of the bride and groom's car (something I recall Archie doing – well, wouldn't he? – at Cass and

Fergie's wedding) has seriously unpleasant origins. It comes from the days when the bride would symbolically take off a shoe and hand it to the bridegroom, who would then hit her over the head to show who, a tad more than metaphorically, would be wearing the trousers. Also there's the office of best man. All he has to do today is get the bridegroom up out of bed, keep the ring safe and tell risqué jokes at the reception. Once upon a time though, when a bride could be seized against her will, it was his job to help the bridegroom with the abduction.[*]

Still the good news, as I said to Magda, was that at least she wouldn't need a best man. 'And I'm sure you won't be wanting any of that patriarchal being-given-away stuff either.' But as always with Magda, it wasn't that simple.

This became clear when, even as we spoke, Rochelle appeared in the back of the shop, sliding in like a little black lizard against the wall but still not silent or slippery enough to evade her mother.

'Darling.' Magda jumped up, receiving her customary filial look of loathing. 'I've got something to ask you. A special favour. Something very important to me.' Her voice became wheedling, almost flirtatious. 'You will give me away at my wedding, won't you, darling?' She'd advanced on Rochelle, holding out her hands, trying to catch Rochelle's own.

The scorn was stamped on Rochelle's face like an emblem, like the pair of crossed daggers on her arm, or a hammer and sickle.

---

[*] Neither are bridesmaids entirely innocent in this respect. Veiled and dressed in the same manner as the bride, they were designed to confuse mercenaries sent by the bride's family to rescue her. Yet another reason to be glad my bridesmaid days are over.

'Yeah . . . right . . . OK . . . like . . . duuuuh . . .' She clicked her tongue and raised her eyes. 'I mean . . . like . . . that is sooooo likely, isn't it?'

I said, 'I think we have to take that as a No, Magda.'

In my opinion most weddings are the wrong food with the wrong drink at the wrong time of day, with the wrong people. And given my bridesmaid career I feel I can speak knowledgeably on the subject. I also have considerable sympathy with Magda over the whole patriarchal thing. Because for myself I've always felt there is something vaguely sacrificial about weddings, something more than a little tribal. Tapping away at my keyboard on Weddings Day at the *Free Press*, transcribing the forms and staring at the photographs, nothing about the habit, not even the glitter of a Las Vegas wedding chapel, can stop it seeming to be inextricably primeval. I stare at the forms, at the pictures, and I wonder. Simply that. I wonder how it was that I never wanted any of this, and I know it was more than simply not wanting it. I can still feel a shiver down to the very base of my soul at the thought of having to pronounce those vows, secular or otherwise, before a roomful of people.

'It's such an intimate thing to do,' I said to Cass. 'Honestly, I don't know why anyone should want to do it in front of other people.'

She was at the sink with her back to me and there appeared to be no reaction.

I said, 'You know, I look at those wedding pictures at work and I think there's something almost, I don't know, sadomasochistic about it, women parading up the aisle in those white dresses—'

'It's not about you.' She hadn't turned (never a good sign) and there was a sharpness in her tone.

'Sorry?'

'You think everything's about you.'

'Hey . . .'

'No. You do.' Now she turned and was facing me, hands on hips. 'I've heard all this stuff from you about weddings a hundred times before. Well, who cares if *you* don't like a wedding, if *you* don't enjoy it, if you think they're crap? It's not for you. It's for the people who are getting married.'

'OK, OK . . .' I was surprised at her vehemence but I wasn't about to give in. 'Still, you have to admit, Magda's got a point. Weddings do have patriarchal overtones. I mean, that whole stuff about the bride being *given away* . . .'

'I'm sure it is. I'm sure it's totally unsound and no one in their right mind would still do it.' Her voice had chips of ice in it now. 'However, all I can say is that the way I remember it, giving me away that day brought Dad one hell of a lot of pleasure.'

If our father's death still affects us, Cass and me, all these years on, then I guess it's not surprising. Running off the road on that bend, albeit on a grimy day with a wet surface, could still have been him taking the law into his own hands. It was, after all, a bend he knew well. And the cancer had already been diagnosed. Almost thirty years on we still pick at it like a scab, talk about it in awkward half-phrases.

'If the car hit a skid . . .'

'If he felt it go . . .'

'Perhaps he thought . . .'

'Yeah.'

Which is the point where we pretty much decide to go no further.

The coroner pronounced it accidental death anyway, coupling this with a glare at the lawyer who'd been sent by the insurance company. And if the coroner just happened to be a drinking buddy of my mother's at the Conservative Club, well, who's to say that this affected his decision? A man who liked his tipple, with a large red nose to show for it, he patted her hand that night at the bar and said, 'Sad business, Barbara, but the way I see it, you're a fine-looking woman. You'll marry again.' All of which, I can assure you, took away the sting for her. The only thing that would have improved the situation was if he'd dropped down off the bar stool on to one knee there and then and proposed to her

Our father put on a fine show of unconcern over the cancer in those last weeks.

'At least I'll get away from your mother.'

Had things been different, I'm sure that Cass and Fergie would have crawled off to a register office. Both hate any sort of fuss. Neither, I'm sure, would have favoured a big white wedding but they did it for our father.

We almost forgot the cancer that day. And Cass is right about it being a great day for Dad. He beamed, bringing her up that aisle, so much it almost took the grey in his face away. When the vicar asked that thing about who was giving Cass to be wed, Dad wiped away a tear as he said, 'I do.' Later, at the reception he was nothing but merry and you wouldn't have been aware there was anything wrong with him. For myself, I felt utterly unreal and jagged that day, like I'd been the subject of some timeshift and had lost my bearings.

I'd been away almost four years by the time I returned

from my travels. My arrival in Hong Kong had been a chill, inauspicious start, but it was as I had known that night, thinking about Nathan. Things got better, and from the following morning. In the end I stayed three years there, working on the colony's English language newspaper. I was in Zamboanga, a paradise at the southern tip of the Philippines, when I picked up Cass's letter breaking the news about our father's cancer and that she and Fergie were getting married. 'Come home as soon as you can,' she wrote. 'I need you.' But to my shame I didn't. Instead I travelled on for another month, pretending I hadn't yet got the letter, the only reason I can give being the obvious one that I didn't want to go home. In the end I arrived with only a week to spare before the wedding, by the miracle of modern travel, in not much more than the space of a day, exchanging a solitary dope-swamped beach for a cold-turkey small-town homecoming. The day after I got back, I sat shivering on the seat opposite the abbey, watching the old green buses dragging up the High Street, listening to the small-town bustle and feeling all this to be more foreign and strange than anything I had experienced on my travels. I felt disjointed, physically and mentally, as though my life was in pieces, none of which fitted together. And that was how it was when I walked up the aisle behind Cass and my father, and when I listened to him making that speech, listened because I couldn't even raise my head from the table to look at him, standing there so firm and tall, and despite that greyness apparent around his eyes, I felt some terrible pain, some hurt inside that I wanted to push down, to run far away from. At the same time I also felt unreasonably angry and resentful. I wanted to be back lying on a beach somewhere with none of this happening, with no need to care or hurt like this. For all these reasons

I drank, heavily, shared a joint too, out back of the hotel, with an accommodating waiter. And for all these reasons, and in this frame of mind, I ended up in bed with Archie.

There's no sensible answer to why I went to bed with Archie. Just the simplest one. Because he was there. Because that's what we did then. Because of the way I was feeling.

I went to bed with Archie because I was drunk and I didn't care about anything that night. In particular I didn't care whether I went to bed with him or not, and in the end, just by chance, I did. I have a vague recollection of a drunken stagger up the wide balustraded hotel stairs, of some noisy grappling at the door of his room and after that some of the same but this time in the darkened bedroom. That I remember nothing about the sex doesn't surprise me. Like I said before, in my experience sex is something that doesn't seem to stay in the memory, particularly sex with people you don't like, which was the way it was with Archie.

Still Archie professed to enjoy it.

'Hey, Riley, let me tell you, you do a bloody good—'

'Shut up. I don't want to hear it.'

If I had to choose the nadir of my life, I tell you, I'd pick that moment, that scrabbling together of the pieces from the night before, the underwear, the Biba bridesmaid's dress, the contents of a handbag. And all this under the stern gaze of a grey dawn leaking in through the crack in the hotel curtains.

'Come back to bed.'

'No.' He had reached for me. 'Leave it.' I slapped his hand away.

'What's the matter?'

'Everything's the matter.'

'What?'

'Everything.'

I was reaching back over my head, trying to pull up the zip of the dress, which had slipped down over my naked shoulders.

'Allow me.' His own tone had cooled. Before I could stop him he had thrown back the sheets, revealing his nakedness. The sight of it fuelled my growing unreasonable indecipherable anger.

'*No.*'

I concentrated on pushing my feet into the mulberry satin shoes, first so I wouldn't have to face him, second to try and master the trembling fury.

'Look. We need to be very clear about something here. This . . . thing. This whole thing. It was a mistake. I shouldn't be here. It should never have happened.'

'Well, well, well . . .' He thumped a pillow hard, lifted it and dropped it against the bed head behind him, leant back luxuriously against it, staring at me. He crossed his arms slowly. To me his face was mocking and smirky. 'Who would believe it? That there we were, last night, having such a good time. Making love—'

'Oh, for God's sake.' I advanced on him with the violence of the words. 'We weren't making love, Archie. We had sex. We were *screwing*.' I was filled with a rush of disgust as I stared at him, the arms still sticklike and boyish, folded over the thin freckled chest. I said, 'It was nothing. It didn't mean anything.' I was at the door by then.

Behind me he said, 'So what happens now?'

I didn't even bother to turn. I said, 'Absolutely nothing happens now, Archie.' But, of course, I was wrong.

*   *   *

294

It was Sophie who said I should tell Archie. Sophie. Surprising me.

'Why? I don't need him.' And I didn't. She'd already offered, unasked – if I wanted it – to lend me the money.

I was staying with Sophie by then, in Bristol, where she was working on the evening paper. I signed up with her doctor, which made the whole thing easier.

He said, 'There are some questions, by law, I have to ask you.'

He was in his thirties with the air of a family man about him, not unsympathetic, merely brisk and businesslike as if he'd thought the thing through and knew this was the best way to approach it.

'Why do you want to terminate this pregnancy?'

'I'm too young to have a child.'

The answered surprised me as much as it did him and yet it was the truth. His brow furrowed. He looked down at his notes.

'But you're twenty-six.'

'Yes.'

'That's the perfect age for a woman to have children.'

'Not for me.'

I made a better fist of it after that, being aware, taking account of my position.

'It's not possible. I'm not long back from abroad. I haven't even got a job yet . . .'

'And the . . . relationship?' He'd cleared his throat as if to make a passage for the words.

'There is . . . was no relationship.'

'The father is . . . ?'

'Yes. Married. I don't even know where he is.'

I was surprised at the lies. How easily they came to me. Surprised too that I felt the need to embroider the story.

Words slip and slide, the poet said. Words escape from the grasp, from the box we try to put them into. Like 'want', for instance. 'Want', defined in the dictionary as 'to feel a need or longing for, e.g., I want a new hat . . .' Only it wasn't a new hat that I wanted.

'If it's what you want,' Archie said finally, staring down at his fingers.

'It's not a case of *want*. I don't want it. I don't *want* any of this.' I shouted the words, making the heads of the isolated early evening drinkers scattered around the place jerk up from their newspapers and their glasses. 'Don't you understand? I don't *want* to *be* in this situation.'

I'd phoned him at his office in London, taking a small bitter pleasure in his swelling joviality on the phone.

'Have a drink with you? Well, yes. Of course. You know I'd love to have a drink with you, Riley.'

I took the train up to town, like I was having a day out shopping, then the tube across to the City where we'd arranged to meet in a pub around the corner from his office. At one stop a young woman who looked about my age tried to get on with a buggy, carrier bags full of shopping swinging off each side of it. As she heaved and pushed, the wheels stuck in the floor of the carriage. She looked close to tears as the doors began to close on her. I rose to help but with one last push she was on. She half smiled her thanks at me, sank down into a seat, putting a hand to her forehead, whereupon, as if by magic, the child's mouth opened in a wide O and he began to howl. All of this seemed like a sign: that none of this was what I wanted.

I let Archie buy us both a drink in the pub, taking a small sadistic pleasure in his grinning assumption that this was a straightforward social occasion.

'So,' he said, settling back into the padded bench, lifting his glass and looking at me over it, 'to what do I owe this pleasure?'

And I told him.

'Sophie said I should come,' I said when I'd finished, and his brow crinkled. He leaned forward and took a sip of his pint, then he leaned back, once to one side, reaching in his pocket for something he didn't find and then to the other.

'You weren't even going to tell me?'

'No.'

'Why?'

'I didn't think it was any of your business.'

'*Jesus.*' He looked away from me sharply as if to hide the disgust but I caught the expression. I was struck by the way it transformed him, by the way, just for the moment, he didn't look like the foolish old Archie.

'It's not your responsibility.'

'Right.'

'It's all under control. I'm . . . taking care of everything.'

'You are?'

'Yes. I've decided.'

'Well . . . in that case Sophie was wrong, wasn't she? Not much point in coming up to see me since it's all *decided*.'

The sarcasm in the word caught at something in my throat, something I wasn't prepared for. I grabbed at my bag, half-rising to my feet, which was when he shot a hand out across the table.

'Look. I'm sorry. I'm sorry. What can I do?'

'Nothing. There's nothing for you to do.'

'Money?'

'No. I have it.'

'I could take you . . . there . . . pick you up . . . look after you . . .'

'No. *No*.'

He reared back at the revulsion in the words.

'I'm sorry. No. It's OK. Like I say, everything's taken care of.' But now there could be no misunderstanding between us.

'Look, I know what you think of me . . .' He was looking down, staring at his fingers, which were tapping on the table top. I knew that none of the words he'd spoken were the ones he really wanted and I knew what was coming. 'But . . . what I mean is . . . I suppose . . . there's . . . no point . . . in me asking . . . if we could talk about this?'

'No.' I made sure I answered briskly. I said, 'I'm sorry. There's no point. I know what I want. I know what's best for me.' I was already getting up, pulling my bag towards me again.

He didn't look at me, just went on looking down at those tapping fingers.

He said, 'I'm sure you do, Riley.'

The hospital was a low brick-built affair at the end of a road down by the docks, more like some industrial compound, the home of some plastics firm, than a hospital. I don't remember much about the twenty-four hours I spent there, but then I don't believe it should be emblazoned on my memory.

The doctor was Indian, handsome in a sari. She said, 'I'm sorry but I have to ask you the same questions. It's not too late to change your mind.' I said, 'I won't change my mind.' She said, 'Why do you not want this child?' and this time the answer came out, without my thinking.

I said, 'Because the father is a fool. I don't want to be linked all my life to a fool because I've had a child by him.' And I knew that was the truth of it.

The operation was on a Saturday afternoon, which seems odd now. I woke up around five when they brought me a meal. Grey mashed potato and some nameless meat. It seemed the finest food I had ever tasted, I remember.

Sophie picked me up the following morning. It was a grey day and early, and the streets through which we drove home were dreary and empty. In the flat she said, 'Are you alright?' I said, 'Yes. But I want to sleep.' I went to her spare room and clambered into bed. By the time she came in with a cup of tea I was fast asleep again.

It was late afternoon when I woke and Sophie was standing over me. She said, 'Archie's here,' and I made a violent movement.

'I don't want to see him.'

'I don't think he'll go away,' she said.

He was looking out of the window, out over the river, when I came in. The suspension bridge was lit up and all the lights of the city were winking.

'Why are you here?'

At the words he turned sharply. 'Why do you think I'm here?' He thumped a fist impotently down at his side. 'I've come to see how you are.'

'There's no need.'

'I wanted to know.'

'When will you get the message? It's none of your damn business now, Archie.'

He dropped down on the chair by the window then, pinched two tired fingers on his nose.

'Riley, I haven't slept. I've just driven a couple of hundred miles.'

'So what? That's your fault.'

He turned a tired, pleading face up to me. 'Couldn't we just be civilised? Couldn't you just make me a cup of coffee or something, Riley?'

I don't believe that anything has tasted as bad as that cup of instant coffee I made that day. I've never drunk the stuff since. All these years on I can still taste that thin sickly chemical bitterness, see the granules the way I saw them then, small round gritty pieces floating on the surface.

Archie put a hand to his head as if shielding his eyes from the light beside him.

'What can I do, Riley?'

'I've told you a dozen times, there's nothing you can do. Nothing I want you to do.'

But his hand had dropped by now and he was staring at me. 'I'm not talking about you. I'm talking about me, Riley.'

I remember to my shame now the rush of disgust I felt seeing the tears form in his eyes. I looked away sharply so as not to see them.

'I'm hurting too, Riley.'

'I don't care. I don't care if you're hurting.'

'You don't?' He was looking at me wonderingly and there was something else in those damp eyes that might even have been admiration. He shook his head. 'I'll give you this. You are something, Riley.'

He bunched his hand into a fist, struck it into the other palm. Then he laid it on his lips in the way someone does when they're choosing their words when they're thinking.

'What do you . . . want . . . Riley?'

'You really want to know?'

'Yes.'

'I want – as far as is humanly possible – never to see you again.'

'That won't be easy. With our connections.'

'We'll manage it.' I dropped down on to the sofa. Like someone making the arrangements for the annual school fête, I ticked them off on my fingers. 'When I know you'll be going to something, I won't go and you'll have the decency to do the same.'

'You don't think they'll notice?' He gave a weak smile, trying to make a joke of it.

'No. They know I don't like you.'

'Oh, right. I forgot.' A sharp snap of sarcasm entered his voice. 'That makes it easier.'

For a long moment there was silence between us, then he struck a hand on his knee. He got up slowly from the chair. 'Right,' he said. 'If it's what you want.'

'It is.'

At the door he stopped with his back to me. His head was bent as if he was thinking about something. He didn't turn but his back straightened as if he'd made some sort of decision. 'There's something I have to say before I go.'

'I'm sure there's no need.'

'Yes. There is.' And now he turned in the open doorway. 'I'm aware of what you think of me. You've made that clear enough. You think I'm a clown and maybe you're right. But I'll tell you this, beneath it all, right from the start, I knew—'

'Stop.' I shouted it at him 'I don't want to hear this. How many times do I have to tell you?' The words came out like a stream of bile. 'I don't care what you think about me. I don't care what you feel. All I know is you're trying to make something happen and it isn't going to happen.' I was closing the door on him, pushing him out into the

301

corridor as I did so. 'What you have to understand is that this has all been a horrible mistake. But now it's over. It's all been taken care of. It's finished. The End.'

On the last words I slammed the door, leant back against it, which is how we both stood, I know that now, him with his back against one side of the door, me with my back against the other.

Twenty-five years on, sitting on the wall of the pub car park, taking the air with the raucous sounds of Fergie's party coming out through the pub window, Archie's head shook slowly in the darkness.

He said, 'All I know is I never want to feel as bad as I felt that day, Riley.'

It came as a shock, coming round, on the pub floor with all the faces – Archie, Fergie, Cass, even my mother – staring down at me.

According to Archie, I went down like a tent: 'Like someone had pulled your pegs out, let down your guy ropes.'

Naturally, being Archie, he was unable to resist boasting about the quick-witted and chivalrous way in which he had acted.

'Lucky I was there to catch you.'

There were judged to be extenuating circumstances for my fainting, i.e., the room was hot, I hadn't eaten much. And there was this virus going around (I'd get it a couple of days later). I was not, however, drunk although there were those who wanted to claim it. 'Tch-tch-tch . . . really, Adeline.' And this from the woman I've poured into the front seat of my car more times than I care to remember.

In fact I had had only two glasses of wine.

The third was still in my hand as I tried to force myself, struggling against the sinking floor and the dying light, to get across the room to David. I went down still clutching it, which is how Archie caught the lot, all down the front of him.

It was fortuitous, as it turned out. The first thing I saw, regaining consciousness, was the stain, blood red, standing out against the cream of his jacket. It provided a perfect cover for the words that I spoke as I reached out to touch it.

I said, 'I'm sorry. I'm so very sorry, Archie.'

X *is for . . .*

So many things. A kiss, for a start, the one you put at the bottom of a letter, or a card, or in lieu of a signature on an e-mail. X is for the X chromosome, the eXtra one which we have as women, instead of the Y which makes a man a man, without which we'd be bachelor boys instead of spinsters, also for the X-factor which they're bound to find hiding away somewhere in that bundle of DNA. X also marks the spot where the treasure is to be found, this in adventure tales (which surely this is). Through the Freudian forest, past the deserted mansion, along by the cave mouth where someone has scrawled, 'Here Be Dragons'.

X is what we put in the box. It marks our preference, the option we select, the choices we make.

X stands for the decisions we take.

I've never told Archie about seeing 'David' at the party.* I didn't tell him sitting on the pub wall following my

---

* The reason for the quotation marks will become apparent.

colourful collapse just after it had happened, and I've not told him in the six months since. There are a host of reasons for this. One is that I think there is nothing to be gained by it, that the vision, the experience, was mine and mine alone, not designed to be shared, you might say.* A second is that I did not want the whole thing – the vision, if you like – to to be misconstrued and I know how easy that would be. In short I didn't want the whole thing to turn into one of those *I always thought it was a boy* scenes. I hate those scenes. I despise them when they turn up in books and plays and films. I find them sentimental, masochistic, full of self-indulgent misery, more often than not born of an agenda. More than any of these things, though, I just didn't know how to explain what happened, how to describe it. I, who make my living with words this time didn't seem to be able to find the right ones. And one thing was for sure, I didn't want to use ones that were wrong.

I was standing by the buffet table at the time, picking at the food, idly watching a group of teachers ebbing and flowing in the middle of the room, Fergie in their centre. They'd not long presented him with his farewell gifts – a cheque, a piece of carpentry equipment I couldn't figure the use of, an engraved tankard, which he now clutched, full of Butcombe, to his chest, smiling amiably.

Naturally enough, being teachers they were talking about pensions. The voice of Archie, standing next to Fergie, rose above the rest.

'Don't even want to think about it. Bloody stock market wiped forty thou off mine last year.'

---

* Although who or what the Designer might be, I'm not prepared to speculate, dear Reader.

Fergie smiled in his customary amiable fashion. He said, 'You can't imagine how much better that makes me feel, Archie.' And that's when the group began to gently swirl apart, several people moving to the bar and the buffet. A gap opened up and the next moment I was looking clear across the room. And there he was. Talking to Jonah.

Look, people talk about other realities, don't they? About how they might be passing us by a mere hand's grasp away but we never see them. All I can say is, that's how it seemed – like I had broken through, like a curtain had been pulled back and now I was looking through into this other reality, into one of those endless other possible worlds, where everything was the same except in this one fundamental, all-encompassing respect, and this thanks to that X I put in the box, the decision that was taken. I felt a kind of tremor as I looked at him, something else too, something beneath my feet like the plates of the earth might be shifting.

I knew immediately it was him and I would expect you to ask me how, and this is one of the hardest things to explain from the whole experience. Because I *knew*, that's all, first because of the likeness in their faces, his and Jonah's, something around the jaw and the lower part of their profiles, the easy way, too, that they leant against the pub wall together, which of all things tore my heart out, knowing that this was because, as boys, they'd been brought up so much together. Also I knew it was him from the long legs in the suit he wore (for, of course, he would have long legs, given his father), one of those vaguely fifties suits in a subdued weave now fashionable, a suit I knew I'd bought for him, and all this a completely different sort of knowing, not something *unearthed*, dug out of memory, not something that had to unfold inside me, but something *there*, like data, something that was a part of me, like I'd been reprogrammed, like I now possessed a different life, a completely different set of experiences.

He looked so good in that suit as I stared at him across the room, that's the thing. I felt my heart swell, another reason I guess I knew it was him. And it was all so clear, that's the point, so real and natural, not like some *vision*, some piece of whimsy, but him there, in front of me, lounging against that wall, hair cut close to his head, fashionably close, dark against the whitewash of the wall, his skin pale as the faces of so many young man are fashionably pale these days, particularly if they're kept from the light, which he would be . . . was . . . (where are the words, which are the right ones?) working in the basement office of a small TV company.

Because I knew *everything*, that's the point, everything from his name upwards. David. And let me repeat, lest you should think it, this in my defence, that I never once, in all the years, indulged myself in *I always thought it was a boy* scenes. The name was there, quite simply, among the rest of the data, the rest of the day-to-day minutiae – where he'd gone to university, for instance (Sussex), what he'd done (English first, then changed to Film Studies) how he hadn't worked that first year, and how I'd called in his father: *You'll have to do something. Dammit, you are his father.* How he had, too, done exactly the right thing, surprising me –

Well, you would be surprised. You're always surprised when I do something right, Riley – getting him into a film production company for a holiday job, so that by the time he left to go back to college he was crazy about getting into the film business and came out with a respectable second.

I could replay all of this in my head, even including all the snide comments I'd made about his father.

So is he still with Feeeeeonah from the events company?

What do you care?

You're right. What do I care?

I even had there in my data base, on my new hard drive, what had happened earlier that day, how for instance he'd sat on one of the stools at home (his home still, in my mind, despite the flat in London), how I was making him a cheese sandwich with lashing of Hellmann's and lots of pepper the way he liked it, how he'd told me as I was doing it – and with a deliberate air – that he'd told Jonah he could stay with him before flying out to Thailand. How I'd rounded on him, the bread knife still in my hand.

I told you before, I don't want you to encourage him.

He doesn't need encouraging.

He's too young.

And you weren't.

Times change. The world's a more dangerous place.

Safer too with e-mails. Mobile phones. You never had that when you were travelling.

I knew I'd turned back to his sandwich, inwardly fuming, reaching for another slice, pressing it down, cutting the whole crossways the way he also liked it, that I was thinking of my next move when he said: *It's selfishness on your part.*

That's not fair.

Yes it is. You're pretending you're thinking of him but actually you're thinking of yourself. You don't want the hassle of worrying about him, that's all.

And I knew then as now, that this was the truth of it.

How did I know it was him? Because I'd been expecting him, why else? Because I'd been expecting him for twenty-six years. Just because I refused to do any of that *always thought it was a boy* stuff, doesn't mean I took things lightly. I always knew there was chance it . . . he . . . might be up ahead waiting for me.

I don't know how long I stared at David. It seemed like aeons, as if whole ages might have passed away but I guess it wasn't even a minute. I don't know why I started to walk towards him either. I can only guess there were things I wanted to say. Maybe I wanted to defend myself:

I knew the whole thing wasn't for me, that's all . . . I just knew it wouldn't have worked. Look on the bright side. I'd have been one lousy, flaky mother.

I'd taken only a few steps when I realised something was wrong. First of all I thought it was just my legs growing heavy, then I realised it was floor, no longer firm but slipping away beneath me.

I might have been walking on the sea, that's how it felt, a strange sea, with a glassy surface that gave way a little more with each succeeding footstep. It had begun to billow, rising in waves around me when I cried out his name and he turned from the wall and held out a hand to me.

He held his wine glass in the other hand as he beckoned. He turned it upside down, laughing. Which is the way I remember him. Doing just that. What any son might do. Shaking the drops out of the upturned wineglass and laughing.

The waves that closed over my head as he disappeared from my sight seemed composed not of water but of a sweet and terrible sadness.

Down, down, down I went, knowing this was the first and last time I'd ever see 'David'.

According to Archie I was about halfway across the floor when I fainted.

'You seemed to be waving to someone. You called a name.'

'Did I?' I said. 'I can't remember.'

I let Archie lead me outside, using the excuse of needing some air. Actually I wanted to say sorry. I said, 'I think I've wanted to say it for a long while. I'm sorry about the way things happened, that's all.' He said, 'Yeah. I'm sorry too,' but there was no warmth in his tone and his voice was flat and unresponsive.

I took offence straight away. I said, 'It's not a *mea culpa*,' but he bit right back. He said, 'Don't insult me. I never thought it was, Riley.'

I said, 'Sometimes you have to face the hardest thing in the world, Archie, the thing that kicks everything else into touch.'

'Which is?'

'That something can hurt, something you did, but you can look back on something you did that hurts but still know it was the right decision.'

He said, 'Sounds good to me, Riley,' but there was that same coldness in his tone. 'Glad you got it all worked out, anyway.'

I said, 'Well . . .' half rising from the wall, irritated that my olive branch had been rejected. He continued to stare down at the ground and appeared not to notice.

He said, 'Do you ever think what might have been?'

'I've thought about it a bit.' I made my voice deliberately brusque. It wasn't the sort of question I wanted to answer. 'You do think about these things, you know, when you get older.' I made a dismissive gesture with my hand in the air. 'It doesn't blight my life or anything.'

'Good for you.'

The bitterness in his voice both shocked and offended me. I said, 'Time to go, I think . . .' but now he was holding out a hand in restraint, an olive branch of his own.

'I'm sorry. It's just that it doesn't make you feel good about yourself, Riley.'

'What?' I could see his eyes clamped hard on mine, shining out of the darkness.

'Having a woman make it clear to you, you're not worthy to be the father of the child she's carrying.'

'It was nothing to do with you, Archie. It was just bad timing.'

The band had started up again. A jangling version of 'Hi-Ho Silver Lining', with singing and shouting and stamping, came out, like the sound of some other world, through the pub window.

I said, 'It happened at the wrong time, Archie, that's all. If it had happened some other time, later say, who knows . . . ? We just got unlucky.'

'Unlucky?'

'Yeah. Unlucky.' I was getting angry now. I raised my voice over the sound of the music. 'That's it. OK. Just the way it fell. But if you want to look at it different, Archie, if you want to wallow in it and feel bad about yourself, well, that's fine by me. Be my guest. Only don't expect me to feel sorry for you. And you know why? Because life's too short. Because it's now that counts and not something that happened twenty-six years ago.'

He said, 'Yeah, you're right,' stuck his hands in his pockets as he got up from the wall. He gave a small sigh. 'Well . . .' he said, 'maybe it all worked out in another reality,' this with a small crooked smile.

I said, 'Yeah, maybe,' but it wasn't a line of enquiry I wanted to pursue any further.

We walked back towards the pub door in what would probably pass, and this for the first time in our lives, as companionable silence.

He said, 'All I want is to be friends, Riley.'

I said, 'Me, too, Archie.'

I'd had enough of the party by then. I needed to go home, to be on my own. I needed that solitude.

I said, 'Hey, do me favour, Archie. I'm going home. Tell Fergie I've gone He won't mind.' I laughed. I said, 'He knows I overdose easily on teachers.'

'No problem,' he said. He was reaching into his pocket. I heard the clink of his keys. 'I'll drive you.'

'No. It's OK. I want to walk.'

'Come on.' It was like I'd never spoken. He clinked the keys in his hand.

'No. Really. I want to walk. I like walking. I like walking through the town at night.'

'I'll walk with you, then.'

'No. Thanks. But I'd rather be on my own. I like to think when I walk.'

'Not a good idea.'

'What?'

'Walking. Not after fainting and everything. Besides, it's too late to be out on your own. This way.' In the half-light the keys glinted in his hand as he pointed them towards the car.

'NO!'

I wouldn't be surprised if they heard that shout right through 'Glad All Over' which was the exercise in sixties nostalgia now coming out through the pub window. I even stamped my foot. At the same time I'd also like to report that the phrase 'spoken through gritted teeth' is by no means mere poetic licence.

'Archie. Just in case you missed it, or I haven't made myself clear, I'm going to repeat everything v-er-y sl-ow-ly. I want to walk home alone. I like walking home alone. Now . . . is there a problem here? Am I speaking in a foreign language? Is there something you need translated?'

'OK . . . OK . . .'

He'd put his hand up. But you know me, folks. I'm a tanker when the dander is up. It takes me six miles to stop. I crash on rocks. I can pollute entire continents.

'I want to walk home. That is to say, I wish and desire it. In fact, at this particular moment, in the light of this conversation, I'd say I pine, thirst and yearn for it. I want to be on my own. I want to have time to think. It is not long past eleven. I am a grown woman. Now. Anything else you want to know, Archie?'

But he was standing quite still now, his arms crossed, and while I dislike the word intensely, feeling it to be the sort of word that turns up like 'gritted teeth' in the worse sort of prose, I'm forced to say he was grinning.

'Imagine.'

'What?'

'I'd forgotten.'

'What?'

'How easily you come to the boil.'

By now I was stalking away from him but with his long legs he was able to lollop languidly along beside me.

'I'll tell you something, Riley.'

'Please don't.'

'You think you're so eeeeeasy and lackadaisical but actually you're strung as tight as a piano wire.'

'Yeah, well, maybe I have to be.' I'd stopped abruptly, rounded on him.

'Oh, really, why?'

'Because I'm a single woman. Because I have to run my own life. Because it can be hard and most of all because in my experience it's positively peppered with patronising arseholes like you.'

'Oh. *Gooood* alliteration.'

He was leaning against the boot of the car with his arms crossed and even in the half-light I could see the previously mentioned grin was turning to that old Archie look of lascivious pleasure.

'What?'

'I'd forgotten.'

'What?'

'Just how much it turns me on when you insult me, Riley.'

I enjoyed that walk back through the town that night. God knows I have a fraught relationship with my home town, still there's nothing like a late night stroll through its old streets, and on an early spring night with the smell of woodsmoke still in the air. On the way home I did what I always did on such a walk, which is to stop for a while, sit on the seat opposite the abbey, ponder its delicate fingers of ruins pointing upwards like a warning.

I thought a lot about 'David' as I sat there that night, and what I saw was the truth of the thing and of all such fond imaginings of other possible/impossible worlds and realities, that 'David' was a mere fabrication, no more than a model put together from the evidence available – an *abstraction* the poet calls it,* not one pinned down by the realities, let loose on the slips and slides of the world, those

---

* What might have been is an abstraction

        Remaining a perpetual possibility
        Only in a world of speculation.
        T. S. Eliot, *Four Quartets*

terrible slings and arrows of outrageous fortune that we read about in the papers, that happen to other people's children, the ones that cause that intake of breath coupled with that instinctive, unstoppable, grateful prayer of selfish thanks: *Not my child. Thank God* . . .

What I saw most of all that night was how important the quote marks were around that 'David' I saw at Fergie's party – how, had he ever really been, he might never have attained the age of that fantasy figure, how instead he might have died from some fatal disease at an early age, or had an accident, fallen off a roof or a cliff, been hit by a car and this at the end of his own street, how he might have drowned white-water rafting or been murdered in the outback on one of those years out travelling, just like the one currently freezing my heart up with fear for Jonah, in any or all of these things, leaving me only half alive and faced with the impossible task of going on living; how, there again, he might never have been at Fergie's party talking comfortably with Jonah at all, and this because he despised everything I was, including my family, how instead, at the very moment I thought I saw him slouched easily and handsomely against that wall with Jonah, he might have been holed up in a squat somewhere, bad-mouthing his mother, and sticking a needle in his arm; how, indeed, he might never have been 'David' at all, but Davina, one of those extraordinary, tough, cold-hearted young women, working in the City perhaps, and with a life-style to match; Davina who each time I rang would take my call without affection, who would never visit even at Christmas, and who would reserve for me, in a more mature and far more terrible fashion, that same visceral dislike, which, with a bit of luck in a year or two, Rochelle will have swopped for fond amusement, which instead she will bestow upon her mother.

'I guess you can't get through life without regret,' Archie said with a small sigh by way of farewell at the gate of the car park. Despite the spat, we managed to part as friends.

'It's not about regret,' I said with a return to my former sharpness.

He said, 'What's it about then, Riley?'

I said, 'It's about the choices you make. Simply that. The paths you didn't take . . . the doors you didn't open.'

'And that's not regret?'

'No, because you took other paths, opened other doors instead.' I said, 'We all got to follow our own yellow brick road, Archie,' and even as I said the words I felt that I'd plucked them from the air, that they'd been hanging there waiting for the taking.

Sitting on the bench, that same one I sat on years ago as a returning traveller, feeling so jagged as all that humdrum small-town life went past me, I wondered where I'd heard the words before.

I was putting the key in the lock of my own front door when I remembered they were Nathan's.

Y is . . . for that old
Yellow Brick Road

He wrote me a letter, you see, the only letter he ever wrote me. I opened it up in my tiny room in the grubby back-packers' hostel where I was staying in Hong Kong.

It said, 'We've all got to follow our own yellow brick road, Riley.'

Nathan, Nathan.

In direct translation, *given of God.*

A scary thought.

'If I believed it. Which I don't.' I said this firmly despite everything.

Danny said, 'I'm so sorry, Riley.'

I'm not sure now what made me decide to contact Nathan again that night after Fergie's party. The reminder of Nathan's letter, perhaps, in the words I spoke to Archie. Probably what had happened with 'David' at the party too, that glimpse through an unopened door of another path untaken. Perhaps, as well, what I saw on TV when I got in, cracking open a bottle of wine as I watched, those lumbering old warhorses that had woken us up all those years ago with their dull, rumbling throb, now rising up from an airbase I'd once camped outside with Magda. Or maybe it was just Danny. Danny, spotting my light still on, rapping on my window, coming in for a glass of wine. Danny saying, 'Come on. Let's do it, Riley,' plumping down in front of my Mac, twenty minute later – this the real magic in this sorcerous town – laying out Nathan's life before me.

He'd seemed a million miles away, across the universe, not just the other side of the planet, all those times in the past when I'd phoned him. Now, staring at the screen beside Danny, scrolling down through all the minutiae – his career, undistinguished I could see that; always *deputy*, always *acting*, his teaching schedule, attendances at university council meetings (never speaking), those still dry-as-dust research papers – I felt like I was spying on him, like I was looking in through his window. I seemed to see him there in the low dark house I'd imagined, that familiar bull-headed stooping figure bent over his desk, low dark serious music playing in the background. He seemed so utterly real and alive I laid a hand on my heart from the sheer shock and amazement of it. I had to get up from the Mac with the force of it. I made an excuse, going into the kitchen to fetch more wine. There I found myself walking up and down thumping a fist agitatedly into the palm of my hand. I was mid-stride, one hand cupped into the other when I realised it was exactly the same action, exactly the same way I'd behaved a decade before. The last time I'd phoned Nathan.

It was not long after Lennie had left. Just how mad and bad I was then I never quite realised until Connie Cheung said, years later, 'I don't think I've seen anyone as crazy as you were then, Riley . . . that is, outside an institution.'

I think it was principally the loneliness that made me call, not the loneliness of losing Lennie but the loneliness of sorting the whole thing out, the loans, the leases, the small print, which seemed endless. When friends asked about it, I'd say, 'There's nothing to say,' which wasn't true, there was everything to say, but I just couldn't bear to go through it, to see their eyes, against their will, glaze over.

I was drunk and stoned that night. I wasn't sleeping much either, so that when I called him it was almost dawn, office hours on the other side of the planet. I figured that if the phone was lifted it would have to be him, and as it rang out the sweat formed on my palm as usual and ran down the receiver. When the tone was broken abruptly I closed my eyes, feeling my throat tighten as I waited for his voice. But instead of that growl it was a woman's voice, someone in his faculty office. She said Nathan wasn't there. He was in London. Researching at the British Library.

I jumped up from the sofa as I put the phone down. I began to stride up and down, thumping that fist and palm together. I rang the station, got all the times of the trains to London, phoned Tourist Information too, booked a hotel room. After that I sat down on the sofa, opened a bottle of wine, fired up a spliff while I tried to figure out the best way to approach him. Whether to leave a letter at the desk in the library, or play the gumshoe, following him to his hotel, spying on him from the gallery.

That was how it continued all the following week, every day checking the train times, cancelling a hotel room, booking another. Every day, opening a bottle of wine, lighting up a joint. Every day that walk, thumping, thumping, fist to palm, unholy palmer's kiss . . .

'Sorry . . . what . . . wait . . .' Danny is leaning forward, his forehead screwed in confusion. 'Are you telling me you never *went*? He was *here*. In England, a couple of hours away on the train and you didn't *go*?' Danny is shaking his head at me.

In fact, I did almost make it once. I got so near, so very near. It was the day before Nathan was leaving. I showered, threw some things incoherently into a bag, took a taxi to the station. There I sat on a bench for a long time watching the trains to London come and go until I began to attract the attention of staff. In the end I walked out, took a taxi home, downed some more wine with some more dope and this time some sleeping pills. When I woke up Nathan must have been somewhere over Asia.

'I couldn't do it. I couldn't go to him when I was strung out over Lennie. It wouldn't have been right. He was worth so much more than that.'

You see, I've done a lot of things I'm not proud of in my life (I can feel myself defending myself to you here, just the way I was doing it to Danny), but at least I've never played the Victorian heroine, never laid my head on a man's chest just until I've got my strength back and I'm up and running and no longer need him.

'Besides which, it wouldn't have worked, I knew that. I knew that if we were ever to meet again I had to be feeling good about myself.'

'I can see that.'

'You can?' I was surprised.

'Sure. But things are different now.'

'It's not that simple.'

'Why not?'

'I've changed.'

'So what? People do change.'

'No. It's more than that. I've tried to explain to you.

320

The whole thing was based on a fantasy. Me the little bar girl, him the professor.'

'But it wasn't what he wanted. And now it's not what you want either.'

But I wasn't saying the things I wanted to say and I knew it.

'He was . . . an old forty. He said so himself. Now he'll be in his seventies.' But these weren't the right words either.

'Also . . .'

'Yes?'

'Supposing he's quite different?'

'Different?'

'Different from what I remember. Dull . . . some old academic stick . . . not at all the glamorous man of my memory.'

'So that would be the end of it.'

'No . . . no . . . you don't understand. I put a hand to my head. 'Don't you see, that would be worse than the end of it? By contacting him again, I'd have destroyed something. Utterly. The memory of it. Of that perfect affair.'

And there it was. The absolute truth. Unvarnished. Out in the open.

'Don't you see, it's all been a stupid game, Danny. Ringing at the wrong time, not going to see him. All of these years I've been holding on to this thing, keeping it alive, intact, away from light: the memory of the perfect affair unspoilt by reality.'

Danny said, 'Sounds good to me. Lots of psychobabble, lots of bollocks.'

He said, 'On the other hand you could just be a good old-fashioned coward, Riley.'

* * *

At the door, laughing, I said, 'Anyway, what the hell would I say if I did e-mail him?'

Danny said, 'Just tell him the truth, girlfriend. Tell him you never married.'

Perhaps that's what did it in the end. It's as good as anything else, anyway. All I know is that a glass of wine later, I wanted more than anything else in the world to e-mail Nathan. And while it's true that was always the way when I contacted him, i.e., I'd always had a little too much to drink, this time it was different. This time everything seemed clear in my head, more than clear – simple, confident. I saw how much easier and more straightforward things were than I'd been making them. I realised I didn't care whether Nathan was old now, which he would be, or boring, which I very much doubted, because none of these things mattered. They didn't matter because I didn't have to be terrified any more. I didn't have to suffer from that old philophobia, and this because I didn't have to worry about getting in too deep or finding myself under some sort of obligation or losing any of that precious freedom or independence. I didn't have to be worried about being tied down either – something he tried to tell me all those years ago – and it had taken me until now, until I'd established and understood the depth and satisfaction of my own spinster life, to realise it. I knew that life could only benefit from the likes of Nathan, at least if he was the Nathan I remembered, as cussed and spikey and ill-fitting as myself.

All this I realised suddenly so that the words came surprisingly easily in the end.

Dear Nathan,

If this e-mail comes as an unpleasant surprise, or is awkward, or in any way unwelcome to you, please ignore it. I am

322

merely writing to say that I have thought of you many times over the years and with much pleasure. I have wanted to contact you and indeed, on several occasions, have made inadequate attempts to do so. The benefits of e-mail, however, now make this so much easier. I hope that you are well and happy, as I am, and wish you all the very best whether or not you choose to reply to this.

   Best wishes, Riley Gordon
PS. By the way, you were wrong. I never did get married!

I have a weird, other-worldly, rather melancholy voice on my Mac. When I do something wrong, she says, 'It's not my fault,' sounding faintly hurt and offended. Since it was late at night when I eventually clicked on Send, the sound of her voice as I rinsed out the wine glass in the kitchen telling me I had mail, this less than ten minutes after I'd sent the thing, surprised me.

Long descriptions of feelings at tense moments are inappropriate. They merely break up the action. Thus I will only tell you that I was shaking when I sat down before the screen, that as my hand had sweated all those times on the receiver, so it now sweated on the mouse as I grasped it.

Clicking on, as the e-mail opened, I registered first of all and almost instantaneously the briefness of the e-mail and a split second later the words 'AUTOMATED MESSAGE'.

What came next seemed to uncurl like some ancient scroll very slowly, as if the two of us, the message and I, were taking the long plodding steps together.

Time bends and shifts and shapes, doesn't it? It falls down black holes. It seemed aeons before the words finally formed themselves into a whole to make sense in my brain.

It is with regret that the University has to inform you of the death of Dr Nathan Feinstein.

Z is for . . . Zing Zing Zing*
(went my heartstrings)

You know what I think. I think sometimes the gods decide to lay it all out before you, roll it out like a carpet, this as if they're saying, Take a look at your life, see the way you've lived it. See if you think you could have lived it any better. That's the way it seems to me now, anyway, when I look back on the night of Fergie's party.

'It's the perfect ending for me, isn't it?' I said to Danny.

He was in the bathroom cleaning his teeth when I banged on his back door. It could only have been ten minutes or so since I received the e-mail but it seemed like I'd read it a thousand times, each time like an archaeologist trying to make sense of hieroglyphics on a cave wall, or a detective poking around for clues in the undergrowth, something that would tell me I was misinterpreting the whole thing,

---

*   Clang, clang, clang went the trolley,
             Ding, ding, ding went the bell,
             Zing, zing, zing went my heartstrings . . .

'The Trolley Song', words and music Hugh Martin and Ralph Blane from the film *Meet Me In St Louis*

reading it all wrong, and that actually Nathan wasn't dead at all but alive and well and waiting to hear from me.

'It's all so nice and *clean*, isn't it? It means I don't have to worry about doing anything, making any sort of emotional effort. Look, I even get to weep these crocodile tears.'

Danny shook his head. 'Give yourself a break, Riley.'

I was sad, you see, just so damn sad, and there wasn't any other word for it. And what it made it worse was the feeling of phoneyness.

'Don't you see, if I'd cared, if I'd *really* cared, I'd have done something about it over the years.'

'We all have regrets, Riley.'

I shook my head. 'It's not about regret.'

Regret just seemed too damned simple.

There was a name on the bottom of that e-mail, a number too, for an administrative assistant, an offer of further information. But I didn't want any further information, I didn't want to know when or how precisely Nathan had died. I didn't want to know if there were any awful ironical strokes of misfortune lying in there. All I knew was what I know now, which is that I want him to have died in the best possible way, peacefully, from some benign disease, the sort that might take off a man in his seventies without too much pain and trauma, this with family or friends or both about him, maybe even his wife, with whom he was reunited, his son too (who may or may not have become a rock star), perhaps grandchildren, or another wife, or a long-term lover, or any or all of these things, but so content with life that he had long since forgotten that autumn of '72 in Bangkok and the woman with whom he spent it. What else could I give him in return for what he had given me? After all, thanks to him, thanks to his dying, I'd be able to do what I'd always wanted to do, which was to keep our affair perfectly preserved in that aspic of memory.

To keep it complete, standing there with its icing and its ribbons and its little silver bells.

Miss Havisham's wedding cake in the middle of the table.

I shut myself away for a week or so after all this. I was due some holiday from the paper and I took it, this thanks to an immediate dispensation from Sophie. As if determined to match my mood it rained for most of the time. There was flooding on the moors, the worst for many years, but I didn't go out so I didn't see it. I didn't even know about it till I saw Danny's pictures some time later in back copies of the paper. Then one morning I just gave the thing up. Pulled back the curtains that had been drawn for a week or so. Because in the end, life goes on, which is the best thing about it, the truly good and amazing thing, Real Life that is, not the *abstractions* that in the end were 'David' and even Nathan.

Speaking of Real Life.

Not.

Magda is now a 'married' woman.

Magda's 'wedding' took place one glorious long midsummer night when the sun scarcely seemed to sink down over the horizon. She claimed she'd picked the date because according to her astrological chart the omens were good, but I happen to know it was the only Saturday she could get the upstairs room in the Jolly Pilgrim.

She went for an ancient Egyptian theme in the end (white dress with a sort of tinsel wig and winged gods on her sandals), this as a tribute to her last days, which were spent in Alexandria after she was carted off to be walled up in the tomb of some pharaoh.[*] This didn't seem to me to be an entirely propitious way to start a marriage; on the other hand I could see that Magda's wasn't going to face the usual trials and tensions associated with the more traditional bipartisan arrangement. (For just this reason I decided against spending long nights with my workbox, cross-stitching 'Never Let The Sun Go Down On Your Wrath' as a wedding present and instead settled for a set of coasters.)

I managed to convince Magda that I was unable to be a bridesmaid since I would be covering the event for the paper.

'Fourth estate, you know, Magda. Editorial impartiality and all that.'

For a full account of the event, I refer you to the *Free Press* of Friday, 11 July 2003, not deep in the paper on the wedding pages either, but slap bang on the front, complete with three-column, eight-inch picture by Danny of Magda making her way up the Tor at the head of the procession.

Both picture and story marked a triumph for Magda in the face of a firm determination by Sophie to have absolutely nothing to do with the event, professionally or otherwise. This commendable aim was entirely thwarted by the fact that by the time the wedding occurred, Magda was a media star, having been on everything from *Woman's Hour* to *Richard and Judy*, not to mention featured prominently on the pages of every national newspaper including my mother's:

---

[*] Have you noticed how no one ever dies peacefully in bed in a previous incarnation?

WOMAN TO WED HERSELF
'IT'S GOODBYE TO BRIDGET JONES,'
SAYS EX-TV RESEARCHER

By the time Danny and I arrived on top of the Tor for the ceremony a small crowd had already gathered, including a small band of Scotsmen who'd taken a wrong turn on the way to Cornwall and were now well down a six-pack of McEwan's. They watched with consummate interest as Bad Ponytail Peter, dressed in his Aleister Crowley outfit, set up his pasting table at the foot of the tower. First came a black bedspread with astrological signs, which he threw over the table, then candlesticks and a dusty old book, all clearly designed to make him look like some sort of magus. Last but not least came something bearing a strong resemblance to an African fly swot, and which at the end of the ceremony he would shake over Magda's head for reasons not entirely clear to the rest of us. As he went about his work one of the drunken Scotsmen nudged my arm politely.

'Wass happening here then, hen? Is it ganna be one of those primeval ceremonies?'

'Pretty much,' I said. 'In a manner of speaking.'

Cresting the Tor, with her flares around her (the torches, you'll recall, not the trousers) Magda looked as all brides should look on their wedding day, utterly radiant. In lieu of the Wedding March, the tantric drummers started up. Most were female and bra-less (we don't do bras too much in our town, particularly among the women). Suffice it to say that the effect of their exertions beneath their flimsy Indian cotton tops could be seen to be quite seriously exciting the Scotsmen. Luckily, however, just when things might have turned nasty, a number of the bridesmaids took to hurling themselves to the ground, rolling around and shouting out invocations to Demeter, Great Goddess of Grain, at whose temple Magda had worked as a vestal virgin. 'Less a divinity, then,' as Danny remarked, 'than a previous employer.' Whatever. All the rolling around and shouting more than diverted everyone's attention from what might have been a difficult situation.

In all this (and confounding the sceptics among you) I'd have to say the bridegroom wasn't much missed, not least by one of the Scotsmen, who watched with an expression of shameless enchantment as Peter bound Magda's hands symbolically with a tatty-looking piece of gold material she claimed was unearthed from some mummy's tomb, but which I happen to know was a scarf she couldn't sell in Hocus Pocus even when it was knocked down from £39.99 to a fiver. He then placed twin silver rings on both her third fingers, kissing them (slavering a little I thought, but then as you know he and Magda once mingled more than their auras after a Friday night channelling session), after which she knelt and raised her hands together sacrificially in the air as he read something over her head from that dusty old book. He told us later it was an ancient Egyptian blessing, although, frankly, it could just as easily have been a recipe for camel curry.

Personally, I would have liked a more traditional service, this because I wanted Peter to have to say, 'Will you Magda take . . . well . . . you Magda . . .' but no such luck. Thus his damn mumbo jumbo robbed me of probably the only opportunity I'm ever going to get in my life of raising my hand and stepping forward in that wonderful dramatic moment when we, the congregation, are asked if there is any reason why these two should not be joined together. 'Hello, yes . . . excuse me . . . over here . . . Um, correct me if I'm wrong, and I know it's a small point . . . but isn't there just the one of them?'

The ceremony being over, there was a great deal of embracing, something in which I couldn't help noticing one of the Scotsmen participated with more than the average enthusiasm. When it came to his turn to kiss the bride, it looked like a tongues job from where I was standing. This might have been considered offensive, not to say reprehensible, were it not for the fact that the newlywed appeared to show not the slightest objection.

After that it was all back to the Jolly Pilgrim. Despite being Pub of the Year and celebrated for its food, the Pilgrim still couldn't rise to the fig fricassee and sheep's eyes in aspic Magda had hoped for, so we had to make do instead with chilli and baked potatoes.

I was surprised to see Fleur waiting for us at the reception, surprised in so many ways, not least at that I hardly recognised her. Gone were the cashmere and pearls. Instead she was all in black leather, a change of image due in small part to the fact that now she was speed-dating.

'Speed-dating?

'Yes.' Her look was challenging.

'But I thought . . .'

'What?'

'Well, I thought that was for . . . professional people . . . you know, busy executives without a minute to spare.'

The look turned severe. 'I'm doing four mornings a week in the shop now, Riley.'

After a couple more glasses of wine she told me her sex life was now 'amazing', this giggling like a teenager. 'Honestly, Riley, I can't tell you what I got up to last weekend,' a vow of silence for which much thanks. On the other hand, taking in the leather bustier and thigh-boots I thought I could probably guess at it. Before I could stop her, she launched into a list of the shortcomings of her sex life with Martin.

'We hadn't done it for months. Frankly, I just couldn't be bothered.'

His main crime, apparently, was that he never did anything *interesting* (and what that might be I chose not to imagine). That in the final reaches of lovemaking he made a sound like a train coming out of a tunnel shot quickly to the top of my list of Things I Would Prefer Not Know In Life and not least because I knew it would spring instantly to mind the next time I saw Martin.

And so it proved.

I was making my way through the bar downstairs on the way to the Pilgrim's Ye Olde Outside Toilets, when I felt a firm hand on my arm and there he was. Before I could protest he'd dragged me on to a seat, put a glass of wine in front of me, which I didn't want, and one in front of himself I judged to be definitely surplus to requirements.

'You can tell me,' he said, his eyes bleary. 'How is she . . . *really*?'

I knew what he wanted me to say. He wanted me to say: 'Martin, she's *devastated*.' He wanted me to say, 'It's all an act she's putting on. She's bitterly lonely. She knows she's made a mistake, only she doesn't know how to admit it.' Unfortunately, however, I couldn't say any of these things. Neither did I feel it was the right moment to reveal that thanks to the speed-dating she was currently trying to decide between a rich, black, beautiful barrister and a big blond über-mensch of a stockbroker so hot to trot it was scary.

Thus I contented myself with, 'She's fine, Martin,' whereupon he gave me an irritated look, which morphed almost immediately into suspicion.

331

'Really?'

'Yeah. Really.'

Not knowing quite what to say next, more as a reflex than anything else, and to fill up the bottomless pit of gloomy silence, I said, 'So how's things with you then, Martin?'

What happened next is a lesson to us all, spinsters everywhere. Beware the mild exchange of pleasantries. More especially beware the dangerous belief that where certain people are concerned, i.e., members of you own extended family, you're entirely safe from surprises.

'Me?' Martin said. 'Me?' like only a fool could ask. 'I'm fine.' He said, 'It's a bull market out there . . . if you understand me,' and he gave me a wink, so frightful, so retro-lascivious I could scarcely believe I'd seen it.

'D'you know,' he said, speaking the words in the firm, confident tones of a man who believes them to be the ones for which I'd been waiting through the long dry summer of my youth, 'I've always fancied you, Riley.' He was staring at me fixedly, or as fixedly as someone can stare, suffering from serious double vision (it was at this point I realised that Martin was totally plastered). He leant back in his captain's chair, its front legs lifting rakishly off the floor, only the broad shameless smirk on his face betraying him as a man who for most of his life had considered morris dancing the acme of daring, but now, just for this moment, for this one terrible glorious moment, believed himself to be a Lothario of matchless ability.

'You and I should get together, Riley.'

By way of response I did what all civilised women of my age and persuasion do when fielding inappropriate advances. I laughed. I said, 'I think it's forbidden by the prayer book, Martin,' (he is, after all, a church warden) half rising to go.

Sadly the scene wasn't over. As I tried, and with some alacrity, to prise myself out from behind the table, he shot forward on his seat, front legs of the chair clattering hard on the floor, and grabbed my hand, sandwiching the tender flesh of my middle finger between the large silver ring that I wear and the hard wood of the table.

'OW!'

He held on fast to my fingers as I tried to pull them away.

'There's no reason why you and I shouldn't have some fun.'

'More to the point, there's no reason why we should.' I ripped my hand from his. 'For fuck's sake. Get a grip, Martin.'

Entirely inappropriate when I think about it.

By the time I made it back upstairs, Magda was attending to the traditional courtesies, complimenting the brides-maids, thanking the guests for coming, raising her glass and saying how happy she and herself knew they would be, all this while fighting off, although clearly not too hard, the attentions of the amorous Scotsman.

He claimed his name was Hamish, something I thought unlikely, even at the time. However, it turned out to be the truth of it, as did the fact that he was a) surprisingly tender in bed and, b) extremely good at mending roofs, this last of particular importance to Magda, since the tree whose life she had so selflessly saved from the wrath of the Carpet World digger had recently shown its appreciation by crashing down on top of her conservatory.

Other useful attributes would prove to be the number and nature of his tattoos (bleeding hearts, skull and crossbones, death's-heads, writhing serpents) which, when displayed by him, arms akimbo behind the counter, and even beneath a genially smiling face, would seriously cut down the incidence of shoplifting.[*] They would also put into perspective what Rochelle had previously thought of as her risqué twin daggers, while an Easterhouse childhood, a kicked heroin habit, and a spell in Barlinnie would have much the same effect on her slavish devotion towards a brace of over-acned young men who had managed to convince her they were cup holders when it came to bad behaviour.

For all this reasons, Hamish is still beneath Magda's roof six months after her wedding.

'Hen,' he is prone to say, still staring at her as though she fell from heaven, 'Ah thought you were the most beautiful thing Ah'd ever seen in that white dress. Ah still do.'

That night, standing beside Danny in the upstairs room of the Pilgrim, and watching the merry band of wizards, witches, astrologers, druids, Grand Vizors, and assembled all-purpose shamans doing what is always done by sixties people at weddings, i.e., dancing really badly, I said, 'I tell you, Danny, sometimes I think we've shot into reverse in this damn town. Sometimes I think we're heading straight back to the Dark Ages.'

What happened to Magda, meanwhile, as regards Hamish, has given fresh heart to my mother. 'It just goes to show.' This said with pursed lips and an eye cocked in my direction and in what I take to be a highly significant fashion. 'It's never too late.'

I don't bother asking her what it goes to show, or what

---

[*] Always a problem in Hocus Pocus. It's a mistake to think those intent on pursuing the Higher Path won't half-inch some Tibetan bells and *The Sayings of the Buddha* to start them on their journey.

it's never too late for, knowing as I do that all such cryptic allusions these days relate to Archie.

To say that my mother got excited when Archie returned a month or so after Fergie's party and took me out to dinner is to indulge one last time in that deplorable habit of understatement.

'Well?'

'Well . . . what?' I reached, appalled, for the alarm clock beside the bed the morning after. It said ten to seven.

'Is he still there?'

'Don't be disgusting.'

I could see her at the other end of the line in her pink quilted dressing gown in the kitchen, reaching for her Nimble and her fat-free spread, making those sharp, irritated movements, hands-free receiver lodged between ear and skinny shoulder.

'So what happened?'

'Nothing *happened*, Mother.'

Cass, frankly, was not much better.

'Nice time?' she enquired later in the day, much too casually.

'Not bad at all. Quite pleasant, in fact.' Both of which were truthful. The nice thing about going out with a squillionaire, as I mentioned to Danny, is that it 'sure takes the heat out of feeling you ought to go halves.'

'I'll say this for you, Riley,' Archie said, leaning back in his chair in the dining room of the Jolly Pilgrim 'You're wearing well.'*

---

* It's worth pointing out here that I had made an effort, little black dress, etc. Plus I wield a mean hairdryer when I try, not to mention face-pack and razor.

'Well, you know . . .' I took a sip of sixty-quid bordeaux, which I seemed to be swallowing perfectly well along with my principals. 'Only one careful owner . . . me.'

'So how's your sex life?'

'None of your business.'

'Mine's pretty thin.'

'I don't recall asking, Archie.'

I took a bite of the fancy *ceps à* something starter. 'What's happened to what's her name, then?'

'Ah ha,' he said in the manner of a man who, if he'd had a monocle would have stuck it, roué-style, in his eye and peered at me through it. 'So you are interested?'

'No. I'm merely making polite conversation in return for this disgustingly expensive wine, Archie.'

In the end we tracked 'what's her name' down to Feeona.

'Good God, that was years ago.'

'Hello?' I held my knife and fork up either side of me. 'I don't keep up with your love life, Archie.'

'Really? I always kept in touch with who you were going out with, Riley.' He looked at me coolly over his glass as he said it.

In fact I had kept up with Archie's love life over the years. Against my will.

'He's going out with her that presents that programme on the television.'

'Well, that narrows it down, Mother.'

He did indeed go out for a while with one of our better-know TV quiz presenters, also a junior doctor, a business studies lecturer, and Fiona the aforementioned corporate events manager (and there's an occupation we'll be able to dispense with, come the revolution). All of which I couldn't help thinking, made my tally of mechanics, painters and decorators, the odd renegade painter and writer (not to mention arch-rascal Lennie) look like a bunch of serious underachievers. Several of Archie's were live-in relationships – business studies lecturer (Linda) and, of course, Feeeeona. He even married one of them. The junior doctor (Marilyn).

'What happened?'

'She went off with an ear, nose and throat surgeon.'

Archie seemed quite comfortable about all of this, tucking into his fillet steak without the least sign of angst or trauma. Looking at him, I had to admit that in the wearing-well stakes, he wasn't doing that bad either. The tan helped, of course. Sophie likes to imply these days that I'm dead from the neck down as regards sex but it's not true. Put a man in a good suit, especially a tall one, cut his hair well and splash some French cologne on him and I can feel that faint familiar stirring as well as the next woman.

Around the third glass of wine, I was in the mood to be generous.

'I guess you must feel pretty good about yourself, Archie.'

'How so?'

'Come on. Credit where it's due. You've achieved what most people only dream of.'

'Yeah ... well ... money ...' His lips pursed in a self-deprecating gesture.

This unnerved me. I wasn't used to self-deprecation from Archie. 'Yeah, money ... you bet money. Don't knock money.'

'Right. And it really impresses you, for starters.'

I considered this, a forkful of fillet in the air. 'Actually, it does although I hate to admit it. Still, enough of being nice to you. Tell me, how did you make all that goddamn money?'

According to Archie there was nothing clever about it.

'Could you knock off the self-deprecation. It's beginning to irritate me.'

'It's the truth,' and I guess it was. There *was* nothing clever about it. Mean, perhaps. Sneaky. But hardly clever. All part of that great Nineties Dot Com Gold Rush. The Greater Fool Theory. All you had to do was to keep your eye on the ball – 'or rather the shit and the fan' – this so that when the two got too close you could off-load your stock onto some poor sap who was unaware of their proximity.

'So . . . you found this greater fool, huh?' And that was when he paused in the action of slicing through his fillet steak and raised his eyes, which were altogether too mocking and knowing.

He said, 'No doubt you find that surprising, Riley?'

I could have let that go. Pretended I didn't get the insinuation. But a lot more water had passed under that old bridge now.

'Maybe,' I said, 'but to tell you the truth I might even get around to revising that opinion, Archie.'

The bill was lying on the plate before him and he was reaching into an inside pocket for his wallet when he said, 'There's something I've wanted to ask you. I hope you don't mind.' He was staring down at the bill, although I had the distinct impression he was only pretending to check it. He said, 'Cass and Fergie, they've never known . . . you've never told them . . . you know, what happened between us?'

I didn't really want this at the end of the evening, to tell you the truth. I'd have preferred it the way it was before, the joking, the careless sparring. It was like someone had rolled something in the middle of the table – not a grenade exactly, more a canister, which was beginning to fizz lightly, emitting a smell, a smoke not unpleasant but still disturbing.

'No. I don't ever want them to know.'

'Why? I'm just curious.'

'Because I never told Cass at the time and now it would break her heart to find out that at that time in my life I never turned to her for help.'

'Right. I see that, Riley.'

I left it there. Actually, there was another reason but I figured it could wait or maybe I would never tell him. That I knew that Cass wanted kids, and that she and Fergie were already trying, and I thought that this might sway her judgement, make her try and talk me out of what I was determined to do.

He was tossing down a credit card now, carelessly, the way people do when they don't have to worry about money. He said, 'There you are, you see,' and now he was looking up at me, and his face was straight and his eyes flat so I couldn't make out if he was joking. 'If I was the nasty bastard you've sometimes accused me of being, I could blackmail you over all this.'

I thought it best to treat it as joke. 'Wouldn't do you any good. Not with my finances.'

'Yeah, but then maybe I wasn't thinking of money.'

'Are you flirting with me, Archie?'

'I'd say we've come too far for that, Riley.'

We decided to walk back to my place where he'd call a taxi to go back to Cass and Fergie's, where he was staying. It was a warm spring night.

He said, 'Tell me something, if you had your time again, would you do things differently?'

'Not a sensible question.'

'Why not?'

'Because if you just had your time again, you'd be the same person, wouldn't you? You'd make the same decisions.'

We were passing the abbey and those same fingers of ruins were still pointing upwards like they were determined to be a leitmotiv for the whole damn story.

I said, 'Now if they let you have another go at it?'

'You'd do it differently?'

'Well, of course. I mean, there wouldn't be any point in doing everything the same way again, would there?'

'Then you could compare?'

'No, no.' I shook my head vehemently. 'Not to compare. Not to see if one was *better* than the other. Simply to do it *differently*.'

'It's a bastard, though, isn't it?' We were at the cottage by then and he paused, his hand on the gate. 'Just getting the one damn go at it.'

'A flaw,' I said, as I pushed it open.

'You'd think someone would have thought of it.'

Inside, as he reached for the phone, he said, 'I guess a wild night of unconditional sex is out of the question.'

I said, 'You know me. I don't put out on the first date, Archie. Anyway, I'm not even sure I remember how it's done.'

'Don't worry,' he said. 'The way I do it, it's much like riding a bicycle.'

It's my guess that you'd like to know what happened then, i.e., the precise details of how we said good night.

Was it:

a) a warm friendly hug, the sort girl scouts give at the end of particularly successful summer camp?

b) those air kisses, one on each cheek, so favoured of Europeans and corporate events managers?

c) a full mouth-on-mouth job, lingering, investigative?

I'd say it was a little bit of all of them. Furthermore, it's none of your damn business.

The taxi was idling when he turned at the gate. His words blew a stream of white into the air.

'I'll tell you something, Riley.'

'What?'

'Bearing everything in mind, your situation, your finances, and everything, you could do a lot worse than marry me.'

It was so full of the old Archie, so full of bravado and with a touch of that truculent air, I crossed my arms over my chest and burst out laughing.

I said, 'Yeah. But let's face it, it wouldn't be easy, Archie.'

It was only later, reporting all this to Sophie, that it struck me what a seminal moment it had been.

'Apart from anything else, it's the only time in my life when anyone's actually asked me to marry them.'

She said, 'Uh-huh,' but I could tell she wasn't really listening. Instead she was studying the manly frame of a thirty-year old army gym instructor keen to widen his experience with an older woman.

Life moves on, like I say, and not least for Sophie. She's back seriously on the on-line dating scene, this because Denis is no more – not dead, just taken early retirement. Unlike Fergie, however, he's not spending it down the bottom of the garden. Instead he's bought a villa, moved with his wife to Malaga.

'Gosh,' I said when Sophie told me. 'The Costa Crime. He'll probably bump into Lennie.'

Sophie's taken this with what I can only describe as total equilibrium, an approach assisted in no small way by the prospect of the likes of of the above-mentioned army gym instructor.

She was browsing among the 'Absolutely Original' (arty, sporty, confident) and the 'Self-employed and Stylish' (friendly, talkative, intelligent), when I said, 'This thing with Archie – I wouldn't want you to think it's a zing, zing, zing went my heartstrings, job.'

She said, 'Of course not,' distinctly drily, turning for a moment from the screen to stare at me over her glasses. 'We all know they're *well* past the plucking.'

I settled back contentedly on her sofa. 'Anyway,' I said, taking a self-satisfied slurp of my wine, 'it would never work with *Archie*.'

She said, 'I'm not clear,' the words surprisingly chill, cutting through the air. 'Why exactly does it have to *work*, Riley?'

They broke over my head, those words, like some sort of clear white light on that old Road to Damascus. Because I saw it then, all these years I'd been telling myself, kidding myself that I was different, a dyed-in-the-wool spinster, and yet each time someone new had come into my life, I'd done exactly the same as the rest of the world, wondered, instinctively, if the thing had a future, if it would *work out*, if it would turn into one of those things, those mysteries, called A Relationship.

'Good God,' I said, 'I'm just the same as everybody else.'

Sophie didn't take her eyes from the screen, just went on clicking away calmly.

'Really,' she said. 'I imagine that must be devastating.'

We're coming to the end of this Spinster's Alphabet now, all the way from Attitude to Zinging heartstrings. I'm still no nearer to figuring out how or why I ended up a spinster, whether I was born or bred to the calling, or whether it was merely accidental, pure serendipity, just falling one side of that solitude/companionship crossbeam rather than the other. Or perhaps it really was all down to that old bridesmaid's curse the way Archie alleged all those years ago when he wanted to save me from it at Cass and Fergie's wedding.

Thanks to Archie, meanwhile, I won't be doing any of that *if it falls to me* stuff I envisaged at beginning of this Alphabet. In short, while many may be the calls for it upon publication of this volume, I won't be forming the Spinster Appreciation Movement.

I don't think so ... (This in reply to one of my e-mails.)
Why not? I see stickers, I see badges ... I see T-shirts ...
My point exactly.
Sorry?
Look, do you really want SpAM across your chest when you go on *Richard and Judy*?

As regards Archie, I regret to say it is exactly as I feared and indeed alleged that day to Fergie. There are indeed olive groves surrounding his villa. I can see them dropping away down the hillside in the jpeg that arrived with his latest e-mail this morning. In addition, I can see bougainvillaea, something you may recall I also foresaw. It crawls up, some might think appealingly, around the roof stanchions of the terrace. In the subject box Archie's typed 'WHEN ARE YOU COMING?' and beneath the picture: 'IF YOU NEED A CHAPERONE BRING DANNY.'

'Ooooo ... now, you never mentioned this,' said the man in question, who unfortunately happened to be passing as I opened it.

Whether I shall go, I don't know yet. Whether, in

particular, I shall be able to conquer my aviophobia to get there, or indeed, and for that matter, any other phobias that you might feel, dear reader – knowing all that you know and having come this far – are applicable to the situation.

Finally, if this has ended up like one of those self-help books, the sort crowding on Magda's shelves, or if it's more like those fake funky sociology tomes with their racy titles and covers, I don't know. But if there's a moral or motto to it all then it's probably this: that there's a little bit of a spinster in all of us, the very reason to stop regarding her as slightly inferior, odd, different.

Finally, as regards the Life of Riley, I can only repeat what I said at the beginning. It's been a good life. Leading apes in hell would be a small price to pay for it, although personally I don't think it's going to happen. I'm with Beatrice on this. I think I'm bound for Spinster Heaven.

I imagine Spinster Heaven like a paradise – white beach, blue sea, and palm trees, like the one in Zamboanga where I opened up that letter from Cass all those years ago, or the one in Southern Thailand where Jonah is now, and which you can see behind the band of beautiful baggy-shorted young men and bikini-ed young women all laughing into the camera with him, he laughing most of all, in the middle of them.

'What do you think?' said his mother. 'Do you think he's alright? What do you think he's doing?'

I said, 'All the things you're supposed to do at that age. All the things we don't want to think about, so let's not do it.'

And this because I knew that 'David' was right, that worry was the price that you pay, and I'd like to cut it down as much as is humanly possible.

Meanwhile, back in my spinster heaven, I'll build a palm-roofed wooden hut, set out my gramophone and my records à la *Desert Island Discs*, my Bible and my Shakespeare along with Cornelia's solar vibrator. I'll scratch out 'Spinster' on a piece of bark, nail it up over the door proudly.

In Spinster Heaven, a demographic time-bomb will have resulted in a serious excess of good-looking, intelligent men, of varying age and all with a terrible sense of humour (this because Sophie, who knows about these things, says anyone who puts GSOH in an ad almost certainly doesn't possess one).

Their hobbies will include wine, water sports and quiet nights around the campfire . . . oh, yes, and the films of Martin Scorcese.

They will have been brought up to believe that women of a certain age and of a certain persuasion are to be prized beyond rubies.

For them the word 'spinster' loosely translates as *The Great Blonde Haji For Whom We Have Waited.*

The Author gratefully acknowledges the financial assistance received from New Writing North through its Time to Write Award during the writing of this book.

Thanks also to Faber and Faber and the Eliot estate for permission to quote from T. S. Eliot's *Four Quartets*.